THE ONE BEFORE THE ONE

Katy Regan worked at *19* magazine for two years before joining *Marie Claire* in 2002 as a feature writer. In 2004 at the height of her career as the office roving reporter singleton, she fell accidentally pregnant by her best mate (who just remained a friend). Seeing the creative possibilities in this unconventional situation, her editor commissioned her to write a column – *And then there were three* . . . which proved so successful it ran for two years and inspired many a reader to write in to Katy with their life story. She has now taken her loyal following to her blog: *The State She's In* on the *Marie Claire* website. Her first novel *One Thing Led to Another* was published by HarperCollins in 2009. She lives in Hertfordshire and shares care of her son Fergus with his dad.

By the same author

One Thing Led to Another

KATY REGAN

The One Before the One

HARPER

Harper
An imprint of HarperCollins*Publishers*
77–85 Fulham Palace Road,
Hammersmith, London W6 8JB

www.harpercollins.co.uk

A Paperback Original 2010
1

A catalogue record for this book
is available from the British Library

ISBN: 978 0 00 727738 4

Set in Sabon by Palimpsest Book Production Limited,
Falkirk, Stirlingshire

Printed and bound in Great Britain by
Clays Ltd, St Ives plc

Mixed Sources
Product group from well-managed
forests and other controlled sources
www.fsc.org Cert no. SW-COC-001806
© 1996 Forest Stewardship Council

FSC

FSC is a non-profit international organisation established
to promote the responsible management of the world's forests.
Products carrying the FSC label are independently certified
to assure consumers that they come from forests that are managed
to meet the social, economic and ecological needs
of present and future generations.

Find out more about HarperCollins and the environment at
www.harpercollins.co.uk/green

For my parents

Acknowledgements

Huge thanks to the amazing team at HarperCollins who worked so hard to make this book the best it can be. I am so grateful. Special thanks go to the very talented Sarah Ritherdon – my editor – for her un-floundering belief in the book, her insightfulness and for laughing and crying in all the right places! To the gifted Lizzy Kremer, quite simply the best agent any writer could ask for. Also thanks to Laura West and everyone at David Higham Associates for their ongoing support. Thanks to Johanna Campbell for the long calls from Australia about the sales stuff. Any inconsistencies are mine! . . . And to Martin Roper and all the sixth formers at Ashlyns School, plus my niece, Charlotte for the txt spk and reminding me what it is to be seventeen. LOL.

As everyone who knows me will know, this was the hardest thing I have EVER done (what? Surely not harder than the first book?!). I am truly grateful to ALL my wonderful friends and family for listening to me go on (and on and on) particularly Rowan Coleman for the writerly advice, encouragement and coffees! However, special thanks have to go to Louis Quail for the morning plot . . . ahem . . . I mean, relaxing coffee meetings and for his continuing love and support. Also, to Greg Knight for the jokes, for letting me in on the cutest Arnold Schwarzenegger story ever and never doubting this book would get written, even when I did. I am forever indebted.

Prologue

September 2008

I knew this would be the day the minute I opened my eyes that morning, the sun pouring through our slatted blinds throwing stripes onto Martin's face. I turned over and examined him, his face slack with sleep, head half turned into the pillow, mouth ajar.

That was it, I decided, tears already threatening. I'd come to the end of the road.

I just couldn't do this any more. It was killing me. Not softly, like the song, but slowly and painfully, sucking the life force out of me like hands around my neck.

I reached over and gently (guilty, probably, at what was about to come) pushed his dark hair, clammy after another Indian summer's night, from his face so that it stuck up, revealing his widow's peak. I'd watched that peak develop. That deepening V was like a measure of the fourteen years we'd spent together. Sometimes I felt like my feelings were receding at the same rate as his hair. *Fourteen* years. More than a third of my life. Did I even know who I was without him? My heart thudded with nerves.

'Happy Birthday, gorgeous,' he mumbled, still half-conscious, before flinging a heavy arm across my chest.

I swallowed hard. It felt like trying to swallow a mouthful of dried leaves.

'Thanks,' I managed eventually. But it was already anything but happy.

The next time I would be in this bed, I would be here alone. What I hadn't predicted at that point, however, was that *technically* I was about to finish with my fiancé, the man I was due to marry in a month's time, the only man I had ever loved or who had loved me, over a present. A present he'd bought for me.

'Here we are birthday girl, one blueberry smoothie and Eggs Benedict with – I dare say so myself – a Michelin star standard Hollandaise sauce.'

It's two hours later (one of those spent perfecting the Hollandaise sauce) so that I'm that unfortunate mix of so ravenous I am annoyed, and guilty that I'm annoyed, Martin places the tray on the duvet in front of me, then sits down on the bed. He tightens the belt of his white 'waffle' dressing gown, a free gift from Boots with a Magimix coffee machine last Christmas.

I look at the tall glass with the sprig of mint placed lovingly on top and then at his face – such a pleasant, friendly face that I knew so well: the neat, narrow mouth, pressed deep into a generous chin that told of a man who was full of *joie de vivre* and liked the good things in life; the slightly upturned nose that he liked to root around constantly when he thought I wasn't looking; round cheeks that made you want to reach out and squeeze them and those small, yet ever-twinkling dark eyes behind tortoiseshell glasses, slightly too far apart like a sheep, and yet filled with so much unwavering love it made me want to cry.

I forced a smile. 'Thank you, honey.'

'My pleasure. Now, does birthday girl want her present now, whilst she's eating her breakfast, or later?'

Martin liked to refer to me in the third person.

'Ooh, I think now.'

'Good choice.' Martin reached deep into his dressing gown pocket and produced an envelope wrapped up in red ribbon. Martin was always an excellent present-wrapper, unusual for a man I'd always thought. A momentary flurry of hope: tickets to the theatre perhaps? Beauty Salon facials? A voucher for John Lewis? It didn't really matter since I'd already decided I won't be able to keep it.

'Come on then, Caro, the suspense is killing me. Aren't you going to open it?' he said, eyes glistening.

I opened the envelope, my hands shaking. A leaflet with a picture of a tree in full autumnal blaze on the front.

'Your Guide to the National Trust', it read in an uninspiring font.

Membership to the National Trust? I momentarily had to catch my breath. If it was membership of the National Trust at thirty-two, what would it be at forty? His-and-her flasks? *The Vicar of Dibley* box set? Jesus Christ, I was about to marry my *dad*. (If my dad were a normal sort of dad, which he isn't).

'So do you like it? he said, nudging closer whilst I held the membership card in my shaking hand. 'I thought after the honeymoon, when weekends are more free, we could start with the Stately—'

'Course I like it!' I cut in, and then an awful, awful thing happened. I started to cry. I started to cry and I couldn't stop.

Martin peered at me, alarmed.

'Caro, what on *earth* is the matter?' The membership leaflet was damp with tears now. 'Please. Tell me. What on earth is wrong?'

And that's where it ended, in what should have been our marital bed. Martin, the only man I had ever known, really, the man who had loved me for more than a decade, who had talked about having children with me, who had held me whilst I sobbed through no end of twenty-something self-esteem crises, who had listened to me moan about my parents and my mental family, who knew the best of me, the worst of me, the ugly truth of me and yet accepted me more than anyone else in he world, was lying next to me, shushing me, stroking my hair.

And I was about to break his big heart into a million different pieces.

CHAPTER ONE

Early June 2009

I suppose you could say that things had barely moved on in my life, nine months later, when my seventeen-year-old sister turns up on my doorstep and I am drunk, alone, on a Sunday afternoon.

When I say drunk, I don't mean staggering-all-over-the-place drunk. God no! That would have been humiliating. It was more like two-large-glasses-of-wine drunk. Okay, possibly half a bottle, exacerbated by two fags and the dregs of a bottle of Prosecco. I'd say, on alcohol consumption alone, I would have just about got away with convincing someone I wasn't drunk. If I hadn't been crying. Or if I hadn't answered the door with said bottle of Prosecco. Or if I wasn't standing barefoot on my doorstep at 4 p.m. on a Sunday wearing a wedding dress and a tiara.

It had been raining, sheeting it down for hours, but was on the verge of brightening up so that the sky glowed, making the row of white terraces behind where Lexi stood and the trees of Battersea Park – full as broccoli florets in the height of summer – look unreal, like a stage set.

She was carrying a trolley case with fuscia-pink lips all over it and was wearing gold leggings, and a silver headband, Grecian-style, around her forehead. In the luminescent light,

I thought how lovely she'd become, a modern take on Wonder Woman, with her gamine crop and kittenish eyeliner. I, on the other hand, must have looked like a contestant for Trailer-Trash Bride of the Year.

'Hi! It's me, Lexi.'

Did she think I had dementia? That I needed to be reminded of who she was before being escorted back to the church where I would get on with the wedding I had clearly wandered off from?

'Sorry, is this a crap time?'

I leant one hand on the top of the doorframe, but missed, so that I stumbled forward and ended up doing a strange unintentional dance on the front step.

'Er . . . no.'

'Right, it's just you —' I was aware I was swaying, that the trees were moving although there was no breeze — 'look like you've been crying. And you're wearing a wedding dress.' I looked down. This was no word of a lie. 'And a tiara. And you're holding an empty bottle of wine.'

'It's Prosecco, actually.'

Overlooking the empty bottle of Prosecco and the fact my house stank of booze and fags and the fact I had Pat Benatar's 'Love is a Battlefield', blasting from the stereo, I think I styled it out well. It was regrettable that my wedding dress had a four foot train and so could not be passed off as evening wear, but like I say, all this was exacerbated by the fact I was drunk and it was the middle of the afternoon.

'So how long are you planning on staying?' We're standing in my kitchen now and I'm trying to sound as breezy as possible.

Lexi leans against the doorframe and looks around her.

'Um, well, I thought maybe the summer holidays . . .?' she says, hopefully.

The summer holidays? I almost heave.

'What? Like, the whole summer?'

'Er, yeah.' She smiles. She still has the same rosebud mouth she had as a baby. Pouty and cherubic. A real Drew Barrymore mouth. 'Why, are you going somewhere?'

'No.'

'Cool,' she says brightly, like, that's that sorted then.

She sits down at the kitchen table, helps herself from the bowl of pistachios. Inside, I'm beginning to panic – this is all a bit sudden, isn't it? A bit unexpected. She's been here half an hour now and I don't feel we've quite got to the bottom of why she is.

'Look, Lex . . .' I say, gently. She looks at me with her big, brown eyes – there's something hopeful about them, so innocent and trusting and I already feel awful. 'I'm more than happy to have you for a while but you have to understand, I have a job, a really demanding job. I'm out all day . . .'

'I'm very resourceful.' She shrugs. 'I'm used to amusing myself.'

That's what's worrying me.

'I often have client events at night.'

'Seriously? Cool. Maybe I could come to a few?'

I sigh. My stomach shrivels like a mollusc into its shell.

'Or help you out at work? I've decided I want to go into business, actually – sixth form's not for me. I was thinking, because I really love shoes, like *seriously* have a passion for them, that I could be a shoe designer. I could design the shoes here, I mean dead funky ones, much better than the pap that's in the shops now,' she says, in her flat Yorkshire accent. I've pretty much lost mine, after someone once told me I sounded like Geoff Boycott. 'I could draw them – Art's my best subject – send the designs to China where a team of people would make them, then get them sent back here!'

She looks at me as if to say, 'Genius, or what?' and a strange nausea passes over me, like this is already becoming more surreal than I can handle. Thankfully, then, there's a noise like a lion roaring. Her mobile. Again.

She picks up. 'Yo.'

She said that last time they called, so I assume it's the same person.

'Yeah, yeah, I'm here now.' *Pause.* 'Yeah, she's cool, yeah, I *think* so . . .' She looks at me and grimaces, apologetically – so she clearly told whoever's on the other line of her plans to come and 'surprise me'. Just not me.

Her voice grows quieter.

'Yeah, I know Carls, I know. I'll talk to him at some point.'

So, boyfriend trouble?

She rolls her eyes and makes a blah-blah-blah sign with her hand.There's a long pause, then a gasp and a 'No way!' then an even bigger gasp and a 'What, like permanent-permanent?!'

After about five seconds and no 'goodbye' that I can decipher, she hangs up.

'What's happened? Is everything Okay?'

'Oh yeah,' she says, cracking a pistachio between her teeth, 'it's just my mate Carly's had her hair dyed, and it's gone totally tits up.'

We sit at the kitchen table, me still in the wedding dress and the start of a hangover.

'So listen, honey, about the sixth form thing. Does Dad know you aren't planning on going back?'

'Yes. Dunno. Don't care. I'm not really talking to him at the moment, or Mum for that matter.'

'What? What do you mean you're not talking to them? You mean to say you came on the train all the way to London and you didn't tell them? Lexi! Right, I'm calling Dad now.'

I pick up my bag and rummage in it, trying to find my

mobile, but Lexi stretches across the table and slaps her hand on top of it.

'Caroline, don't. Please.'

She lowers her eyes at me, looks at me from under silky black lashes that I was always so envious of as a teenager.

'Back away from the bag, Caroline. Away from the bag, come on . . .'

She slowly takes the bag from my grasp, like I'm a self-harmer and it's full of razors.

'Please don't call Dad. They know I'm here – Dad drove me to the station.' She looks a bit sheepish. 'And gave me the money to get the train. He gave me a bit of cash too, you know, for the holidays?'

'Oh, did he now? And did he think to, you know, call me about this?'

She wrinkles her nose.

'Mmm, yeah. But I think you had your phone off.'

I am about to protest about the ludicrousness of this comment when I remember, yes, I did. I always switch off all methods of communication when I'm indulging in a maudlin-fest. One gets so much more out of it that way.

We sit in silence for a minute. I look around at the kitchen, at the disarray – the Flora margarine carton with fag butts in it, the empty bottle of Prosecco (with a fag butt in it), the little sister, helping herself to pistachios, announcing she's staying for the summer. The *whole* summer. God, I hate summer, and I am suddenly taken hold with a sickening grip of panic, a sort of vertigo like I'm in freefall.

Then Lexi's phone goes again. This time she looks at the screen and runs upstairs to take it.

Brilliant. A lovesick teen on my hands.

I get straight on the landline to Dad. It rings three times before the answerphone kicks in. If they've sodded off on one of their yoga holidays to an obscure Greek island, I'll kill him, I really will.

'Hi, this is the happy home of Cassandra and Trevor Steele. I'm afraid we've been currently called upon elsewhere, but if you'd be so kind as to leave us a message . . .'

Then: 'Helllooo!'

These days, Dad sounds like he just leapt off a yacht in the Carribean to answer the phone, he's so ecstatic.

'Dad, it's Caroline.'

'Ah, lovely Caro! I was just about to call you.'

'Were you? Good.'

Resist temptation to rant. It never works with Dad.

'Do you think you might be able to tell me what's going on?'

'Ah. Lexi?'

'Yes, Dad, Lexi.'

'The thing is, honey, I've been trying to call you all afternoon but you're always so unavailable.'

(Note: emotional blackmail three seconds into the conversation.)

'I see, so you thought you'd just send her over?'

'No! It wasn't like that. Look, I can tell you're excited . . .'

'Am I? I don't feel that excited.'

'So just take a moment to relax. A few deep breaths. Would you like me to call you back?'

'No, I'm fine. I want to talk about this now.'

'Okay, all right.' (Dramatic sigh.) 'The thing is, honey, Lex is . . . how can I put it . . . "at sea" at the moment. She's in a transitional phase, there's a lot of inner conflict. She's been off the rails recently, raging against the world. All the normal teenage stuff, but also some sadness, some searching; her mum and I feel, some un-met needs.'

I hold the receiver away from my mouth for a second and swear, silently and enthusiastically to the heavens.

'Dad, do you think I could have this in plain English please?'

'Basically, she's decided . . .' (sigh) 'Lex has decided she doesn't want to go back to sixth form next year and finish her A levels.'

Well, that's a relief. By the way he was carrying on, you'd think she'd signed up for a sex change.

'Basically, she dropped out of school last month, been moping around the house ever since, lots of tears, very hostile. As you can imagine, her mother and I are very concerned and we thought – well, actually it was Lexi's idea – that she'd really benefit from spending some time with you. You lead such a stimulating life down there in London.'

'Do I?'

'And you've always been so driven, such an achiever, Caro, done your A Levels, gone to university. Always done everything so right. You'd be a great role model for Lex, who needs some direction right now, so I invite you to take this opportunity, Caro. Cass and I invite you—'

'Stop inviting me, Dad,' I interrupted, 'it's not a bloody party.'

He makes this noise, and I know he's tapping manically at his forehead, which he does when he's stressed.

'I guess what I'm trying to say is, can you talk to her? Please, darling? She's mighty upset about something, and *something's* happened for her to just drop out of school, of life, like this . . .'

'Probably just boyfriend trouble, Dad. She's seventeen, these things often seem like the end of the world . . .' (Like I knew anything.)

'Ah, but it's not. You're wrong there, because . . .'

There's an enormous racket as Lexi thumps down the stairs.

'Look, she's here now.'

'I know, and I'll talk to her in a minute, but just . . . Will you do this one thing for me, Caro? Will you talk to your sister? Her mother and I just don't want to see her throwing her life away like this. It would give you a chance to get to know her better, besides anything else, and she's a good kid, a *great* kid.'

Why was he talking like he was in an episode of *The Waltons* all of a sudden?

'I will, Dad, okay? Course I will. Anyway, here she is . . .'

I hold out the receiver.

'It's Dad,' I say. 'I think you should talk to him.'

Lexi's on the phone for ages. She sits, curled up like a cat, in a puddle of evening sun by the window, fiddling with the phone cord. I watch her as she talks, and I have to admit she's very pretty. She has thick, dark hair, painstakingly styled 'bedhead', a neat, snub nose – her mum's nose, not the size-able Steele honk I inherited, and then those eyes, wide-spaced, chocolate-dark, a flick of black eyeliner accentuating their feline quality, and framed by slightly too bushy eyebrows, which give her a naturally exotic look, like she might look ridiculous in too much make-up.

She talks to Dad for ages. At first there are the usual sullen grunts and rolls of the eyes and a 'Yeah, all right, Dad, don't give yourself a nosebleed about it.'

But then her voice becomes much quieter and softer and when I next look, a big fat tear is rolling down her face.

'I know that, Dad,' she's saying. 'I know it's coz you care . . . Course I'd tell you if there was something. You know I tell you everything . . .'

Liar, I think. Girls don't tell their dads *any*thing. At least, I didn't, but then, that's probably because Dad was always doing the talking.

'But there isn't, I promise,' she carries on, wiping her nose on the palm of her hand, and something, despite myself,

12

squeezes my heart. Even if this was just boyfriend trouble she was gutted, really upset – and she'd dropped out of sixth form. It *must* be serious.

Eventually, she says, 'I will. I miss you, too. Yep, love you too.' Then she hangs up and looks at me, mascara running down her cheeks. 'God, look at the state of me,' she says, laughing through the tears. 'What sort of total minger must I look now?'

'Wanna talk about it?'

I'm sitting down beside her now.

'No. Honest. I'm all right.'

'Sure?' I nudge her with my elbow. 'I might be able to help, you know. Especially since I am such an exceedingly sensible, level-headed and mature person.'

Lexi looks at me in my wedding dress.

'Yeah, right!' She laughs. 'I used to think you were – now I'm not so sure.'

There's a pause.

'Anyway,' I say, eventually, putting my hand on her knee. 'We'll sort this out, yeah? Me and you, whatever it is, we'll get you back on track.'

'Okay.' She sniffs. 'Thanks. You're very nice to me.'

'Oh, I know – my benevolence knows no bounds.'

'I'll be okay,' she says. 'I just need some time out of Doncaster, to be honest, some time away.'

Then she leans her head back on the radiator and studies me, her dark eyes still glassy from crying.

'And d'you know what?' she says, absentmindedly stroking the fabric of my wedding dress. 'It's all right to get dumped. We all get dumped. Carly's just been dumped, so it doesn't make you a freak.'

I don't know whether to laugh or cry.

* * *

13

It's only when Lexi's in bed that I do what I've been dying to do all day. I sit back on my pillows, take my notebook – all perfect in its lovely, stripy hardness – out of my bedside-table drawer and I begin, asterisking new items.

To Do:
MINOR
*Make something with Quinoa
Pluck eyebrows
Get spare room painted
Sort out photo albums (buy photo corners)
*Get drippy tap fixed
Get involved in local culture: this coming weekend: installation by interesting sounding German artist at The Pump House Gallery. (Toby to come? Impossible. Shona and Paul? Possible. Martin? Pretty much a cert. Call him tomorrow.)
Learn how to use i-pod that have now had since Christmas. Just do it!!
*Do 3 x 12 squats and 3 x 12 sit ups before bed (start tomorrow)
MAJOR
Incorporate two hours of admin into every weekend. No excuse!
Every day, do something for self and de-stressing, even if just breathing (alone, concentrating on, rather than just breathing breathing.) for ten minutes.
Work: Step things up a gear. Seal deal on two new clients per week.
FIND OUT WHAT'S WRONG WITH LEXI ASAP!!!
Fix it. Then send her back to Doncaster asap.

Was only joking about that last bit . . . Kind of.

14

CHAPTER TWO

I should say that when I say my 'sister' I actually mean half-sister. Lexi was born when I was fifteen – which makes her seventeen now – about seven months after Dad moved in with Cassandra, which means he must have got her up the duff whilst he was living with Mum. My mother never lets me forget *that*.

I remember the day she was born – 12 September 1991. It was a Thursday morning, a school morning, and Mum was putting a load of washing on. Mum was forever putting a load of washing on, back then, especially after Dad left. It was ridiculous; she was either stuffing it into the machine or hanging it out, like some manic, nervous tick, which I now realize it was.

She had her bottom in the air, and was wearing the aqua elasticated trousers that couldn't have helped in Dad's final decision to walk, that's for sure!

'Well, your father's had his second daughter,' she announced. 'God help her, Caroline, with two lunatics for parents! Alexis Simone, they've called her, poor little sod. Surely the work of the She Devil.'

The 'She Devil' was what Cassandra was known as in our

house, which, even at fifteen and abandoned by my dad, I felt was a little harsh, but what did I know? Mum's a black and white kind of a woman. It's love or hate with her.

I remember an immediate pang of envy that she'd got Alexis Simone, where as I got Caroline Marie, something you'd surely call a canal barge. But then there was another emotion that took me by surprise: excitement. Surging, dizzying excitement that made me unable to swallow my Weetabix. I had a sister! I'd always wanted a sister. Especially since I'd always felt short-changed by my brother, Chris, whom I strongly suspected was off the autism scale and whose one great love in life was his biscuit-infested Nintendo.

'And is she okay? I mean, is she healthy?' I asked. I liked to think I was a caring sort who rose above personal politics even then, mainly out of necessity, since if anyone had two lunatics as parents, it was me.

'Oh yes, she's fine . . . *physically*,' Mum said, ramming the soap-powder dispenser shut. 'Only time will tell what they do to her head.'

I don't know what I expected having a half-sister would be like. I guess I was thinking along the lines of swapping clothes, discussing boys, although since Alexis – Lexi, as she quickly came to be called – was a day old, I'd have to wait years to do all that.

I was travelling from Mum's in Harrogate to Dad's (well, Cassandra's house) in Doncaster every other weekend back then. Cassandra was a flamboyant American who could talk a glass eye to sleep and had a good line in enormous dresses that looked like she'd had a run in with a box of water-colours. Dad had met her on a residential course called Heal Your Life at the height of his midlife crisis.

Anyway, I was desperate to get to Dad's that weekend so I could meet this new, coolly named sister of mine. My little sister. My very own confidante! Someone to save me from

16

my mental family and, above all, myself and this altogether below-par existence I was leading.

As soon as I walked in, however, I realized the other thing I hadn't thought through – as well as the fact that it would be approximately sixteen years before I could discuss my concerns about still being a virgin with my sister – (and at the rate things were going, I'd still be a virgin then) – was the fact that my father would be madly in love with this new bundle and that this would bring my already crumbling world crashing down.

Cassandra was breast-feeding when I arrived and Dad was sitting next to her on the sofa, stroking Lexi's head. I stood in the doorway, my throat constricted with an all-consuming jealousy.

You'd have thought, what with Cassandra being a life coach and Dad now transformed into a yoga-loving, therapy addict who used terms like 'closure' in normal conversation, that they might have been more sensitive and given me time to adapt. But no. Cassandra simply lifted Lexi straight from her gigantic breast, which dangled out of a bra the size of a pillowcase.

'Caroline, meet Alexis Simone, your new baby sister. Isn't she adorable?'

She was so light, she almost fell through my fingers.

'Yeah, she's, um . . . nice,' I said, holding her like you might hold a bundle of firewood, trying to keep all the tiny bones, the bits, together. I was appalled, shocked by how tiny she was. What use was this to me? How could this downy, squawking thing that bore more than a passing resemblance to a newborn ape save me from anything?

Cassandra was smiling at me, head cocked to the side. Then Dad started with the camera. This was so embarrassing.

'Put her next to your breast, sweetie,' urged Cassandra, massive knockers still dangling like water bombs. 'Babies love skin-to-skin contact, it makes them feel safe.'

Yeah, well, it didn't make *me* feel safe, it made me feel like a total moron. I touched the top of her head – just because I felt I ought to really – but it felt like an over-ripe peach and made my legs turn to jelly. Then the baby started head-butting me. This wasn't panning out well at all.

'Aaah, look, she's rooting,' gushed Cassandra.

'What do you mean?' This sounded like something a badger did.

'She thinks you have milk, sweetie, she's hungry. She thinks you're her mommy, too.'

Dad was still snapping away: 'My two little girls,' he kept saying. 'My two, gorgeous girls,' which for reasons I am yet to fully understand made me suddenly so mad, and so sad, it was all I could do not to punch him.

We had tea, eventually, around 9 p.m., with Lexi being passed between Dad and Cassandra and the Moses basket. Nobody asked me a thing, except for Dad, who asked when I'd started to get psoriasis on my scalp. Then I went to bed, an hour earlier than normal, and balled my eyes out, all the time listening to Lexi do the same.

So Dad, as much as I loved him, was never a father to me or Chris, and yet, here he was being one to somebody else. And that hurt. That hurt like nothing else had ever hurt in my life, and if I'm honest, my realisation that day that Alexis Simone was not, as I'd hoped, my very own baby-sister-shaped saviour but a usurper, stayed with me. If I'm *really* honest, it's probably still there.

CHAPTER THREE

The morning after Lexi arrives in London, I wake up to the sound of something throbbing. At first I assume it's a hangover, but then decide I feel nowhere near rancid enough, since mine are largely of the vomit-on-waking variety. I remove my earplugs and fumble around on the floor for my glasses, morning being a gradual reintroduction of the sensory world to me, my myopia at a level where I have been known to say hello to my own reflection.

It doesn't take me long to realize the thumping is music and it's coming from downstairs.

It's only then that I remember I have a guest.

'Lexi?' I'm banging on the bathroom door in my pyjamas now. 'Lexi, are you in there?'

'Yeah,' comes a muffled voice from inside. 'Come in if you want. I'm fully dressed.'

I push open the door. It's steamy and warm. I just can make out Lexi hovering over the sink but not much else.

'Er, music?' I shout with what I hope is a vaguely humorous I-am-so-cool-with-your-rock-music-at-seven-in-the-morning but there's an accusatory rise at the end of the sentence.

'Gossip!' she shouts back

'I'm sorry?'

19

'GOSSIP!' She stands up from the sink. 'The MUSIC. It's GOSSIP. Why, do you like them?'

'CAN'T SAY I'VE EVER HEARD OF THEM!'

'WHAT?! BETH DITTO IS A FEMINIST ICON OF OUR TIMES!'

'I THOUGHT YOU SAID IT WAS GOSSIP?'

'IT *IS*. BETH DITTO IS THE LEAD SINGER OF THE GROUP, GOSSIP.'

'OH . . .'

'WHY ARE WE SHOUTING?'

'I DON'T KNOW. I CAN'T HEAR BECAUSE I CAN'T SEE AND I CAN'T SEE BECAUSE I HAVEN'T GOT MY GLASSES ON. I THINK I LEFT THEM IN HERE!'

'Oh my Lord,' giggles Lexi as I edge right up to her face. 'You really are blind, aren't you?'

She fumbles around near the sink, hands me my glasses, and I put them on. Only then does everything become clear. Well, almost clear, there's still something obstructing my vision. Lexi has her hair wrapped in a Tesco bag, dribbles of purple dye running down her forehead, around her ears. My sparkling white, Italian designer bathroom basin – *obscene* amounts of money from a place on Lavender Hill – is splattered with purple dye. As is the wall. As is the towel around Lexi's neck. As are, I discover, my glasses. Hence the dark spots in front of my eyes.

'Um, the sink,' I squeak, thinking, keep a lid on it, Caroline. Keep things in perspective.

'The sink?' says Lexi.

'It's covered in *dye*.' I put a specific emphasis on the word 'dye'.

'Oh!' She bites her nail. 'Shit. But it'll come off, right?'

She goes to rub at it with dye-covered fingers.

'Er, Lex, don't do that?' I'm trying to sound calm, whilst suppressing the hysteria that's bubbling within me.

20

'If I just . . .' She licks her fingers and goes at it again.

'Stop!' I mean it to come out normally but it shoots out of my mouth like a small, hard pellet. 'NOW. Please. Lexi.'

'All right, missus.' She's brightly rubbing at it with my flannel now. 'Calm your boots. I'm just going to give it ever such a little . . .'

She wipes away a drip of dye that's rolling down her forehead and then goes to pick up the flannel again, at which point I crack. I literally slide, cartoon style, across the bathroom floor in my towelling bedsocks, grabbing the side of the sink. 'FOR GOD'S SAKE JUST LEAVE IT OKAY? JUST . . .' I gather myself. '*Leave* it.'

She stops rubbing.

'Oh, okay. Sorry,' she says. Does she actually flinch?

Something tells me this little arrangement may not pan out that well. Something tells me I have lived alone for far too long.

My sister turning up for the summer aside, I do occasionally worry what it says about my life that I look forward to coming to work on a Monday. The hating weekends thing crept up on me, really. For the fourteen years that Martin and I were together, weekends were okay. Well, they were much the same as anyone else's – any other couple's, that is.

Endless rounds of barbecues and visits to the almost in-laws; Sunday afternoons spent at the Tate Modern, even though neither of us really liked anything in there so we'd end up in the shop where I'd buy another Dali postcard and Martin would buy his mum her birthday present in advance – usually another Liberty-print oven glove.

Post break up, there were about three months where I revelled in my new-found freedom. When the novelty was over, however, and my concerned friends, who had rallied round went back to their neglected boyfriends, I began to dread weekends. Especially summer weekends. Bank holiday weekends are the work of the devil. The two in May, a torture device. Because what I envisaged about summer in London: Tooting Lido, picnics on Hampstead Heath, Shakespeare in Regent's Park, didn't hold that much appeal on my own and sometimes, although I hated to admit it, I would feel lonely. Panicky, even. And at times like that I'd start to think that maybe I'd made a huge mistake with Martin – well, actually, I still sometimes wonder if I've made a huge mistake with Martin. I kind of missed the 'schedule' after all. At least he was enthusiastic about doing stuff, even if it was Duxford Aerodrome. Also, Martin Squire is, quite simply, the nicest bloke in the world. Which is probably why he wasn't the bloke for me.

I get out my mobile to call him. I miss 'us' most in the mornings, sitting here at Battersea Park station, the heady, oily smell of a London summer in the air, the sky already a brilliant blue. Maybe it's because it reminds me of the summers we sat here together, Martin giving me one of his early morning pep talks: 'Caro, nobody's dying, you've still got me. What's the worst than can happen?' he'd say. 'You lose a client. You fail.'

I'd go into voluntary spasm at the thought.

The phone rings and rings, which is strange, because Martin always picks up. I leave a message.

'Hello you, it's me. Why aren't you answering your phone? Wanted to know if you fancied coming to see an exhibition with me on Saturday? Thought I'd get you early. It's by a German artist, some sort of conceptual thing – I saw it in *Time Out*. Might be crap but it would just be nice to see you. As ever. Also, you'll never believe this, but guess who just rocked up on my doorstop last night, announcing she's staying for the whole summer? My bloody sister! As you can imagine, I'm freaking out. I need a Martin pep talk. Oh yeah, and the exhibition. You'll probably want to know–'

'Where it is,' I'm about to say, but then a cargo train approaches and by the time it's passed, the space on the answer machine has been used up and there's just a flat tone ringing.

Shona's the only person in the office when I arrive. She's on the phone and I know exactly, by her straight, tense back and clipped voice, who to. She presses 'hold', gives a little shudder and puts her fingers to her head, mimicking a trigger. Shona's not one for hiding how she feels about people, especially how she feels about Darryl Schumacher.

'It's Darryl Bum Smacker,' she hisses. 'Wants to discuss a date for the pitch for Minty Me – and to take me to dinner, obviously.'

'Tell him I'm not here yet. Tell him I'll call him back, okay?'

'She'll call you back,' says Shona.

Then, more irate: 'I *said* she'll call you back!'

Even more irate: 'I don't think what I'm doing at the weekend is really that relevant to the oral hygiene market, do you, Darryl?'

She slams the phone down.

'Cock,' I hear her mutter under her breath before taking another call. God, I love Shona. I wish I could be more like Shona. Doesn't suffer fools. Never gets stressed. *Never* puts her job before her principles – which is maybe why she's still the sales' team's admin exec after seven years at the company. If we let her loose on selling anything we'd be in liquidation by now.

Darryl Schumacher is head buyer for Langley's supermarkets, notorious for making women physically sick but also for driving the hardest bargain in the oral hygiene market. For weeks now, I've been chipping away at him, toeing that fine balance between what our boss calls skilful sales and 'the sledgehammer effect' (i.e., all punch and no result). I sell oral hygiene products to supermarkets for a living. I know it's not saving the world, but I love my job and seem to be quite good at it. But then I guess, without blowing my own trumpet, that I'm pretty good at most things if I put my mind to it. 'Caroline is a very capable young lady,' teachers would write on my report. You know the sort: three As at A Level, First Class degree, head-hunted on the university Milk Round to join Skidmore Colt Davis's graduate scheme – a geek, basically.

This is a crucial time with Schumacher. If he catches me off guard, I could lose the sale, but if I play my cards right, we'll have Mini Minty Me breath freshener on the shelves of all branches of Langley's by next week, meaning profit for the company and a stab at being nominated as Sales Person of the Year in August's Institute of Sales Annual Awards – not that that's a highlight or anything.

So now, when I've just walked into the office and I'm not on my guard, is not the time to deal with Schumacher. I'm distracted by Lexi's arrival and I want to mail Toby.

To: toby.delaney@scd.co.uk
From: caroline.steele@scd.co.uk
Subject: Teenage Mutant Sister invasion at 64 Coombe Gardens. Argh!
So, on Sunday I am knee-deep in admin [small, white lie but he doesn't need to know this] when the doorbell goes. You will never guess who was there, announcing she's staying for the summer?!

There's a sudden pressure on my shoulders and then a familiar schoolboy giggle.

'Writing love letters to me *again*? Give it a rest, will you? They're clogging up my inbox.'

'Jesus, Toby. You nearly gave me a heart attack.'

24

He laughs, chomping on a pastie. I've never known anyone eat as much as Toby Delaney, and still have a concave stomach.

'I tend to have that effect on women,' he says, sitting down at his desk.

There are bits of pastie all down his tie but even that, unfortunately, doesn't seem to take away from his breathtaking attractiveness. In fact, it seems to add to it, which I find exhilarating and demoralising all at the same time. The less he tries, and he never does, the more delectable he seems to become.

I lean back on my chair, assuming an air of nonchalance. It's something I've perfected after nearly a year of sitting opposite someone who it's all I can do not to strip naked and eat.

'So how was *your* weekend?' I say.

'Oh, you know . . . *missed* you,' he mouths, chucking a pen in front of me.

'Shut up, Delaney!'

'I did!' he says, clutching at his chest with mock hurt. 'Anyway, pick up that pen, will you? I want to see your pants.'

I chuck the pen back at him

'What about you?' he says. 'Good weekend Steeley? Or are you keeping it a secret?'

But then there's the familiar 'dong' as his computer sparks into action. I wait for him to carry on the conversation but he's too busy squinting at his screen.

'Caroline still topping the sales targets,' he reads, in a South African accent, mocking our boss's email. 'You bitch.' He shakes his head. 'You total spawny cow.'

I'm about to respond with some devastatingly witty come-back when a familiar figure looms over our desks.

'What's that I hear, Mr Delaney? Spawny cow?'

Janine Cross. Our boss. At least five foot ten of South African sinewy muscle and balls. I speak metaphorically, of course,

25

although it wouldn't surprise me if, tucked into those skintight Joseph trousers, she does, actually, have a pair of iron balls.

'Do I detect a smidgen of jealousy?'

'Um . . .' Toby can't speak. More due to food bulging from his mouth than anything else.

'Or just a healthy competitive streak?'

'Oh, just the, er, streak,' says Toby.

Janine shakes her head at him then smiles at me. 'So, you got Morrisons? Well done. Very well done, in fact. Just Schumacher to get in the bag now, Caroline, but I have no doubt you'll crack it. If you carry on like this you'll definitely be in the running for Sales Person of the Year.' She taps Toby on the shoulder. 'Look and learn, Toby, and don't think I've not noticed that you were late twice last week and haven't reached your target for three weeks running.' Then she strides off on her racehorse limbs towards a slightly scared-looking marketing team.

Toby's shaking his head at me.

'You're such a lick-arse, Steele.'

I am about to reply when a high-pitched 'Eeek! Eeek!', unmistakable as the sound from the shower scene in *Psycho*, interrupts us.

'What the hell's that?' exclaims Toby.

'What?'

'That noise like the shower scene from *Psycho*.'

'I've no idea.'

Toby looks around him. 'Well, it's not coming from me.'

The noise continues, grows louder, more urgent.

'I didn't say it was coming from you.'

'So where is it coming from, then?'

'I don't know!'

'It's coming from you, Steele!' Toby slides back on his chair, pointing at my bag.

I pick up my bag and open it, look inside.

26

'Have you got a rape alarm in there? That'd be typical of you.'

'What the hell do you mean by that?'

'A bomb, then?'

'Don't be bloody ridiculous.'

'What is it, then?'

'I don't know!' I hold up the bag a metre away from me. 'But I'm not looking – you can.' And I walk over and thrust it onto his desk.

'Oh, nice. So I get the bomb-in-a-bag,' says Toby, shaking it up to his ear. He opens it. 'Jesus, there's like a whole eco-system in here.'

He rummages a little and then, a smirk spreading across his handsome face, lifts out my mobile phone, the 'Eeki Eek!' becoming ear-splitting as he does. He stands up and hands it to me. LEXI is flashing in silver.

'Hello?'

'Hiya!' says the Yorkshire voice on the end of the line. 'What d'ya reck to what I've done with your ringtone? It's awesome, isn't it?'

'So how long is she staying?'

Toby is highly amused but trying not to show it. Shona is sitting on her desk, biting hard on her pencil, trying to come up with a solution, because this is what Shona does in every problematic situation.

For some reason, Toby seems to have orchestrated a 'crisis' meeting and skidded over next to me on his office chair, which is causing all manner of problems, mainly in the pelvic region, since I can smell him: a clean, just-had-a-shower smell, but made purely of pheromones and mixed with something reminiscent of fresh, sugary bakery goods. Something delectable. Something flutters between my legs.

'The whole summer,' I say, pretending to look

conscientiously at my emails, when really I'm picturing Toby, in bed, naked, and me, burrowing my head in his chest hair.

'What, like July and August?'

'That's the whole summer, isn't it?'

Toby sucks air between his teeth. 'Oh, Steeley,' he says, squeezing my shoulders. The something fluttering between my legs is positively flapping now. 'Sharing your space with a whole other person? How are you coping?'

'Not very well, actually. There's stuff all over my flat.'

'Oh no. Not stuff. In flat?'

'Piss off!' I nudge him in the side.

Shona groans. Poor Shona. She's worked with Toby and I nearly a year now and the constant sexual tension by proxy must be beginning to wear thin.

'And what about her not leaving the cushions lined up symmetrically? Leaving the tap dripping? Spoiling your one-woman efforts to save the Great Barrier Reef?'

I slap him over the head as he twinkles his swimming-pool-blue eyes at me.

'You're so rude! And this morning she dyed her hair in my bathroom – purple dye all over my brand new Italian bathroom.'

Toby bursts out laughing. 'Fuck, I'm surprised you made it into work.'

'How old is she?' asks Shona

'Seventeen.'

Toby almost falls off his chair.

'Seventeen?' Health and Safety Heather swings around and sighs dramatically, but we all ignore her since she does this several times a day. 'You didn't tell me you had a seventeen-year-old sister!'

'*Half*-sister,' I correct.

'That is so cool,' says Shona. 'I would have killed my three brothers for a sister when I was a kid.'

28

Toby and I frown. Shona often saying things that make people frown.

Toby put his feet up on my desk. 'So what's she like? Is she a—'

'Delaney!'

'God, Delaney,' agrees Shona.

'*What?*' he says, wide-eyed at the injustice of it all. 'A student, was all I was going to say. Thanks a lot, you two.' He stabs at a ball of Blu-Tack with his pen 'What do you two take me for? I'm a responsible, married man.'

'Well, since you're such a fan of responsibility, maybe you'd like to volunteer as a fire marshal? Eh? Clever clogs. Whaddya think about that?'

Our 'crisis meeting' – obviously just an opportunity for Toby to laugh at me – is suddenly cut short by Heather, playfully hitting Toby across the head with her Fire Safety manual.

'Fifty quid for the first three takers and an hour with me, to show you the ropes.'

'That, H, is a very hard offer to refuse,' says Toby, as Heather swings back and forth on her court shoes, clearly delighted by her opening gambit. 'But I think I'm going to decline, on this occasion. It's more Caroline's sort of thing, isn't it, Caroline?' And then he smiles in a way that makes me want to punch and snog him all at the same time.

So that's how I get roped into being one of the office's three fire marshals – me, Heather and Toupee Dom from payroll. I spend the next hour learning how to use the fire extinguisher and sitting in a special chair used to evacuate disabled people from the office, whilst Toupee Dom almost knocks me out with his body odour. I try Lexi several times but, worryingly, get no answer until, finally, around lunchtime – just as I get stuck into my PowerPoint presentation, in particular a very well-executed pie-chart, detailing what's currently driving the growth of oral hygiene goods in Asda – comes the shower scene noise from *Psycho*. I immediately grab my phone from the table, but it flips about in my hand like a live trout.

There's a text.

Am up town. This oldie just tried to flog uz xtc! I WMPL!
C u l8r
DWBH. [smiley face]
Ha ha. lol. Lex xxxxxx

What?
'Am up town' is all I can make out. So she's in town, but where in town? Soho? Shoreditch? The arse-end of Hackney?
I immediately email Toby. He's got a nineteen-year-old brother. He'll know what she's on about.

To: toby.delaney@scd.co.uk
From: caroline.steele@scd.co.uk
This text from Lexi, do I need to worry?
Am up town. This oldie jst tried to flog uz xtc! I WMPL!
C u l8r
DWBH. [smiley face]
Ha ha. lol. Lex xxxxxx

Five seconds later, an email pings into my inbox.

Subject: translation services from down-wiv-the-kidz
From: toby.delaney@scd.co.uk
She's been offered class A drugs by a geriatric. This made her wet herself laughing. She says, don't worry, be happy!

30

To: toby.delaney@scd.co.uk
Don't worry? I am SO worrying. I don't think I can hack this responsibility for another human being/space-sharing thing, you were right.

He emails back.

From: toby.delaney@scd.co.uk
Relax woman. It could be fun. I sure wish I had a seventeen-year-old lolling about my gaff all summer. Although, it has occurred to me, I don't know whether it has you. Does the fact you've got your sister staying change the book club? Like, do we need to re-locate??!

I email back.

That, Mr Delaney, is the last thing on my mind.

CHAPTER FOUR

When I get home from work, Lexi's in the back garden, sunbathing. It's only when she removes the copy of *Time Out* she is reading to talk to me in comedic deep voice (I am finding she rarely uses her normal one) that I realize she is topless.

'Afternoooooon. You're early; good day at the office?'

'Yeah, good, thanks.' I don't know where to look, so I take a sudden interest in the doorframe. 'Very productive.'

'Great.' She smiles brightly. Her long legs are stretched out on the sun lounger. She's wearing bright red lipstick and enormous square shades. 'So, what do you think?'

'About what?'

'My tattoo, you chump!' She sticks her right arm out in front of her.

I look in horror at the anchor (an anchor?) splat in the middle of her upper right arm. I can't believe this. Dad will kill me. I have an overwhelming desire to head-butt the wall.

'You got that done today?'

'Yes, don't you like it? It's like the one Amy Winehouse has, kind of ironic, you know, sailor iconography?'

'Who did it to you?'

'A tattoo artist *did* it to me.' She laughs. 'A very sexy, Paolo Nutini lookalike tattoo artist, if you must know.'

Who the hell was Paulo Nutini?

'Where?'

'Camden Market. That place is awesome. I could have spent a fortune. And guess what? I got a job!' She sits up on her elbows and I have to look away so it doesn't look as if I'm leering at her bosom. 'I met this guy called Wayne.'

'Wayne?' I grimace. 'Unfortunate name.'

'I know, but he had *the* most wickedest shop – well, it's not his, it's his mate's, but he's working on it part-time. We got chatting, coz he's originally from Sheffield and his accent stood out. I said I'd just landed for the summer and he said he needed some help at weekends and occasionally during the week, so . . .'

'Hang on. Who *is* this Wayne?'

'He runs a shop in Camden Market, like I said. And he lives in Battersea!'

'Where?'

'On a boat, how special is that? Anyway, do you wanna see the stuff I bought?'

'Yeah, sure.' I decide to come back to the Wayne thing later; this was all going way too fast. So then she's up, padding across the garden, legs as skinny as a stork. She gets hold of my hand.

'Come to my boudoir,' she says, which sounds ridiculous in her thick Yorkshire accent, and I follow her, helpless.

We go through the lounge.

'Soz about the mess,' she says, trampling all over the cushions she's tossed on the floor earlier. 'I was trying my new stuff on and was just about to start tidying up when you came home.'

'That's okay!' I lie, quickly replacing all the cushions on the sofa.

We get to the guest bedroom.

'Okay, you stay there,' she says, hands on my shoulders,

pushing me against the wall. And then she goes inside and closes the door so I am left staring at it, suddenly feeling like a stranger in my own home. Five seconds later, music is on.

'Ta-dar!' She flings open the door.

'Nice,' I say. 'What is it, exactly?'

'It's a playsuit, divvy. A vintage one.'

'So when would you wear it?'

'Anywhere, shopping?'

Not shopping with me you won't!

'Hanging out in cafés, in Battersea Park, maybe with some high-heeled sandals,' she says, doing a funny pose like one of those vintage postcards of ladies in 1920's bathing suits.

'And I got these . . .' She shoves a pair of shoes in my face. 'And this . . .' she puts on a purple trilby. 'Cool, or what? And there were loads of stalls and some right nutters selling stuff. There was this bloke, right, he came up to me and he was going, "marijuana", but pronouncing it with a "J" which cracked me up. So he was like, "Do you wan-na, some maru-ju-ana?"' She puts her hand on her hip and says it with a convincing Jamaican accent, which, despite myself, makes me laugh. A little. 'Then he was like, "Do you wan-na some Es?" That's when I texted you.'

Es? At Camden Market? Why was I never offered Es at Camden Market? Well, could be I've never *been* to Camden Market . . .

'And, guess what? Jerome was there!'

'Who on earth's Jerome?'

'A guy I met on the way here on the train – you know, the one who rang me yesterday?'

So that's who she was going all coy with.

'Anyway, he's somethin' spesh, he is. Such an inspiring person. He says he wants to photograph me. He says I have a very interesting look.'

'Lexi,' I groan. I get that feeling, like stop the train, I want

34

to get off. 'You can't just meet up with randoms off the train and let them take your picture. This is London. A big, scary, dangerous city.'

I've been thinking all day about what Dad said on the phone, but it's only later, when I've drunk the best part of half a bottle of wine, that I pluck up the courage to talk to her.

'So, Lexi . . .' She's slumped on the sofa in the playsuit; laptop open, one eye on Facebook. 'I think we need to chat.'

'Wow, sounds serious. Are you about to dump me?'

'*No!*' Sometimes, Lexi strikes me as very sophisticated. Then she says things like that and she sounds about twelve.

I reach over and slowly close her laptop.

'Look, you know you're very welcome to stay . . .' I start.

'But,' she says.

'But?'

'There's a "but" in there, isn't there?'

'No, not exactly.' God, I'm crap at this. 'It's just, Dad's worried about you. *I'm* worried about you. I think we need a plan for this summer, that's all.'

'What sort of plan?'

'A plan, you know? A goal. An aim.'

'God, now you sound like Mum and Dad. They can't go to the toilet without a personal goal.'

I resent this comparison. I hardly think me suggesting a few things for Lexi to concentrate on constitutes a 'motivational talk' on a level with the talks (that'll be evangelical lectures) Dad and Cassandra give as key speakers with the Healing Horizons Forum (that'd be cult) that they run. And anyway, it was Dad who insisted I talked to her. I would quite happily have avoided anything of the sort.

'I made a list,' I say, finally.

'Not another one! You're obsessed with lists.'

'Oh, that's unfair.'

35

'I don't think it is. I've seen them all over the place. You make so many lists, I'm surprised you have time to do anything on them.'

'Lists help you to focus,' I say, grabbing my notebook and opening it at the page that says LEXI'S FIVE POINT PLAN.

'Number one, your room.'

'Oh, you've seen it?'

'Yes, and I nearly had a seizure, so please sort it out. Moving swiftly on. Number two, you need to get a job. If you're not going back to sixth form – which, incidentally is number three, we need to discuss sixth form properly – then you need to know what else you're going to do. I thought we could draw up your options.'

'Make a list you mean?'

'Number four,' I sigh. 'You need to call Dad.'

'I'll call him tomorrow.' She shrugs

'Good, well that's all of them.'

'That's it? That's the list?'

'Yup. Told you it wasn't serious.'

'But you said there were five points,' she says, edging closer.

'Did I?' I move my hand so that it covers up the fifth point. The bit Dad told me to do. The bit about finding out what's actually wrong with Lexi.

She uncurls my fingers from the notepad.

'Find out what's wrong with Lexi,' she reads out. 'God!' She flops dramatically onto the sofa. 'Did Dad put you up to this? He did, didn't he? There's *nothing* wrong with me, except that everyone keeps *asking* what's wrong with me, and my parents treat me like I'm depressed, or a total mentalist or like it's not totally normal for a seventeen-year-old to not know exactly where she's going or what to do with her life.'

'Of course it's normal,' I say. 'I'm thirty-two and I still haven't really got a clue what's going on with my life.'

'Liar!'

'It's true! It's just, Dad said—'

'I don't care what Dad said. He's such a moron sometimes. I mean, I love him, but he doesn't understand me. He and Mum, they're always like: "You could do anything you want to do, Alexis. The world is your oyster!" But what if you don't *know* what you want to do? What then?'

'I thought you said you wanted to be a shoe designer?'

'Oh, I don't mean that really. I'm crap at Art A level.'

'I'm sure you're not.'

'I am. I'm crap at *all* my A levels.'

Her face goes bright red and she looks like she might cry.

'Look,' I say, realizing this isn't going anywhere. 'We don't have to talk about it now.'

'Good,' she says, 'because there's no big secret. I just came here to have fun, that's all. I just want to have a good time.'

So why are you crying? I want to say. But of course, I don't.

CHAPTER FIVE

Caroline. Sorry, can't do exhibition tomorrow. Got an unavoidable appointment. Enjoy though.

I stare at the text again. The umpteenth time in two days. Why didn't he just call me? Caroline, too. Martin never calls me Caroline. And no kiss. Not even a friendly exclamation mark.

I call him one more time but it goes straight to answerphone and this time I don't leave a message. Still, Martin doesn't know how to be enigmatic so maybe he does, actually, have an unavoidable appointment; probably something to do with his wisdom teeth.

It's been almost a week since Lexi arrived, and, since the hair-dyeing fiasco and the tattoo, she's been on best behaviour. She seems to love this job with Wayne, who has already achieved guru status in my house.

'Wayne reckons people who write obsessive To Do lists are masking unhappiness,' said Lexi the other day, as I added 'dry-clean rugs' to the list pinned to the fridge.

'Does he now?' I said, thinking does anyone actually talk like that? And anyway, since when was a complete stranger qualified to comment on my state of mind?

'Yeah. He reckons they're just avoiding the big stuff.'

'Oh, right. I see. And what is this big stuff, according to Wayne?'

'Dunno, life I s'pose. He didn't really go into that bit.'

I rolled my eyes.

'That'll be because Wayne – who I am sure is lovely but who basically runs a jumble sale for a living, let's not forget – doesn't really know what he's talking about.'

In truth, I don't really care what Wayne says, as long as Lexi enjoys working for him and he gives her some focus. I'm still pretty worried about her. She won't talk to me, not really. We've chatted a bit about how she hated sixth form, a *lot* about her friend Carly and her disastrous love life, but nothing about hers. Once or twice, late at night, I've heard her having hushed, stressed conversations on the phone but I think I've finally worked out what that's about.

The other evening, quite out of the blue when we were watching *How to Look Good Naked*, she announced, 'Carly thinks she's pregnant.'

'You're joking,' I said, one eye on the telly. 'What's she going to do?'

'Dunno,' said Lexi. 'She hasn't done a test yet.'

'No way! If I was worried I was with child there's no way I could sit around wondering. I'd have to *know*.'

'Really?'

'Definitely. Anyway, I thought her boyfriend had dumped her?'

'He has, which is why it's a complete nightmare.'

There was a long pause. I was too busy watching the bit where they make her walk down an aisle, naked in a shopping centre, to really be listening, then she said,

'Anyway, Carly reckons she's decided she doesn't want to keep the baby if she is.'

'Oh. Right.'

'What's the furthest gone you can be before you have an abortion?' she added, after a long pause.

'Dunno. Twenty weeks? But then the problem is that some women give birth not even knowing they're pregnant, especially teenagers whose bodies don't even change that much.'

'What, so you could just think you're a bloater when really, you're like, eight months up the duff?'

'I s'pose so, yes.'

Then we watched *Celebrity Big Brother* and that was the end of that.

And so, what with Martin and his enigmatic 'unavoidable appointment' and Shona having to stay in and wait for a washing machine to be delivered, it's just Lexi and I who find ourselves standing in the starkness of the Pump House Gallery in Battersea Park, staring at a square of turf.

'So, by actually filming the grass growing . . .'

The curator, Barnaby Speck (I always read the accompanying leaflet from start to finish) is a bald, fleshy-lipped man who gives a little jump on words he finds exciting, like 'growing'.

'. . . Rindblatten is saying something about the mysterious, unseen nature of time. Time not experienced by us, time of the –' He jumps so much on this word, I see his red socks leave his shoes – 'Other of Otherness.'

'Eh?' Next to me, Lexi screws her little nose up. 'How do you go from a piece of grass, right?' I nudge her in the ribs, which she reacts to with a comedy death rattle under her breath. A woman in a green beret turns round and tuts.

'In short . . .' Barnaby Speck clears his throat in our direction. 'By actually witnessing the growing of the grass, Rindblatten forces us to acknowledge the events taking place in places we cannot or see, and thus expresses beautifully . . .'

40

I am suddenly aware of Lexi's warm, minty breath in my ear. 'What about that one there?'

I shoot her a sideways glance.

'What one?'

'The tall one with the dark hair and glasses.' She gestures in the direction of a man near the front of the crowd, peering intently at the installation – essentially, a napkin-sized square of turf surrounded by four camera lights, entitled: *Otherness. The Other. An Objective Study of Displacement* by Jergen Rindblatten. Lexi grimaced when I read from the leaflet: 'I smell a bollock,' she sniffed in that left-field way she has with words. 'But we can go if you want.'

I crane my neck to get a proper look at the man who is lanky, wearing a cardigan and looks about twelve.

'Nose too small.'

'What?' Lexi frowns. 'What do you mean, nose too small?'

The woman in the green beret turns round again and purses her thin, crimson lips at us. Then, thankfully, Barnaby Speck moves on from talking about the grass and we are encouraged to disperse and look at Jergen Rindblatten's accompanying sketches on the subject of 'Otherness', which line the wall of the sun-flooded gallery.

'Can't do a small nose; it looks like it belongs on a doll and makes mine look even bigger.' We stand, admiring a sketch entitled, *Untitled*. 'Also, he looks about your age.'

Lexi sighs and looks around. I study the drawing, which looks like a square to me but I'm sure it's layered with meaning if you know how to interpret these things.

Suddenly, Lexi gasps.

'Ohmigod!' She nudges me in the elbow. 'I might actually have found my future husband.'

I look to where she's indicating, to see a lean, black guy, record bag draped across his broad chest, looking intently at the drawing next to us.

41

'Good God, no, he's wearing a gold chain.'

'Yeah? And? He's gorgeous! I'd 'ave him. He looks like Dizzee Rascal.'

'Who the hell's Dizzy Rasta?'

'You know,' says Lexi. '"Bonkers"!'

'Bonkers?'

'The song, "Bonkers".'

I roll my eyes at her. Who in their right mind would bring out a record called *Bonkers* for crying out loud.

Then she starts singing:

'Some people think I'm bonkers, some people think I'm mad. Some people think I'm crazy but there's nothin' crazy 'bout–'

'Lexi!' I grab her by her rapping arm. The tattooed arm. 'Just concentrate on the art, will you?'

We make our way around the gallery, which sits at the top of a spiral staircase in a tall, old pump house in the middle of Battersea Park. Outside, down below from where we're standing, I can see two swans gliding on a lake, which glitters with hot, afternoon sun, and a young couple standing arm in arm on a wooden bridge.

I turn my attention to another drawing, which depicts what looks like a mound of cow dung.

Lexi moves in next to me, head cocked to the side, pretending to read the accompanying commentary.

'Another hottie,' she suddenly hisses into my ear. 'Ten past two. Your ideal man.'

'Soz,' mumbles Lexi. We're walking across the park towards the river now. 'It just wasn't my thing. When you said "art", I thought you meant proper art, like paintings, sculpture, something where they'd splattered paint on canvas and it meant "happiness" or "death" or something.'

Half of me wants to protest. Half of me thinks: this *was*

art, proper conceptual art, if you must know – not bloody Monet's water lily paintings. You wouldn't get this in Doncaster! Honestly, you try your best to show someone some real London culture and this is the thanks you get. I wasn't sure Lex and I were really going to agree on much. However, I must admit that the other half of me did kind of agree – *Otherness. The Other. An Objective Study of Displacement* didn't quite live up to my expectations, either, and, in fact, I'm wondering, if I took, say, a fork, bashed it about a bit and then wrote something about how this represented the domestic unrest I experienced as a child, I, too, could be an acclaimed artist with a 'ground-breaking' exhibition at the Pump House Gallery.

Also, I think to myself as we walk across the park, dodging rounders' teams and men in rugby shirts and cropped trousers attempting to light barbecues, we had to leave. I couldn't have tolerated one minute more of Lexi's 'talent-spotting'.

It's all my fault. I should never have humoured her 'Find Caroline a Boyfriend' project, which was born last night, probably as a distraction from the Lexi Five Point Plan Project. (I wonder what Guru Wayne would make of *that* little manoeuvre.)

I didn't have the heart, when she was looking at sad dating sites where sad people gather to meet other sad people, to say, 'Look, Lex, I don't want a boyfriend, I really don't. All that having to get your bikini line waxed and worrying if they'll call. I just can't be bothered.'

We're still walking across the park. Lexi won't let the match-making thing lie. 'He was your ideal type, though, wasn't he?' she says referring to the blond man in the gallery. 'Tall, blond, handsome. He was well sexy, you should have given him your number.'

'He was nice,' I say, dodging a couple, their legs entwined on a picnic rug, 'but like I say, I'm happy being single.'

'If you say so. Although nobody's really happy being single, let's face it, not for long anyway. Wayne says single people suffer more depression than those who are attached, that it's part of being human to want somebody.'

Praise be to the God of Wayne! Maybe Wayne should write his own self-help book.

'The most Carly's gone without a boyfriend is twenty-five days and that was only—'

'You're single, aren't you?' I say, turning to her. It's more of a question than a statement. Something boy-related is going on, I'm sure of that, but then something's always going on in a teenager's love life.

We've stopped walking now, Lexi is looking at me.

'Yeah,' she says. 'I s'pose I am. Well it's a bit . . .' She looks the other way, like she might be about to cry, and I have a sudden desire to hug her. Not that I did the whole messy teenage business of falling in and out of love, not even having a boyfriend until Martin at eighteen. But I recognize that if-you-prod-me-I-will-break look, so I smile.

'It's all right, Lex,' I say. 'You don't have to explain yourself to me.'

I'm about to carry on walking when my eyes are drawn towards the men in the rugby shirts trying to light barbecues. One man in particular looks familiar. It's the legs that do it. Stocky, with no ankles. Those are *Martin's* legs.

Just as this thought sinks in, he looks up from the BBQ he's poking, gives an awkward smile, and starts to walk over.

'Bloody bugger!' I say, squinting at him.

'Caroline,' says Lexi. 'Language, please!'

Martin grins sheepishly and waves as he walks over, that same slightly lolloping walk of his. 'Unavoidable appointment'? Likely story!

44

'Hello, you.' He's standing right in front of us now, holding out his barbecue prongs like we should shake them or something. 'I didn't expect to see you here, Caro.'

He's had his hair cut since I last saw him three weeks ago, into a bizarre little quiff that doesn't really suit him. However, he's tended to it like he does to everything, with meticulous precision so that it is a perfectly symmetrical, topiary-like construction on the top of his head.

'Clearly, Martin Squire. So what's the unavoidable appointment, then?' I prod him jokily in the stomach. 'A barbecue with your mates? You could have just said.'

'I know I could, it's just . . .'

'Sorry, you know Lexi, my sister, don't you?' I say, when I can see he's struggling. 'Lexi, you remember Martin?'

'Oh yeah, I remember Martin.' I shoot her a look – why the rude tone? Oh. I know why the rude tone. 'We met a few times,' she carries on. I feel the blood rise in my cheeks. 'The last time when you were actually *engaged* to my sister.'

Martin's eyes dart to mine. Mine dart to the floor.

Why didn't I just tell her it was me who broke off our engagement?

'So, er, how's tricks, Caro?' says Martin, after a very awkward pause. 'Just having a walk?'

'We've been to see an art exhibition, actually.' Lexi folds her arms, indignantly. 'It was at the Pulp House–'

'The Pump House, Lexi.'

'It was brilliant, really inspiring.'

God, Lexi, just shut the fuck up.

'You should go if you get the chance, although probably best to go with someone, you know, if you can.'

'Right,' says Martin, staring at me with something combining boy-caught-out and confusion. This is dreadful.

We stand in awkward silence until I see a blonde, plumpish

45

girl in flip-flops and a cotton shirt dress walking towards us, smiling.

'Hello . . .' She puts her arm around Martin's back.

A girlfriend?! Martin has a girlfriend?

'Oh, hello P.' P? Pee?! Bloody hell, were they already on pet names and he hasn't even told me he's seeing someone? 'You made me jump. Caroline, Lexi this is Polly. Polly, this is Caroline and her sister, Lexi.'

'Hi!' She smiles. She has a ruddy complexion, well-bred teeth and earnest, uncomplicated eyes.

'Hi,' I say, my face fixed into something I hope resembles friendliness. I look over at Lexi, urging her to say the same, but she's chewing the inside of her cheek and looking Polly up and down.

'Anyway . . .' I say

'Anyway,' agrees Martin.

'We'd better get going.'

'Yes, we've got so much to fit in today,' says Lexi. 'Shopping, having dinner . . .'

'Nice to meet you, anyway, Polly,' I say, squeezing Lexi's hand tighter. 'Have a lovely barbecue.'

'We will,' says Martin, somewhat feebly.

And then we carry on across the park, and the soundtrack of a summer's day in London – planes flying into Heathrow, roller-bladers' shrieks of delight, the laughter of friends on picnic rugs – is drowned out by the sound of my brain trying to fathom how I feel about what just happened.

CHAPTER SIX

After a bus ride, where Lexi goes on about how I am so much prettier than Polly and how Martin wanted me back, she could see it in his eyes, we end up in a Mexican on the King's Road.

Lexi studies me over her menu, twiddling her fringe.

'Are you all right?' she asks.

'Me? Fine.'

'Are you upset about Polly?'

'No. *No,*' I say, totally unconvincingly. 'It was going to happen sooner or later.' Although I didn't expect it quite so soon. We only split up last September. That's nine months ago. Nine months to get over a fourteen-year relationship? I thought I might have made a little more impact than that.

'Can I ask you a question, then?'

'Fire away,' I say, forcing a smile.

'Was I right?'

I scour the menu, pretending to be making vital decisions between a burrito and a taco.

'Right about what?'

'The dress.' She puts the menu down now and folds her slim, tanned arms. 'The wedding dress? Look, I know it's none of my business but I think the reason you were wearing

47

your wedding dress when I turned up and that you were drunk . . .'

I wince at the drunk bit.

'. . . and sh-mok-ing . . .'

'Now you're just rubbing it in.'

'. . . was because you were upset about Martin, you know, and the fact −' she cocks her head to the side sympathetically, which makes me feel even more terrible − 'the wedding didn't happen?'

'If only it were that simple,' I say, in a you-wouldn't-understand-you're-only-seventeen kind of a way.

But clearly she does understand, because then she says, 'Caroline. How many times have you had that dress on?'

'Why? What's it to you?'

'Come on, I just wanna know. How many times have you had it on in, say, the past six months?

I don't know how the wedding dress thing happened, it just did, a self-indulgent little ritual that got out of control. It was a bit like how some people feel the need to get all their hair hacked off when a relationship ends, or go out and get drunk.

That dress was gorgeous, too, a vintage-style gown with silk sleeves sliced to the waist and a four foot train. I pictured myself walking down the aisle, smiling and radiant on my wedding day, arm in arm with Dad, who, for just that one day, would be there for me. Just *me*. I would be a success story. Because someone wanted me and loved me enough to marry me.

But, in the end, that dress, which was supposed to represent My Future, just smells faintly of cigarette smoke and regret and sits at the top of my wardrobe only to be brought out after another romance bites the dust, so I can wallow in could-have-beens.

Of course, Lexi's right; the first time it came out was two months after Martin and I finished, which was one month after the wedding that never happened, which, like I say, was almost a year now and I'm still wracked with guilt . . .

'Hello?' Lexi says. She's got her 'computer generated' voice on. 'Calling Caroline Steele to planet Earth. Calling Caroline Marie Steele—'

'Three times, okay? I've had the dress on three times.'

She raises an eyebrow.

'Okay, possibly five. And, yes, if you must know, I did once put it on and get drunk and listen to Pat Benitar because I was upset about Martin — but that wasn't really why I had it on when you arrived.'

'Right, got yer,' says Lexi. 'So who were you crying about, then?'

Who was I crying about? It's hard to tell. Since Martin and the first outing of the dress, there's been a wake of casualties: Nathan — a Kiwi I met on a client do who I fancied like mad but who then asked me if I wanted to come and visit his mum in New Zealand *three* weeks after I started seeing him. I made a sharp exit in the opposite direction. There was Mark — I had hopes for him, could have really fallen for his green eyes and penchant for obscure French films, but then I realized he was just pretentious. In the end, I could no longer tolerate him calling me Carol-eeen (if he had actually been French that would have been fine, but he wasn't, he was from Walsall). And of course there was Garf, lovely Garf, who I dumped at his sister's wedding, which was held at Walthamstow Dogs Track (not that his family's love of dog racing was a deal-breaker or anything). He was the sweetest of the lot and he could have really loved me, but I couldn't love him, probably because I was already falling for someone else by then, I just didn't know it yet.

So, a pattern emerged. Every time a relationship ended, I

would find myself getting sentimental and morose and drinking alone in my wedding dress. But really, I wasn't upset about Nathan or Mark or Garf, I was just upset that, at thirty-two, I was no closer to finding The One, and asking myself whether I'd made a huge mistake letting Martin go. After all, I still loved him, even if he was a bit middle-aged, had over-bearing parents and could spend three hours making the perfect pesto. I just don't know whether I was ever *in* love with him, that's all, not after the first few years anyway. But the older I get and the more complicated life becomes, I am beginning to wonder whether I could settle for 'love' rather than 'in love', which everybody knows is the solid, reliable concrete that remains beneath your feet, when the sparkling snow has melted away.

Still, I reasoned, it could be worse. At least I had the book club . . .

CHAPTER SEVEN

Toby leans coolly against my bedroom window frame, takes a slow, deep drag on his cigarette, his eyebrows smouldering as he does. I swear he's putting that on now.

'God, you really look like James Dean doing that.'

'Do I?' he says.

'Yes, except for maybe the socks.' I squint at his feet. 'Are they actually South Park socks?'

It's a rare man that can pull off nudity *avec* South Park socks with all the style and nonchalance of a Hollywood sex god, but Toby Delaney manages to.

I sit up in bed and pull the sheet up so my nipples don't escape. It's 8.08 p.m., still broad daylight outside, the hum of traffic from Battersea Park Road just audible, and Toby is smoking a post-coital cigarette out of my bedroom window. It's something he's done every other Wednesday for the past five months, a ritual of the 'book club'. Except, it isn't a book club at all. It's more, well, it's more of a fuck club. With just the two members: Toby and me.

Rachel, Toby's wife thinks it's a book club. She thinks that every second Wednesday, Toby comes to my house in Battersea to discuss the naked prose of M. J. Hyland, when really, he's just there to get naked with me.

I sink further down into the duvet and take a moment to savour his physical form. I never know when it might be my last chance, after all. When all this might implode. When he, or I, decide we can't do this any more. His long, slim legs, which drive me crazy, his bum, possibly less firm than it could be but that's because he spends so much time sitting on it. Lazy bugger. His . . . Yep, he's got a very nice one. Surely it spells trouble if you're starting to find their flaccid penis attractive?

My eyes move up his body to that flat, boyish belly of his, which he's always stuffing but which never increases. It incites a sort of erotic envy in me. His chest, lean yet broad, that perfect smattering of darkish hair and then that bizarre, mutant third nipple, tiny like a baby's, which apparently is very common and which I find thrilling because when he's at work I know it's there, under his shirt. Our little secret. And, finally, his face. The bit I crave the most when he's not here: that gorgeous line from his Adam's apple to his chin to his jaw, emphasized by a two-day shadow, which I know he's kept for me because I've got a thing for facial hair. (A throwback from a crippling crush on Tom Selleck in *Three Men and a Baby*). The fine, distinguished nose and the sexy quiff of a fringe. Then the famous Delaney eyebrows, which I love and despise all at the same time because they give away all of his feelings. They frequently disappoint me.

Toby sucks hard on his Lucky Strike.

'So what did you tell your sister again?' he asks.

'That I was hosting a book club. That it would be full of geeks reading *War and Peace* and that she'd hate it.'

Toby laughs.

'Steele, you're a genius. And did she buy it?' He exhales the last of his cigarette and gets back into bed, slipping his cool, hard body next to mine.

'Oh yeah, totally. She was like, "yawn" and other teenage expressions denoting boredom.'

Toby smiles, amused, snuggles under the duvet and grabs my bum.

'Anyway, she said she was going swimming followed by some body combat class at the gym, thank God. Otherwise, I don't know what I would have said to get her out of the house.'

'Like I said, Steeley, perhaps we'll have to de-camp.' Toby puts one arm across my chest then pulls me on top of him.

'Decamp what?'

'The book club, of course.' He cups my boobs in his hands and gives them a squeeze. 'I can't do without my book club, no way. I'd go crazy with lust.'

'Really?' I say, with more hope in my voice than I'd intended.

'Er, *yeah*. Let's see.' He frowns up at the ceiling in mock concentration. 'Firstly, with whom else would I get to discuss whether *Pride and Prejudice* is, in fact, the perfect novel?'

He gives one of his infectious schoolboy giggles and I kiss him on the lips.

'How would I get through the week without hearing what a genius – who's that Japanese bloke you love?'

'Murakami.'

'Yeah, him. What a genius he is. Where would we be without having to make it through another fucking Joanna Trollope novel?' We both burst out laughing. 'Shit, I mean, seriously!' We're both snorting now. 'Enough to make you want to open a vein. And then there's that Houellebecq dude. What a barrel of laughs he was.'

He assumes a deep, pompous voice. '"I found *Atomised* very nihilistic text."'

I bury my head in his chest and shake with laughter.

'Don't be mean! At least Charles was actually taking it seriously, unlike someone I know.'

'Who was just there because he fancied the arse off a certain book club member? A member who, as well as exquisite taste in literature, also happens to have the best norks in London.' He squeezes them again and we end up snogging.

I guess this is how I manage to square all this in my head (which most of the time I don't, meaning I spend my waking hours swinging between ridiculous excitement at the prospect of the 'book club' and feeling like a wanton whore who is destined for hell). There once was an actual book club. Once upon a time, that wasn't a lie. It was Marta's idea, Marta being the office martyr, arranging countless, thankless, work-bonding events. We needed a venue, so I volunteered. It had been two months since Martin moved out and I liked the idea of the house being full once a fortnight. I imagined we'd sit around a roaring fire, sipping vintage Merlot and discussing so-and-so's use of personification and whether we identified with such-and-such protagonist. What actually happened was that we'd discuss the book for ten minutes, get slaughtered on Blossom Hill. Then have a row.

What was supposed to be a bonding exercise ended up dividing the office. It was 'us': Me, Toby, Shona and Charles from marketing ('The ones with degrees,' Toby would comment with typical scathing humour) and 'them': Marta, Health and Safety Heather and Toupee Dom ('the plebs' – Toby, again). The plebs thought our book choices were pretentious. We thought theirs were lame. Everything came to a head when Toby said that Heather's choice – admittedly it was *Flowers in the Attic* by Virginia Andrews – had less literary merit than a McDonald's menu, and she fled from the club in tears.

And so, one by one, people fell away until it was just Toby and I who found ourselves in my lounge, books in hands. I knew immediately this was a bad idea. We were reading *Intimacy* by Hanif Kureishi (my choice). An account of the night before a man leaves his wife, charting the unravelling of a relationship; how you can look at someone you've known for ten years and feel nothing.

'How can you be married to someone for ten years and feel nothing?' I said. We were sitting at my dining table. I'd lit candles – something I'd never done when everybody else was here.

'Oh, it's possible, believe me,' said Toby, those eyebrows smouldering, fixing me with his hypnotic blue eyes 'And it doesn't have to take ten years.'

I read a passage aloud. The drunker we got, the more seriously we were taking it. Or perhaps it was because discussing the book meant we didn't have to acknowledge the strangling sexual tension in the room. I could feel Toby's eyes burn my eyelids as I read. I looked up from the book and he was still holding my gaze. I read on, my heart thumping. Then there was a line where the narrator says how he never found a way to be 'pleasurably idle' with his wife; how she was always so busy, wanted too much out of life.

'I know that feeling,' said Toby. His gaze was intense, penetrating. Gone was the usual, puppy-dog Toby; he was serious. 'Feeling neglected, unimportant.'

The room had gone deathly quiet and I pulled a face. No doubt wholly unattractive, but nerves do that to me.

Then Toby said: 'You know what, Caroline (he never called me Caroline, only Steeley)? I think you may be one of the few women who *does* understand me.'

I downed a glass of red in one. Then Toby sat down next to me, moved his face millimetres from mine and kissed me, but I'd not had time to swallow the wine so a dribble ended up in his mouth.

'Sorry!' Another bit escaped down my chin, so I now resembled an incompetent vampire.

'Don't apologize,' he said. 'Red wine and Caroline Steele. Two of my favourite things.'

Things went from nought to sixty in about ten minutes. We abandoned the books and my top and started on the vodka (the beginning of the end). The next thing I know, I'm lying on the lounge floor smoking Lucky Strikes whilst Toby showers my belly with kisses (the end of the end) and he's telling me he thinks I'm 'enigmatic' and I'm telling him I find it hard not to touch him at work, that I think he looks like James Dean. At which point, I imagine, I ceased to be enigmatic.

And then he says, giving me the most gorgeous, stubbly kiss, 'Well, if I'm going to live fast and die young I'd better get the snogs in now . . .' And a small explosion took place in my groin.

Then we ended up in my bed.

'We need condoms!' I said as he pulled my tights off. 'We need condoms and we need fags!' That's the last thing I remember. I woke up, with just my bra on, a Lucky Strike – you live, or you die, the in-joke of the evening – lodged between my cleavage.

In this case, I died. Of utter embarrassment. Talk about out of character. Toby, on the other hand, thought it was hysterical.

'And I thought you were stuck up,' he said, laughing and laughing in the office kitchen the next day, as I stood, face in hands.

'This can never, ever happen again,' I hissed. 'You are bloody well married and I . . . I want to be single.'

He raised his James Dean eyebrows at me. My cheeks burned furiously.

'Not that I was suggesting . . .'

'Oh, Steeley,' he said, with his sexy little lisp, taking my hand. 'Take a chill pill. It'll be our little secret.' Then he sighed. 'But yes, you're right, we can't do this again'. He grimaced in a way that told me he didn't mean this at all. 'You are, however, sexy as hell. Remember that.'

I did. Oh, I did.

I shuffled into work later after a horrifying, near-vomit experience on the tube where I heaved, but nothing came out, so that people on my carriage just parted, like a wave as I made a sound like a dying walrus. I was green and the heel of one shoe was missing. Last seen, rolling down the escalator of Marble Arch station.

As the day wore on and the alcohol wore off, the reality of what I'd done hit me. I'd slept with a married man. In the space of five months, I had dumped my fiancé, dumped a string of men and slept with someone else's husband.

And it had all started off so well, too! For the first four years of working together, I was the only person out of twenty-two graduates on the Skidmore-Colt-Davis graduate trainee scheme who hadn't had so much as a party kiss with Mr Delaney. This was my first grown-up, 'proper' job, after all, and I was in the thick of a ten year, *very* grown-up relationship with Martin Squire. So whilst all my new colleagues were out drinking till 3 a.m. and jumping into one another's beds, I was batch-cooking risotto.

'Two birds with one stone, Caro!' Martin would proudly announce, like batch-cooking actually elevated him to a higher spiritual plain. 'This will do us for tea *and* five days of lunches!'

It has come to light since – I know because he's told me – that Toby was somewhat fascinated by me. He was the unmistakable heartthrob of the grad scheme. His unique blend of raw sexiness and little-boy-lost look had all the girls wanting to soothe his hangovers, then roger him senseless and bear his children, me included.

And yet I never stayed behind to get drunk, always went home to the boyfriend. That wasn't to say I didn't have the same filthy thoughts as everyone else, I was just a pro at self-control. On the few occasions that Martin and Toby met at work drinks, I would squirm, then feel *terrible* for squirming. They would talk about music – nobody is less sporty than Martin and it seems to be sport or music with men. I would be trying to concentrate on whatever conversation I was having whilst overhearing Martin going, 'David Gray, Toby, *he's* your man!' whilst Toby raised his eyebrow at me over Martin's shoulder and tried not to laugh.

Then, in 2004, four years after Toby and I met on the first day of the grad scheme, he was head-hunted and we didn't see each other for another four years. But then, one day in the October of 2008, I heard a familiar voice in the office: loud, slightly husky, with an adorable lisp. My stomach turned upside down.

So now we're here, with me snogging a married man in the living room of the house I used to share with my fiancé. Like I said, it was all going so well . . .

Perhaps, I reasoned, that now I was going to hell anyway, I may as well get the best seat there, because despite my resolve, come a fortnight later, when Toby kissed me outside the tube station, cocked his eyebrow and said, 'Back to yours?' I dissolved.

Well, that was it. I had lost face, dignity, any enigmatic qualities I might have ever possessed. I was damned if he thought he was just going to continue to get me drunk, then have his wicked way with me any time he wanted. I was damned if I was going to get involved. If we were going to play this game, then there were going to be some rules. The book club rules. My house, every other Wednesday. Out by 9.30 p.m.

So, in an effort to show Toby Delaney that I am not the sort of girl he can just get slaughtered then shag, I have become the sort of girl who makes a fortnightly appointment to sleep with someone's husband. Which suits me fine, of course. Sex with someone who is already taken. I couldn't get involved if I wanted to.

We're dozing in bed now. Beside me I can see the red digits of my clock winking, menacingly: 8.16 p.m. Forty-four minutes until he has to go.

'Would sex vixen of SW11 care for a glass of wine?' asks Toby.

I roll on top of him and sigh.

'Is it that time already?'

''Fraid so, treacle.' He smacks my bottom. 'Wine time, home time . . . Worst luck.'

I kiss his nose and get out of bed. 'You don't mean that,' I say, turning towards the window so he can't see my smile.

We get dressed and go down to the kitchen. Post-coital, ice-cold Sauvignon Blanc being one of the book club rituals.

'Do you know what I love about you most, Steeley?' says Toby, pouring me a glass.

'No, go on, what do you love most about me?'

'You're like a bloke.'

'Oh.'

'Oh, baby!' he says, seeing my face fall. This time his schoolboy snort is a little irritating. 'I don't mean in the way you look – you're foxy as all hell, you know I think that – I just mean in the way you are.' He pushes me gently against the worktop and kisses me. 'You have a rare gift for a woman.'

Our noses are touching now; I'm staring right into his blue, blue eyes.

'Really? And what's that?'

'You're able to compartmentalize things. Get what you want, when you want. You're in control of things. It's ridiculously sexy . . .' He puts his hand between my legs. I remove it.

'Stop that! You'll set me off.'

'Like, take a look at this. This book club. This little fuck club of ours, young lady.' He's putting his hands through my hair piling it on top of my head.

I open my mouth to laugh but nothing comes out.

'Don't pretend you didn't orchestrate all this. This suits you down to the ground, doesn't it? You schedule me in on a fortnightly basis. Three hours. Your house. Nice and tidy.'

I prod his stomach, look at him saucily.

'Now you're making me out to be some sort of cold fish.'

'I'm trying to give you a compliment, actually. All I'm saying is that you're not governed by constant, irrational emotion like most women, are you, Caroline?'

'Oh God no. No, no! Never been like that.'

'Not like Rachel. Jesus! She's such a woman, is Rachel.'

I lean against his chest. The mention of Rachel − which doesn't happen often − incites a sort of fascinated fear in me. Like I want him to shut up and carry on all at the same time.

'What do you mean by that?'

'I just mean it's constant, you know?'

'Constant what?'

Don't dig too much. Remain nonchalant. Nonchalant and not governed by constant, irrational emotion.

'Constant woman-ness with her. It's *all* about her, Steeley. If she's not spending the whole bloody weekend counselling some boring friend about her drama, she's having a drama herself. Or we're going to yet another do with the boring

Uni Girls, or yet another boring awards ceremony for her. Or she's working, always working.'

I feel a stab of insecurity. Rachel is well-known in the industry for winning awards. When she first met Toby she was selling soft drinks and used to sweep the board at the Trade's Awards, twice being named Sales Person of the Year.

'Sex has gone completely off the radar, she's not interested.'

'How . . .' I kiss him '. . . can that be possible when you're such an irresistible sex god?'

He laughs.

'She's uptight. Doesn't let herself go, like you. If we do have sex, it's like something that's got to be factored in to her tight schedule, something on her fucking endless To Do list, do you know what I mean?'

I shake my head. To Do list. Who would reduce their entire life to a To Do list?

'To be honest, sometimes,' he says, 'I feel like an extra in the show that is Rachel's life.'

'Well,' I say, slipping a hand under his shirt. (Must balance fine line between wanton sex goddess and only-woman-who-understands-him.) 'We can't have that.'

Toby cups my face in his hand.

'Fuck me, I fancy you,' he says. 'What is it about you, Caroline Steele, that means that when I am around you, I just want to have sex with you?'

Our top halves are off in seconds, the bottom two of Toby's shirt buttons sent skidding across the floor. Toby pushes me backwards against the fridge, sending magnets and papers flying. I cover his chest with kisses, his hair smells incredible, that shower-fresh, sugary, bakery smell, times about five hundred. I inhale as he pushes my hair back and kisses me, hard; on my face, my neck, my breasts. There's the feverish undoing of belts, which is awkward since I am wearing one of those fabric ones and for some reason he keeps squeezing

61

it the wrong way so that my insides are getting squashed. Finally, after much giggling, I'm up against my fridge, naked, jeans around my ankles. A woman possessed. Possessed by a harlot in my own kitchen.

I want him so badly now. I drop down and take him in my mouth. His pubes smell delicious, clean, with a faint muskiness that sparks another explosion that spreads from my groin, right down my thighs.

'Jesus, you're good at that,' he says, leaning back onto the fridge, and laughing, a sort of half-laugh, half-groan. His eyes are closed, his whole body rigid, except his hands, which are gently pushing my head, and his knees that are bending, along to the same rhythm as me.

'Stop,' he says, softly. 'Stop. I won't last two minutes if you carry on like that.'

Then we're on the floor, he wants me on top of him and I happily oblige. I am possessed, again, by someone who writhes and swishes her hair and her hips, like a belly-dancer, there, next to the whirring fridge, as, outside, the birds break out into evensong and, inside, I think I might explode with desire.

We're lying on the kitchen floor now – me on top of Toby in a breathless, sweaty, elated heap.

Then I hear the door go.

'Fuck!'

'What?' says Toby alarmed.

'It's Lexi, she's back!'

'You're joking?'

'Do I look like I'm joking?' I'm scrambling off him now. Toby's spread-eagled, naked except for a large erection and the South Park socks.

'Get up!' I hiss, flapping my arms about.

'All right keep yer knickers on.'

'I would if I could find them!'

I'm flitting about the kitchen now. Toby's standing, scratching his head and smirking at me. He thinks this is funny.

'Right, you through the utility room and into the bathroom,' I say, spotting my knickers scrunched up like a sleeping rodent next to the fridge.

'What?'

'Just do it!' I push him, still sniggering through the door and kick his clothes in after him.

I hear Lexi slam the front door shut and call down the hallway,

'Hel-lo-oh! I'm back!'

'Just using the loo!' I shout back. It's lame but, frankly, I need anything that's going to stall her.

I manage to get one leg in one hole of my knickers, as I hear her drop her bag on the hallway floor, then follow Toby, limping, into the bathroom.

'I can't find my pants,' he whispers, rummaging through the pile of clothes.

'Well, just wear your trousers then. You'll have to go commando.'

I hear Lexi cough, dramatically, and drag her heels towards the kitchen. Just those two sounds tell me she's drunk. Body combat class, my arse.

Then she's hammering on the bathroom door.

'Hurry up, Missus. I'm gonna piss my pants! Can't make it upstairs!'

Toby's buttoning his shirt, his face red with the effort of not laughing.

'Won't be long!' I shout. Fuck. Fuck. Fuck it! How was I going to get out of this one now?

'In the bath,' I mouth to Toby

'The what?'

'It's leaking out!' moans Lexi.

'All right, can you just hang on a second?'

'Not su-re!' She's singing the words now, intermittently leaning against the door and making it bang. 'There might be a little puddle in your kitchen if I don't get in there soo-oon!'

Eventually, I get Toby crouched safely down behind the shower curtain, flush the toilet and open the door.

'Ohmigodimgonnapissmyself,' Lexi barges right past me clutching her crotch.

I hear the toilet cover go up, then Lexi sigh, heavily, as she announces. 'Oh Lordy,' over the longest, loudest wee ever known to man. 'I fucking needed that.'

To be honest, at first I'm so relieved that Lexi didn't catch me riding Toby on the kitchen floor that I forget to be annoyed that she's drunk. But she is. Leathered, in fact. My little sister is totally pissed.

I managed to persuade her upstairs for a few minutes by presenting her with a pile of laundry, thus freeing Toby up. As far as she's concerned when she comes down, he just emerged from the lounge.

Lexi stands, arms folded, giving Toby the once over.

'So. Who's this then?'

'This is Toby Delaney.' I've no idea why I give him his full title. Like we're in a Jane Austen period drama or something.

'Hello, Toby *Delaney*,' she says.

She's wearing a black, stretchy minidress, pointy shoes with bows on them and a leather biker jacket. In my mother's book this would definitely qualify as a look that says, 'On the game.'

Toby's sitting up on the worktop, hands clasped neatly in his lap in a gesture that says, 'Do I look like a man who was just having sex on the kitchen floor?'

'Hi . . .?'

'Alexis,' she says.

Alexis? Since when did she ever want to be called Alexis?

She pulls out a kitchen chair and sits down, stretching out her long, bare legs. If I didn't know any better I'd say she was flirting.

'Cool name,' says Toby. 'So how was the body combat class? Back when us two old timers were young . . .' Ha! He's got a cheek. Less of the 'old timers' and the 'us two' thanks very much. 'It was aerobics or step class. Everyone was lugging these step things about.'

Lexi giggles. A mixture of nerves and a certain thrill, perhaps, that a handsome, older man is talking to her.

She leans forward and rests her dainty chin on her hand so that you can see her perfect B-cups resting in a floral lace bra.

I check Toby. His eyes dart upwards. Caught!

'Eh, so you're that Toby off the photo aren't you?' she says, her accent even stronger now she's obviously had a drink.

Oh, that's great, that is. Now he's going to think I'm obsessed with that photo.

'What photo's that?'

'Brighton,' I say curtly. 'Anyway, hadn't you better be getting a shower or something, Lexi?' I glare at her but she ignores me or she's just too pissed to take a hint.

'It doesn't do you justice,' she says. She's looking up at Toby from under mascara-smudged eyes. She *is* flirting. God, I could kill her! 'You know how some people look better in a photo and some people take a rubbish photo but look much better in the flesh?' she slurs on. 'Well, you're definitely the latter type.'

Toby laughs, flattered. I shoot him a look.

She takes off her leather jacket and puts it on the back of her chair, sliding it back from the table slightly. That's when

I see them. Toby's Tommy Hilfiger boxer shorts, caught under the front right chair leg! I look over at Toby. Had he spotted them too?

'Thanks very much,' says Toby. 'If that is a compliment, which I think it is. It's all your sister's fault, anyway . . .' He winks at me, which I respond to with a tight smile and cock of the head in the direction of the floor. 'Shoddy photography.'

Lexi mumbles something but she's already thinking of the next question. She has her audience and she's determined to keep them.

'How was the book club, anyway?' she pipes up. (How much longer was this going to go on?)

'Great,' we say in unison.

'So where is everyone?'

'They left,' we say, again in unison.

'But they were here,' I add, totally unnecessarily.

Lexi nods, uninterested, and looks around the room, her eyes finally landing, unfocused on Toby.

'Sowhatsyerjob?' she slurs

God, when was she going to shut up? I look again at the pants, the chair's moved slightly now, so that more material is on show. My heart's beating ten to the dozen.

'I'm an account manager. I sell stuff to supermarkets the same as your sister, but I'm much better at it than she is,' he says, to which I roll my eyes.

'Wow!' says Lexi.

Wow? She's never said *my* job is wow.

'So that must mean you have to do a lot of like, speeches?'

'Present—'

'—ations,' he was going to say, but then Lexi kicks off her shoes, which land with a slap on the wooden floor, inches from the pants.

I see Toby do a double take as he spots them; his eyes

linger there for a second before he looks up at me, mouth open.

'What's wrong?' Lexi giggles. Her eyes flit about the room and rest on the floor for a second. I clench my stomach muscles, hold my breath.

'Nothing. Er, just saw the time, actually,' says Toby, brightly. 'I'd better get going.'

'Really?' Lexi's face falls, her eyes drunkenly following him as he gets his jacket.

I'd normally see Toby to the door, catch one more lingering kiss before he has to go but I can't risk it this time. Besides anything else, leaving Lexi alone with the pants could be potential suicide.

'Good book club this week, Delaney,' I opt for, lamely, as he puts on his jacket.

'Best book I've had . . . sorry, *read,* for ages,' he says, which is a joke he wheels out every book club. 'Hope your head's not sore tomorrow, Alexis,' he adds as he's walking out. I watch as he opens the door, closes it behind him and goes home to his wife.

CHAPTER EIGHT

Lexi goes to the tap to get some water and I immediately see my opportunity, grab the pants and put them in the kitchen drawer. She sits back down, nearly missing the chair. God, I think, I really don't need this.

'Lexi, are you drunk?'

'No.'

'Well, yes, you are, actually. It's totally obvious.'

She rolls her eyes and gives a little teenage wobble of the head and I suddenly feel very tired. I've come over all black of mood and pretty miffed that she thinks she can just turn up here with her minxy little ways and flirt with my, my – what was he? – my lover? My partner in crime? My . . . well, *mine* anyway, that's what he was. And I resent her making me feel like this, actually: a horrid mix of jealous big sister – a very unattractive emotion – and a nagging, joyless mother when she's my sister and I just want to go to bed, go to work and get on with my life like I was doing before.

'What happened to the body combat class?'

'I bumped into a friend.'

'Lex, come on. This is London. I've been here for a decade and never just bumped into friends.'

'Well, I did, okay?'

'And who is this friend? Is it a male friend?'

'Might be.'

'Is it that Jerome bloke you met on the train?'

'Might be.'

'Is it Wayne?'

'Nope.'

'Lexi, don't be like that.'

'I'm not being like *any*thing,' she sighs, rolling her eyes dramatically.

'And what was that flirting in aid of anyway?' It comes from nowhere but it's out now and I can't take it back.

'What flirting?'

'Oh come on, Lexi, you were flirting like mad with Toby! Batting your eyelashes, kicking your shoes off.'

'I was not! I was just chatting to him.'

'Chatting? You were thrusting your cleavage in his face!'

She looks visibly wounded. I feel a stab of guilt, but not much.

'That's bollocks. And anyway, *he* was flirting with *me*.'

'That *is* bollocks. You're just pissed and imagining things'

'What do you care anyway?'

She had a point; why did I suddenly care?

'He's my colleague! I have to work with him.'

'Whoopdee-do, he's not your boyfriend is he? And so what if I have a little flirt with a nice bloke who's who's . . .' she starts crying now, which seems a little OTT. I know I should probably hug her but I don't feel like it, I just don't. 'Nice to me and asking me questions?'

I roll my eyes. 'For God's sake, Lexi. It's not really that, it's the fact you're drunk out of your head and I'm supposed to be bloody well looking after you! You're supposed to have come here to sort your head out and I don't even know where you've been.'

Just then the phone goes. We both stare at it, then stare at each other.

'If it's Dad, I'm not in,' says Lexi

'You bloody well are.'

I pick up the phone.

'Hello?'

'Oh, hi there.' It's a man's voice – a man's, not a boy's. 'Is Lexi there?'

'Who is this?'

'Tell her it's Clark,' he says. His voice is northern, rich, and really quite attractive.

'It's Clark,' I say, flatly, holding out the receiver, but Lexi's face darkens immediately.

'No. No way,' she says, shaking her head. 'Tell him I'm not here.'

'She's not here.'

Lexi has shrivelled into the wall, gone a dealthly pale all of a sudden.

'Are you sure? Because I really need to talk to her.'

I hold out the phone to Lexi again.

'He really needs to talk to you.'

Lexi shakes her head.

'Tough shit.' She's really crying now, tears are streaming down her face. 'Tell him I don't want to talk to him. And while you're at it . . .' she stabs a finger in the direction of the phone. 'Tell him to go fuck himself. I wish he, and you, for that matter, would just leave me alone!'

Then she runs upstairs, leaving me holding the phone, wondering what the hell all that was about.

I gingerly take my hand off the receiver.

'Clark? She's drunk and really upset about something. I'd call back another time, if I were you.'

'I will,' he says.

* * *

The next day, I wake up feeling irritated. Like if my life were laid before me it would all be in tiny little fragments, like nothing's in control. Call me selfish, but it's one thing agreeing to take my half-sister in for the summer but not if she's going to come home off her face, taking out her boyfriend troubles on me. And clearly we can't have the book club at mine if Lexi's going to walk in any minute, so perhaps we shouldn't be having it at all. Why did that thought suddenly fill me with panic? Anyway, I've got a big presentation to give to Schumacher today – if I play my cards right, I could seal the deal between us and Langley's, meaning I'm in with a chance of Sales Person of the Year, and frankly, although I can already feel sisterly guilt breaking down my resolve like a hairline fracture, I can do without Lexi's boyfriend dramas, too.

I take my To Do list from my bedside table. This is what I need. Nice orderly lines of writing, clear tasks and a chance to prioritize. I feel better already.

This is my Master list, I also have a Shopping list, a Must-see Cultural Events list, an Admin list, Presents to Buy list and a Long-Term Goals list.

I take my notebook out of my bedside table and set about updating.

<u>To Do:</u>
MINOR
Make something with Quinoa – still to do.
Pluck eyebrows – done. (Do again when start to join up.)
Get spare room painted – Never going to do it, give it up!
Sort out photo albums (buy photo corners) – Still to do, but seriously, when?
*Call council about recycling – Done! (Although I still maintain there's some smug little arse down at Wandsworth Council with 'Head Foxer' as his job-title since it seems one needs a degree to recycle correctly.)

Get involved in local culture: this coming weekend: installation by interesting sounding German artist at the Pump House Gallery. Done! What next? (See Must-see Cultural Events list and pick something else. Aboriginal Ceramics?)

Learn how to use i-Pod that have now had since Christmas. Just do it!!

(Have developed a dislike of people who buy me things that I then have to find the time to learn how to use, which is just wrong on so many levels.)

Do 3 x 12 squats and 3 x 12 sit ups before bed (start tomorrow) – start tomorrow.

*Join actual book club

MAJOR

Incorporate two hours of admin into every weekend. No excuse! (This is looking pretty unlikely now I have a teen on my hands.)

Every day, do something for self and de-stressing, even if just breathing (alone, concentrating on, rather than just breathing breathing) for ten minutes. Chance would be a fine thing.

Work: Step things up a gear! Seal deal on two new clients per week: work in progress. If I nail this meeting with Schumacher today, I could be half way there.

FIND OUT WHAT'S WRONG WITH LEXI ASAP!!

At present, I don't really care what's wrong with Lexi, to tell you the truth, which I'm worried makes me the worst sister in the world.

I give her a knock before I leave for work anyway, just to check she's still alive.

'Lex?'

No answer

'Lexi, are you awake?'

Nothing.

'We'll speak later in the day,' I say, presuming she's sulking. 'I've left a cup of tea by your door so don't, you know, step straight into it and get the mug stuck on your foot.'

I wait a few more seconds and when I get no answer to my moronic ramblings, I leave for work.

Victoria tube station is rammed with tourists carrying cameras and backpacks. It used to make me feel nostalgic when I saw tourists *en masse* like this; reminded me of a time when London was new and exciting for me, too, when Martin and I were fresh-faced from the cosy confines of the rolling hills of Yorkshire and everything and everyone seemed exotic.

Now I'm just one of a million other jaded Londoners who wishes they'd all bugger off, stop treating my city like a holiday destination and taking up space on my journey to work.

A train approaches and I curse the 20-strong team of rowdy school children blocking my way to the door. 'HOLD YOUR BUDDY'S HAND!' a blonde woman with no chin is shouting as the children shuffle, dazed, onto the tube. 'And remember we're getting off at Vauxhall.'

Vauxhall? Christ. Did I have to put up with this until Vauxhall?

The tube creaks into action and I look down from my spot jammed up against the armpit of a man who smells of fried chicken to see a pale, ginger-haired girl staring up at me, tasting the snot that streams from her nose with the tip of her tongue. This is what I resent most about the tube: the fact you pay a fortune to be subjected – totally out of your own control – to the most vile of human habits at 8 a.m. in the morning.

I eventually get a seat and ask myself when I turned into such a wizened, grouchy old woman. I'm sure I used to be a sunny sort of a girl who took delight in the minutiae of life and gave selflessly to others. Or something.

Perhaps it was just that I was happier back then. Or younger. In fact, perhaps happiness is actually just youth. It's funny, isn't it, how your experience of happiness changes as you get older? When I was young, happiness came in bursts of unadulterated joy, moments that stuck in my memory like diamonds in a rock-face: a walk onto the university campus on a sunny October Friday, knowing Martin was coming to visit in a matter of hours; running into the sea, drunk on Bacardi in just my knickers on a girl's holiday to the Costa Brava. (Now I wouldn't be seen dead in a bikini even if I drank my own weight in Bacardi.) Driving through the Yorkshire Dales in my clapped-out Polo with Pippa, my oldest friend from school, chain-smoking out of the window. Where was Pippa now? Last I heard, she was shacked up with some builder in Otley, a baby on the way, and what was I doing? Living in London, the great flat, the big job and shagging somebody else's husband. Oh GOD. It made me feel sick just thinking about it.

Yeah, these days, happiness to me is more like an unreliable weekend dad. You never know when it's going to turn up, and even when it does, you never know how long till the next time.

Mum used to say: 'You wait till your thirties, Caroline! Your thirties are the happiest time in your life because you'll know who you are and what you want.'

Sometimes, I feel like that is the biggest piece of misinformation I've ever been fed. In fact sometimes, I get this feeling like is this it? Is my only stab at happiness over already?

Perhaps that's what Toby feels like when he talks about his marriage. And I can relate to that; this is why I understand him. Because if grown-up happiness means knowing *anything* for certain, I'm about as far from it as humanly possible.

We grind to a halt at Green Park. I think about Lexi, tucked up in bed, no doubt brooding about life, about Clark, about our row last night. She's probably sticking needles into a voodoo doll of me as we speak. Maybe this boyfriend trouble was why she dropped out of sixth form – I suspected as much the day she arrived. She probably thinks it's the end of the world, too. It's only when you get to thirty-two and look back that you realize it had only just begun.

CHAPTER NINE

'Meet Aaron. Aaron is twenty-eight and at the top of his game.'

Rule number 1 of the perfect sales pitch: HUMANIZE. Especially when pitching to Darryl Schumacher. Darryl can't resist the human touch. It makes him believe (wrongly, so wrongly), that he possesses it too.

'Aaron is a successful insurance broker. He works in a swanky high-rise in the heart of Manchester.'

(Cue picture of a swanky office block in Melbourne. Shona couldn't find one in Manchester.)

'He owns a wharf apartment in the city's hip Canalside district, drives an Audi convertible, drinks Staropramen, Budvar, shops in Ted Baker, Diesel, Reiss.'

Darryl fingers the length of his tie. Must get myself down to that Reiss, you can see him thinking, see what all the fuss is about.

'Image to Aaron is everything and that's because IMPRESS . . .'

The word flashes fuscia pink on my laptop. Darryl's piggy eyes widen.

'. . . is Aaron's middle name. By day, he needs to impress clients. By night . . .'

Darryl taps his chewed biro on his notepad. 'The laydeez. . . .'

'Quite,' I say, suppressing the desire to be sick.

I take a deep breath, turn my eyes to the screen.

'Aaron is talking to people twenty-four-seven. The last thing he needs is to feel unconfident. But he is also a fast-living guy in his twenties. He works hard, plays hard, does everything to the max.'

Darryl loosens his shirt. 'To the max . . .' According to what scale, exactly, I can hear him thinking.

'He likes a double espresso to kick-start his morning, more than a few Marlboro Lights to relax him post-work. His post-lunch café crème cigar is as much a part of his image as his Armani cufflinks. In short . . .'

Rule number 2 of the perfect sales pitch: Introduce humour. Especially when pitching to Darryl. Darryl likes to think he's a very humorous man.

'. . . without help, Aaron's breath's going to smell like a camel's bottom.'

The picture of the camel's gigantic arse flashes up. For some reason, Shona had no problem sourcing that one.

'Hahahahahah!' Darryl throws his head back and guffaws. 'Love it!' A roll of neck fat spills over his shirt like a pie-crust. 'I can always trust you to provide the laughs, Miss Steele. A girl with a sense of humour. Rare in this game, very, rare indeed.'

I shudder inside. Darryl carries on laughing. Then coughing, like he might cough up a blackened lung right there on the beige, static carpet.

'So,' I almost have to shout over the hacking, 'this is where Mini Minty Me comes in.' I pick up the tiny silver bottle from the table and hand it to Darryl.

'It's got all the benefits of the Minty Me mouthwash: kills 99.9 per cent of oral bacteria, prevents tartar, reduces plaque, but it comes in a slick little atomizer that Aaron can slip into his pocket along with his wallet. A mouthwash-cum-breath freshener, all in the size of a lighter. Revolutionary, Darryl, I'm sure you'll agree.' I flash my best QVC channel smile.

Darryl is nodding, rubbing the stubble on his top lip, which is pale ginger and for some reason reminds me of my old guinea pig, Graham. Me having been the sort of child to call a guinea pig Graham.

He holds the bottle up to the light. Paws it with his sausage fingers.

'Is he single?' he says.

'I'm sorry?'

'You don't say if Aaron is single.'

'No, he is not single!' I am not sure I like where this is going.

Darryl cocks his head to one side. 'Oh?'

'I mean, yes! Yes, of course he's single. Single, but looking for The One.'

'Ah, likely story. Good looking mover and shaker like Aaron? Come on . . .' Darryl's red-rimmed piggy eyes are looking straight at my chest. 'Okay, how many women has he slept with this year?'

'I don't know.'

'Fifteen? Twenty?'

'No! No way.'

'Ten, twelve?' urges Darryl.

'Definitely not that many.'

'How many then?'

'Three.'

'What? An Alpha Romeo like Aaron?'

'Okay, six maybe. Oh God, *I* don't bloody well know. He's not *real*, I made him up!'

Darryl laughs again. I feel my cheeks burn.

'Anyway, Darryl, Mr Schumacher,' I say, closing my eyes.

Don't blow it now. You're almost there, this sale is so in the bag . . .

'Back to the product, a great product, which all your competitors without exception will be stocking come mid-August. I'd say there's an opportunity of 1.2 million pounds here for Langley's with a margin of 35 per cent, which is higher than your average category margin.'

'I'm sold.' Schumacher slams shut his notepad and folds his porky little arms.

'Oh!' *That was easy.* 'That's great. Really great.'

'I'll order 600 units to be in all of the 57 stores by August.'

And there it is. The kick. The high. The fizzy little bubbles of achievement that start in my belly and rise to my face, which is beaming now. It's the reason I do this job. The reason I get up at 6 a.m. some days, work weekends, work all hours God sends. Because this feeling, it's gold. Sales is the crack cocaine of the corporate life if you ask me. Although, on reflection, even I am concerned that getting this euphoric about mouthwash may not be altogether healthy.

I shake Schumacher's hand. He has a handshake like salami: damp, limp and fatty.

'Thank you, Darryl.' He carries on shaking. 'I'll get the paperwork to you for tomorrow. Of course, it won't all be done and dusted before the contract's signed and it's all, you know . . .'

'Bona fide,' says Darryl, flashing a set of tartar-covered teeth.

'Exactly,' I say, hoping he doesn't see me wipe my hand on my skirt. 'Well, I'm looking forward to working together,' I lie.

'Yep, we're onto a winner, Caroline. Awesome,' he says, eyes boring holes in my shirt. 'Now, I've got some mail to fire off, so I'll see myself out.'

'Great, speak soon,' I say, making towards the door.

As I close it, I see him breathing into his hand, covering his nose and sniffing it.

'Yes! Get *in*. Schumacher *in* the bag!'

It's only when I stop punching the air that I see that Shona and Toby are looking at me.

Toby bursts out laughing.

'Fuck me, you really do get excited about selling mouth-wash, don't you?'

I feel suddenly ridiculous.

'Shut up you, you're just jealous.'

'I can't believe you can even be in the same room as that man,' says Shona. 'Look at him . . .' She watches him through the glass. 'Letching at us all with his little piggy eyes.'

'He's all right,' I say. 'Schumacher and I, we have, a personal understanding.'

'Uh. Grim!' Shona shakes her head, grimly.

'Man, your face though,' laughs Toby.

'Yeah. Ab-sol-utely-fucking-hilarious,' agrees Shona.

'Were you spying on us?'

'Course we were!'

'Well don't! Especially when I'm in with Schumacher. He kept making irrelevant sexual references and then there was the picture of the camel's arse. GOD knows why I thought that was a good idea. The last person I want to be sharing a joke with – especially a joke about an arse – is Schumacher. He kept laughing, like a braying donkey. And then, you know how I get the dark, twisted thoughts that just pop into my head and then I can't get rid of them?'

'Sure do,' says Toby, raising an eyebrow.

'Well, I kept thinking of Darryl and a camel.'

'*Oh Jesus.*'

'Yes. I know, I am sick, sick in the head. Then I kept thinking he was going to make a move on me.'

Toby's snorting with laughter now, Shona's got her head on the desk and one eye open.

'Your face was like this . . .' Toby says, assuming a grimace, somewhere between shocked and offended: flared nostrils, wide eyes.

'You looked like a cross between someone who had poo smeared on their top lip,' adds Shona, thinking hard, 'and a hamster in rigor mortis.'

'Thanks.'

'You're welcome.'

'Hey, but I got the sale though and that is all that matters.' I raise my hand for a high five. Toby slaps it, somewhat reluctantly. 'Six hundred units to be in every store by next month!'

'What?' He wasn't expecting that. 'You spawny cow. If you win that award, I'll kill you.'

I feel a guilty little thrill of competition. So it's not just Rachel who wins awards, actually, thank you very much.

I look at Shona.

'It will be an award tainted with dubious morality, which is unfortunate,' she says.

'God, people! It's breath freshener I'm selling, not children!'

'But well done,' Shona adds. 'Because I know how much it means to you. It's just, don't think that just because Schumacher is now officially on board, that I will ever engage in any conversation with that prick that isn't ab-sol-utely fucking necessary, okay?'

'Loud and clear, Shona. Loud and clear.'

'Well done, Caroline.' Janine has a new super-short fringe that makes her look even more like a German lesbian than she did before. 'You officially kicked ass.'

'Thanks,' I say, dumbly. I always feel like a disappointment whenever I'm in Cross's office.

But it feels great all the same. Sealing the deal. Who would think selling breath freshener could make your heart race? But I think that's it. The simplicity of it, the lack of anything major at stake. I doubt, for example, if I'd feel this way if I worked for a charity, or as a teacher where real hearts and minds were on the table. The fact we could all quite happily survive well into our nineties without breath freshener allows me to put a hundred per cent of me in without feeling there's going to be any emotional fall out. And that's great, because sometimes it feels like work is the only place in my life where I feel safe to operate; like it's the only room in the *Titanic*, not yet sinking.

I bump into Toby as I'm coming out of the loo. He's got an important meeting at Tesco's HQ today and is wearing his best grey, sharp suit. He looks devastatingly, ridiculously handsome, like he should be in an advert for Lynx.

'There you are,' he hisses. 'Been looking for you. So come on, what happened?'

'About what?'

I know perfectly well about what, but I just want to keep him this close for as long as possible. I just want to sniff him.

'My pants, silly,' he lisps and I melt. 'Did she see the pants?'

'No, no. Pants all safe in the kitchen drawer.'

'You're so clever, CS.'

'I know. Multi-talented, me. Can seal deals, hide pants . . .'

He leans right into my ear.

'Give amazing head,' he whispers, so despite my resolve to be an insouciant, *femme fatale* at all times, I turn purple.

'Unfortunately, Lexi and I had a row once you'd left,' I say, desperate to change the subject. Toby never seems to mind discussing overt sexual matters in the office, which I find absurdly flattering, whilst intensely embarrassing all at the same time.

'Shit, really? Did you bollock her for coming home pissed?'

'Yes, I did, actually. I'm not having that. I don't know whether it's going to work, her being here for the summer, you know. I have my life to live too.'

He tidies a strand of hair behind my ear.

'The book club to run.'

'Well, yes, and that,' I say, trying not to smile.

He edges in closer. 'Due to the pants fiasco, I think we may have no choice but to upgrade the book club to an epic bonkbuster in a London boutique hotel, what do you think?'

Here's your chance. Calm, aloof. You are woman-in-control. A woman able to 'compartmentalize' things.

I draw back and fold my arms.

'We'll see, shall we?' I say, before tidying his lapel.

Then I stride off, all heels, skirt and swinging hips. That was good, Steele, that was very, very good.

'Caroline,' he calls after me three seconds later.

'What?'

'You've got bog roll on the bottom of your shoe.'

It's still boiling hot when I leave the office. The Edgware Road is being re-laid and the air is thick with the smell of tarmac. I weave through the rush-hour crowds, towards the tube, past the Arabic hardware stores and halal cafés where white-robed men sit smoking pipes and playing cards, smiling to myself about the conversation with Toby and thinking that soon, very soon, I'm going to get to wake up next to him. And then it's onwards from there.

CHAPTER TEN

I see the note as soon as I get in. It's propped up on the kitchen table next to a vase. The hand is that typical teenage sort: fat, squidgy, with circles for the dots of Is. I try to refrain from taking a pen and correcting the mistakes. (Especially the 'your' when it should be 'you're'.)

Dear Big Sis!
Have managed to sort it out with the Ex and have gone home. Sorry for the hassel. Your really nice to let me stay especially since I know your so busy. It was great to see you. Am sorry if I spoilt it at the end.
C u soon (I hope!)
Loads of luv
Lex xxx

The 'sorry if I spoilt it at the end' brings a slight lump to my throat but, to be honest, the overwhelming feeling at reading the note is relief. She's sorted out her problems – obviously the reason she was here in the first place – and now she's good to go. Maybe the little break I facilitated was all she needed.

It does cross my mind it's a little strange that she didn't

just text or call to tell me but you know what teenagers are like. Dramatic. She probably didn't want to water down the drama of me finding her exit note.

I go into the kitchen and experience a sudden feeling of calm, having the place back to myself again. I absentmindedly line up the tea, coffee and sugar holders the way I like them, and decide to de-Lexi the kitchen of the stray Rice Krispies, some of which found their way into the kettle, and the splatters of red on the tiles from her daily fruit-smoothie making. Before I know it, I'm at it with the toothbrush inside the taps. Lost to the call of the kitchen. Bliss!

I sit down with a large glass of wine about seven. Fortified by my cleaning stint, I think about going on Facebook, where I like to torture myself by looking at photos of Toby and Rachel together. I keep hoping over-exposure will eventually mean immunity and also there's the one of her with a double chin that always makes me feel better. I've also noticed she wears quite badly cut jeans. (Stop it, stop it, stop it!)

Then it occurs to me, maybe I should give Dad a quick call just to check that he's picking Lexi up from the train station. It would be shoddy form if I didn't even check. Dad picks up. He sounds muffled and yet somehow ecstatic. High. High on Motivational Speaking.

'Hi, Dad. It's Caroline.'

'Hel-lo, Caro!' He says it all sing-songy and OTT like he's cooing a baby. 'How's my favourite girl?'

'Oh fine. Yeah, fine.'

I've never been very good at humouring Dad's new persona since it's so different from the one I grew up with.

'Where are you, Dad? You sound muffled.'

'Ah yes. Well. Funny you should say that . . .'

He does his nervous laugh. Three, short, entirely false 'Ha!'s, which irritate the hell out of me, but I have to stay calm. I can't let him think there's any sort of crisis here.

'Cass and I were invited to talk in–' He says something so quickly I don't catch it, but it sounds like London.

'What, you're in London?'

'No . . . Atlanta. We're in Atlanta.'

'Atlanta?! What the *hell* are you doing in Atlanta?!'

It's only when I've got over the shock that he's in Atlanta, USA, that I start to put two and two together: if he's there – where is my sister?

'It's not for long.'

'How long?'

'Um . . . thirteen days'

'So a fortnight, then?'

'Well, just short of.'

'It's a fortnight, Dad.'

He clears his throat.

'Right. Everything's okay there, though, isn't it? I mean, we told Lex where we were and she sounded fine about it. She *is* fine, isn't she?'

My mind is already doing overtime: drug dens, cobbled alleys, wheelie bins.

'Yes, of course she's absolutely fine.'

'It was last minute, sweetheart, and we did try to call you, it's just . . .'

'My phone was off.'

'Yes, your phone was off. And it's a golden opportunity, we'd be fools not to have taken it. If we crack America . . .'

Who does he think he is now? Susan Boyle?

'. . . then we could be really taking Healing Horizons to a whole new level.'

He goes on, but really, once I know the situation I just want to get off the phone. It's just me and Lexi now and one half of us is missing. I have a sickening feeling this is all my fault.

* * *

First things first: I try her mobile but it just goes through to the bizarre answermachine message again with Lexi shouting 'Lexi Stee-yel!' like she's at the top of a roller coaster about to go down. But then, I am fast discovering that Lexi lives most of her life as if she *is* at the top of a roller coaster about to go down.

I leave a message. The third.

'Me again. Look Lex. I know you haven't gone home coz I just rang Dad and he's in Atlanta – as you know – so PLEASE call me. I'm sorry about the row last night, I'm not angry with you and you did nothing wrong . . . Well, except go out and get drunk instead of go to the gym and you wouldn't tell me who with. This is why I'm panicking now, because I don't know who you're with and London's not like Doncaster. You can't just–'

Beep. Beep. Beep.

Fuck it. Run out of space. I sit at the kitchen table with the phone in my hand, scratching at the patch of eczema on my hand that seems to be spreading by the day. What would the police do in this situation? Has she even left London? Is an hour of knowing she's gone enough to report a person missing? I figure I should have a stab at it myself, first. Nothing will be achieved sitting at this kitchen table. I need a list, a P of A. I rip a page from an A4 notepad and begin:

* Carly. She'd know where she is. But no idea how to get hold of Carly. Don't even know her surname.
* Email: could hack into Hotmail and track her movements but no idea of password.
* Facebook: Genius! Lexi is one of my 'friends' so should be able to access her Wall.
* Failing all: I go out and trawl the streets of London myself.
* I call a search party.

* I call Martin. No, can't call Martin, he's not my boyfriend, he's somebody else's.

I call Martin.

He's over in twenty minutes, by which point the images of wheelie bins are getting the better of me and I'm sitting on the sofa, head in hands.

Martin's standing over me, hands in pockets, his belly popping out from under his maroon GAP T-shirt, making the odd soothing 'mm-mm' noise.

'It's all my fault,' I'm saying. 'I was supposed to be looking after her, I was responsible for her and then we had a row last night but then I was so obsessed with bloody work and To—'

I stop myself just in time.

'To . . . tally everything that I forgot she hadn't called back and then it was too late and now—'

'I think less self-pity, more action is what's needed here, Caro, mmm?'

He's right of course. He always is.

We try Facebook first. All I see on her Wall, however, is a string of dialogue between Lexi and Carly Greenford. So that's her surname. Carly seems to be mightily pissed off, but then I'd be pissed off if I thought I might be pregnant and my boyfriend had just left me.

In Carly's profile picture, she has wavy blonde hair and puppy-fat cheeks. She's cherubically pretty. Then she writes:

Carly Greenford to Alexis Simone Steele: Have decided that C stands for one thing: C**T. He woz s'post to be meetin' me 2day but no show so he can GFH now. I am officially over him. Who am I kiddin? I'll never be over him!

88

Alexis Simone Steele (big fur coat, shades, pout) to Carly Greenford: Move on GF! Ur worth more than him. DGYF! And I, 4 one, luv u meercat. Mwah xxxx

Carly Greenford to Alexis Simone Steele: Aaaaw! I luv u 2, meercat. Wot r we like? Gorge, clever ladeez like us letting feckers like that mess with r headz. Grrrrr. U woz also far 2 gud for him. The boy is dead to u 2, CM, okay? Mwah xxx

'DGYF?' mutters Martin, confused.

'Damn Girl You're Fine.' I know, because Lexi texted it to me, too.

'Oh right. So CM?'

'Call me.'

'Right,' he says, sounding pleased with himself. 'It's not that hard once you get started, is it?'

'So, Lexi's been dumped. That's what's wrong with her,' I say, half to myself.

'Eh? How do you decipher that?'.

'Because Carly says, "he's dead to you".'

'Dead to you?' Martin pulls his chin back when he's puzzled, which I've begun to think gives him a look of Gordon Brown.

'Yeah, dead to you, you know.'

Man, we're going to run into problems if we can't even de-code teen speak.

'It means, you're over him, he doesn't matter to you. People say it to you when someone dumps you to make you feel better.'

'Do they? Nobody said—'

'Ohmigod!' I cut him short as I read something that sets my heart racing faster than it already is.

Alexis Simone Steele to Carly Greenford: U know wot u shd do? Internet dating. It's the biz! Just met a right hottie. He's twenty-nine but looks much younger and u know how I luv an old timer. Been on one date.'

'Fuck!'

I slap my hand to my mouth.

'What?' says Martin, alarmed. 'What's the matter?'

'I need to hack into Lexi's email,' I say, flapping my arms about. 'You're an IT man, you know how to hack into someone's email.'

'You might not need to,' says Martin, calmly. Always with the calm. 'If you know her password.'

'I don't! Why the hell would I know her password?' I snap, and then I feel awful. Poor Martin. He didn't need to come over tonight. He's got a girlfriend and here I am snapping at him like *I'm* his girlfriend. I haven't even *asked* him about his girlfriend! God, I am awful.

I rest my head on his shoulder. 'Sorry. I really appreciate you coming over. I'm just stressed that's all.'

'I know. But we'll find her, okay? Put your energy into guessing her password.'

I try Carly. No. I try Simone. No. I try meercat, since that seemed to be some sort of in-joke between them, but it's not that either.

'Try Caroline,' says Martin.

'Are you joking? I must be her most hated person on the planet right now.'

'Just try it.'

So I do, and it works. And somehow, just that small thing, that surprise indication of my little sister's feelings for me, means that by the time I'm walking behind Martin towards Battersea Park station tears are streaming down my face.

* * *

90

It's possibly typical of a seventeen-year-old that if she was planning to elope to Notting Hill with a man twice her age she should cover her tracks, ludicrously badly. Thank God. Five seconds rooting around her inbox and we know the following things:

- She's meeting a guy called Tristan who she met on Match.com
- He sounds like a prize twat.
- He lives in Notting Hill. Course he does.
- They're meeting at Shoreditch House. (A quick Google search reveals this to be a five-storey, uber members bar near Liverpool Street.)
- I have to rescue her.

Martin and I hardly speak on the way there. Martin knows I can't do conversation when stressed, so all the way on the tube, he whistles, Martin being one of those people who finds silences awkward even with someone he's known for thirteen years. Then, we're pegging it along Bishopsgate, in the heart of the City. It's 9.15 p.m. and the towering glass office blocks that surround us, sleek as shark fins, are ablaze with the setting sun, the last of the be-suited City workers making their way towards the tube after another long day.

Martin's running in front of me, his GAP jacket flapping around his sides.

Me, shouting after him: 'What are we going to do if he's already slipped the Rohypnol in? I'll never forgive myself!'

Him: 'Now you're just trying to scare yourself. Worst case scenario is she's drunk, it'll be okay.'

Me: 'But she's seventeen.'

Him: 'Well, think when you were seventeen/eighteen. You weren't a complete idiot, were you? You could look after yourself?'

Me: 'Yes, but I had you by the time I was eighteen.'

Him: 'True.'

We're both gasping for breath by the time we get to Shoreditch House. The doorman – a mountain of a bloke with a blond moustache – eyes us suspiciously.

'Have you seen a . . . a girl? Skinny, . . . short, dark hair, probably wearing next to nothing, ridiculous tattoo up her right arm?'

He raises his eyebrows at me.

'Well, you've either seen her or you haven't?'

'We think she's with someone,' Martin cuts in, hands on knees, trying to get his breath back. I know what's going through his head: I'm screwed if I'm getting into a fight with this guy. 'Any idea who that might be?' The man on the door is of that breed of customer care that doesn't deem eye contact necessary.

'Some tosser called Tristan.'

Martin nudges me with his elbow.

'Tristan Banks. Mr Banks is one of our most respected customers.'

'I'll bet he is,' I say. 'Look, can we just come in and look for her?'

I try to barge past but the man puts his arm out.

'This is a members only bar, madam. That means, you have to be a member to come in.' He looks Martin up and down. 'Besides, I'm afraid your friend is not dressed appropriately.'

I look at Martin in his faded GAP T-shirt that doesn't stretch over his belly and the crappy beige GAP jacket that he buys in bulk and I feel a stab of pity and love all rolled into one.

'Look, to be fair, I didn't know I'd be coming to Shoreditch House when I set off to my . . .' he looks at me. 'My *friend's* house today,' says Martin. 'With all due respect, what I'm wearing, isn't really my concern. What *is* my concern, is my friend's sister who's only seventeen and in there with a man she doesn't know and we're worried about her. Please let us in.'

Martin lifts his chin up triumphantly and I suddenly want to hug him.

The doorman nods. 'They're up on the rooftop,' he says.

In any other circumstances, this would be awesome. When the lift opens, a vast, Colonial-style lounge area with white-wicker furniture and dark-wood floor greets us. In the middle is a tower of logs, supposedly for the wood-burning stove one won't be needing during a London heatwave, and behind that, a low, granite bar behind which a girl with an Afro idly shakes her hips to an Ibiza-esque chill-out tune. I scan the clusters of white-leather chairs, where couples, legs entwined, enjoy what is, no doubt, an extortionately priced sundowner, but I can't see Lexi. Then, behind me I hear Martin say, 'Jeez, check it out.'

I turn around to see what he's talking about − behind glass sliding doors, which have been opened, is the rooftop pool. It's a tropical turquoise and set against the most breathtaking view of a London evening skyline, where cranes are silhouetted like prehistoric creatures and high-rise windows glow and flicker like the lights on a sound system.

Then, a high-pitched squeal of delight and a . . . 'Don't! Me bikini bums are gonna come off!'

My heart stops.

'She's in the fucking pool!'

'What are you on about?' asks Martin.

'Lexi. She's in the swimming pool.'

I unglue my feet and use all my strength to push the doors open. I'm standing there now, Martin behind me, taking on what feels like the whole glittering city, which opens out before us. Except it's not the city I'm taking on, it's my pint-sized sister. She's flapping about in the pool with Tristan Banks.

Her jaw drops when she sees me.

'Caroline!'

Good God, she's inebriated.

'Whashyou doin' here? I didn't know you were a member of Sawdish House.'

'I'm not. I'm your sister and I've come to collect you. Now get the fuck out of that swimming pool and get dressed. We're going home.'

'What?' She's intermittently treading water and occasionally going under. I spot two large cocktails by the side of the pool. 'Why? We're having the best time. Sherious. Tristan's in A&R. Tell 'em about all the people you've signed, Trisht. Hey, tell 'em about that night with the Kills and Kate Moss in that hotel in Miami. That was *sick*.'

'Lexi, get out of the pool.'

'Hey guys!' Tristan (American, obviously) who's been avoiding eye contact until now, swims to the side and lifts himself out in one slick move. He's six foot three at least, lean, extremely hairy, and wearing a thick, silver chain around his neck. He gives a staged flick of his hair so that it lands, rock-and-roll style, across his forehead. He is very good looking, I'll give her that.

'I'm Tristan Banks,' he drawls. 'Like, is everything cool or do we have a problem here?'

'We have a problem and it's you,' I say.

Behind me, Martin emerges, hands on hips, with three inches of beer belly sticking out

'Oh God, it's you!' says Lexi. 'I don't know who you think you are, what right *you* have—'

'Lexi,' I cut in, worried she's about to start going on about the engagement thing. 'I'd prefer it if you were *not* rude to Martin.'

I turn to Martin. 'Look, I think I'm okay here. I'll handle this. Thanks so much for coming, but I think, you know . . .' I reach out and squeeze his hand.

'Cool, sure,' he says, backing towards the glass doors. 'Well, you know where I am if you need me. I'll just, er . . .'

'Great,' I nod, urging him to go.

'Go home then. Call me if you . . .'

'Course I will. Thanks, Martin.'

'You know your problem? You're frigid. You're anally retentive. You wouldn't know fun if it poked you up the arse!'

We're standing on the corner outside Shoreditch House now, and Lexi is incredibly, dirtily, horribly drunk.

'Wayne says that people who are obsessed with trying to control their surroundings are often just crying inside . . .' Her voice teeters off as she stumbles over her own feet and nearly falls flat on her face.

'Lexi, just get in the cab, please?' What the hell had she been feeding this Wayne?

The driver has eyebags like elephant skin. He's leaning against the bonnet, smoking, knowing he's in for the long haul.

'No, I won't!' She's stumbling all over the place on her high heels. 'I won't have you tell me what to do, crashing my date. Tristan was a really nice bloke, actually.'

'He was old enough to be your dad and stone cold sober whilst you were pissed out of your head. Don't you know what that says?'

'He doesn't need alcohol to have a good time?'

'Wrong. He's a total wanker, taking advantage of you.'

'Oh, stop being such a drama queen! So I'm pissed, so WHAT?' she shouts as I put my hand on her head and bundle her into the car.

'Pissed in a swimming pool, Lexi. Have you any idea how dangerous that is? What sort of person would allow that to happen to you?' I ask as I fasten her seatbelt.

'You don't know how to live you don't. So fucking BORING!'

'No, Lex. You're the one who's getting boring.'

We're speeding over London Bridge now. Lexi's sunk down in the seat, glaring at me, antagonistically.

'Just be quiet now, please,' I sigh. 'It's 10.30 p.m. and I'm knackered.'

'I just wanted to come to London and have a laugh for the summer – a laugh!' she slurs. 'But I guess you wouldn't know what that is.'

The driver looks at me through the mirror, raising his eyebrows as if to say, 'You've got a right little cow on your hands there.'

We drive in silence for a while, past the Dickensian gloom of a deserted Borough Market down past the offices of Southwark Street, a ghost town at this time of night. We get to the crossroads with Stamford Street and Blackfriars Road, about to turn left towards Elephant and Castle, when Lexi suddenly says:

'Stop the car!'

'Don't be ridiculous, Lexi, you're not getting out here.'

'Shtop the car,' she slurs. 'I'm gonna puke.'

Now, I'm rubbing Lexi's back as she hurls into my toilet bowl.

'I'm dying,' she groans.

'Oh, I think you've got a few years yet. You'll make it through the night at least. You'll be wanting a glass of wine by this time tomorrow.'

'UURGHH!' She hurls again. 'NEVER! I'm never drinking again! I'msuchatwat,' she slurs. I look skywards. How long was the self-flagellation going to go on? 'I mean, look at me! I'm rubbish, I'm stupid, I'm fat. A total fucking mess . . .'

'Lexi, you are *none* of those things . . .'

'Nobody loves me, nobody fancies me,' she sobs. 'I'm not surprised he did it. I'm not surprised he dumped me,' she says, at which point I take notice.

'You're not surprised who did what? Who dumped you, Lex?'

'Him!' she shouts, raising her head in an involuntary drunken jerk, and it accidentally catches the side of my face. 'Loser, cunt-face, prick-head, wanker!'

I bite my lip in order not to laugh. It's just my little sister, so pretty, so elfin, swearing like a trooper, as drunk as a wench . . .

'Do you mean Clark? The guy who called?'

She looks up at me, eyes wandering, cheeks smeared with mascara,

'Like I shed. Loser, cunt-face, prick-head, wanker.'

Then she falls asleep on the toilet seat.

I eventually get her to the sofa and switch on the telly: some late night documentary about a girl who cries blood. An hour later, a small voice speaks into the darkness.

'I'm sorry.'

'Oh, you're alive, then? Feeling any better?'

'Headache,' is all she can manage. 'He kept feeding me Island Cream Teas.'

'Long Island Iced Teas, you mean. That'll be the headache, then. And the spectacular projectile vomit in the taxi that reached as far as the windscreen.'

'Noooo!'

'And parts of the driver's head.'

She covers her face.

'He was a bad 'un, wasn't he, Tristan?' She grimaces.

'Oh, he probably wasn't an axe murderer, but not boyfriend material, let's put it like that.'

'I'm sorry . . . And also, you know, for anything I might have said.'

'That's okay, but will you promise me something? Don't go meeting any more strange men from the Internet. You nearly sent me to an early grave.'

Then there's a long pause, before she says, 'Caroline?'

'Yes?'

'Can I ask you something?' I look to see her small, pale face above the duvet. 'Do you not want me here?'

I swallow. God, had I been that unwelcoming?

'Course I want you here,' I say. 'And anyway, neither of us have much choice now because our useless father and your useless mother have absconded to bloody Atlanta, so you're stuck with me, kiddo.'

She manages a laugh.

'I'm kind of glad,' she says.

'Yeah, me too.'

And in a strange way, I was, I really was. Perhaps it was nice to be needed. I felt one step closer to finding out what was really bothering Lexi, too. I just needed to find out who cunt-face prick-head wanker was, whether he *was* Clark, and what exactly he'd done, and we'd be all right. We'd be sorted.

I find the leaflet quite by mistake ten minutes after she's gone to bed.

Her mobile had gone. I'd thought I'd better see who it was, just in case it was Dad. I rummaged in her bag, among the tissues and the make-up, and then my stomach rolled. Everything started to fall horribly into place.

What To Do If you Think You're Pregnant, said the leaflet.

How could I have been so dumb not to realize she wasn't talking about Carly, that she was talking about herself!

I'm starting to think I may have bitten off more than I can chew.

CHAPTER ELEVEN

'I don't need to hear the details, we just need to know, because only then can we draw up a P of A.'

'What's a P of A?' shouts Lexi over the traffic.

I'm marching her down Battersea Park Road towards the pharmacy. She's wearing the vintage playsuit, flip-flops and a flower in her hair. She looks like she's going to a carnival.

'A Plan of Action!' I shout back. It's a Martin term and one that I'm glad to have at my disposal.

'A P of A is a tool, Caro,' he always used to tell me when I was scared and overwhelmed, 'a way of feeling in control.'

And I do feel in control, which is strange, taking into consideration the disaster potential of this latest drama.

'I'm having an abortion if I am pregnant.'

It's broad daylight, 9 a.m. in the morning and Lexi shouts this at me with all the gravity of: 'I'm having my ears pierced whether you like it or not!'

'Let's just see if you are first, shall we?'

'There's no way I'm having a kid at seventeen. I'm still a kid myself.'

That much is clear.

'Anyway, a girl at school had an abortion.'

'Poor her,' I shout striding ahead of her.

'She was at school in the afternoon. She said she was just put to sleep. She didn't feel a thing.'

'She might have been okay physically, but I'm sure she was in turmoil emotionally.'

'She wasn't crying or anything. We all expected her to be in a right mess. But—'

'Abortion's not something to take lightly, Lexi!' She's annoying me now and I stop and face her. 'It's not something you decide to just do, like having Botox or getting a tattoo.'

(The tattoo wasn't real. I discovered that on Thursday night when, convalescing on the sofa, half the dye came off onto my spanking white duvet, smudged by the swimming pool. 'Can't believe you thought it was real,' she said, managing a snigger even in her near-death state. I could have bloody hit her.)

Lexi glares at me, but there's that look in her eyes again, behind the usual defiance, a kind of unfathomable sadness like you'll never be able to reach her.

'I'm still having one,' she says.

'How can you say that? Until you know if it's a reality or not? You'll need to think it through, there'll be a counsellor to talk to . . .'

She stops. Stamps her foot like a child having a tantrum.

'I don't *want* a bloody baby, all right!' Her anger seems to come from nowhere. 'And I definitely don't want . . .' She hesitates.

'What?'

'I don't want . . . Oh, for fuck's sake!'

She starts crying now: Big, frightened, gulping sobs and I'm sort of glad. At least that's normal.

'There's no way I could cope with a baby crying all night. I can't change a nappy. I've never changed a nappy in my life. I'd do it all wrong. I don't wanna get fat and never be able to go out with my mates. I know I'm not clever. Not like you. I've fucked up my A levels already, and I won't be going to uni. But I have got stuff to offer, you know. I'm not totally useless.'

'You're not useless at all!' It disturbed me when she talked like this.

'Wayne says I've got potential – and I've got loads of stuff I want to do. I've got ideas . . .' She can hardly speak for hiccupping sobs now.

'Lex, course you have.'

'I've decided I want to move to London. I decided that on day two. I love it here,' she says, eyes burning with enthusiasm. 'I want to go travelling and get a really good job and show Mum and Dad, make them proud of me. I don't want to end up a teenage mum with my life over at seventeen!'

'And you won't, that's not what I mean.'

'So why are you saying I should have the baby? If there *is* a baby that is?'

A Chelsea couple, her pashmina, him with a striped shirt and the collar turned up, approach with a baby in a pram, the woman looking Lexi up and down. What you looking at? I want to say. Never seen anyone discussing abortion at the top of their voices in the street at 9 a.m. in the morning?

'Oh, Lex, come on.' I go over and hug her but she holds her arms stiff by her side. 'I'm not saying you should definitely have the baby. All I'm saying—'

'I feel like you're judging me. Like the fact I want an abortion makes me weird or a bad person. It is a woman's right to choose, you know.'

'Of course it is. Absolutely it is.'

'And just because you're all grown-up and sensible and would never have ever been so crap as to get in this situation in the first place, just because I'm a fuckwit . . .'

She lifts her head up, folds her arms, and looks the other way towards the mews houses of Chelsea in the fuzzy

101

morning light. Shall I tell her? Would that just be making this about me, when it's Lexi in crisis here? But I want her to know that I understand at least, that I'm not judging her, that these things happen – even to 'sensible' big sisters like me, so I say:

'Actually, I did.'

Lexi sniffs. 'Did what?'

'Get pregnant.'

She laughs. 'Yeah, right.'

'I'm not joking. I was twenty-three, it was Martin's baby. I messed up on the pill, something to do with antibiotics, these things happen so, you see, I do mess up. All the time, as it happens.'

'So, what happened? Did you not even talk about keeping the baby? I mean, you were twenty-three, it's not seventeen, is it?'

We pass a café with a few tables outside; the sound of relaxed chatter and the clinking of china, the sound of the weekend, and I get that feeling I've had before, like I'm watching myself, like everything was calm before this. Before Lexi turned up.

'Oh yeah, we talked. For three weeks. It was horrible, I've never cried so much in all my life.'

'God, you must have shat yourself,' she says with usual Lexi decorum.

'I think that would be a fair description.'

'So why?' She's shaking her head, dying to ask.

'I didn't want a baby.' I shrug. 'I guess that's what it boiled down to. It was the wrong time and I was like you, I was ambitious.'

'I'm not ambitious!'

'Yes you are,' I say and she looks at the floor. 'I had so much I wanted to do. I was obsessed with work . . .'

'You're *still* obsessed with work!'

'This is true,' I say and she manages a smile.

Lexi bites her thumbnail. 'God, I feel awful now.'

'Don't be silly, you don't have to feel awful. Much.'

She gives a little laugh.

'I was just telling you so that you know I have some idea about how all this feels. That I'm not some lecturing do-gooder sister. Well, I have days off, anyway. And anyway, you may well not be as unlucky as me. You might not *be* pregnant. So shall we bite the bullet and find out?'

She gives me a dead arm

'Let's do this,' she says.

It occurs to me, as we walk the rest of the way towards the chemist, that that was the first time I've ever told anyone about the abortion. It's not that I'm ashamed of it, or have any regrets myself; it's just I was once pregnant, and I decided not to see it through. There doesn't seem a reason to speak about it, really.

That's not to say I don't think about it. I think about what would have happened if I had kept the baby – was it a girl or a boy? They'd have been nine years old by now! Maybe with a baby in the picture, Martin and I would have made it work because we'd have had to. Maybe I would be a different person now, be less demanding of life, more content?

I've shut out those few weeks before I made my decision – even though I know I made the right one for me.

I had morning sickness from the moment I found out. 'Hey, that means the hormones are strong,' Martin said, excited as I lay on the bathroom floor groaning. 'That you know, it's really taken.' Which made it sound a bit like a hair dye, but I knew what he meant.

It was then that it struck me – my God, he really *wanted* this baby. I hadn't said either way yet. I was too in shock and hadn't wanted to commit to anything. Maybe the hormones will kick in? I thought, and suddenly cull my desire to take over the world in sales of handwash (the department I was in at the time on the grad scheme, desperate to impress Janine and make my mark). But they never did, and a fortnight later I finally told Martin I couldn't do it.

'It's your body, I love you and I'll stand by whatever you decide,' he said, and I cried and cried because I knew how hard it was for him to say that; that deep down he wanted to scream: 'Don't do this to me!' I was *so* lucky. 'After all, we've plenty of time,' he added. But I suspect I already knew we didn't, that we weren't going to last the stretch, maybe that's the real reason why I couldn't do it.

Either way, my decision to not keep the baby was the first nick in the tear that was going to run through our relationship, eventually splitting us in two.

The dispenser at the chemist is a large African lady with berry-coloured lipstick and grey hair. We exchange a knowing smile as I hand over the pregnancy test with Lexi shuffling about behind me, pretending to look at shampoos.

'Tell her there are two in there,' she whispers. 'How late is she on her period?'

'About a fortnight, could be more. Basically, she's missed a whole one.'

She gives me a sympathetic grimace.

'I know,' I say. 'It doesn't look good, does it?'

'Well, stress can do a lot at that age. Is she stressed?'

'I don't know, it's hard to decipher from the five hundred other moods she seems to experience on an hourly basis.'

The lady laughs, silently.

'Tell her they do counselling at the Women's Wellness centre, you know, if it's not the news you were hoping for,' she says with a sympathetic smile.

'Thanks, that's really kind,' I say, thinking, Lord, please no. No, no, no! There's already been more drama in two weeks of this summer than I have had in the past year. I'm not sure I can take much more.

'Do you want me to come into the bathroom with you?'

We're at home now. Lexi shakes her head.

'Do you want me to stand outside or just go and do something?'

'I think, yeah, just go and do something.'

'Do you know what you're doing?'

'Just wee on the stick?'

'That's right, then put it on the side and wait for a minute.'

Lexi pauses, bites her lip.

'What shall I do for that minute?'

'Er, I'd pray, probably.'

She gives a weak smile then disappears behind the door.

Of course I don't go and do anything. Instead, I stand bolt upright against the wall, next to the bathroom, bricking it. What if she *is* pregnant? Quite frankly, it's looking likely. Two weeks late 'about' she told me. *About?* I thought. Good God. If I were as much as a few hours late on my period I was down the chemist doing a test.

I run through the P of A if she is. Just picturing the bullet points in my head, helps me, it slows down the heart rate.

· Phone Dad. Am I *insane*? Of course I wouldn't call Dad! Did I call Dad when I found out I was pregnant? No. No way. Mind you, did I call Mum? Nope. Mum would have kicked my head in and Dad would have burst into tears. Both useless, which is basically the way it was in our house.

· Organize session with a counsellor to 'talk through her options'. Not that I saw any counsellor. Martin was my counsellor. Just thinking about the hours he dedicated to me over those dark few weeks still makes

105

my stomach lurch. Still, it was my body, that's what he said, didn't he? My body. My decision.

There's a creak as the bathroom door gently opens and a, 'Can you come in here please?' Help. Here we go.
She hands me the stick. I look at her, but her face is grave, it doesn't give anything away.

I take the stick in my hand. I close my eyes. Then, not until I've said a prayer and apologized for any past sins, including evil thoughts about Rachel and her double chin and her badly cut jeans, I open one eye. I remove my thumb from the display window, then I open the other.

Not Pregnant it says in bright blue letters.

I shake my head

'You little shit!'

Lexi starts to giggle, then laugh, which starts me off. Before we know it – must be the rush of adrenaline, the dizzying relief – we are both collapsed on the bathroom floor in stitches, wetting ourselves laughing at something that, let's face it, would have completely transformed the summer. Not in a good way.

'I think you'd better come into work with me from now on, do some work experience. I'll get it organized next week.'

We've both been lying on the bathroom floor, staring up at the ceiling, for approximately fifteen minutes.

'Alexis and Caroline have been lying on the bathroom floor for approximately fifteen minutes,' Lexi says, in the Big Brother Geordie accent.

'I'm serious!' I say, punching her in the leg.

'I know you are and I think you're right.'

'Twenty-four hours left to your own devices and look what happens, Lexi.'

'I've said I'm sorry, haven't I?'

'I forgive you. This time.'

There's a long silence.

106

'Caroline?' she says eventually, turning to look at me.

'Yeeess?'

'Can we make a pact?'

I narrow my eyes at her.

'What sort of pact?'

'You never tell Dad about today and I'll never tell him about your abortion.'

'I should think so, too.'

'I s'pose that's not exactly a fair exchange, is it?' says Lexi.

'Not really, but I guess it's a deal. Can I ask *you* something?'

'Go on.'

'Who's the loser, cunt-face, prick-head, wanker?'

Lexi explodes with laughter. 'What? What you on about?'

'You said it on Thursday night when you were drunk.'

'Did I?'

'Is it the guy you thought had got you pregnant?'

'Oh,' she groans. 'Maybe, I don't know. I'll tell you about it one day. I'm too tired now.'

She lies back down and her breathing slows. I wonder if she's asleep, exhausted from the drama.

I lie there for a while, thinking about the events of the last forty-eight hours. I've never thought of myself as someone who copes well in a crisis and, yet, this has been the biggest crisis since when Martin and I split up, and I feel I did okay, *better* than okay. You were officially awesome in a crisis, Miss Steele. But then, maybe I've avoided anything like a crisis since Martin; held everything together, all tight, so that nothing, nothing could get in. But perhaps you can't stop it coming in, can you? You can't stop life worming its way through. It's how you deal with it that matters.

Martin used to tell me that, too.

CHAPTER TWELVE

The man behind the reception of the Malmaison has a bleached blond crop and a name badge that says 'Antoine'.

'*Alors* . . .' He scans a computer screen. 'Mr and Mrs . . .?'

'Steele,' I say.

Toby squeezes my hand. It's the first time he's held my hand in public and it feels lovely: protective and reassuring.

'*Bon*, Mr and Mrs Steele. Welcome to the Malmaison Lond-on.' He hands me a key. 'You are Room 314, which is just up on ze zerd floor, turn to your right and three doors alon-g.' I can see Toby staring at him. Surely he is putting it on? Nobody has a French accent that strong.

'Would you like a newspaper in the mornings?' Antoine looks at me, then at Toby, who looks at me. I go red.

'Um, maybe just tomorrow. We're just here for the one night,' I say.

'Of course, sorry, just the one night. Très bi-en,' says Antoine, slowly stapling some sort of receipt together and looking us up and down from beneath his pierced eyebrow. '*Pas de probleme. Pas de probleme du tout.*'

Antoine flounces from behind the reception area and shows us into the lift, where Toby and I promptly burst out laughing.

'You is 'ere just for ze massive shag?'

'Stop it! There might be cameras in here!' I squeal, putting my hand over his mouth.

'Monsieur Steele, 'e 'as un grand one?'

'Pack it in, Toby,' I say, creasing up. 'I'm gonna wet myself!'

The room is huge, softly lit, with an exposed brick wall behind a gigantic bed and bed linen in muted tones of stone and taupe. A huge rosewood wardrobe stands beside a similarly imposing dressing table. There is a bottle of mineral water by our bed and a small box of chocolates.

We open the door to the bathroom and swoon: monochrome sleekness, free-standing bath, shower head the size of a dinner plate.

'Post-coital power shower, baby,' says Toby.

'Really?' I say, excited. 'Was thinking more of a bath.'

Toby walks into the bedroom and turns around slowly.

'Steeley, you have surpassed yourself,' he says, opening his arms widely.

'Do you think so? Do you like it?' I say, hugging him.

Despite everything, the excitement today has been killing me; turning me deranged. I've been dropping everything, forgetting to forward messages, been completely unable to concentrate.

'What the hell is *with* you today?' said Shona eventually, after I'd left the stapler in the office fridge. It took all my strength not to just blurt out: Guess where I'm fucking well going after work? Only the fucking Malmaison Hotel with Toby fucking Delaney. *Arrgghh!*

In front of Toby, however, I am determined to exude a slight air of intrigue, at least. 'It was a stab in the dark, as it were,' I say. 'I just Googled "romantic hotels in London" and this one came up.'

'I love it,' he says, pushing me back on the bed. Looks like the air of intrigue isn't going to last long.

'Hang on a minute! I haven't got my shoes off yet! I'm

going to get the duvet dirty!' I squeal, batting him off as he covers my neck with kisses.

'Since when did you worry about being dirty, CS?' He takes one shoe off and flings the other across the room.

'Now, let's get these prissy little ballet shoes off, shall we? And this skirt and all these bloody . . .' He gestures for me to lift my arms so he can take my top off. '*Layers*. What is it with girls and layers? Because we are going to be getting really quite dirty.' He unhinges the back of my bra and throws that across the room. 'Very dirty indeed.'

'So what do you reckon we should be reading today?' mumbles Toby.

We're lying naked, salty damp bodies entwined in one another, a shaft of evening sun warming the bed.

'Why, is this like an extended book club, this overnight stay?'

'Oh God, yeah,' he says, still breathless. 'My reading credentials tell me that was already of the highest, epic standard.'

'Epic bonkbuster?'

'Exactly, Steele.' He laughs.

'Mmm, I guess we should be reading *Lady Chatterley's Lover*?' I say, sleepily.

Toby laughs. 'Very good. But how about *Madame Bovary*, since we're in a French hotel?'

'You'd have to poison me with arsenic, though, then watch me die a slow and painful death, which I don't think would be too romantic. How about *Les Liaisons dangereuses*?' I suggest, stroking his chest hair.

'*The French Lieutenant's Woman*?'

'Wow. We *have* come over all literary this evening.'

'Yeah, fuck that,' says Toby, rolling over to kiss me. 'Is there a book version of *Debbie Does Dallas*?'

* * *

110

We order wine from room service, then take a candlelit bath, me leaning back on Toby's chest as he gently strokes my hair. I feel divine, content, so relaxed it's all I can do not to fall asleep.

'I feel like Julia Roberts in *Pretty Woman*,' I murmur.

'What, like a hooker?' asks Toby.

'Charming. You've got all the lines, you have.'

Toby laughs, the vibrations of his voice sending shivers down my back to my feet.

'Why do you say that anyway?' he says.

'Because there's a scene where she and Richard Gere take a bath, a candlelit bath like this, it's all very romantic.'

'So what happens then?'

'Well, they cross the boundary of client–prostitute, I guess. They form a relationship. They fall in love.'

He doesn't say anything. There's just the sound of rippling water as I sway my knees from side to side. Then, Toby says, 'Well, you're my pretty woman, anyway,' and I turn my face to kiss him.

'Thanks, but I cost a bomb,' I say. 'I'm extortionate, actually.'

'I bet you are. But you're gorge, so you're worth it.'

'Who are you now?' I laugh. 'Cheryl Cole?'

We kiss, drink wine, and Toby washes my hair. Then we chat in the bath for what seems like hours, until the water is cool and the sky we can see through the window fades to a dusky blue. The only light is candlelight.

Toby tops up the hot water with his toe again and I sink down further in the deliciously soapy water, feeling the wine and a sudden burst of happiness surge through my veins. I seize it. I am determined to enjoy the moment. I know that soon, like a drug addict coming down, the paranoia and guilt will set in and the reality of what I'm doing will hit me. For now though, here with Toby, I can pretend this is a film. I can live in the moment.

Tonight is the first night that Toby and I will spend the whole night together and the web of lies is growing thicker by the second.

'It's book club tomorrow night,' I told Lexi whilst she sat painting her toenails last night. (Since the pregnancy scare, she's been lying very low.) This was LIE 1.

'And it's being held at Angela's house in Barnet.' LIE 2 AND 3, since Angela doesn't exist and she certainly doesn't live in Barnet.

'Oh, okay, so what does that mean?' asked Lexi.

'It means I'll be staying over and not coming home.' LIE 4.

'Who's Angela?'

'She works in the post room so you won't have met her.' LIE 5.

Then I drank almost a bottle of wine to myself because the lying made me feel so agitated, but now, just in this moment, it all seems so worth it.

Spending the night together seems like a huge milestone in mine and Toby's relationship, and yet the fact I call it a 'relationship' at all also seems like a milestone – one that shouldn't really have been reached at all. When the snogging first happened, I could convince myself it was short-lived, a blip. I could stop any time I wanted to – I just didn't want to yet.

It was a bit like a smoker who convinces themselves that if they only do it when they drink, then they're not a smoker at all. The book club was for two hours, once a fortnight, for God's sake. An appointment at the hygienist had more spontaneity and romance. Plus, this was how I liked it, didn't I? He had a wife, so I couldn't get involved if I tried. After the casualties that followed Martin – Mark and Nathan and Garf – this was all I could handle, and it was perfect. All the thrill of the sex, someone to flirt with at work but without the commitment.

But lately, especially since Lexi arrived and made the logistics of the book club difficult so that we have had to decamp to romantic French hotels, it feels like our relationship's been stepped up a gear without me even realizing.

Of course, any sensible person might have marked the day their sister arrived on their doorstep needing guidance as the day they stop 'extra-curricular' activities. Ordinarily, that would be exactly what I would do, but that's before emotions were involved, that was before I accepted I was actually having an affair. Now I feel like there are four things I know about this (and about a million that I don't):

a) I love it.
b) I hate it.
c) I am *so* not proud of it.
d) I think I may be in love with him.

That last bit *definitely* wasn't supposed to happen.

In fact, I think as I lie here, feeling Toby's hands caress me, the rise and fall of his chest beneath my head, that of all the people in all the world, I could safely say that my friends would consider me: Woman Least Likely to Have an Affair with a Married Man.

I have far too big a guilt complex, for a start. My brother always said I should have been born a Catholic. I am the sort of person who on hearing a police siren, becomes convinced it's me they're on their way to arrest for that arson attack I must have committed several years ago but which my memory has clearly erased. As teenagers, my friend Pippa tried to embroil me in shoplifting – it was Anti-Capitalist, she said; Dorothy Perkins had loads more money than we did and, therefore, why should we ever pay for anything they sold? It made sense when we were fourteen, but I just couldn't do it. The one time I attempted to nick some bangles, I got

113

as far as the next shop, broke out in hives, then had to go back and say that I'd just recovered from brain surgery and, therefore, had forgotten to pay. Pippa was not impressed.

So there's all that – the fact, I am what an investment broker might call 'utterly risk averse', along with the small matter that my mother's entire life was ruined by someone like me; someone who slept with married men. It's the reason her insides are like the roots of an ancient tree, they're so gnarled up with bitterness.

So, how am I *doing* this? How did this *happen*? And why, if I am so controlled in all other areas of my life, can't I make this stop?

CHAPTER THIRTEEN

And . . . zoom out. And . . . zoom in. Rachel's chin normal, Rachel's chin(s) huge.

And . . . Zoom out . . . And . . .

Oh.

It's only when my mobile vibrates that I realize it's been lodged between the sun lounger and my left buttock for approximately an hour.

I can just read 'mum' beneath the film of sweat.

'Hi, Mum, how are you?'

'Oh, hello. It's only your old mum – I'm not interrupting anything am I?'

No, no. Was only on Facebook blowing my lover's wife's face up.

'No, no. I'm just in the garden, sunning myself,' is what I actually say.

'That's nice. I'm glad one of us is getting the chance to relax. [Note the martyrdom; anyone would think Mum was calling from the spike she sleeps on.] You always seem so busy, so hard to pin down.'

Shit! She rang five days ago and I never called her back.

'Well, I have been *extremely* busy, Mum,' I backtrack. 'I still am. In fact, I'm sitting here in the garden with the laptop on my knee, working whilst I sun myself. Also, I've had a visitor for a while . . .'

'What, *Martin?*'

The excitement in her voice is just heartbreaking.

Since Martin and I broke up, Mum has lived in hope that he'll change his mind. That's because, like Lexi, Mum thinks it was his decision to call off the wedding. She adored Martin – Martin being the kind of capable, solid man she should have married instead of my dad, and I haven't had the heart (or the guts) to tell her that it was *I* who rejected *him*. In the circumstances, you'd think she'd assume he was a total bastard who left her darling daughter in the lurch. Not so. On hearing the wedding was off, her words, verbatim, were: 'Well, what did you do? You must have done *something*.'

'No, not Martin. Lexi's here for the summer,' I say. I wish I hadn't.

'Oh, don't tell me! Your father and the She Devil have gallivanted off to one of their witchcraft meetings [Mum has gone literal on the demonizing front], dumping Alexis with you?'

'Well, sort of.'

'Doesn't surprise me in the slightest. That man is *unbelievable*. In fact, the two of them are just abominable. Utterly selfish. No sense of duty.'

'It's not all Dad's doing, Mum. Lexi wanted to come. Dad said she needed a bit of support.'

'Needed? Don't talk to *me* about needs. I had my needs un-met *for twenty-two years married to your father* . . .' I can pretty much mouth it these days. 'It's any wonder you turned out as okay as you did, although you obviously didn't get off scot-free. Nobody's single at thirty-two for no good reason.'

Good old Mum. I can always count on her to make me feel like I am an emotionally scarred freak destined never to

116

be able to form normal relationships due to my philandering father.

'Mm, well never mind. Anyway, how's you?' I say, changing the subject. 'How are the Lovely Ladies of Harrogate?'

The Lovely Ladies of Harrogate are more the Separatist Spurned Sisters of Harrogate, bonded in their bitterness and acute hatred of men. Mum spends most of her time with them.

'Oh fine, we're all battling on. We don't have much choice, do we? Life goes on.' [Does it? She seems to have been stuck in the same bitter mind-set for seventeen years now.] 'Anyway, when are you coming up?'

'Erm . . .' Oh God. I knew that was coming.

'Because you did say May, then it was June, and now it's July.'

'August, I'll definitely come up in August.'

'Okay, it's just I won't have seen you for eight months by the time August comes around.'

Oh, here we go. All aboard the Guilt Trip. It's not that I don't want to see my mum as such, even if she does make me feel like a dysfunctional freak who'll never have a normal relationship (a therapist once called it projection), it's just, the thought of going to see her in that depressing dormer bungalow she rattles around in where seventeen years of bitterness seem to ooze from the furniture doesn't exactly fill me with glee.

'I promise August, Mum, okay? And I would have to bring Lexi.'

'Well, I don't suppose you'll have much choice since her own parents don't seem to care where she is.'

'You could come here,' I say.

'Oh no, there's nowhere to park and you know me and driving in London.'

Not that she's ever tried it in ten years of me living here.

'Your dad always used to do the driving, I've never been very confident.'

'Yes, I know, Mum. I know that's difficult for you.'

'Well, I'll look up train times then, shall I? Maybe if I book one in advance, you'll get it cheaper. We could go for lunch with the Ladies?'

'Yes, Mum, that would be lovely' Although last time I went for lunch with the Ladies, Brenda went on for an hour about how she beheaded her ex-husband's prize chrysanthemums after she found out he'd been unfaithful to her. Maybe this time she'll confess she actually beheaded *him*.

I eventually get rid of Mum, close the laptop and sink back down on the lounger. It's the most beautiful summer's day. Blue skies, the smell of sweet peas in the air, the odd hum of an aeroplane coming into Gatwick, and I'm here embroiled in self-torture on Toby's Facebook page. Sad, sad cow. God, I miss him now. I miss him so much at the weekend when I can't see or call him and I know he'll be at Kew Gardens or swanning down the Southbank when I'm sitting here obsessing over photos of him and his wife. The thing that gets me is that it doesn't actually add up, although I've never brought this up with him – the less asked the better, I think. The way he tells it, Rachel is some kind of militant wife who never has time for them as a couple, but the page is full of photos of them having a good time: diving in some far off place, heads poking out of a tent, chins cupped in their hands, New Year's Eve . . .

''Iya!' The pitter patter of flip-flops on the garden steps. That'll be Lexi back from the newsagent's.

She stands over me clutching a copy of the *Guardian* and a pint of milk.

'What you doing?' she asks.

'Oh, just a bit of work.'

'Hey, guess who I saw in the shop?'

'Who?'

'Wayne!'

'Ah, yes, now we need to talk about Wayne,' I say, as she sits on the end of the sun lounger, blocking out the sun. 'I think after the Tristan Banks fiasco that I should meet Wayne.'

'He'd love that. He's the best. Very laid-back. I feel I can tell him anything. What about tonight?' she says, excitedly. 'I could ring him now!'

'I can't tonight. I'm going out with a friend.'

'Oooh,' she says. 'A friend? Likely story. You're on Match. com, aren't you?' She grabs the laptop. 'You sly little fox.'

'Give me that!' I say, snatching it from her. 'I certainly am not. It's Martin, actually.'

She rolls her eyes at me and groans.

'Why you seeing him? You're mental, you are. He dumped you and you want to be his best friend? I don't get it.'

Tell her now, why don't you just tell her now? The words are on the tip of my tongue, but for some reason they just won't topple out and, just like the situation with Mum, the longer I leave it, the harder it is.

'Look, grown-up relationships are complicated,' I say. 'It's not black and white. You'll see when you get older.

'Yeah, yeah,' she says, getting up and going into the kitchen. 'It'll all end in tears! You just listen to Lexi, she may be seventeen but she does know some stuff.'

The Duke of Cambridge pub is one of those London 'gastropubs' that gets away with charging twenty-five quid a main course just because it has flocked wallpaper and a chef who 'trained with' Marco Pierre White (i.e., probably went to Scouts with).

Martin's standing outside when I get there, ten minutes late. (Martin believes it's rude to sit down at a table before your female companion has arrived. So sweet and gentlemanly, but sometimes I just wish he would, so I wouldn't feel so bad about my persistent, low-level tardiness – a chromosomal blip in an otherwise thoroughly anal DNA profile.)

He's got his hands in his pockets and is rocking back and forth on his heels, which I know to be an expression of strained patience.

'Sorry, Lexi was in the bathroom for ages so I couldn't get ready and then the phone went just as I was leaving and–'

Martin ruffles my hair. He knows I can't just say, sorry I'm late. (*Note to self: must work on this.) 'Come on, let's eat, shall we?'

The pub's packed, mainly full of the Sloaney Chelsea types – the girls with their ballet pumps and fringed scarves, the SW11 boys with their Pink shirts – with the odd, cool Bohemian thrown in. Possibly from the nearby houseboats moored just off Battersea Square.

We decide to have an aperitif in the bar before dinner. It was a ritual we followed when we used to come here as boyfriend and girlfriend, which was pretty much every weekend: Kir Royale, followed by wine with dinner and then a Quarante Tres as digestif, and since neither of us are great fans of change, it's a ritual we've stuck by.

'Great look, by the way,' says Martin, into my ear, putting his hand on my back as we're standing at the bar.

'Do you think so? You don't think my hips are too big to wear a pencil skirt like this?'

'No. You've got gorgeous hips.'

'Not too Miss Jean Brodie?'

'Too who? No, you look a million dollars.'

'But what about the blouse – you once said that Pussy Bow blouses were the work of the devil.'

Martin frowns. 'Did I? Well, I suppose it depends who's wearing it. Like I said, I think you look great.'

Martin doesn't look too bad himself tonight. It can go one

of two ways with Martin, depending on the shirt and the facial hair situation. When he's got a couple of days growth of stubble, it disguises his rapidly developing thirty-something slack jawline, and when he's got a good shirt on, like tonight – a navy blue number over well-cut dark jeans – it disguises his rapidly developing thirty-something waistline. So, he looks good tonight, handsome. A cuddly bear kind of handsome, but handsome all the same.

We get our drinks and sit down in the conservatory, which is filled, as conservatories should be, with cheese plants and wicker furniture.

'So, this is nice, we haven't done this for ages, have we?' says Martin brightly, straightening his shirt.

'Well, I thought you were officially under the thumb what with P on the scene,' I say, looking at him coyly over the top of my glass.

I've been dying to ask him about Polly since we bumped into them in Battersea Park, but there's never been a good time. I thought he might offer information the last time we met, but then I didn't probe for any information since I was far too wrapped up in my lost little sister – something I feel a bit bad about now. Still, he did turn up that evening as soon as I called, so I'd begun to wonder if I'd read the situation wrong.

'Polly's just a friend,' says Martin. A friend? Oh. I try not to smile.

'Oh, but you looked kind of close when we saw you in the park together the other day.'

'She goes to the same pastry class as me'

I can't help it, I burst out laughing.

'What? You bonded over shortcrust?'

'Yeah, something like that. Why what's it to you?'

'Nothing I just . . .'

'Come on, you know you're dying to say it, so you may as well spit it out.'

121

'She just looks like the sort of girl who might go to a pastry class, that's all.'

Martin laughs. 'And what, Caroline Steele, is that supposed to mean?'

'Nothing! She's just, sort of homely.'

'Fat?'

'No! Not fat.' (Yes, fat!) 'Domesticated-looking. Domestic Goddess.'

'Mumsy?'

'No!' (Yes, mumsy!) 'Warm. That's what I meant to say. Warm and friendly and really approachable.'

'Well, she is,' he says. I'm aware of a prickling up my back. 'Warm, approachable. All of the above.'

'Not the uptight ice-maiden that I am then, evidently?'

'Did I say that?' We're both laughing now but both of us know it's in a nervous, loaded kind of a way.

The waiter calls us to a table. A candlelit one at the far end of the modern, high-ceilinged gastropub. There's a hatch right behind us, where bombastic French chefs are shouting out orders – all adding to the relaxed charm of the place, or so I thought.

We sit down. The waiter goes to put Martin's napkin on his knee but by the way Martin's pursing his lips, I know what's about to come.

'Sorry, I . . .' He puts both hands up, like expecting us to sit here is akin to putting us in the laundry room to eat. 'Would it be a problem if we moved?' he says. I roll my eyes. 'It's just . . . Caroline, what do you think?'

'I'm fine here.'

'Really?'

'Really.'

'Oh, well I'm not. I'm sorry.' He grimaces apologetically. 'It's too noisy with the hatch so close and the plates clattering.'

'I'm sorry, sir, this is the only free table. We're fully booked,' says the waiter.

This is a rigmarole we used to go through practically every time Martin and I went for dinner. If I am anal about everything else, Martin makes up for it ten-fold with his seating-in-restaurants and food obsessions. He once moved not once, not twice, but three times in a restaurant we then had to stop going to and Martin has been known to serve Christmas dinner at midnight, so anal is he about the 'perfect chestnut stuffing'.

That's possibly why we worked. Or didn't. I could never make up my mind. I would certainly say there was empathy where Martin and I were concerned. Both of us as bad as each other but in our own separate ways, which is why Martin has never once, ever, suggested I 'just chill out', something I love him for.

'Look, Martin, it's fine, let's not . . .'

'Nope. No. Sorry we'll *have* to move.'

'You can sit *here* if you like.' We turn round to see a man with dirty-blond, thick hair and wearing an awful, baggy jumper, standing up from his table. 'We're going.'

He's with a tiny, dark-haired woman who hasn't taken her jacket off and who is still sitting at the table, looking down at a full plate.

'Are you sure?' I say. I know when Martin's made his mind up, it's best to just get it over and done with.

'Yeah, course, not a problem.' The man has rather nice deep creases around his eyes when he smiles.

The man's sliding his chair back under the table now. The girl is gathering her bags. She hasn't said a word.

'That's really kind of you, thank you,' says Martin, standing up to shake the guy's hand. Martin's handshake is a both-hands-nearly take-your-arm-off kind of shake but the man reciprocates graciously.

'Sorry about him,' I whisper as I make my way to the seat, our chests almost touching. He smells distinctive, a woody, earthy smell like he's been sitting around a campfire. 'Awfully fussy.'

He laughs as Martin calls behind him: 'Kettle, black, Caroline Steele! Kettle black!'

We're finally seated now, menu in hand, a glass of wine down, and I'm aware of a lovely feeling, of being utterly and totally myself. I look over at Martin. He's studying the menu in that way he does, head in hands, as if it was a medical consent form and the choice he has to make is a life and death matter, and I think how he is really the only person in the world that I feel that way with.

I'm not myself with my parents, with whom I seem to regress to teenager mode since I didn't get much of a chance to do that when I actually was one. I'm not with Lexi, since she *is* the teenager and therefore I have no choice but to be the grown-up, even though I didn't exactly offer myself up for that role. And, I realize now, I'm not even myself with Toby, any more, trying desperately to exude an air of not being governed by irrational emotions when I'm beginning to feel anything but. God, it's exhausting.

So yes, Martin is a very rare thing, a true friend, a soul mate, really, and I don't know what I'd do without him.

'So, why don't you go out with her?'

It comes out of nowhere.

'What?' He laughs. 'Why don't I go out with who?'

'Polly,' I say, dipping my bread into the oil. 'Why don't you ask her out on a date?'

'She *is* a lovely girl.'

'Well, *you* obviously think so.' I seem unable to fully eradicate the spikiness from my tone. 'So why don't you ask her out?'

'Oh, it's complicated . . .'

'Come on, Martin.' The wine's gone to my head and I'm full of bravado. 'You either fancy her or you don't.'

'Oh, I do fancy her.'

'Oh.'

'What?' he says.

'Nothing!'

'Why are you so desperate for me to ask her out?'

'I'm not!'

'You'd rather I didn't then?' Martin puts the menu down and cocks his head.

'I don't care either way.'

'You girls . . .' Martin smiles at me – I'm not sure what sort of smile but it makes me feel a little uncomfortable – and polishes off his wine before pouring us both more. 'You think us blokes can't see right through you.'

The starters come. Olive tapenade for Martin, a confit of duck for me. Martin approves of a restaurant with confits and tapenades on the menu. I'd be quite happy with bar food at the local, but Martin is very suspicious of any establishment that serves 'bar food' and considers a carvery as criminal as, say, organ trafficking. It's something I always found both exasperating and attractive about him. A man with high standards.

Martin picks up the menu again and peers over it at me.

'So, what about you?'

'What about me?'

'Been seeing anyone lately?'

My stomach turns to liquid.

I don't know what goes on in Martin's head, to tell you the truth, and I'm not sure I want to. As far as I can tell, he's okay, he's getting on with his life, he seems happy with his job at BT and his ongoing dream of opening a restaurant. Yes, he compliments me often, which I love, I have to admit – what girl wouldn't? But I don't think he's still in love with me. It's been a year now, anyway, and he seems to be getting back into the dating game, which is good, isn't it? Great. Yes, fantastic. Good for you, Martin! Way to go!

Oh, who the hell am I kidding? The thought of him falling for another girl fills me with a sickening dread, not really because I can't stand the thought of him having sex with another girl; strangely that doesn't seem to bother me, but because, deep down, in the part of me I don't like to venture often, I can't stand the thought of him telling another girl he loves her. Also, I know that the minute he gets a girlfriend − or I get a boyfriend, for that matter − we can't carry on like this, that never works in the long run. But Toby doesn't count as a boyfriend, does he? He is someone else's husband, so how could he?

Martin gives a little laugh, breaking my train of thought.

'You look like you've seen a ghost,' he says. 'Sorry. I shouldn't have quizzed you like that. You don't have to answer that question.'

'Yes, you are quizzing me, Martin Squire,' I say. 'But no, no I'm not seeing anyone.'

'Great!' says Martin. 'I mean, not *great*, but you know cool, as in cool, that's cool . . . Shall we just change the damn subject?' He laughs and I laugh too, relieved that's over.

'So dare I ask, how is Lexi?' asks Martin as we're tucking into our pudding. 'After her run in with Mr Banks?'

'Well, after a full scale row outside Shoreditch House where she called me a frigid cow then proceeded to throw up all over the taxi, I think I got the message through to her that Tristan did not have her best interests at heart.'

'You're joking?' says Martin. I don't tell him about the pregnancy test, that would be one step too far.

'Unfortunately not. Although now we seem to have another problem with some ex called Clark who keeps calling her and something's obviously happened between them because she never wants to talk to him.'

Martin pauses. His bread halfway to his mouth.

'Wait a minute, did you just say Clark?'

'Yes, why?'

'Clark Elder?'

'Yes, that's his name. I saw him as one of her friends on Facebook.'

Martin sucks air in between his teeth, which Martin always does when he's about to offer some sage advice, which he does often.

'She wants to watch herself with him,' he says. 'He was notorious in Doncaster: drug-dealing, fraud.'

'You're joking? Shit!'

'He was inside for a while, think it was GBH. And he's definitely done time for drugs.'

'Fuck, that's awful. I wonder if Lexi knows all this,' I say. 'Either way, she's worked out he's a baddun because she doesn't want anything to do with him, thank God. He seemed so charming when I spoke to him on the phone.'

'Oh yeah, he was always good at *that*,' says Martin. 'That's why he's probably got hundreds of illegitimate · children running around Doncaster.'

I think about the pregnancy test. My stomach turns inside out.

'And I think he was associated with date rapes some years back.'

'Okay . . .' I think about this for a minute. 'Well, I'm not going to worry too much because Lexi wants nothing to do with him. She won't even take his calls.'

Martin is an excellent drinking partner. A *bon-vivant* boozer who only gets jollier the drunker he gets. We drink two bottles of red wine. We laugh, we talk so easily it's like old times but better, more special; the kind of special things become when the pressure to make things work has gone, but the mutual love and respect remains.

It's funny, isn't it, how the things that make you fall in love with someone often become the things that make you want to hit them over the head with a mallet in the end?

When I met Martin, when he was a youth worker and I was a swotty sixth-former doing my Silver Duke of Edinburgh Award, I fell completely in love with his resourceful spirit. Him erecting a tent in a force ten gale could leave me nauseous with desire. He was three years older than me, twenty-one to my eighteen and the sight of his bottom, so hunky and capable in his combat trousers, was, to me, the epitome of manliness.

I would marvel at how pleasant he was to his parents (something I still struggle with now), how he could put up shelves whilst talking on the hands-free to his mum, in fact, do *anything* whilst talking to his mum.

That was probably the first niggle I had with Martin – his obsession with his mum. Martin's parents, Martin and Martine (all true! It was like they were a species in their own right) are lovely, lovely people; it's just that whilst I could accept that Martin was his father's best friend, I never quite understood why this meant I had to be his mother's best friend too.

When Martin played golf with Martin Senior, Martine and I would be expected to go shopping. When Martin booked a golfing weekend at a country hotel with his dad, Martine and I were booked in for facials. Eventually, we could hardly put the bins out without it having to coincide with a visit to his parents. (They moved down south to be with us a year after we went, which was the first nail in the coffin.) What with Sunday lunches, Saturday teas, shopping trips and facials, there wasn't much time for friends of our own age. They were all too busy doing what normal twenty-somethings do, like spending Sundays hung over in bed with their other halves, not in Morrissons watching him agonising over the three-for-twos.

I began to feel stifled, embroiled in a relationship where the dynamics were all wrong. Perhaps it was that, deep down, I knew that Martin loved me more than I loved him. But it's been two weeks since I've seen him and I've missed him. When the rest of my life is so complex, so unsure, Martin is a constant, and sometimes, when I'm being drunk and nostalgic and when I put on that wedding dress, I see it as the biggest tragedy of my life so far that things didn't work out between us.

'We're okay, aren't we?' I say, putting my hand on his. I'm aware of the echoing clatter and chatter around us and yet it feels, like it often does with Martin, that we're the only people in the room.

'What do you mean?' he asks, putting his hand on mine.

I send a finger around my wine glass.

'I mean, you're okay, aren't you? You know, about us, the wedding. I still feel sad about it, Martin . . .'

'Now, Caro . . .' Martin pats my hand. 'Don't start getting maudlin. It's fine. I'm okay. I'm getting on with my life and we still get to do this, don't we? I still get to see you . . .'

'You're lovely, Martin.' I'm drunk now, and nostalgic and sentimental.

'Thanks. And you, too, my dear, you too.'

'I'm so sorry it didn't work out and that I hurt you, it. I . . . I think about you every day.'

'Caro*liine*.' Martin lifts up my chin. 'I thought you promised you weren't going to get maudlin?'

'Sorry, it's just sometimes . . .'

'What?'

I look at his eyes, those grey, kind eyes that look at me with a love that nobody's matched since.

'Well, I wonder if you know, I was just too scared . . .' Oh God, here I go.

Martin shrugs.

'Maybe you're right.'

I feel my eyes fill up with tears. Don't cry, not now.

'Oh, Caro,' he says. 'Don't be sad, hey? It's all right, you'll be a spinster till you're seventy and then, one day, you'll wake up and think, you know, that Martin bloke wasn't all that bad after all.'

I laugh, shyly, and wipe away a tear. Then he says:

'You haven't told Lexi it was your decision, have you?' It comes out of nowhere and catches me off guard. 'She thinks I called off the wedding. That's why she's rude to me, she's mad with me, isn't she?'

'No!' I say. 'No, no, no . . .'

Shit, shit, shit.

'Course I told her, back when it happened. She's just a teenager that's all. And teenage girls are the worst. Very moody for no apparent reason.'

'You're sure?'

'Course I'm sure,' I say, thinking, that's it. I really have to get round to it. What's the big deal, anyway? So I broke it off. I failed at something, it happens. Then he says:

'Oh well, you've still got me, haven't you? I always want you in my life, even if just as friends.'

'Me too,' I say, raising my glass. 'To friends. Special friends.'

CHAPTER FOURTEEN

On the following Saturday, when Lexi is working on the stall with Wayne, I decide to go and *introduce* myself. That's what it was. It wasn't prying. Prying would be sneaking around and watching her from afar, getting on the same bus as her and following her there, like a paranoid mentalist of a big sister. And I wasn't paranoid – was I? Only a healthy amount. I just wanted to suss him out, that's all. He could be any old unsavoury market trader.

Anyway, she knows I'm coming and she's really excited.

'Wayne's the business, you're gonna love him,' she keeps saying, which for some reason is making me nervous, ramping up expectations. What if I positively hate him? (Don't be ridiculous, I keep telling myself, Why on earth would I hate him?) But I've always had this slight nervy thing about meeting new people – I get it from Mum. Not so much cynicism, as a lack of confidence – will he lik*e me*? Or does he already have me down as a list-obsessed, anally retentive freak who is masking some terrible unhappiness?

Either way, I realized as I sat for what seemed like an eternity on the Northern Line, I hadn't even been to Camden Market before. In ten years of living in this city, that particular cultural attraction had never been ticked off. I worked out that that was because I'd lived with Martin for all that time and Martin is a particular breed of conventional man who thinks that Camden Market is full of 'crusties', people with 'dreaded locks', as he calls them. It was the same with Spitalfields or Portabello, and God forbid I wanted to go to Notting Hill Carnival. 'Just so predictable, so touristy, Caro,' he'd say, 'and full of ethnitat.' I guess when you spend ten years with someone, attitudes like that begin to rub off and I, too, had become suspicious of anything second-hand, of leather jackets that smell of joss sticks.

So it's a surprise to me that I love Camden Market. Can't get enough of it. I feel like the kid of a health freak let loose in McDonalds. I love the stalls selling chunky silver jewellery and necklaces with enormous coloured stones that look like boiled sweets. I lose an hour in the shops selling frosted glass bottles and bongs and wondering how you used one – was it too late for the Bong Years? I am entranced by the raven-haired, kohl-lined stallholders with their piercings and their funny fat trainers; the punks and goths and gangs of teenagers wearing Ray-Bans who look like they've just come straight off the set of some beatnik film.

I wander for an hour, forgetting even to look for Lexi, immersed in a new, psychedelic London that makes me feel strangely alive. It's warm and the scent of food is everywhere. Any kind you want: golden crepes sizzling on a plate, huge terrines of bubbling curries from goat to mutton to dahls and baltis; pizzas and fragrant vats of creamy, Thai curry. There's a squat, muscly man tattooed from head to toe, (including his face), shouting, 'Encilladas! Two for a pound!' I buy one, dripping in soured cream. Why had Martin never brought me here?

I lose at least fifteen minutes at a stall selling old books, thumbing through first editions of Thomas Hardy novels, deliciously yellowing copies of Shakespeare plays and sonnets of the Romantic Poets. I keep my eyes open for Lexi, but it seems like every stall is run by a hip, pretty young girl, sitting in the sun, and I decide there's no rush anyway, I'm having a ball all on my own. I wander on, spotting an archway that looks intriguing, dimly lit, like a rabbit warren, with emporiums of books and clothes and records branching off a main gangway. There's a stall on the left, a little shop in its own right with dinky, frosted windows, like an old Dickenisan curiosity shop. Music is coming from inside – something soulful and crackly, playing on an old gramophone. I stick my head in and it goes back far further than the front would suggest. It sells mainly vintage furniture: a couple of beaten leather sofas, old-fashioned hairdryers and retro coffee tables. In the far right corner, a single, antique bed is elevated like it's been hurled about in a typhoon and landed there. There are shabby-chic standard lamps lighting every corner and piles of vintage Wedgwood china stacked precariously in any spare space. Near the back there are rails of leather jackets and fur coats in all colours, vintage shoes lining the floor, and sparkly, embroidered handbags dripping off every hanger. It's the sort of shop Martin would drag me from, tutting: 'What is it with girls and their obsession with stuff their grandma would wear?' It's also the kind of shop that makes me feel vaguely intimidated, whilst at the same time tantalized, like will they sniff me out in a second? In my George at Asda sundress?

There doesn't seem to be anyone there though, so I venture in, self-consciously eyeing up the leather coats, stroking the dresses in all their strange, coarse, patterned fabrics. 'Looks like a pair of old curtains.' I can hear my mother now.

But I've always secretly admired those girls who can wear vintage; those girls who have a 'statement look' or who can pull off hats like they were born wearing them. The sorts of clothes Lexi wears. I have never been very good at fashion. Not for want of trying. I'd go out shopping, determined that, this time, I'd get an 'outfit', a 'look', wow my friends with some left-field, edgy ensemble, then come back with another beige cardigan from Next.

But I'm feeling adventurous today – maybe I could pull off a vintage dress after all? Perhaps Toby would find me irresistible in a cute, insouciant Sixties number? I leaf through the rails, feeling self-conscious.

I find a fur coat – toffee colour, amazing – and hold it up to me in front of the mirror, then put it back when I try and fail to imagine me walking around SW11 wearing anything of the sort. But this! *Drool* . . . I pull it from the rail: A gorgeous little Sixties shift dress. It's midnight blue with cute capped-sleeves and a wide, boat neck with leaf patterns in silver thread. I take it off the rail, stand in front of the mirror, holding it with one hand, piling my hair on top of my head with the other, imagining how it might show off my clavicles. My strong point, Martin once told me.

'You can try it on, if you like,' says a sudden voice behind me. Flat northern tones. Yorkshire. Can spot it a mile off.

'God, you nearly gave me a heart attack.' I laugh, turning crimson. What was I doing in the mirror? Was I actually *pouting*?

'I was pouting, wasn't I?' It just topples out.

The man – I assume it's the stallholder – leans against the clothes rail and laughs, a throaty genuine laugh.

'Yeah, proper fancying yourself in that, you were,' he says, and I feel my face burn. 'I bet you'd look great in it, go on, try it on.'

He's wearing a faded grey, vintage T-shirt, jeans and trainers – blue and bright green, with the laces trailing.

'Oh no, I won't . . .' I feel suddenly mortified. The fact he's so handsome isn't helping one bit. Tall, pale-green, searching eyes with deep creases around them so that when he smiles – which is often – they meet up with the creases

134

around his mouth. There's something about those creases that are familiar. I bet he does loads of outdoor pursuits, I think. Skiing? No. Too bourgeois. Probably kayaking or mountain climbing, or maybe those laughter lines come from riding a motorbike for hours at high speed on the open road.

His hair is straw-coloured, highlighted by the sun and unconsciously bouffant against a swarthy, slightly oily complexion. But it's his smile that gets me – I can't stop looking at it: wide, mischievous with a slightly chipped front tooth. One could get lost in a smile like that, I think. Hours could be lost.

He walks off, sipping from the takeaway coffee, as if he's just had an idea. 'Here,' he says, coming back seconds later with a large floppy hat and a scarf, 'try this' He puts it on me. '*Very* Marianne Faithfull,' he says, 'very foxy.'

I shake my head.

'Oh no. I couldn't. I could never carry off something like that.'

He folds his arms, stands with his feet apart and looks at me intensely so that I laugh nervously and look away. 'Actually, I beg to differ,' he says. God, was he flirting with me?

I look at myself again. I'd never be seen dead in it, but it was cute. Very cute . . .

'You reckon?'

'Reckon? *I know*,' he says with mock-seriousness.

'Oh, go on, then,' I groan, coyly. 'Your flattery sales technique's working a dream on a sucker like me.' And then I take the dress to the dressing room – a bit of old curtain pulled-to at the back of the shop. What the hell. Live a little, Caroline. So what if it ends up at the back of your wardrobe? Maybe you could save it for the book club. For Toby's eyes only. I feel naughty at the thought, and even have a little hum to myself as I shimmy out of my Asda dress, and pull the shift dress over my underwear (dodgy and not matching today, which somewhat spoils the experience). I look around for the mirror. No mirror. Shit. Now I'm going to have to go out and greet him without being able to check for any obvious problems like bra fat or the fat you get when your knickers dig in. Still, you can't stay here all night, Steeley, I say to myself, taking a deep breath. Come on, got to *do* this. I pull back the curtain and walk out.

He's sitting on a chair now, looking very serious. It makes me giggle.

'Okay, you've got to get the dress. With legs like that? Wow.'

I roll my eyes, but I was secretly loving this. 'Now you're just flattering me to get the sale. I may be blonde but I'm not dumb.'

'Oh come on! Get the damn dress. Anyone can see you look utterly gorgeous.'

I fight it, but a smile spreads involuntarily across my face. Gorgeous? Utterly so?

'Are you always like this with your female customers?'

'No,' he says. 'Absolutely not.'

I tut coyly and go back to looking at myself in the mirror. My legs did look quite good, quite shapely. Goddamn it . . . maybe he was right.

Then suddenly, from the back of the shop: 'Oh, you met each other then?' And my sister emerges from a rail of clothes.

'Lexi!' I pull at my hem. I feel like a schoolgirl caught snogging behind the bike sheds.

Wayne looks at me, amused realisation creeping across his face.

'Wayne, this is my big sister, Caroline. Caroline, this is Wayne . . . Quite literally, the coolest boss in the world.'

'Pleased to meet you, Caroline.' Wayne presses his lips together like, 'Oh dear, we got that wrong didn't we?'

'What, you didn't know who each other was?' says Lexi.

'No, um no.' I am trying to ignore the fact that I am blushing furiously. 'But I was just admiring Wayne's stall. Great stall, Lex. Love it, some really cool stuff.'

'Your sister was particularly loving our Sixties collection,' Wayne says, suddenly businesslike.

'So I see.' Lexi looks me up and down. 'Are you going to buy that dress?'

I look down at it and suddenly come to. What was I thinking? Toby would *hate* it. He'd think I shopped in a jumble sale. I have a sudden urge to run into the changing room and rip it off

'No,' I say, making towards the changing room. 'I think I've changed my mind.'

We're all sitting down in the middle of the shop now, clutching cups of tea.

'So, how did you two meet again?' I've been staring at Wayne since I realized who he was. How on earth could someone that good-looking be called 'Wayne'?

'Right here, Lexi was browsing round the shop,' says Wayne.

'Is it your shop?'

'No, it's Dave's – the guy I live with – but he doesn't like being front of house so I do all the selling and he does the business side.'

'Oh,' I say, slightly disappointed. So it wasn't even his own shop.

'Anyway,' says Wayne, possibly sensing this, 'I knew Lexi had the killer sales instinct even then, didn't I?' he says, nudging Lexi, and the creases in his eyes get deeper as he smiles.

'Oh my God!' It suddenly comes to me. '*That's* where I've seen you before. Last week. The Duke of Cambridge? You gave up your seat for us.'

Wayne frowns.

'Oh yeah,' he says, eventually. 'You were with your boyfriend.'

Lexi coughs.

'He's not my boyfriend,' I say.

'Really? You looked like girlfriend and boyfriend.'

'Yeah, they're weirdos,' says Lexi, and I shoot her a look.

'No, we're not. He's just a friend, a very good friend.'

'Cool,' says Wayne, nodding like he knows he's touched a nerve and needs to change the subject, sharpish. 'Just a friend, that's cool. That's absolutely great.' There's a rather too long pause, then Lexi says, 'So anyway, what do you reckon to the furniture? This is the stuff I'm mainly selling, isn't it, Wayne?'

She gestures to a pearl-coloured standing lamp. 'I think you'll find this is Danish mid-century,' she says, doing her best *Antiques Roadshow* voice now, 'And this, madame, is an original Borge Mogensen 1960's sofa.'

I look at Wayne for approval – she's only worked for him a short time, surely she couldn't know that much already?

'She's spot on.' He shrugs. 'I think she's really got something. The selling X-factor. A head for design and strange Danish designers!'

Lexi's face lights up every time she speaks to him, but not in any sexual way, I am confident of that. Yes, Wayne is gorgeous, if one can overlook the Eighties name (and a total flirt, it turns out, but we'll brush over that) but I think I'm a good judge of character and he's a good guy, anyone can see that. I'm glad she's found him.

'Really? Wow. Could we have a Sales Person on our hands?' I say. 'That's so cool, Lex.'

'I know,' she says, grinning.

I feel a bit awkward, like now we've done our introductions I should go and leave them to their thing.

'Well, I should be going,' I say, standing up. 'Great to meet you, Wayne, seems like you have a very willing apprentice there. I'll see you back at home, okay, Lex?'

'Hey, but wait,' says Wayne as I make to leave. 'If you fancy – I mean, I'll be shutting up shop in an hour – you could come round to mine for a beer on the deck? I don't know if Lexi told you, but I live on . . .'

'A boat near Chelsea Pier. Yeah, she did,' I say, (as well as the fact you're from Sheffield, are a Sagittarius, think people who make lists are masking a deeper unhappiness. Although, having met him now, I found it hard to imagine him being judgemental.)

'Oh, great. Well if you're not anti boats, then . . .'

He smiles encouragingly but I am aware I am pulling a face. Maybe I was anti people who lived on boats and just didn't know it? Sometimes it worried me how much I had morphed into Martin, to what extent his own prejudices might have rubbed off on me.

'Do you fancy coming over? Beautiful sunset on a night like this. If you want, you could go and Lex and I will meet you later, so you don't have to wait for all the boring packing up bit.'

I think of the alternative. Another night in, itching to text Toby, torturing myself with images of them cooking together, snuggled up on the sofa. Plus my sister is nodding her head excitedly. 'Why not?' I say. 'That'd be lovely.'

It's only when I actually get there that evening that I realize that when Lexi said Wayne lived on a boat, I was imagining a posh yacht not this huge cargo carrier. A rusty, barnacle-covered eyesore dredged up on the side of the Thames like an ancient, ailing walrus. I'm trying to keep an open mind though – eradicate any thoughts of dread-locked, mangy-dog-owning types. Wayne may think he can comment on my lifestyle, draw the conclusion that I am a control freak, but I'm bigger than that. I can do 'bohemian'.

I didn't imagine we'd have to risk our lives just getting onto the thing, though.

'Whoa! Lexi, bloody hell! Will you watch where you're going?' I'm standing on the banks of the Thames watching Wayne guide her across a rotting plank of wood.

'She's cool, I've got her. Now, it's your turn,' smiles Wayne, reaching out his hand.

It's big and covered in what looks like charcoal or oil, as is the jumper he's now changed into. Not exactly dressed up for the occasion.

'But it's rotting. That plank of wood is *rotting*!' I protest.

'Come on, get yer bum over here and stop being a gaylord!' shouts Lexi, from the deck.

Wayne holds his arm out further.

'You're okay, I promise. I've got dry clothes if you fall in. Dave might even have a skirt you can borrow somewhere.'

'Not funny!'

'Sorry.' Wayne smiles, winking at me.

I take his hand. It's rough and warm and I finally make it across, not without almost crushing his hand in the process.

The sun is just setting and he was right, the view from the deck is amazing, everything reduced to charcoal smudges against a watermelon sky. To our right, past Battersea Bridge and a stretch of wide, inky river, the lights of Albert Bridge glitter, and the steeples of Battersea Power Station seem to rise from the banks like pearly turrets of some mystical castle.

'Isn't it awesome?' I can just see Lexi's knickers from where she's leaning over the side of the boat, her skirt billowing in the breeze.

'You don't look so sure,' says Wayne, peering at me, amused.

'Oh no, it's gorgeous. I'm just recovering from my near-death experience, that's all.'

Wayne rolls his eyes and leads us below deck.

The inside of the boat is far more homely than the outside would suggest. A cavernous space, an extension of the market stall, really, with countless lamps, a big shaggy rug and empty bottles of wine stuffed with half-melted candles all around the edge. A mustard, Seventies sofa takes up much of the living space, and dotted around it, all manner of curiosities, from old baths, to coal scuttles, to the same style 1950's sideboard that I saw at the stall. There's a wood-burning stove in the far corner, giving off a smell, like bonfires, like the smell I smelt on Wayne in the Duke of Cambridge.

'So, what do you think?' Lexi looks at me with bright, excited eyes.

'Well, it's certainly not your Barratt home.'

Wayne gets us a drink and introduces us to his boat-mate, Dave. Dave's an artist, as well as owning the Camden Market stall, the sort to have his finger in lots of pies. He and Wayne met in a bar in Battersea Square three years ago, hit it off, then decided to rent a boat rather than a flat because it was cheaper. He has a Loyd Grossman accent, a thick ginger beard and is wearing a beanie hat, white vest, sunglasses and several gold bangles. Dave thinks Wayne is one of the most 'awesome human beings in this godforsaken city'.

Dave likes to say things like 'godforsaken city' a lot. Along with 'crap-hole' and 'crock of shit', and, with each Americanism, I can see Lexi's face light up, as if she's thinking: 'Man . . . [She picks up 'man' within a nanosecond of meeting him] could this get any cooler? I'm on a boat, in London with some American artist dude – this is more *like* it.'

Wayne takes a bottle of wine from the kitchen – an old sink and a two-ring hob, behind a beaded curtain.

'I take it big sister doesn't mind little sister having a tipple of a weekend?' says Wayne, holding the bottle out towards me, and I feel the first shiver of annoyance. Was I really that uptight? What had she been telling him?

'I'm eighteen in ten weeks,' says Lexi

'She's eighteen in ten weeks,' I repeat, the joke being that she sounds about twelve when she says that.

'Well, that's sorted then. I think you've earned yourself a glass of wine this week. Just go easy on it, yeah?' says Wayne, handing her a glass. 'We don't want anyone overboard.'

I scan the room.

'I love this,' I say, nodding towards an ornate writing bureau. 'Do you sell these on your stall?'

'Yeah, very expensive though. Edwardian antique mahogany, set you back nearly eight hundred quid, wouldn't it, Lex?' says Wayne.

'Eight hundred quid? Jesus. And you live *here*? Sorry. Not that I'm saying . . .'

'No offence,' says Wayne, laughing. 'It's not to everyone's taste, that's for sure. Anyway, I'm sure Lexi could get you one at a discounted price once she's proved her selling worth.' He looks at Lexi who's still grinning like I've never seen her grin before.

Wayne claps his hands.

'Well, shall I give you the official tour then?'

'Yes please!' says Lexi.

'Yes please!' I agree, as genuinely as possible, and everyone laughs.

'It's okay, you can just make the right noises,' says Wayne. 'Just "umm" and "aah", nobody will ever know.'

I start to relax.

Ginger-bearded Dave makes Lexi laugh, a lot. After a tour of the boat, and his room – a cabin that consisted of a mound of clothes and a hammock up high, pretty much like Wayne's – he offers to do a portrait of her, and Wayne and I go up on deck. It could feel awkward considering our earlier frisson, a bit like we've spent the afternoon tipsy and now we've sobered up, but it doesn't. I feel comfortable with him. I feel like I could tell him anything.

'He's quite a character, is Dave, isn't he?' I say, as Wayne hands me another beer. 'Got quite a look going on.'

'Sort of covered himself in glue and ran into Accessorize?'

I crack up laughing.

'Exactly, although I rather like a man in a bangle.'

The red sky has turned to violet now, and, save for the odd cry and creak from Chelsea Pier shipyard, the night is perfectly quiet. How nice it would be if Toby was here, I think. How ironic that I should find myself in such an almost clichéd romantic situation with someone – a good-looking man, I'll give him that – that I'm not romantically involved with. Typical of my life, I think. It's at times like this that I feel sort of *cheated*.

'So, what do you do again?' says Wayne, breaking my train of thought. 'Lexi tells me you work way too hard, by the way.'

I lean against the boat, next to him.

'I'm in sales, for my sins. I sell mouthwash and breath freshener to the supermarkets. So, hardly changing the world.'

'Oh, I don't know about that,' says Wayne. 'Some would say that ridding the nation of halitosis was a very noble cause. I would bet that, in a roundabout way, you've played a part in getting many budding romances off the ground. Beats pushing buttons for a living, anyway.'

'Why, is that what you do? I mean apart from the stall?'

'I used to – I used to live in Leeds and work as a website designer for such fascinating clients as timber merchants and freezer manufacturers.' He laughs. 'It nearly killed me! Now I just run the stall and write in whatever time I have left.'

'Oh, you write?'

'Yes, I'm writing a novel, which is partly why I live on the boat. It's cheaper, you see, which means I can afford to have a low-paid job selling second-hand stuff, have time to scribble and still survive.'

'Seriously? Wow!' I say this with all the enthusiasm I can muster, thinking, isn't half of London writing a novel? Doesn't 'I'm writing a novel and living on a boat', equal 'I'm bumming around'? 'How much have you written?'

'Thirty thousand words.'

'How far is that? Sorry, means nothing to me.'

'What, you mean to say *you're* not writing a novel?' he says, his green eyes widening playfully.

'Ahem, no. People may say everyone's got a novel inside them. I doubt I've got a paragraph in me,' I say, and he laughs. 'So what sort of book is it?'

'Oh, some rom-com rubbish. *Brian Jones's Diary*.'

'Shut up!' I laugh, nudging him in the side.

'It is!' he protests 'Well, let's just say, it's no Martin Amis or William Boyd.'

'I *love* William Boyd.'

'Are you serious? I've never met anyone who loves William Boyd. Well, not a girl anyway.'

'Oh yeah, *Brazzaville Beach*, *An Ice-Cream War* – definitely in my top ten.'

'You're quite the reader then?'

'Believe me, with parents like mine you wouldn't have survived without the escapism that books provide.'

Wayne laughs again, and fills up my glass.

I'm tipsy now. I know I'm tipsy because I'm beginning to find Wayne, despite his oily jumper, and his bad name and his chipped tooth, rather attractive.

We sit down together on deck, leaning against the hull and Wayne rolls up his sleeves. He's got nice forearms: sculpted, covered in fine dark hair. Forearms belonging to someone not shy of physical work. He lifts his glass to his lips and, as he does, I notice he has a tattoo, the full length of his left forearm. It looks like a name. I can just make out a J in the dwindling light but not much else.

'She's a cool girl, your sister.' He sighs contentedly as he pours beer into his glass and then into mine.

'Yes, she is.'

'Do you get on well?'

'We have our ups and downs. It's complicated, you know, half-siblings. Lexi's also having a few issues at the moment . . .'

'I know,' says Wayne. 'But she looks up to you, you know?'

'She looks up to you, too,' I say. 'I tell you, you have guru status in our house.'

'Give over!'

'You do! "Oh Wayne says people who make lists are masking greater unhappiness",' I say in my mock-therapist voice. Wayne groans.

'Oh my God, that's taken so out of context!' he says. 'I'll wring her neck later.'

We drink more, we chat, we laugh easily as the light fades and I begin to feel there's something about Wayne, something that makes me want to confide in him. The drunker I get, the more I'm thinking of Toby and our situation. He's a man, I think, he'll have some insight.

'Can I ask you something?' I say, when there's a break in the conversation. It's pretty much dark now and I can only make out a silhouette of his face. 'I know I'm probably going to say too much, but I don't have anyone I can really talk to about this and I sense something wise about you, Wayne, I really do.'

I realize what I just said and we both start laughing.

'Yeah, such a wise old owl, me!' says Wayne, self-deprecatingly. 'Such a fountain of all knowledge.'

I take a deep breath, look up at the sky that's punctured now with a rash of stars.

'In your opinion – you know, just as a bloke, not one who philanders – do men who have affairs ever actually leave their wives?'

He laughs, but in a different way now. A way that tells me I've shared too much, that I've possibly embarrassed or unpleasantly surprised him.

'Well, I-I-don't know,' he stutters. 'I guess that depends on whether he loves his wife; or he doesn't but he didn't have the balls to tell her before he jumped into bed with someone else. Either way, I'd say it's pretty lame to be having an affair in the first place.'

'*Really?*'

'Definitely,' he says, flatly.

'Even if your wife is overbearing, does nothing but work and makes you feel like crap?'

'More so. I mean, if she's that bad, surely any half-wit would be able to do the decent thing and end it? Who'd respect someone who let someone treat them like that?'

I think about this. It's not an angle I've considered before.

There's a long pause that would be far more awkward if I weren't so drunk.

'So, I take it the guy you're seeing, he's married, right?' says Wayne.

'Yes. I'm a Mistress. A *Mistress*! Jesus,' I say, 'I've never said that out loud before. That's how much it pains me.'

Then it all comes out. Poor Wayne. Too much wine and fresh air, I imagine. I tell him all about Toby and the book club that's really a fuck club; about how I'm playing the part of enigmatic temptress but really, inside, I'm more Glenn Close in *Fatal Attraction* and worried Toby's going to see the real me one of these days, the one that knows she's falling for him. I tell him about Martin and the wedding we never had – because of me – and the fact I still love him, just not like that – and can't bear the thought of him loving someone else. Then I stop to draw breath and it's only then that I realize Wayne has done nothing but nod and 'mmm' and stare into his drink for at least half an hour.

'Sorry I . . .' I stop. It's a good job it's dark because I feel my face blush.

'It's cool,' Wayne says and shrugs. 'Honestly, it's fine.'

'I don't usually . . .'

'Look, don't worry about it,' he cuts in and gives me a curt smile.

'Okay.' I regret ever opening my mouth.

'Where are you . . .?' 'going', I was going to say as he suddenly stands up.

'Just below deck,' he says. 'I won't be a minute.'

I watch him disappear below deck; cursing myself for my emotional vomiting. This is how it feels to be me these days. I hold it together. Just. I exist in an airtight funnel. And then sometimes, just sometimes, the pressure gets to much and – bam! – I'm in my wedding dress, getting drunk alone and listening to Pat Benitar or emotionally splurging over some poor innocent bystander with no warning at all.

I lean back, look up at the stars, thinking about what Wayne just said. Why *didn't* Toby just get rid of her, if she's so bad? He had a point. But then nobody knows the real reasons somebody stays with someone, do they? And nobody knows both sides of the story.

My vision's blurred now. I'm getting the feeling this vetting-Wayne visit hasn't really turned out like it was supposed to. I should go, I think. Go before I emotionally seep even more and Wayne starts to wonder what sort of madwoman his protégé's come to spend the summer with.

I take a last look at the view – just dark shapes now and the lights of Albert Bridge, soft and bruised looking after far too much wine. I finish my drink.

'Lex!' I call clambering clumsily down the ladder of the boat. 'Lexi, we should go, it's nearly eleven o'clock . . .'

Then I stop on the bottom rung. I blink hard, and I try to compute what I see. My sister, eye make-up smudged, leaning louchely against the dresser, a glass of wine in her hand and Wayne, his hand slap bang on her left breast!

'Alexis Steele!' I shout, at the top of my voice. 'Get your stuff. We are going home. NOW!'

CHAPTER FIFTEEN

It's been ten days since the Wayne debacle and Lexi is adamant I read it all wrong.

'It wasn't what it looked like,' she kept saying, the following day. We were in Debenhams trying to buy tailored trousers for her first week's work experience with me where I could keep an eye on her. I hoped it meant that she wouldn't feel the need to work for wandering-hands Wayne (I should have known better with a name like that), although Lexi's having none of it: 'Wayne's about as far away from a pervert as it's possible to get.'

What that was exactly, I didn't really know. What I did know was that a hand on a breast is a hand on a breast and I didn't want her working for someone who puts his hand on her breast. Why she's sticking up for him, I'll never know.

To think I was actually starting to listen to her and Wayne's nuggets of wisdom about the lists and 'avoiding the Big Stuff'. Knob. And now she's got this bizarre idea that Wayne fancies me.

'The thing is, I think he likes you.' We were standing at the sales counter, buying her a dress. (Lexi, rather eloquently had said she'd rather eat her own excrement than buy tailored trousers.)

I laughed out loud.

'Oh yeah, because groping my little sister would be a sure way to my heart. Not.'

Lexi sort of growled.

'Can you just shut up about the groping thing? He wasn't, he didn't! Didn't you see the look on his face?'

'Yes, guilt.'

'No, he was mortified! Think what you like but you're wrong. Wayne's lovely, and he fancies you.'

'How do you know?' I said. (Why did I *want* to know?)

'I just do,' she says. 'I have instincts for such things.'

I roll my eyes. If Lexi's instincts about men so far this summer were anything to go by, I wasn't going to listen.

'The thing about men like that, Lexi,' I said, 'is that they fancy everyone. They think they can just ply you with booze then take advantage. And I don't want you working with him. I just don't think it's a good idea.' I shrugged. 'And anyway, Dad would kill him if he knew.'

It struck me as I said that that Dad wasn't really a chivalrous type and would be more likely to offer him therapy to deal with his sexual deviance issues than kill him.

The trip to Debenhams was last Sunday, then, on Monday, Lexi started work experience at mine. Something I'm not sure was a good idea either.

Marta stirs her coffee and sighs, dramatically.

'I won't be here this afternoon as I'm at the consultant's again.'

It's never just common or garden doctor with Marta, always the consultant.

I'm not really listening. I'm too busy watching Lexi from in between the blinds of our office kitchen where, ten minutes ago, I got cornered by Marta. Marta's been suffering from a mystery 'personal' illness for three months now, and since nobody bothers to actually ask, she has no option but to hint.

'They'll be scanning me at the hospital,' she adds, hopefully.

'Great,' I say, opening the blinds a little wider.

Since Lexi started at SCD, I've had to watch her like a hawk in case she does something inappropriate (which is often). Whenever she picks up my phone, my heart's in my mouth. Why I included answering it as one of the key requirements of her job description, I'll never know. I meant *answer* the phone. Not have a half-hour conversation with whoever's on the other line.

'What's that, Marta?'

'I said, they'll be scanning me at the hospital. So depending on the results, I might not be quite myself tomorrow.'

Lexi's over at Shona's desk, chatting now. Then I see the red light of my phone start flashing and Lexi move towards it, as if in slow motion and it's only as she does that I realize: 'Shit. That'll be Schumacher.'

Marta sighs, very audibly this time.

'I'll soldier on in though, don't worry, even if the news is bad.'

'Good. I mean not good.' You really have to concentrate when talking to Marta, otherwise you drift off and end up saying something completely inappropriate. 'You really don't have to, Marta. Look, can we talk about this tomorrow? It's just . . . LEXI!' I'm banging on the kitchen window now, trying to get her attention before it's too late. 'Lexi, leave that, will you? Just leave . . .' *Oh bollocks.* Then I'm legging it towards my desk, just as I hear Marta say:

'The consultant says I'm probably polycystic.'

Lexi's reached my desk now.

'I'll get that, Lexi! I'll get that, just . . .'

Too late.

'Oh, *hi*, Darryl.'

It *is* Schumacher. Shit.

'Yeah, I'm still here.' She rolls her eyes. 'No, they haven't found out about the criminal record yet.'

Oh God.

'Sorry, what's that?' She's sticking her fingers down her throat now and Shona's shaking her head, Shona having taken Lexi on as her protégé in her silent war against Schumacher. 'Has anybody asked me out yet? Urgh. Letchy or what. I don't think . . .'

'Thank you!' I yank the phone from Lexi.

'Hello, Darryl. Terribly sorry about that. Now, how can I help?'

I'm fast learning that the biggest problem with taking on a seventeen-year-old intern is that 'Professionalism' is not a concept they get. In the past week alone my sister has asked Janine if she was dyslexic (she is). (Most of us don't dare to ask Janine the time, never mind if she suffers from a learning disability in full earshot of the office.) Then she went out to get Janine lunch before announcing Janine owed her ninety-five pence. Janine hasn't bought her own lunch since about 1989 and has no idea how much things cost. Every other intern has just kept quiet. Not Lexi, no. Not my little sister.

After day two, we had a little chat about office politics; about how one doesn't talk to Janine unless spoken to, let alone enquire about her health.

'And I'm sorry, but as irritating as he is, Schumacher's a vital client,' I said. 'If I fuck up this Minty Me thing, the company loses out, never mind me and my chance of winning Sales Person of the Year, which is important to me, Lex, you know?' I reasoned with her. 'So, no matter what you think of him, unfortunately, you have to be polite at all times.'

'But he's a *disgusting*, sexist sleazebag,' she said, genuinely baffled by my desire to engage with him on any level.

'I know, but this is business.'

So it's been a stressful week for many reasons. The longer this Toby thing goes on, the harder I'm finding it to hide my feelings in the office. Since the glorious night at Malmaison, I feel like barriers have been broken and we don't know where the lines are any more; like we're in danger of slipping up at any given moment.

In some ways this is thrilling because I feel like I'm having an actual relationship; like the looks he gives me are more loaded. Then again, the last thing I want is this to come out at work. If we're meant to be together, then I want it to happen the proper way. I want him to leave his wife and us to be able to have a normal relationship that we don't have to conceal as a book club. In this way, then, the slipping up thing at work is a real issue. Especially now with Lexi around and her sixth sense for such things.

The other morning, when Toby said something funny at the photocopying machine, I caught myself touching his face.

Lexi was sitting opposite and started laughing.

'What are you doing?' she said.

'What?' I said, innocently.

'You just stroked his face!'

'No, I did not.'

'You did!'

'I didn't.'

This was becoming like a pantomime. Then Toby saved the day.

'Come on now, Steeley you did, don't be ashamed. Although we were discussing my outbreak of eczema, so, not exactly romantic.'

I could see Lexi looking for any evidence of a skin disease on Toby's flawless face. I stared straight ahead.

Then this afternoon, after the Schumacher telephone debacle, Toby and I are looking at some figures on the white-board when Lexi comes out with:

'So you know this book club thing. What's it all about? Does everyone in the office come?

I nearly gag on my tea.

'Um.' I look, alarmed, over at Toby for support 'Well it depends . . .'

'On what?'

'On what week it is,' I say, feebly, grasping at straws.

Toby leans against the whiteboard and sucks air between his teeth.

'Oooh, I wouldn't mention the book club in this office, Lex. Political hot potato. Messing with fire,' he says, taking his lighter out of his pocket and lighting it for added punch.

Lexi wrinkles her nose.

'What you on about, weirdo?' Since she started at SCD, Lexi's started a little sister/big brother over-familiarity thing with Toby, which I'm not that keen on, but then I guess it's better than the outright flirting I saw in my kitchen.

Toby folds his arms and leans in towards Lexi, whispering in her ear.

'Let's just say, it's caused rifts in the past.'

'Yes,' I add. '*Enormous* rifts. Rifts like, God, like . . .'

'Rift Valley,' says Toby, seriously, and I have to try hard not to laugh.

'Why would a book club cause rifts?' asks Lexi. Toby and I are both twitching on the words 'book club', aware that Shona's walking over here now and, as far as Shona's concerned, the dissolution of the book club happened months ago.

'Oh, you'd be surprised,' says Toby. 'Literature can bond and break people.'

154

'So, was there a massive fight? Was it like book club warfare?' Lexi asks, suddenly excited.

'Ssh!' Toby interjects, loudly, putting his finger to his lips. I almost want to laugh now. I've never seen Toby like this. 'Like I say, it's wise to just, you know . . .'

He taps the side of his nose.

'No,' says Lexi.

'Just don't discuss the BC thing, okay, Lex? People get very funny about it in this office.'

As soon as Shona is back at her desk and chatting with Lexi, I email Toby in a panic.

To: toby.delaney@scd.co.uk
Subject: And the Oscar goes to . . .
You were sensational, De Niro, but seriously, what are we going to do? Got away with it last time but what about next? She's going to start asking to meet this Angela from Barnet and I won't be able to lie.

From: toby.delaney@scd.co.uk
Method acting, darling, that's my advice. I was pretty awesome, wasn't I?! But yes, your sister is a fucking liability. What to do? No idea. But in the meantime, meet me in the meeting room to discuss it. I simply cannot live another second without touching your tits in that top.

'So what are we going to do, Steeley?'

We're in the meeting room now, standing against the wall, Toby tenderly tidying a strand of hair behind my ear.

'Call it off?'

'No way!'

'Oh, well if you say so.'

'I do. I couldn't do without my fortnightly fix of these

little puppies for a start.' He puts his hands on my boobs and I feel a shiver of arousal, as well as one of slight disappointment. Didn't he want more than a fortnightly fix? In an ideal world?

'And every fortnight does seem a long time to wait, don't you think?' I say, hopefully.

'God yeah.' He puts his hands around my waist and pulls me close. 'I missed you this weekend.'

'Really?'

Missed me? He's never said that before.

'Rachel was working all weekend as usual, so I just sort of hung around like a spare part. But listen, I've got something serious to talk to you about on the Rachel front.'

'Oh yeah?' I say excited. (Oh my God, could this be it?)

'She wants to meet you.'

'Oh! No way. No *way*!' I say. 'Are you mad?'

'She wants to ask you over for dinner,' he says and winces.

'Well, I won't go.'

'But she won't let it lie.' He kisses me, as if that will butter me up. 'She keeps saying, "When am I going to meet Caroline? When are you going to invite her round for dinner?" I keep putting her off, but she'll start getting suspicious if I do it much longer.'

He pulls me closer, starts nuzzling my neck.

'Toby.' I giggle, pulling away. 'What are you doing? You can't snog me here. You can't get round me like that.'

'Who says?' he kisses me again.

'*I* say.'

'Cut loose a bit, Steele, don't be uptight . . .'

'But what if someone walks in?'

'God, I so fancy you,' he says, plunging towards me for another kiss. I give in. I've totally succumbed. Toby's got his hands in my hair and we're just going for it now, up against the wall of the meeting room. I can hear the blood rushing in my ears and the sound of our breathing, quickened, faster. Then . . . disaster. Massive, huge, humongous disaster. I hear the handle go and time seems to slow down. I can see the handle turning. I make a last ditch, frantic plea for Toby to stop by nipping his buttock and trying to speak but he's suckered to my lips so it just sounds like I've been gagged and I think he thinks I'm just being kinky. Then it's all over. Shona walks in, a look of absolute horror on her face.

'OhmigodFUCK!' She covers her eyes.

'Fuck!' Toby springs apart from me, wiping his lips and leaving the top two buttons of my blouse undone.

'Bra,' I say, eyes squeezed shut, not sure what that's going to achieve.

'Jesus, you two,' says Shona and slams the door shut.

Shona eyes me seriously from over her coffee cup, her brown eyes full of concern.

'Mate, I'm just shocked, I'm just worried. It's not that I think you're a bad person or anything,' she says, in a stage whisper.

The SCD canteen is a hive of gossip. God knows how many torrid office affairs must have been played out across these flimsy, wipe-clean tables, how many conversations with confidantes, just like this one. I feel like a cheap cliché.

'Don't lie to me. You don't have to lie to me, Shone. I *am* awful – and it's so unlike me.'

Shona nods her head.

'*So* unlike you,' she says. 'Of all the people, all the friends . . .'

'I am the woman least likely to have an affair with a married man?'

'Yes! Don't take this the wrong way, but you're not exactly the most fly-by-the-seat-of-your-pants person in the world, the most reckless person I know.'

157

I smile, feebly.

'So come on, what brought it on?' she says.

'I don't know. It just happened one night when nobody else turned up to the book club and before I knew it, the book club had become . . .'

'A fuck club?'

'Yes. I guess so. A fuck club.'

She's looking at me as if there's more. She *knows* there's more.

'I guess after Martin and that whole hideous experience and feeling like I'd broken this man's heart and ruined his life . . .'

'Gosh, you really flatter yourself, don't you?' She laughs. 'Just waiting for the suicide call, were you? The Martin Squire found hanged in his wardrobe?'

'No!' I roll my eyes. 'It wasn't *like* that. It's just after Martin and then Garf – remember sweet Garf? Well, I decided I couldn't do this any more, I just couldn't. I couldn't get involved with anyone because hearts always got messed up . . .'

'Which is generally what happens in relationships,' says Shona.

'Maybe.' I sigh. 'But I didn't want it, couldn't deal with all the upset.'

'But that's the fun bit,' she says, taking my hand in hers. 'That's what makes you feel alive and like there's a point to it all.'

'I know but . . .' I can see that Shona doesn't really get where I'm coming from. 'I felt wretched about Martin, never wanted to do that to anyone ever again. I guess I thought a bit of harmless sex with a married man would be perfect, in a way, at least I couldn't get involved.'

'Mmm.' Shona folds her arms 'But things aren't that cut and dry, though, are they?' she says.

'Look, it's all under control. I'm not in love with him or anything.'

'So it's just a sex thing?'

'Oh *yeah*.'

Liar, Liar, Liar . . .

'Well, that makes me feel a bit better.'

'Look, Toby's not very happy at the moment,' I carry on. 'Rachel works day and night. He feels lonely and neglected, plus you know . . .' (I know by the way Shona's frowning at me that this isn't going to wash but I'm going with it anyway.) 'Rachel's with HunterHewitt now, and she's selling Ice-Maiden breath freshener and . . .'

'No!' says Shona, strictly

'Oh.'

'You can't justify sleeping with a married man by the fact that their wife works for a competitor, sells a competitor's product and therefore in someway deserves it.'

'Oh,' I say again. (Damn it. Why was Shona so bloody mature and reasonable sometimes?) 'Look it's all going to end soon, anyway,' I say, squirming, thinking I just want to get out of here now. 'It'll run its course and that will be that.'

'Good,' says Shona

'It will be,' I say. 'But will you do me a favour?'

'Go on.'

'Don't tell anybody about this please? Especially Lexi, okay?'

CHAPTER SIXTEEN

I'm staring out of the kitchen window, idly going through the To Do list. I usually carry a copy in my handbag, adding to it when things come to me, but lately, what with everything going on, I've let it slide. Maybe Wayne was right. Maybe lists *are* just a distraction from what's really important. And what's really important, right now, is Toby and I.

Outside, the sky is that fierce blue you only get in high-summer, the grass parched, the scent of my yellow roses filtering in through the open window.

What a difference a year makes. It's 10 July today. Martin's birthday. On this day last year, a soggy July day to match the other thirty-one soggy days of July where the only sound inside the house was the drip, drip of relentless rain, I decided to call off the wedding. I decided I had to leave him. It took me another two months to finally get round to it, but I remember that day so clearly, the feeling of not being able to breathe.

It's funny how you remember the smallest details about such momentous times in your life, as if your conscience is trying to block out the worst of it. I'd booked for us to go to the Ritz for afternoon tea. We sat on the Number 19 bus in the rain, Martin with his hand on my knee, tapping in time with his singing: 'We're going to the Ritz. So put on some glitz.'

I remember the way the rain ran in rivers down the window, the screech of the windscreen wipers like nails running down glass. I thought I'd hate July for ever because of that day, having to endure a birthday tea with Martin – something that should have been fun – knowing the dreadful thing I was going to have to do to this man that I loved, but just wasn't in love with.

And now, look. A year on. And I am in love with someone else and summer feels full of possibility.

A bird lands on the windowsill, breaking my reverie. I get back to the list, asterisking items.

* Buy new skirt for Brighton
* Join actual book club
* Give T until end of August to leave the wife, otherwise, move on! (you total loser, mug, fuckwit)

I hover over the last one with my pen, before scribbling it out so absolutely that the pen mark is raised from the paper like scar tissue. I can't commit it to paper like that, it's way too risky.

Going to Brighton to a hotel together was entirely Toby's idea. Absolutely no hinting or nagging from me. After the awful day where Shona caught us kissing in the meeting room, we went for a de-brief after work.

'We should stop this,' I said. 'Now. Before it gets out of hand.'

'But I don't want to stop this,' said Toby. 'It's *already* out of hand.'

He actually looked serious – very disconcerting. There was no cheekiness, or sarcasm, or flirtatiousness, just sincerity.

I tried to appear calm, whilst inside a fanfare was going off, fireworks were erupting, an entire brass band had taken up residence. For crying out loud, was he saying he loved me? Was that what 'out of hand' meant?

I was staring at him, grinning inanely.

'I want to take you away. I want to treat you, Steeley, really spoil you. For us to have some time together.'

'Okay.' I beamed. 'When?'

So much for 'stopping this before it gets out of hand'.

It's a bloody good job I scrubbed out the bit about Toby leaving his wife on my To Do list because later that day, when I'm hoovering the lounge, Lexi shouts from the kitchen.

'Hey, Caroline, what's this? I thought you were already *in* a book club?'

My heart stops. The list. I fucking left out the list!

'What's that, Lex?' I shout, the blood draining from my face.

'I said, I thought you were already in a book club. This To Do list up here says, "must join book club".'

'It's old, that list!' I shout back, frantically searching the corners of my mind for an explanation.

'So, why you've only just stuck it up on the fridge?'

Luckily then, the phone goes.

'Hi. Caro my love, it's Martin.'

I feel irritated. Then I feel guilty for feeling irritated. Is it the fact he just called me 'my love' like he's my dad? Or that I secretly wished it was Toby on the phone. Either way, it's not a pleasant feeling.

'How are you? Happy Birthday!' I say.

'Yeah, thanks,' he says. 'Another birfday, another year older!' 'Birfday' was always a Martin-ism, along with 'mind stew' for 'mind you' and 'ickle' for little. 'Look, I'm not doing much this morning and so I thought I'd come and fix your drippy tap?' he says, cheerfully.

162

'Drippy tap?'

'Yes. You said you had a drippy tap.

'Oh. Did I?'

I vaguely remember some drunken conversation last week at the Duke about the To Do list that keeps growing, needing a man in the house. God, I can't believe I said that.

It's been ten months since Martin moved out of this house (the house that I bought because Martin didn't earn enough in his job at the Electricity Board when we first moved down to London and he paid me rent for, but which was to be our marital home all the same) and he still loves to do odd jobs for me. He'll still come over with his Woolworths toolkit to fix a fuse here, put up some blinds here. I'm very grateful of course, justifying it in my head with the fact that he enjoys it. Spending half an hour fixing a drippy tap, to Martin, is like half an hour having a relaxing cappuccino to most people. But this time I feel uncomfortable him doing things for me, and not just because it's his birthday and why on earth does he want to fix a tap on his birthday? I have a deep, queasy feeling in my stomach, like I'm doing something wrong by accepting.

'Oh no, Martin, it's okay,' I say. 'It's your birfday! Surely you're doing something far more exciting. Aren't you meeting friends for lunch or anything?'

His silence tells me no, and anyway, if he were, I'd know about it as I'd be invited. Then he says:

'Look, I'm in the area, so it's no skin off my nose. Only take me a jiffy.'

'Jiffy?' I think. Who says 'jiffy'?

But I need my drippy tap mending, he likes mending drippy taps, so I say:

'Um, well, if you don't mind.'

'No. Course I don't mind.'

Fifteen minutes later he turns up with his toolkit, wearing

the Gap jacket and his Paul Smith T-shirt with the monkey on the front. Not that I can talk in my enormous fluffy bear slippers and dressing gown. This is what's great about mine and Martin's relationship; there's no shame in large bear slippers and a dressing gown at 11 a.m. on a Saturday morning.

Martin is holding a pint of milk (why he doesn't just let me provide the milk, I don't know) and gives me a kiss on the cheek.

'Ah. I see you've got your cute slippers on again?' he says, hands on hips. 'Now, which is bear left and which is bear right?'

I laugh, admittedly slightly less enthusiastically than the last five hundred times Martin's delivered this joke.

There's an awkward few moments, like there always is whenever Martin comes over where we stand, in what was once our hallway where his trainers sat on the shoe rack and his coat up on the peg, and hover around each other not quite knowing what to say.

This time it seems even more loaded, though, and Martin's smiling at me like I'm supposed to be saying or doing something. It occurs to me, did I say too much at the Duke the other week? Get drunk and over-sentimental? You're a bugger for that, Caroline, I think to myself. You really must rein yourself in. Saying all that stuff about how I still wonder if it could have worked, when I know it couldn't have worked, I was just pissed and getting nostalgic. Still, Martin knows me. He knows what I'm like after a few drinks. He comes to expect the whole 'oh it's such a shame we didn't work out talk!' so I'm probably just being paranoid.

Martin wanders through to the lounge where Lexi is sitting, munching on a slice of toast. I watch as her eyes follow him. Not him again, you can see her thinking.

'Hi, Lexi. Not seeing two of me this time?' says Martin.

164

Lexi gives him her best surly look. 'Never was, Martin, never was.'

'Hormones?' says Martin, as we go into the kitchen.

'Probably PMT,' I say, feeling awful. I'd forgotten, *again*! I'd forgotten to tell her.

Martin's been lying on his side under my kitchen sink now for three quarters of an hour, and you can see about an inch of builder's bum.

Lexi wanders in and puts her toast plate on the side.

'Nice bumcrack,' she says.

'Ta very much,' says Martin. 'I like to think I'm pretty buff myself.' I cringe. Don't try to be all down-with-the-kids, Martin, you really don't have to. 'Anyway,' he says, clattering around with some sort of tool or other. 'I've got a bone to pick with you, Lexi.'

Lexi arches her eyebrow at me. I shrug as if to say, nothing to do with me.

'What's this about you liking a bad boy?'

'Dunno,' says Lexi. 'What is this about me liking a bad boy?'

'Your sister says you've been on the blower to Clark Elder.'

Lexi shoots me a look. 'No, I haven't been on the phone to Clark Elder,' she says, defensively. 'That's the point. I don't want to talk to him.'

'Well, good, that's good then,' says Martin. 'Because you should steer well clear of him. He's bad news, is Elder, very bad news.'

'Why've you got such an opinion on the matter?' she says, sulkily.

'Coz I know him. I'm of his era, remember? He's about thirty-five like me, isn't he?'

'Thirty-five? You didn't tell me he was thirty-five, Lexi!'

She bites her lip sheepishly.

'He's not, he's thirty-two.'

Martin continues, 'Well, anyway, he lived around where I lived, when you were only a whippersnapper.'

Lexi shifts from foot to foot.

'So, what's he done that's so bad?' You can tell she's quite interested now, or was that scared?

'Oh just stuff that's not good, I mean *really* not good, so just steer clear of him. That's all I'm saying.'

Lexi looks at me, blinks as if this is all news to her.

'Yeah, well, he's changed now,' she says. 'He works for my dad on the Healing Horizons courses doing motivational speaking, so he must be okay. Dad vets all the speakers. He's always banging on about achievements and personal goals and people with drive.'

I say, 'You're not speaking to him, so this is all irrelevant, anyway, right?'

She nods.

'Good, just checking.'

Martin seems to hang around for ages, fixing this and that, having endless cups of tea. He picks up a photo. It's of me, sitting outside the Duke of Cambridge about eight years ago.

'Ah, I remember that day,' he says. 'That's the day you got the job at SCD and I ordered champagne at the Duke.'

'Mmm,' I say, 'so it is.'

He carries on, looks through my CD rack. 'Do you still listen to this?' he asks, picking out David Gray's *White Ladder* album and I cringe, slightly. 'Fond memories I have of that, summer evenings in the garden, too much rioja, eh, Caro?'

I'm starting to feel a bit uncomfortable. He smiles at me – that same smile he had in the Duke. The one I'm not sure I like.

'So,' I say, brightly. 'Seen Polly again lately? Fixed up a date?'

'Why?' he asks, a teasing, rising inflection in his tone.

'Just because.' I shrug. 'Because she looked nice.'

'Right,' he says, with a blank expression. 'No, I haven't set up a date with her, I've been really busy.'

There's a slightly awkward silence then he touches my arm and peers at me, smiling.

'Was that the right answer?'

'Martin, there is no right answer.'

He finally leaves and I wander back into the kitchen where Lexi is defacing my kitchen walls by making a smoothie with my hand blender.

'He so still loves you,' she says, over the noise.

'He so does not!'

'He so does. Any idiot can see that. Why else would be give up his Saturday to come and sit under your sink?'

Deep down, I know she's right. I just don't want to accept it. I'll tell her now, I think, I'll tell her when she's finished the smoothie.

CHAPTER SEVENTEEN

I guess I'd forgotten about the proposed dinner party of horror, or maybe I'd just erased it from my mind. Then, on Tuesday, there it is, sitting in my inbox.

From: rachel.delaney@hunterhewitt.com
Subject: *Newsflash* Husband cooks!!!
(And she's quite funny too. I hate her already.)
Hi all
I'm sure you won't be surprised to learn that despite me bending his ear for the past six months, Toby seems intent on never sending this email so I'm doing it myself! Him and I would love to have you round for a summer barbie on Saturday. Very chilled out. Just bring a bottle and your lovely selves. Haven't met some of you before but in a rare event, Toby's cooking so I'll be the one reclining on the sun lounger, beer in hand!
Hope you can all make it.
Rach x

I slump back in my chair and read the email over and over again, combing it for clues about her, their relationship. In just one paragraph, I manage to outline three major personality flaws, which is quite a lot for one person, never mind one email.

1. *I'm sure you won't be surprised to learn that despite me bending his ear for the past six months, Toby seems intent on never sending this email so I'm doing it myself!* Patronising and not very empathetic. Maybe he doesn't want to have a bloody barbecue and invite me. That's why he hasn't sent the email.

2. *Him and I would love to have you round for a summer barbie on Saturday. Very chilled out. Just bring a bottle and your lovely selves.* Bossy (have heard about this) and tight.

3. *Haven't met some of you before but in a rare event, Toby's cooking so I'll be the one reclining on the sun lounger, beer in hand!* Lazy. And making a joke at someone else's expense.

Oh God, who was I kidding? She sounded nice. Lovely, in fact, and she was inviting me to her house. Could this get any worse? Well, yes, it could, actually. It could if I actually went, which I'm not going to. That would be insane.

To: toby.delaney@scd.co.uk
Subject: WTF???!!!
I can't go. I'm sorry, I just can't. I will saw off my arm before I ever face your wife. God, what are we doing??!!
PS She sounds really nice. Why didn't you tell me she was really nice?!

I watch him as he receives it, flops back in his chair and looks at me as if to say 'get a grip, woman'. I could have predicted everything.

From: toby.delaney@scd.co.uk
Subject: Get a grip woman

Steeley, now calm down. It's only a barbecue not tea with the Queen. Shona and Paul are coming too so it won't be just me, you and Rach.

Please come you gorgeous, gorgeous creature. For me? PLEASE. She'll start to get suspicious if I keep refusing. We don't want that. That'll mean the end of the book club and there's still so much ground to cover. (In terms of reading material, obviously.)

PS She is nice. Just not that often to me.

PPS God, you look sexy with your hair up like that.

Rach. I didn't like 'Rach'. What man who was falling out of love with his wife, still used abbreviated names? And I was getting a little tired of the book club, too. Hadn't we moved on from there? The tedious book club/fuck club joke? Once you've slept (spent the night with) someone, taken a bath with them, watched TV in bed together and he's plucked a stray hair from your cleavage, doesn't that promote you to something more than stupid email flirting and in-jokes?

And since when was it good that Shona and Paul were going? That's still two couples and me. Not in a couple. As if I didn't feel bad enough, now I would be lying not just in front of Rachel, but Shona. The friend to whom, only days ago, I promised I'd call this whole thing off.

Sort of wishing I had now. At least then I wouldn't have to endure the Barbecue of Horror.

Just as I am thinking this very thought, Shona emails me.

From: shona.perry@scd.co.uk
Subject: WTF?!

Oh My God, 'tis the email of horror and doom. Not that it's any of my business in the grand scheme of things, but have you dumped him yet? You KNOW it'll end in tears. Either way, I think you have to go. Not to go would look way too dodgy.

From: caroline.steele@scd.co.uk
To: shona.perry@scd.co.uk
I'm not going.

I decide to just call Toby. Some things one has to discuss.

'You know I'm not going, don't you?' I whisper, eyeing him over the screen

Toby fixes me with his eyes. Shit, he was gorgeous. Why was he so gorgeous? All this would be so much easier if he looked like Bernie Ecclestone.

'Oh, you're talking to me, then?' he says. 'You've been ignoring me all day.'

'Lexi said she thought I was obsessed with you.'

He laughs, irritatingly. 'Well you're only human'

'Shut up Toby, this is serious. I'm not coming. It'll be hideous and . . .'

I'll burst into hysterical tears the minute I see you with your wife.

'I'm doing something on Saturday, anyway,' I say, thinking backtrack, backtrack. If he thinks I'm that obsessed, he's wrong.

'What?'

'Staying in and watching chick-flicks with Lexi.'

'Liar.'

'Bully.'

'Just bring her, too. Rach won't mind.'

There he goes with the Rach thing again. I'm gonna punch him if he says that again.

'Do I have to come?'

'No. But she'll only ask again and start getting suspicious.'

171

'God, is she always this pushy?' It just pops out. I've always prided myself on never saying anything negative about Rachel. I do not want to become the embittered mistress; it's bad enough being the mistress at all.

'What am I supposed to do? She harasses me night and day and I'm counting on you. Please?'

I pass on the tube that evening and walk into Oxford Street, wander around Waterstones and gather my thoughts. This was getting a bit too tricky for my liking. I was beginning to feel that horrid feeling again, like nothing was in control. Up until now, Rachel has been a mythical figure, a presence in the shadows that if I tried hard enough, I could pretend didn't exist. I could pretend what I was doing was almost okay, too. This *used* to be a book club, right? It morphed into something slightly different, but that's not what it set out to be, that wasn't my intention.

I hover around the 3 for 2 counter with its summer block-busters, the wedding rom-coms, the Barbara Taylor Bradfords and the Costa award winners. I used to love coming here after work, sometimes as late as 9 p.m. if I'd been working late, and browse for possible book club reads; search for those I'd read about in the *Observer* books section, the ones advertised on the tube, or recommended by friends. I'd pick out books at random too, doing my 'first page' test to see if it grabbed me, pulled me into its world.

Sometimes, Toby and I would take a little trip to Waterstones at lunchtime to buy the book club book together. After the book club turned into a fuck club, we'd then trail the aisles, giggling at all the possible 'ironic' book club reads: *Notes on a Scandal*; *The End of the Affair*. I used to love those lunch-hours. They were illicit liaisons all on their own where just the two of us could be together, without anyone being suspicious as we huddled in the aisles − the hushed tones, the in-jokes, the intimacy that comes of sharing ideas and a private joke.

Now, however, the book club joke doesn't seem that funny any more. I don't even come here now that the space that used to be taken up by books has been taken up by Toby. And Toby never even buys the supposed book club book any more. Could it be that he wants to get found out?

I don't feel like rushing home, so I walk down Carnaby Street, via Liberty, where I buy the poshest bottled fake tan I can find, through Golden Square and down Piccadilly to Green Park. It's one of those London summer early evenings where the hot air has built up so that the entire city is swathed in a tobacco-coloured fug that sits above the skyline.

I take the Number 19 home, deciding Toby may have a point. The only way I am possibly going to get through this Barbecue of Horror, is if Lexi comes with me. At least then she can wow them with her youthful charm and I can just melt into the background, only opening my eyes when the whole sorry event is over.

That evening over dinner, however, Lexi's reaction isn't exactly what I was hoping for.

'Go to a *barbecue*? Eeugh!' she said like I'd just suggested she join me at a Tantric sex workshop or a BNP march. (Lexi's grown in confidence since she started at SCD and acquired an air of cheek). 'When?'

'Saturday. Why? What's the big deal about a Saturday barbecue?'

'It's a bit *thirty-something*, isn't it?' she said, poking around at the food on her plate. In an attempt to be a proper big sister who sets an example of wholesome living, I had finally got round to making something out of quinoa. It was egg-fried quinoa, a variation on egg-fried rice, just, it turned out, a lot less nice.

I laughed.

'What's so wrong about thirty-somethings? If your taste in men is anything to go by – Tristan Wanks, Wayne, Clark – you actually prefer them to your own age group.'

Lexi sighed.

'How many times do I have to tell you? I don't fancy Wayne!'

'So, what's the problem?'

'I dunno. What do you talk about at these sophisticated affairs?'

'Christ, it's a barbecue, Lexi, not tea with the Queen,' I say, stealing Toby's line. 'What do you *think* we talk about?'

She thinks about this very seriously.

'The Recession,' she says, her brown eyes all innocent. I try not to laugh. 'Politics. House prices. You lot are obsessed with mortgages.'

I couldn't help it, I snorted with laughter.

'What do you take us for?' I said, thinking back to a particular 'relaxed afternoon barbecue' at Shona and Paul's where Shona got so drunk she fell sideways into a bush.

'Where is this barbecue, anyway?' she asked, changing the subject.

A bit of quinoa seems to get lodged in my throat.

'Toby's.'

'*Toby's!* As in Toby Delaney, your 'colleague'?' she asks, doing a sarcastic in parentheses with her fingers. 'The man you're obsessed with.'

I feel myself go red.

'Lexi, shut up! I am *not* obsessed with Toby Delaney.'

'You touched his face. And you email him all the time at work. I know, because I can see you watching to see when he gets them.

I fight the rush of blood that threatens to take over my face. I'm sure this was supposed to be the other way round.

'Lexi, give it up, the man is married for a start. Look, will you come? I just want some company that's all and it'll be all coupley with Shona and Paul and Toby and . . .' For a horrid second I forget her name.

'Rachel,' prompts Lexi.

'Yes, Rachel. So will you come? Pretty please? Please please please?'

Lexi narrows her eyes at me.

'Only on one condition,' she says.

'What's that?'

'That I don't have to finish this quinoa. I'm sorry, it's just—'

'Foul?' We both start laughing.

CHAPTER EIGHTEEN

I'm lying in bed hoping death comes quickly. It is morning, just after 7 a.m. (when I last threw up) and the room is dark, just a strobe of light from the gap in my curtains, but even that seems to burn through my head, cauterizing the main artery in my brain, which probably still oozes Sauvignon Blanc.

The barbecue was horrendous. Never mind the Barbecue of Horror, this was more the entire box-set of *Nightmare on Elm Street*, only live.

I reach for the glass of water on my bedside table. My throat feels like I'm trying to swallow a hedgehog – but I can't sit up far yet without the room spinning, so end up throwing half of it up my nose, nearly drowning in the process.

Sleep it off, that's what I need to do, although all I see when I close my eyes, is me (ridiculously drunk) going:

'*Fever Pitch*. Yes. That's what we're reading, it's an iconic novel of our times.'

Idiot.

Then Rachel, (ridiculously sober) going: 'It's not a novel, it's a memoir.'

It's not novel it's a memoir. It's not a novel it's a memoir. It's not a novel . . . You get the picture. That's basically on repeat play until I can't take it any more and have to self-medicate some more with ibuprofen in the hope of oblivion.

In my defence, *Fever Pitch*-gate only happened because the book club conversation happened in the first place, and the book club conversation only happened because, despite everything Toby had told her, Lexi brought it up.

We were just finishing off the monkfish kebabs (this was no standard bbq, not a burger in sight) and I was already almost a bottle of wine and several vodkas down due to nerves and a whole catalogue of previous, equally excruciating *faux pas*.

Rachel finally sat down after hours of hosting, since Toby's idea of 'doing the bbq' as far as I could tell, amounted to chucking meat on there then forgetting about it whilst he got more drunk.

'Can I just say, Toby,' said Lexi — scanning the bookshelf that lined one wall of the kitchen, which looked out through French doors onto the garden — 'considering you go to a book club and are meant to be some sort of bookworm, you haven't got many books, have you?'

It was a typical flying brick comment from Lexi and one that had me down a glass of white in one.

Toby took a swig of beer, Rachel laughed. 'Toby? A bookworm?' she said. 'I think the only thing he'd ever read before he started that book club was Allen Carr's *How to Stop Smoking* and even then he borrowed it from some mate and had to buy another because he'd got a fag burn in the cover. Isn't that right, hun?' she teased. 'That's why I couldn't believe that he was so into this book club malarkey.'

I look over at Toby. This was news to me. He'd always made out he was quite the bookworm to me — or did he just want to worm his way into my knickers?

'You have no idea what books I read in my spare time,' he said, folding his arms indignantly

'What spare time?' laughed Rachel. 'You work, then you

177

come home and play Tomb Raider on the Playstation.' Rachel licked her fingers seductively like Nigella Lawson and swung her tanned limbs over the bench to sit down. 'Anyway, thanks, Lexi, that's reminded me, I haven't even asked you: How *is* the book club doing these days?'

Toby actually laughed – nerves most probably. I wanted to stab him with my kebab prong.

'It's cool,' shrugged Toby, sounding anything but cool.

'It's a good club,' I slurred, at the height of my communicative powers.

'Shona, do you enjoy it?' said Rachel, turning to Shona.

'It's . . . yeah, it's fun,' agreed Shona, face like she'd just had something stuck up her bottom.

'How do you know?' suddenly piped up her boyfriend, Paul. 'You don't even go any more.'

So much for Shona's idea that Paul was always so stoned he never noticed when she went out. Lexi had gone quiet now. This was going from bad to worse.

'I do!' Shona protested

'No, you don't,' Paul said.

'I've just missed a few weeks, that's all.'

Shona shot me a dagger and I closed my eyes. For a God-awful moment, the room fell silent.

Rachel took a long sip from her homemade lemonade. She was on a 'health kick'. Course she was. No shameful daytime binge-drinking for her.

'So, who *does* go?' she said, cheerily, as I gulped down another glass of plonk.

'Me,' said me.

'And me,' said Toby

Lexi wrinkled her nose at me. 'That's not much of a club. You told me . . .'

A glare that could have frozen water stopped her short on that one. God, would she just let the book club thing lie?

I wanted to leave but I couldn't, so I took the mature, executive decision just to drink some more.

'So . . .' You could almost see right inside Rachel's smooth forehead and watch the cogs whirring as she served out more salad. 'It's just the two of you, then? Just you and Caroline?'

'Um, yes.' Toby nodded sagely.

'Yeah,' I mumbled lamely. 'I guess it is.'

'And what are you reading?' asked Paul, as the cube of monkfish I'd just swallowed almost came back up. He was doing well, having provided the two conversation clangers in as many minutes.

'Do you know, that's a good question.' Rachel was still trying to retain her air of breeziness. 'When Tobes first started at the book club, he went on about it all the time. Now I don't think he even buys the book, do you, Tobes? I think his commitment is wavering,' she said, giving his arm a playful nudge.

Toby didn't even flinch.

'I read it at work, *actually*, Rach.'

'Read what?' said Rachel. 'Come on, what's the book?'

This is where it all went wrong. Horribly, desperately, tragically wrong. Nobody said anything. After her brief foray into alibi territory, I could tell Shona was hating every second and I can't say I blamed her. Time stood still. The room span. I practically inhaled the wine from my glass. STILL nobody said anything. Then I spotted the bookshelf. My saviour in pine. I scanned it. My eyes flickering desperately for something I recognized. Anything, anything at all. Everything went into a blur.

'*Fever Pitch*!' I said.

'*Fever Pitch*?' Paul laughed. 'But that's a book about football, about Arsenal.'

'Actually, I love Arsenal,' I said. I've no idea why.

Everyone's eyes fixed on me; Lexi had gone very quiet.

'Look, I know people think it's just a book about football,' I slurred on, 'but actually it's an iconic novel of our time.'

That's when Rachel pointed out it was a memoir. That's when I wanted to die. That's why I then reached a whole new level of drunkenness and why I am now merely slipping in and out of consciousness.

Perhaps it wouldn't have been so bad if that had been the only conversational disaster at the Barbecue on Elm Street, but oh no. It was not.

I slide my Virgin in-flight mask up my forehead and open one eye to look at the time: 9.08 a.m. now. More than two hours since I last threw up. Hopefully, that's the end of that at least. Maybe in another hour, I'll be able to sit up without tasting bile.

I go through the catalogue of other events in my head. A sort of sadomasochistic torture session.

1. The most ill-advised aperitif of all time.

I would say it all went wrong the moment Rachel got out the Sangria but it started way before then – back when I dragged Lexi into the Sun in Clapham Old Town for a pre-dinner 'loosener'.

'Are you all right?' she said, frowning, sipping on her Coke whilst I downed a vodka, then ordered another.

'Yes, fine, why?'

'You just seem weird, that's all.'

'Weird?'

'Nervous,' she said.

'Nervous?' I laughed. Ha ha ha! 'No, I'm not nervous. It's just you can't turn up to a barbecue sober, Lex, everyone knows that.'

So, that'd be why, when Rachel answered the door ten minutes later, stone-cold sober, and offered us a drink, Lexi piped up:

'Don't worry about her, she's already half-cut. She's had two vodkas on the way here.'

2. The misleading double-chin photo.

As soon as Rachel answered the door, I realized she was beautiful. Not just pretty, but utterly beautiful. It turned out that the double-chin photo I'd seen of her on Facebook was hugely unflattering and bore no resemblance to her in real life. All the other ones, the ones I'd detemindly only glanced at, were the accurate ones. Only just not as gorgeous as Rachel in real life, with her flaxen blonde hair, curves in all the right places, sumptuous Billie Piper mouth and a few, sexy laughter lines around kind, hazel eyes. She was barefoot and wearing cool harem pants and a slinky little sun-top that showed a glimpse of tanned, smooth midriff. It was a look that said: I am still breathtakingly stylish when just chilling in my urban garden and totally at ease with myself in a genuine, non-pretentious way. My look — culottes (I know, I know) and what was basically a twin-set from Jigsaw — said: I have just won an award from the Guide Dogs for the Blind and am about to have tea with the Queen.

Still, I wasn't the only one disgracing myself in the fashion department, thank God. It was clear as soon as I saw Toby, hiding behind the barbecue in their garden (I say garden, it was like something out of *Grand Designs*: decking, plants like triffids, high walls painted with brightly coloured murals) that he was over-compensating. He was wearing an Hawaiian ensemble: Bermuda shorts halfway down his bum and a sombrero and a wide open shirt that clung to his firm, broad chest.

'Hey!' he said, throwing his arms wide open. (How could he look so damn *relaxed*?) 'So, you made it out of Battersea? Feeling homesick yet?'

Lexi kneed him in the goolies.

'All right, Munter,' she said. 'What's with the Club

Tropicana get up? Liking the Tommy Hilfiger's, too,' she said, giving him a wedgy. Then she wandered off, leaving me stuttering something about a marinade and wanting to snog him so much I had to cross my legs so that I didn't just hurl myself at him.

3. The Grand Tour.

I'd probably say, in retrospect, that on a list of Things You Would Rather Avoid When Visiting the Home of Your Married Lover (if you had to go in the first place), seeing their marital bed might rate number one.

'Hey, I'll give you a tour, if you like?' said Rachel, after I'd stood in her hallway and said something inane about her achingly-cool flamingo-print wallpaper.

'That'd be great!' I lied.

Highlights included having to pretend to be pleased to see their amazing, glossy, kitchen extension and hear how they really went to town on it because 'we spend so much time as a couple here just hanging out, entertaining mates, having lots of parties'. (Bully for you, I wanted to say, bully for you . . .) This was made far worse by the fact that, halfway through her telling me this, Toby wandered into the kitchen, put his arm around her and started stroking her back. Speak? It was all I could do not to cry.

Then came the bedroom. The marital bed! Could this get any worse? Well, yes it could, because whilst Rachel went into detail telling me how this was a Louis XV-style French antique bed, which they bought at a Parisian flea market on a romantic weekend away, Toby stood in the doorway, beer in hand, as I tried to 'mm' and 'aah' in all the right places and make sure my face didn't go into spasm with the effort.

Then Rachel went to close the window. 'Sorry, is it draughty in here?' she said, touching me on the arm. 'It's just Toby likes a fag out of the window after . . . well, you know . . .' She giggled.

182

Yes, I knew.

And there I was thinking post-coital cigarettes out of the bedroom window were an idiosyncrasy of the book club. Silly old me. Stupid little Steeley.

I decided I needed a breather after that, but even on the toilet I was surrounded with pictures of them: them moving into the house, them skiing, one of Rachel asleep on Toby's shoulder – that was the killer. I composed myself and left the bathroom, only to bump into Toby on the landing.

'Hello, gorgeous,' he said as he put his hand down my top.

'Toby,' I hissed, 'what the hell are you doing?' He looked divine (James Dean gone Hawaiian). But seriously, in his own house? With his wife downstairs? Did he have *any* shame?

4. Then they tried to matchmake me.

By the time we ate, I was a lost cause, and already seeing two of the monkfish kebabs. Thankfully, Lexi, as I'd hoped, was hogging the limelight with her hilarious anecdotes of teenage life, so I could sink down in my chair, fade into the background and just get more drunk until this was all over – couldn't I? No, I couldn't. Because then Rachel piped up:

'Do you know, we were just saying whilst you were in the bathroom, how can such a babe like you (why did she have to be beautiful *and* nice?) possibly be single?'

Lexi made some sort of *hear! hear!* noise. Shona made a sound like a dog about to be sick.

'Well, I . . .' (am clearly morally void, shagging your husband and destined for hell) was on the tip of my tongue, but then Rachel started: 'Tobes, come on, what men do we know? We must know *someone* we could match Caroline up with?'

I couldn't even look at Toby. I concentrated very hard on my seventeenth glass of wine. Then Rachel got out the photo album. I was about to enter a sort of dating agency in my married lover's house. This couldn't get better if I tried.

'Now this is Jamie,' she was saying, pointing at someone who looked like Ian Hislop. 'What do you think of him? And this is Hamish, nice bloke, bit autistic. Oh, what about Daniel, Tobe?' she was saying to Toby who was actually leaning over her shoulder. 'He's quite a catch, no?'

Toby looked at the picture.

'Oooh yeah, Caroline loves a bit of stubble, don't you, Caroline?' My mouth fell open. Was the man I have had an affair with for six months, the man I am in love with, actually being active in setting me up with someone else?

I chewed on my kebab. What had once tasted like succulent white fish, suddenly felt like trying to eat custard powder. I had to get out of there fast, which I did, five minutes later.

'Won't you stay for pudding?' said Rachel, concerned, following me out as I bundled Lexi out of the door. 'It's summer fruit brûlée.'

'Sounds lovely, but no, I'm stuffed!' Then I tripped up on the front doorstep and stubbed my toe.

The worst thing is, as I lay here on my death bed, I can't talk to Toby and I certainly can't talk to Lexi.

There's a soft knock on the bedroom door.

'Does the patient want a drink?' enquires Lexi.

'No,' I groan, crawling further down the duvet.

She opens the door quietly and sighs, all motherly, and I get that feeling again, like I'm sure this is supposed to be the other way round.

'You were really drunk, weren't you?'

'I am like a highly trained animal, Lexi,' I mumbled from underneath the duvet. 'I am in such peak condition that I am very sensitive, that's all.'

I pull back the duvet.

'You look like shit'

'Thanks. I feel it'

184

'Can I ask you something?' she says, coming to sit on my bed. 'Is there something going on with you and Toby?'

I feel the bile rise in my stomach again. I toy with the idea of telling her – what's the big deal, really? I mean, we all make mistakes. But I can't, not now, I don't know why. I'm supposed to be her big sister, aren't I? I'm supposed to set an example. I take a deep breath.

'What on earth do you mean?'

'It's just, you seem to really like him, that's all, and you seemed so nervous yesterday, so not yourself.'

I opt for something in the middle ground.

'Yes, I find him attractive,' I say. 'Who wouldn't? He's a very attractive man. But he's married, Lexi. I could never do that. Never in a million years.'

She sighs. 'Okay, well, I just thought I'd ask. Also, I want to say sorry.'

'Sorry? What for?'

'For bringing up the book club thing yesterday, after Toby had said it was a political hot potato.'

I manage a smile.

'Oh don't worry about that,' I say.

That, I think, is the least of my troubles.

CHAPTER NINETEEN

'Let's just get this straight. I am *never* doing that again!'

I had already had the official telling off from Shona over the weekend but was still in the throes of acute alcohol poisoning at the time, so couldn't properly concentrate until now, 9 a.m. on a Monday morning, under the harsh strip lighting of the office canteen.

'I am *so* sorry.' I reach over and squeeze Shona's hand. 'I know how much you hate lying, how rubbish you are at it.'

'Thanks a bunch,' scoffs Shona. 'I did my best yesterday, under difficult circumstances, I'll have you know.'

'Oh God, I know you did, Shone. Course you did. I didn't know my sister was going to open her big gob, did I?'

Shona frowns and blows air sharply out of her nose.

'I'm not sure that's really the point, is it? I mean, the fact is, you're still seeing him and he's still married. What are you going to do, Caroline?'

I sink further down in my seat, steeling myself for the next lie that's about to fly out of my mouth.

'Finish it,' I say.

'When?'

'This week.'

'*When* this week?'

'This weekend.'

'Good, because you know this is all going to go wrong, don't you?'

'She was lovely,' I mutter. 'I mean, why did she have to be so lovely? It's not fair.'

Shona looks at me – that look she does, a mixture of motherly concern and dismay – like, how could you be so incredibly stupid? Life to Shona Parry is simple: clear-cut, black and white. She doesn't judge – I know she doesn't like me any less for what I'm doing – but she will tell you, if only with a look, when she thinks your behaviour sucks, and this is definitely one of those looks. A look that says, 'Oh. And I thought you were better than that.'

I thought I was better than that, too. I thought I was bigger than that, but the longer this goes on, the smaller I feel like I'm actually diminishing before my very eyes.

Things had hit a whole new level when, in the midst of post-drinking depression yesterday, after I'd managed to drag myself from my pit of self-loathing and check my emails, there was this from Rachel:

From: rachel.delaney@hunterhewitt.com
Subject: Apology. (I had to blink hard to check I'd got that right.)
Hi Caroline
SO lovely to meet you finally on Saturday although you ran off a bit suddenly! I'm just checking . . . we didn't scare you off did we? I'm so sorry if Toby and I got a bit intense on the match-making front – you've got to watch us two, terrible like that!
Anyway, I really hope we didn't and that you and Lexi

will come back again for dinner soon. Hope your head wasn't too sore this morning and that you had a great rest of the weekend.

Rach x

I sat there, festering in my tartan pyjamas, and felt a new wave of nausea wash over me; a different, un-alcohol-related nausea, a kind of spiritual shrivelling like throwing a piece of paper in a fire. I liked her. She was a warm, lovely person. She was smart but not smug, gorgeous but not obviously aware of it. Not exactly the overbearing, limelight hogger that Toby made her out to be. In fact if anyone was an overbearing limelight hogger at that bbq, it was Toby himself with his Hawaiin outfit and stupid drunken jokes about the kind of men I go for. Why was he being such a tit all afternoon?

'It was a double-bluff of course!' he says, when I corner him in the office later that morning, as if I must be thick not to have worked this out already.

'What do you mean?' I said, unable to hide the hurt in my voice.

'If I was seen to be trying to set you up with other blokes, then how could she suspect, silly?'

I looked at him with big eyes.

'Are you sure? Because it looked like you didn't care to me. Like you'd forgotten yourself and were getting some sort of twisted kick out of your little "Let's matchmake Caroline game".'

His eyebrows did a little flicker of alarm. I could almost read his mind: she's not getting needy, is she? Paranoid? Emotional? Could it be that she's like a normal woman after all? That she's not the enigmatic, in-control Steele I knew and loved? And the thing is, I can feel it, I can feel my barriers disintegrating and it's scary, raw and out of control. Now I've met Rachel, been in their house and seen their bed, I feel stupid, like the 'other woman' that I am. How can I compete with that? Five years of marriage. An entire life shared. I feel vulnerable, stripped naked, like my skin is translucent and my nerve-endings are exposed. If this is what being in love is like, I'm not sure I like it.

End it, I think. Now, before things get really messy. He's married! What the hell did I think I was doing? But then, as I am stirring my coffee, he comes up behind me, kisses the back of my neck and there it goes, I can feel it, one more inch of my defences dissolve. 'Now come on,' he whispers into my ear, kissing my cheek. 'Don't get all paranoid and silly. Are we still going to Brighton?'

I stroke his hand then kiss it.

'Yes.'

'Good, because I think this little lady needs some spoiling and I think I know the perfect place.'

Needless to say, I have far too much on my mind that morning to deal with a grovelling email from Wayne. Something about being so sorry about what happened the other night on the boat, but he can explain. And can he buy me lunch to apologize? Oh, and he has something important of Lexi's to return.

To be quite honest, I'm not even that offended any more. Wayne drunkenly groping my sister is beginning to pale into insignificance after the events of the weekend. I'm hardly a pillar of morality, sleeping with someone else's husband. And, Toby? Well. If a fumble with a girl a decade younger than you is a seven out of ten on the dubious morality scale, then cheating on your wife, has got to be at least an eight.

Wayne suggests a patisserie on Marylebone High Street. He's sitting outside in the sun, reading when I get there, wearing Aviators perched on his head, and a silly little retro jacket.

'Hi.' I stand in front of his table, blocking the sun. I'm

189

really not in the mood for this. In fact, I suddenly realize, I couldn't be in a worse mood if I tried.

'Hi!' I make him jump and he closes the book, embarrassed. 'Sorry, I didn't see you there. Please . . .' he gestures to the seat opposite. 'Sit down. I hope this isn't too rustic for you.'

Wow, he really did think I was an uptight, unimaginative philistine who couldn't deal with anything even vaguely left of centre. It was a patisserie, for God's sake, not an Estonian dumpling house.

'It's fine, thank you.' I sit down but I don't take off my jacket. 'What are you reading?'

He shows me the cover: '*The Promise of Happiness* by Justin Cartwright. I just bought it from that little second-hand bookshop down there whilst I was waiting for you,' he says, shadowing his face from the sun with his hand. His eyes aren't half lovely . . . 'Can't seem to leave the house without buying a book.'

'Me too,' I want to say. I'm dying to ask what else he saw in the shop but I haven't come for a friendly chat. Besides anything else, I'm still reeling from the Barbecue of Horror, my head still regurgitating the catalogue of disasters like a sick, retching dog. 'Double bluff,' Toby said. He had looked like he was finding it all far too humorous for a double bluff.

There's an uncomfortable silence, then I say:

'*Anyway,* like I said, I can't stay long. I've got back-to-back meetings at work this afternoon.'

He smiles at me, that irritatingly disarming smile of his.

'You really are a workaholic, aren't you?'

And you really have a cheek. Just because you laze about a boat all day 'writing a novel', or sitting in your smelly little shop charming the ladies. 'I value my job, yes, if that's what you mean,' I say, curtly. 'So anyway, you said you wanted to see me?'

'Yes, look, about the other night. I don't know what you think you saw but I assure you, it wasn't what you think.'

'Oh. And what would I have thought I saw? You groping my sister's boob?' I say just as a waiter comes to the table with a basket of bread.

'Yes. I mean no! I absolutely did not grope your sister's boob.'

'But, Wayne, I saw it with my own eyes. I saw your hand on my sister's left breast.'

'It was on her heart,' he says.

I burst out laughing. I may be thick enough not to know my novels from my memoirs, but I wasn't that dumb. 'And you expect me to believe that?'

'I was comforting her,' he says.

'Now, that's just silly,' I say, annoyed. I was getting sick of either wallowing in self-loathing myself or having the piss taken out of me. There didn't seem any middle ground any more. 'Do you think I was born yesterday? That you could get me down here, impress me with a posh little patisserie and then relieve your conscience by spinning me some half-cocked story that you had your hand on her heart? She's seventeen, Wayne. She's still legally a minor and more than a decade younger than you. She's a kid, basically. She hasn't got a clue about life and you think I am going to sit back and watch someone like you lure her into a false sense of security about being a natural Sales Person, having "potential", when really the only potential you're thinking about is her as a potential shag!' I was on a roll now, what the hell, I'd left any sort of poise or dignity I ever had on Toby's front step and I even tripped over that.

Wayne stares at me, his jaw pulsating. I can see him clenching his teeth, trying to control himself, trying not, perhaps – remembering our drunken conversation on the boat – to bring up the small matter that I am not perfect, either.

'Have you finished?' he asks, after a long pause.

'No,' I say, 'I don't think I have. I wouldn't bloody mind, but you've got a girlfriend, too.'

'A girlfriend?' He screws his face up. 'I haven't got a girlfriend.'

'God, you're pathological. I saw her with my own eyes.'

'Where?'

'In the Duke of Cambridge. The dark-haired girl. The one you were having dinner with?'

'That's not my girlfriend.'

'Who was it then?'

'My ex-girlfriend.' Wayne looks at me and shakes his head. 'Look, think what you like,' he says, 'but it honestly wasn't what it looked like. It was one of those things that got misconstrued, that got . . . Oh God, I don't know!' He rubs his face wearily.

I want to believe him, I really do.

'Well, tell me please. Think about it carefully, because I'd really like to know.'

'I can't say too much,' he says, sighing. 'It's really none of my business but I feel compelled to say something at least.' He pauses. 'Basically, Lexi's got a few issues at the moment.'

God, he was patronising. As If I didn't know that.

'I know!'

'But have you asked her about stuff? About men and, you know, boyfriend stuff?'

He sighs heavily as if he's having to cover ground now that he'd really rather not.

'Course!' I say. Did he think I never talked to my own sister?

'Well, anyway, she's upset and she's confided in me recently, when we've been at work at the weekends, about the issue with Clark and you know . . .'

What issue with Clark? The prolonged lover's tiff they were having? Lexi would tell me if there was a real problem, surely?

'So, she was a bit upset and I was talking to her and . . . God, you're going to think I'm more of a deluded hippy than you already do.' He folds his arms. He's got a T-shirt on today and I can read the tattoo. JUSTINE, it says.

'Basically, I was saying to her "only you know what's in your heart" – ridiculous I know – but I put my hand on her heart, don't ask me why, and then you walked in.'

'And do you make a habit of just putting your hands on peoples' hearts?' I ask. 'Do you fancy yourself as some sort of faith healer as well as a novelist?'

Wayne shakes his head and gives a defeated little laugh. It wouldn't surprise me if he thought I was suffering from some kind of personality disorder after this, I'm being so vile. But I've had enough of feeling like an idiot all the time and so *emotional* like I have perpetual, chronic PMT. If I'm not longing for Toby, I'm insanely jealous of his wife and now this Clark business, not to mention the fact that I still find Wayne distractingly attractive – what sort of sister did that make me?

'Look, I've told you the truth,' says Wayne. 'So it's up to you whether you believe it or not. I can't do anything more. Oh, except this.'

He opens his jacket pocket and takes out a small floral book. Lexi's appointments diary.

I flick through the pages. 'Have you been reading this?' I say.

'Christ,' he says, 'give me *some* credit.'

I feel myself soften. Something tells me he's telling the truth. He's come all the way from Battersea to Marylebone High Street, on one of the hottest days of the year so far – why else would he come?

'I just wanted to give you it back, that's all, and say I'm concerned about Lexi. I think you should talk to her, especially about Clark.'

'Okay, I will,' I say in the end.

I feel awkward, like now he's said his piece there's really not much else to say. Then he looks at me and hesitates.

'Look, I hope you're not going to take this the wrong way,' he says eventually. 'But I felt so bad that I had even given you cause to think that I would do such a thing as grope your sister that I brought you something . . .' He takes something wrapped in tissue paper out of the satchel hanging off his chair. 'Think of it as a sort of wearable olive branch.'

Please don't let it be underwear, I think, suddenly alarmed. Surely not? But a smile spreads across my face as I open the package. It's the shift dress I tried on at the market. It still smells of his stall, reminds me of the day.

'I just thought it suited you so much,' says Wayne, watching for my reaction, hesitantly. 'It had your name on it.'

'Thanks,' I say, feeling a strange mixture of embarrassment from remembering the way he complimented me on the dress at the market, annoyance that I can't be angry with him any more and pleasure that he's given it to me at all. I still love it.

He takes a breath.

'Maybe we could meet at an auction one day and you could see how we buy stuff for the stall. I could impress you with my knowledge of 1950's Danish sofa-beds.'

His eyes twinkle humorously. Was this him asking me on a date? Maybe Lexi was right, maybe he did like me.

'Maybe,' I say.

He shrugs, disappointed. 'Okay.'

I walk back, clutching Lexi's appointments book in my hand and thinking about what Wayne had said. What could she have told him that she didn't feel she could tell me? Didn't she feel she could confide in me? Wasn't I approachable? I thought, after the pregnancy scare and the drunken confession that Clark had dumped her, that this was it, that we'd got to the bottom of it, but maybe I was wrong.

194

CHAPTER TWENTY

I did feel guilty about lying through my teeth to Lexi about going to Brighton – horribly guilty, especially since she'd asked to come with me – but, at the end of the day, I reasoned, this could all be worth it in the long run. It felt a bit like the lying you do before you throw someone a surprise party – horrid and necessary all at the same time.

All the more horrid because she'd asked to come with me.

'Brighton?' she said. 'For two days?' Her little face fell and I felt a stab of guilt, like an irresponsible parent lying through their teeth so that they could elope for a dirty weekend with their lover, which, of course, was what I was basically doing.

The story went like this: Toby and I were going to see a potential client in Brighton on the Friday and Saturday. The entertaining might run over on Saturday night – these people are quite the party animals, we've heard – so we'd spend Saturday night there as well as Friday night. Rachel was away on business in Scotland so she wouldn't know a thing.

'Can I come?' she asked, and my heart flipped.

'No, Lex, sorry, it's a serious work thing – no time for play.'

I spent the best part of thirty quid on DVDs for her and

pizza and a bottle of Lambrusco, and then I left her on Friday morning just before she went off to work.

'I'll call you, okay?' I said.

'Okaaay,' she said, not even looking at me. And then I had to run, so that I wouldn't turn back, feeling like I was leaving her at the gates of a boarding school.

Toby is standing next to WH Smith, when I get to Victoria Station, reading the paper.

'Hello,' I say, leaning in to give him a kiss, but he pulls away.

'Not here,' he whispers. 'Not here, Caroline, where someone might see us.'

I feel a little miffed. Did he have to be quite so guarded? Wasn't I worth a little risk? I mean, what were the chances, after all?

'Sorry.' I look at the floor.

'It's okay, let's just get on the train, shall we? Let's just get there.'

Yes, let's just get there, I think, feeling a little better. Let's just get there and it will all be fine.

I've played this scene over and over in my head. We get on the train, we sit next to each other in the sunlight, me leaning my head on his, as the city rolls into suburbia and into the familiar, faded glory of Brighton.

There'll be the constant, romantic cry of gulls, a brilliant blue sky against the white-washed pavilions and cavernous seafront houses as perhaps we doze, contented, his breath warm on my face, the rise and fall of his chest next to mine.

In reality, we can't find a seat next to each other. It's the summer holidays, and the train is packed with noisy kids, squabbling siblings and harassed parents with bags of sandwiches and backpacks bulging with children's plastic toys. We end up sitting, me on a table seat with a family and Toby on the other side of the carriage next to a woman working on a laptop. We can't even speak to each other. I try to catch Toby's eye, but he's reading the paper, completely immersed, unreachable so I have no other option but to stare out of the window, the knot in my stomach growing tighter. Was he thinking about Rachel? Feeling guilty? Because I sure was. It was becoming very inconvenient. I'd be doing something, like now, just leaning against the train window trying to relax or dropping off to sleep when she'd appear in my head with her beautiful smile and her kind eyes, speaking that line from her email: *SO lovely to meet you finally on Saturday although you ran off a bit suddenly! I'm just checking . . . we didn't scare you off, did we?*

It was so much easier before I'd met her, so much easier when I couldn't picture her, when she wasn't real to me.

As we step off the train, into the vast Victorian arches of Brighton Central Station, which smells of sun cream and holidays, however, my heart lifts. The sun is shining, warming the station like a tropical indoor garden. Toby takes my hand. 'You ready for the seaside, then, Steeley?' he says, kissing my head.

The hotel couldn't be more perfect: a boutique-style, double-fronted villa, opulently decorated with swathes of red velvet and plush cream upholstery. Our room is tasteful and bathed in sunlight, with a view of the sea from the long sash window.

I put my bags down and lean against the windowframe, looking out over the view; the sea glittering with sunlight, the old, burned-down pier like a gigantic, many-legged spider rising from the sea, the sky, a clear swimming-pool blue with just the one cloud floating across it, like a lost spirit from another world. Toby comes up behind me and wraps his arms around me, kissing my neck.

'We could just stay here for the afternoon,' he says,

punctuating each word with a kiss. 'Have endless sex, Martini on the rocks, take a bath like we did in the Malmaison hotel . . .'

I unwrap his arms and wander into the bathroom.

'They've only got a shower,' I say. 'Anyway, I quite fancy going out.'

'Really? Now?' He says,

'Yeah, come on.' The knot in my stomach is stubborn, it won't seem to lift. 'We haven't come all the way to Brighton to sit in our room all day.'

'Oh. All right, cool,' says Toby, nodding his head slowly. 'Well, what do you want to do?'

'Gosh, there's loads of stuff to do,' I say, shifting from one foot to the other. 'We're at the seaside, we do seasidey things.'

'Right,' says Toby. 'Yes, of course.'

'Paddling, the pier, fish and chips, wandering around the Lanes.'

'What's the lanes?' says Toby

'The shopping bit,' I say. 'Didn't you have a wander round when we were down for that think-in weekend in April?'

'Um, yeah but I didn't much take it in, you know . . .'

We walk down to the seafront, dodging rollerbladers on the promenade, street cartoonists angling for business.

'Let's get our portraits done,' says Toby, spontaneously.

I look at him, incredulous. 'Are you serious?'

'Yeah, why not? It'll be a laugh and we're at the seaside, aren't we? Isn't that what you do at the seaside? Eat candy-floss, get portraits done.'

I wonder if this approach may be missing the point.

'Well, I don't want mine done,' I say, searching his face for signs that he might still be joking (there are none). 'But you go ahead, I'll watch you, it's fine.'

So I sit down on a deckchair next to Toby who sits on a stool that's far too small for him, so that his legs come right up to his chin, making him look rather ludicrously like a garden gnome. The man silently sketches away and Toby arranges his face in a fixed grin, as do I. It seems to take ages.

This was bizarre. Did he think I was mad? That I would actually want to pay someone to make me look ridiculous, accentuate my already big nose and the height of my forehead? I think I'd rather die.

'There we are, sir. Do you like?' After what seems like an eternity, the cartoonist turns the paper around to reveal Toby in cartoon form: bushy eyebrows, accentuated quiff, enormous chin, gigantic toothy smile. He looks like a cross between Bruce Forsyth and Tintin.

Toby starts guffawing. 'Look at it! Hilarious! That is brilliant.'

I laugh too.

'That's brilliant,' I say, not quite being able to muster enthusiasm. *Now can we get the hell out of here before the man starts sketching me?*

The afternoon is close and warm and we while away the hours, like young lovers on their first break away.

We roll up our jeans and paddle in the sea, where Toby splashes my jeans till they're soaked to the knee, then lifts me up and pretends to throw me in. We get ice creams with flakes and wander down the pier, giggling as we try to eat them before they melt. We sit outside a bar called Hercules, hand in hand, listening to the people inside doing karaoke in the air-conditioned darkness whilst the sun blares outside.

Eventually, woozy with lager, we make our way to the amusement arcade, where plump, sunburnt couples, the women with dumpy knees and wearing strappy vests too tight for them, the men with stomachs like beachballs, put coin after coin in the fruit machines. I win £1.22 on the penny waterfall and buy us each candyfloss. Then we go on the waltzers where I turn puce and Toby laughs at me.

Anybody watching us might think we were in some sort

of British rom-com, a film about two young lovers on a lost weekend, but inside my head I know the soundtrack's not playing. I know I'm not feeling it.

We go for coffee at a fish and chips restaurant on the front. The clouds have closed in now, a breeze has picked up, and what was a dazzling, blue sea before, dancing with sunlight, now looks rather brown and flat.

I watch Toby carrying the coffees over to me. He's smiling and I smile back, but I'm aware of an unpleasant feeling seeping through my bones, a sense of detachment, like I'm here in body but not really in mind. Like I'm watching myself, just going through the motions.

Toby puts the coffee down in front of me. 'You all right?' he says. 'You look a bit peeky. Still feeling sick from the waltzers?'

'I'm fine,' I say, forcing the corners of my mouth upwards.

He sits down, his face lit by the light of the window and I think how incredibly handsome he is, with his fringe in a sea-swept quiff, the two-day shadow, the perfectly arched eyebrows, the way his front teeth rest slightly on his pouty bottom lip, giving him a vulnerable quality, a boyishness.

He starts talking to me – *Wasn't it funny when,* he's saying, and I'm nodding and saying something or other, but other sounds – the ever-present cry of gulls, the echoey clatter of cutlery as the white-haired, gummy couples eat their fish and chips in silence – are drowning him out, as is the voice inside my head. Because here, in this rather shabby café with its tacky, jarring posters of Hawaiian scenes, I am suddenly seeing things as they really are.

This is just an illusion. This is not real. We can come to Brighton, have mad passionate sex in an expensive hotel, lark about on the pier, play at couples all we want, but we are not one. Christ, outside of the bedroom, we even struggle with knowing what the other likes to do. So what's the point,

200

I'm beginning to think as Toby is rattling on, of being here, of him bringing me here, of me fancying him and loving him at all, if nothing's going to actually happen, if nothing is to change? Sometimes I feel like this is all so futile, like I'm putting all my energies into something that eventually will be nothing but a speck on Toby Delaney's relationship history. But I've burnt my bridges with this one. All the courting is over and the coy games. I'm too far under.

'Do you love her?' It just flies out of my mouth.

'Love who?'

'Rachel, Toby. Your wife – remember her?

He laughs, awkwardly. 'What's brought this on?'

'I just want to know. Do you, or not?'

It strikes me as I say this that I've always assumed he doesn't, and how absurd that is now I've met her, since she's beautiful and charming and I can't see what there is *not* to love about her and what does it say about him if he doesn't? But then, I am also terrified he's going to say 'yes'. So, this is a pivotal moment. This moment, in this decrepit café, basically decides the future for us. If it's 'no', then what? He has to leave her. Things must change. And if it's 'yes', then I must leave, get on a train and go home. Either way, I'm aware that, for the first time in my life, I feel totally out of control in a relationship. Not just at the mercy of somebody else's feelings, but their feelings for somebody else. Then he says:

'You know, it's shit, really. We don't have sex any more. We sleep in separate bedrooms, we don't really talk . . .'

I remember the tour around the house. What Rachel said about the post-coital cigarette and having to have the window open.

'But Rachel said . . .'

Toby wafts his hands.

'She was just covering up,' he says. 'She's always fucking working, Caroline. Working, working, working. Not that I'm complaining about that, of course. It makes it easier to see you, to do this.' He puts a hand on mine. 'We've had a good time today, hey? Just you and me, different place, not having to worry about people seeing us. I've had a ball.'

'Me too,' I say. 'But don't you, you know . . .'

'What, gorgeous?'

His voice is so tender, it kills me.

'Worry about this? About what we're doing? It was sort of okay before I met her, Toby, but now, it's a whole new level, isn't it? A whole new level of lies and deceit. I mean, doesn't she suspect?'

'Who, Rachel?'

'Yes!' Sometimes I wonder if Toby has even forgotten she exists. 'I made such a fucking idiot of myself at the barbecue, got so drunk.'

'Come on, you weren't that bad, and it was funny.'

'Funny?' I can't believe he just said that. 'It wasn't funny for *me*, I was dying in there, Toby. First, it was the tour around your marital home – I had to stand there and listen whilst she filled me in on your morning ablutions. Then, there was the trying to pair me up with people in your photo album.'

'Oh, Steeley! I've told you I was double-bluffing.'

'Whatever, it was awful. How do you think that made me feel? Anyway, then to top it all off, as if the whole thing wasn't totally hideous enough, I went and blurted out the *Fever Pitch* thing and it was so bad and so obviously plucked out of thin air and so clear we hadn't fucking read it or read anything for the book club, she MUST have said something!'

Toby shakes his head.

'Nothing.'

'Really?'

'Not a word. She suspects nothing. Seriously. You have to

remember that Rachel is a woman who's very wrapped up in her own world. She's not home till 9 p.m. most nights; she spends two weekends a month working away – which is why we can do this trip. I mean, we don't do stuff like this, for example, just sit in a café and have a chat. I can't remember the last time we did that, in fact, or got a takeaway together or had fun. We've had so much fun today,' he says, and I realize he has, that he has not a care in the world. 'The truth is, Rachel never bloody talks to me, CS, never mind wonders whether I'm seeing someone else.'

'Oh.' I say. I guess I hadn't really seen that in her, but I mean you can be beautiful and friendly and charming, but it doesn't mean you're a good wife, does it? It just proves, one never knows what's happening behind closed doors.

We go back to the hotel, Toby with his arm around me and the last of the day's sun finally making it through the clouds, and I feel a little better about things, still raw but more connected, like the not unpleasant exhaustion you feel after a good cry.

I have a renewed sense of looking forward to our evening together; maybe a snooze on the bed would be nice when we get back, or maybe ordering room service and watching TV in bed wearing the hotel's fluffy dressing gowns.

I put my head against Toby's. I love how my head only comes up to his chest.

'Shall we just go upstairs?' I whisper, looking up at him.

'I think that might be wise,' he says, kissing me on the head. But just as we're going towards the lift, a lady on reception calls, 'Mr Delaney?'

Toby turns around.

'A Mrs Delaney called earlier . . . But I see you've found each other?'

* * *

'Why the fuck did you book it under your name?'

We're in the lift now. I'm absolutely astounded.

'I don't know,' says Toby defensively, 'habit I guess. Look, it's fine, calm down. Nobody will twig.'

'But what if the woman on reception had said something to Rachel? Like, oh, hello, how are you enjoying Brighton?'

'Don't be ridiculous, Steele. They're more discreet than that. What has got into you this weekend? You're so worked up. I'll have to call her, you know. I'm sorry,' he says.

'I know that, Toby, you don't need to apologize.'

Don't bloody patronize me, I think. I don't need to be handled with kid gloves. 'I'll just go in the bathroom and make myself scarce and you just do what you have to do, okay?'

So I do just that, stare inanely at myself in the bathroom mirror as he calls his wife. I feel like I look different recently, like I've aged, the contours of my face not as firm as they once were. I pull at my temples, imagining what I'd look like with a face-lift, wavering between wanting to hear everything and nothing at all. In reality, I can't hear any actual words but the tone sounds anxious. Both anxious and tender.

'Is everything all right?' I ask, coming out of the bathroom when I hear him hang up.

'Yeah, sure,' he says, with a tight smile. He looks pale and fidgety. 'Everything's fine, she just had an important meeting today and wanted to tell me how it went.'

'Are you sure?'

He puts his hands in his pockets and grins.

'Course.'

'Because you look a bit weird, a bit nervy. There's nothing wrong, is there? Do you need to call her back?'

Toby groans and rolls his eyes.

'Caroline, Caroline, Caroline . . .' He takes me by the

204

shoulders and kisses me on the nose. 'What's with all the insecurity today, hey? All the—'

'Constant irrational emotion?' I say, remembering our conversation in my kitchen all those weeks ago, thinking, See, I'm just the same as all women, Toby. It was all a front to impress you. I love you, you moron.

He laughs. I don't think he quite grasps what I mean, but then, quite out of the blue, he gets hold of my face and starts violently snogging me, eating my face.

'Toby!' I'm trying to say, but his mouth is suckered to mine. 'What on earth are you doing?'

'Kissing you, what do you think?' he says. 'God, I really want to fuck you right now, I really, really do.'

He pulls me closer, starts undoing my skirt at the back, running his hands all over my bum.

'Toby, calm down!' I'm half saying, half giggling. 'We've got all evening, you know.'

'Okay, well let's order bar service, then.' He eventually comes up for air, wipes his mouth. 'I could do with a drink, what do you say?'

I laugh at him. 'We've got a minibar,' I say. 'I'll make you one, if you like, if it's going to stop you behaving like an animal on heat.'

I go to the minibar and mix a gin and tonic, whilst he smokes out of the window.

Good, I think. Maybe a drink and a smoke will chill him out a bit, because I'm not in the mood for sex. The phone call has made me feel exposed and on edge.

He smokes two cigarettes in succession, then takes the gin and tonic and downs it in one.

'That better?'

'You bet,' he says. 'Feel a million dollars now and incredibly horny, as it happens.' He sticks both hands up my top and cups my boobs. 'Let's go to bed, CS.'

'Oh, Toby, I . . .' am really not sure I feel like it.

But he's already lifting my top above my head. 'I don't know why you're resisting me,' he says. 'You are a very, very lucky girl.'

Within seconds, he's got me down to my underwear and on the bed, his tongue down my throat and his hand down my knickers. I lie back and stare out of the window at the fierce blue sky against the white facades of the buildings and, for the first time in my life, I don't want to have sex with Toby Delaney. Not this sort of sex, anyway, this rampant, raw, animalistic fucking like I'm a prostitute or a one-night stand. He's being almost aggressive, his touch rougher than usual, more selfish and detached. This is the sort of sex that seedy men have with their seedy mistresses and I don't want to be a seedy mistress any more.

'Toby, stop!' I say, pulling away.

'What's wrong?' he says. 'What's wrong, my darling?'

'I'm just not in the mood,' I say, pulling the sheet over me. 'I'm just tired, that's all. Must be all that sea air.'

'Oh,' says Toby, sweeping the hair from my face. 'It's okay, don't worry.'

He lies down beside me. We don't say anything for a while. Outside, I can still hear the gulls cry.

'I guess I feel a little bit strange,' I say. 'All this, it's a bit weird.'

'What do you mean?' he says.

'I mean, I don't know where this is going.'

'Oh, Steeley,' he says. 'Come on, let's just lie here.'

So we do; we don't say anything for a while. I stare at the light fitting on the ornate corniced ceiling, my head in pieces, not knowing what to think. Maybe I should just leave, just leave now, put all this behind me. Go home to Lexi, forget him, get on with my life.

Then he says, 'I love you Caroline.'

My heart thumps

'What?' I whisper, turning to him. 'What did you say?

'I said, I love you.'

I feel a swell in my chest, hot tears in my eyes. I touch his face.

'Really?' I say.

'Really,' he says.

'Oh, Toby . . .'

Then, before I know it, we're making love.

Leaving him at Victoria Station on Sunday afternoon, knowing he's going home to Rachel, is agony. I'm exhausted from a million different emotions, the sliding emptiness of Friday afternoon before the elation of that night and the 'I love you'. I LOVE YOU!

That's what he said.

People do leave their wives, I think when we're on the train, this time with me leaning on his shoulder and it feeling so right. It happens, it happened to my own mother! Was I the most awful woman in the world for even thinking that? But this could be a whole new chapter, I think to myself. The promise of things to come. When I kiss him at the taxi rank at Victoria Station, he doesn't pull away. I can still smell the sea air in his hair, hear the cry of the gulls. We say goodbye, a long, lingering one, and this time it feels like a film but the sound-track is playing and I'm not watching myself, I'm fully in role.

We get into separate taxis and I feel happier than I have in years. I take out my mobile, my hands are shaking. 'I love you too' I text. The giddiness builds gloriously inside me as my fingers touch the keys. 'Sorry for going wobbly on you! Sorry for being insecure. xx'

I wait for the reply. Nothing. Maybe he's run out of battery, I think, or fallen asleep. Then the realisation washes over me.

I feel sick to the stomach – he never did tell me if he loved her, did he? He evaded that whole question. Did he just tell me he loved me so we could have sex?

My mobile goes just as we're driving down Battersea Park Road.

'Hello?' I slam it to my ear, not even looking who's calling.

'There you are!'

Martin. My heart sinks to the floor.

'I was beginning to think you'd emigrated.'

'Oh,' is all I can manage.

'Are you all right?' he says. 'You don't sound very good.'

'I'm fine.' You can hear the wobble in my voice, I can feel tears pricking my eyes and I don't want to cry, I really do not.

'Well, you don't sound very fine,' he says. 'I know when my Caroline doesn't sound fine.'

The concern in his voice only makes things worse, and I blink back the tears. Do not open your mouth, I think, do not say a thing. Whatever happens, do not emotionally spew, not to him.

'I'm fine,' I say. 'Just tired, that's all. I've just come back from a client do in Brighton. Didn't get much sleep.'

'Oh,' he says. He sounds deflated. 'Well, you won't want to be going out tonight, then?'

'Go out where?'

'It's a cookery event,' he says. 'Very late notice, I know, but I just got tickets on the spur of the moment, thought it might be up your street.'

'Where is it?'

'A restaurant just off Regent Street.'

I think about tonight – even getting that far without caving in and calling Toby and I feel depressed. I could do with something to look forward to, something to take my mind of him, a bit of good old TLC from Martin to bolster my spirits.

'Yeah, okay then,' I say. 'Sounds really nice, Martin. Text me the details and I'll drop my bag off and meet you there.'

When I get home, I dash up the stairs and call for Lexi, but there's no answer. Off working with Wayne in Camden, I think, more than a little relieved that I don't have to have a conversation with her just yet. Not with thoughts of Toby's 'I love you's filling my mind.

CHAPTER TWENTY-ONE

The 'Cook Italiano!' event is held in the kitchens of a small Italian restaurant on Heddon Street. It's hurling it down by the time I get there – a summer evening storm – and Martin is standing in the doorway, his beige Gap jacket wet through and his glasses steamed up.

'I'm so sorry I'm late!' I'm panting, having legged it like a madwoman from Oxford Circus. 'Some sort of suicide on the tube.'

Martin's lips twitch.

'Some *sort* of suicide, eh?' he says, giving me the look that says I've known you for fourteen years, don't you think I know by now that you're ten minutes late for everything? 'I don't know, these selfish, depressed types, throwing themselves in front of trains?' he ruffles my hair. 'Now, shall we cook Ital-ian-o?'

Martin's good at planning original, interesting things to do. This was always one of the many plus points of going out with him. It's one of the things I miss. Whereas most of my friends would complain they could barely get their man dressed of a weekend, Martin and I would already be embroiled in the first of the weekend's many planned activities come 10 a.m. on a Saturday morning.

Over the course of our fourteen year relationship, I have learned how to make sushi, how to mix a 'Hemingway' cocktail, had tea at the Ritz and lunch on board the London Eye. I went horse riding, paint-balling and did a tutorial on French wines at Vinopolis, London's wine museum. Most of the time it was fun and he got it right (apart from, possibly, a Victorian re-enactment day – five hours in a boned corset that was almost the death of me.

This time, he clearly didn't read the small print.

I know something's wrong the minute we get inside. It's something about the clientele: Too diverse, too oddball, too excited, too *nervous*.

It strikes me: why on earth would you look this terrified at the prospect of cooking a meal? Then I see it, in huge, bright-pink letters on the far side of the kitchen.

'FLIRTING WITH FLAVOUR! COOK. DINE. YOU NEVER KNOW!'

I laugh out loud at first, with shock more than anything. The sheer farce of it all. Then it dawns on me, did he? Would he? Surely not.

I look over at Martin, but he's still engrossed in taking the beige jacket off and hanging it on the back of a chair with . . . *his name on*. I look behind my chair and realize mine has my name on, too, as does everyone else's. This is turning out to be like some hideous *Come Dine with Me/Blind Date* hybrid.

Eventually, Martin looks over at me. I'm pointing frantically over at the banner, but he frowns; he hasn't got a clue what I'm on about.

'Bravo! Okay, people!' At that point a lanky Italian man with greased back hair and wearing chef's whites marches into the room, clapping his hands. 'I'm Stefano Melzi and I'm your host for zis evening of Flirting wiv Flaveeeuur!'

211

The audience break out into a lame trickle of applause. There's a 'woop woop!' From a horsey girl in a pashmina. Some dude in surfer shorts and Birkenstocks starts hammering the table with both fists.

I look over at Martin, who's staring, open-mouthed, up at the banner now and I know by the pale sheen on his face and the expression like he just had the results of a paternity test on live television that no, he had no idea what this was when he booked it.

'Okaaaay!' Stefano Melzi flings his arms open as if he's about to start singing an operatic solo. 'Let's get cooking Italiano! On your right, you will find ze tantalizing menu I have personally put together, carefully planned to set your senses alight, ladies and gentlemen, to increase your powers of seduction, to . . .' he raises one black, arched eyebrow and spreads his fingers like a magician, 'arouse.'

The horsey girl in the pashmina starts snorting with laughter, which makes everybody else except Martin – ten of us in total – join in, including me. I check Martin again, po-faced, a trail of sweat now making its way down the side of his face and I think, come on Mart, it's not that bad, is it? We can laugh at this, can't we? It's not such a big deal?

He looks over at me and swallows.

'I'm sorry,' he mouths

'Don't worry,' I mouth back. We were here now. If I could relax and see the funny side, surely he could?

'Now,' continues Stefano, parading around the kitchen, chest puffed out. Something tells me, however, that this might get worse before it gets better. 'In your drawers are all the utensils you shall need to produce tonight's dinner and in the silver fridges . . . Do you like my silver fridges, ladies and gentlemen?' He runs both hands down one. 'Pretty sexy, ha? You will find all the main ingredients you need, the rest will be in the cupboard. IF!' He stops, sends a finger theatrically around the room . . . 'you are not sure whether your dish looks or tastes as it should, do not ask me!' He bangs on one of the tables for emphasis. 'Zis is not ze way to flirt with flavour! Instead, be brave! Be bold! Ask the person next to you. Stick a finger in your bowl, then stick it in zer mouf!'

'Eh, Stefano, are we allowed to stick what we want, where we want then?' honks the dude with the surf shorts and ponytail – Australian, unsurprisingly. Nobody laughs back.

Stefano wags his finger at him. Surf dude rearranges his greasy, bleached ponytail.

'Please,' he says, ''ave some decorum. This is a sophisticated evening of seduction and let me tell you . . . people –' he lowers his voice right down to a whisper – 'I demand courtesy, manners and, above all, romance! I 'ave 'ad many, many couples leave this room hand in hand at the end of the night then come back the following week to the COUPLES' event!'

There's a round of 'woo-hoos!' Some shrieks from one table. One guy – corduroy jacket, about forty-two and probably still a virgin – is staring at me in a rather intense way. Still, I think, this is okay, this could be a laugh. We might both get a little flirting in, and where's the harm in that?

But Martin's staring down at his table. Then he looks at me. 'I'm so sorry,' he says again, shaking his head.

Despite the initial disaster, however, Flirting with Flavour turns out to be fun. Ten minutes into it, I realize I'm really enjoying myself. Martin seems to be, too. He's been accosted by an Italian woman called Gisella, who has wild, wiry hair and an extremely loud voice.

'Zis,' she is saying to Martin as he hacks into the bone of his guinea fowl, 'is a very hard bird to crack, Martin! Ha ha ha!' She laughs, throwing her head back, and Martin laughs too. He looks over at me and I raise an eyebrow at him. Could it be that Martin Squire has found an admirer?

It's 9 p.m. by the time Stefano finally releases us from his

213

clutches and us 'Flavour Flirters' spill out, heady from too much Italian red, into the balmy London night. We gather on the cobbled area outside La Tavola under the glare of a street lamp, promising we'll do this again, congratulating each other on our efforts. With the absence of anyone else who's under the age of thirty and gagging for it, Surf Dude Dan seems to have made a beeline for Horsey Pashmina.

'Mwah! Mwhah! Ciao, Martin!' Gisella, kisses him theatrically on both cheeks, nearly suffocating him with her hair.

'Goodbye, Gisella,' says Martin, back rigid, hands in pockets. 'Lovely meeting you. Hope your fowl goes down well tomorrow.'

Martin watches as Gisella strides off into the night on shiny red stilettos, then looks at me.

'What?' he says.

'Nothing,' I say, feeling my lips twitch as I burst into a giggle. 'You're just so *cute* sometimes!' I kiss him on the cheek.

'Cute?' he says, flatly.

'The way you phrase things.'

'Oh,' he sighs. 'Did that come out all rude?'

I giggle. I feel a new sort of lightness for Martin of late. When I first called off the wedding, it was anything but light, it was hard work to see him and there were many ill-judged excursions. In particular, a trip to Ikea to kit out Martin's new bachelor pad, where Martin burst into tears into his Swedish meatballs. Those times were dark, full of strained conversations. It's amazing how you can suddenly become like strangers after you've known someone for fourteen years, like the path of conversation is so riddled with potential potholes and no-go areas that there's nothing safe left to say.

But lately I feel like we've turned a corner, and tonight was an accidental milestone. I genuinely didn't care that Gisella was flirting with him; in fact, I thought it was rather sweet. Yes, Martin Squire and I have successfully made the transition from lovers to friends and it feels *good*. I'd rather be a hundred per cent friend to him than a fifty per cent girlfriend.

I take his hand.

'Hey, it was great tonight, don't you think? Despite the um . . . initial shock.'

'Sorry about that,' says Martin. 'Teach me to read the small print next time, eh?'

'So anyway, Mr Squire . . .' I say as we walk away from the restaurant. 'You and Gisella, eh? I reckon she had the hots for you, did she not?'

Martin rolls his eyes.

'But she so did!' I say. 'And I saw you both chatting all cosily, you telling her about your ravioli triumph, swapping pesto recipes, mm?'

Martin looks at the floor and gives a noncommittal grunt.

'Even *I* got flirted with,' I carry on. 'Did you see him? That Howard bloke? He said, and I quote, that my guinea-fowl was pretty damned near perfect.'

'Did he? Coz it looked like a burnt body part to me.'

'Although did you see his hair, bless him?' I carry on, deciding to overlook that comment – out of character for Martin, who has never dissed anything I've done. 'No points for guessing why Howard was single. Trust me to always end up with the goons.'

'Thanks,' says Martin

'Oh shut up,' I say, 'you know what I mean.'

The air is warm and fragrant, the rain long over. I'm enjoying not thinking about Toby for a night, just having fun with someone who feels like family now, and I don't want the evening to end.

'Come on,' I say, 'let's go to the Shakespeare, just me and you, like we used to, remember? Like old times?'

He screws his face up. 'I think, actually, I might just go home.'

'Oh, really?' I'm disappointed. It's only just after 9 p.m., surely we can't go home yet?

He takes his glasses off and rubs his face 'I think I'm probably getting a migraine. A combination of too much red wine and my wisdom tooth playing up, no doubt.'

'Oh. Well come back for a coffee then, at least,' I say. 'Or we could go to the local near us?'

Martin sighs, looks the other way and I feel suddenly a bit silly as if I'm forcing him to do something.

'I'll come for a coffee,' he says, eventually. 'But just a quick one and then I'll walk back home.'

I know something's up the minute we walk through the lounge door. It's the way the lounge is eerily untouched, no cooking smells, no TV, no DVDs scattered around, or Lexi, for that matter, curled up on the sofa with her heart pyjamas on. There's music coming from upstairs, some sort of jazz – since when did Lexi like jazz?

Martin puts the kettle on. He always used to do that when we lived together, walk into the house and put the kettle on without even taking his coat off. I open the fridge and take out the milk.

'Just a sec.' I walk to the foot of the stairs. 'I'll just see what my sister is up to. Lexi, I'm back!' I shout. 'Are you going to come downstairs and say hello?'

No answer, so I leave Martin making coffee and go upstairs. The music is louder now, the erratic beat of some avant-garde jazz or other that sounds incongruous in this house, like going home to Mum's to find she's playing Nineties trance. I knock on Lexi's door, which is ajar; put my hand on the handle with its little silver dolphins hanging on a pink ribbon. A lucky charm, Lexi said, for the summer.

It's funny what we miss when we're not looking for it. It's almost like I know, even as I'm entering the room, that if I

216

could have played the previous few seconds of events back, I wouldn't have gone in there at all, because all the signs were there: the coat on the banister, the tobacco and Rizla papers near the back door that I missed, the faint smell of cigarette smoke wafting through the house, the smell of a foreign body, coming now from inside her room.

But like I say, I haven't registered those things yet. My body is ahead of my brain. So I walk straight into her room . . .

'*Caroline! Like fucking knock first, please!*'

And it's only then that I see she's in bed with a man.

I say 'in bed with a man', but it's not exactly that. Perhaps if she had actually *been* in bed with a man it might have looked more normal. The man is lying on his back on the bed, naked, arms behind his head, whilst Lexi, who sprang back when I opened the door, is crouched by his feet, legs up by her chest, like a small, frightened animal. She's wearing her knickers and a small, cropped pink T-shirt with a silver circle on the front. Her hair looks post-coital.

I stand paralysed for a second, milk in my hand. The man very slowly covers himself with the duvet, but like it was an afterthought, like he's only really doing it for *my* dignity.

'God, I'm sorry!'

'Well, close the door then!' says Lexi, but there's fear, not annoyance in her voice. She has her hands between her knees, she looks terrified.

'Oh, for fuck's sake!' The man stands up now, the duvet wrapped around him, looking for his clothes. He's tall and lanky with shaven dark hair and several angry-looking spots across his shoulders.

Then, Martin is beside me, breathless from running up the stairs. He takes one look at the man fastening his belt now.

'Oh. It's *you*. What the fuck are you doing here?'

Lexi is crying now. 'Look, can he just fuck off, please?' she says, gesturing to Martin but looking at me. 'What is he doing here again? It's like he's fucking following me.'

'I think you should just leave, Clark, okay?' says Martin. (Clark. Why the hell was Clark Elder in my sister's bed?) 'Get your stuff and go.'

Lexi seems to retreat further back, tears streaming down her face.

'I'm just gonna go, Alexis,' says Clark, and I recognize the voice from the phone now, northern and rich, at odds with the gruff, hollow-eyed face. 'These people are insane.'

I've retreated to behind the bedroom door now, which Martin is holding out for Clark with a dignified silence.

But then Clark stops; he's putting on his hoodie. 'I don't know what the big fucking problem is. I mean, she's seventeen, she can see who she wants, she's my girlfriend for fuck's sake. She's not a little girl.'

I am suddenly overcome with anger and something like fear. I don't like this man. I don't like the feeling I'm getting from him.

'Yes, she is,' I say. 'And she's *my* sister, and this is *my* house, so go please.'

Clark looks at Lexi but she says nothing. There's just the sound of her crying. Then he shakes his head, puts his bag over his chest and looks Martin square in the eyes as he brushes back past him.

'You've always had a fucking problem with me, you have.'

'And we all know why that is, don't we?' says Martin.

Then he walks downstairs and out of the house. I feel the blood drain from my face. So whilst I've been gallivanting off to Brighton with some bloke who's not even my boyfriend, my sister has been doing God knows what with a man who, according to Martin, has a string of criminal convictions. It suddenly occurs to me: maybe she didn't even want him to come? Maybe that's why she asked to come to Brighton, and I just *ignored* her? My eyes sting with tears of shame.

Lexi still hasn't said a thing. She's crouched on the bed, crying, head bowed.

'Lexi, he's bad news,' says Martin, quietly. 'You do *not* need a man like this in your life.'

'God, I'm so fucking sick of you!' She stands up now, grabbing the duvet to wrap around her, her dark eyes furious. 'You are so up your own arse, aren't you? You think you can just follow my sister around, telling *me* what to do, passing judgement on people you've never even met before. I wouldn't fucking mind but you're hardly the model boyfriend yourself, are you? Dumping my sister just months before her wedding? She still dresses up in the dress, you know! You shattered her dreams.'

Martin looks at me, with a look in his eyes I will never forget. My stomach rolls inside out.

'Martin, listen, seriously, I just hadn't got round to it, that's all, I just . . . *shit*!'

But he's gone. I hear him run down the stairs two at a time then the front door slam.

'Happy?' I say to Lexi. Then it all unravels.

'Oh, that is rich!' Lexi's voice is stone cold. 'That's a fucking joke, coming from you. I *know* about you and Toby, Caroline.'

'What?'

She's standing in the middle of her bedroom now.

'Yes, you heard right. I know about your affair. I've known from the beginning. You remember that first time when I came home and I was drunk because I'd been out with Tristan?'

'Yes,' I say, and I'm crying too now.

'Well, I saw the pants, Toby's Tommy Hilfiger pants? And I saw you whip them away in the drawer. I couldn't really

219

work it out, then, I just thought I was being stupid, that there must have been some other reason there was a pair of Tommy Hilfiger pants in the kitchen drawer. But then I saw Toby wearing them at the barbecue and, anyway, loads of things had started to fall into place. The book club that's not a book club at all. The list you left out saying "join book club" – why would you write that if you were already in one? The way you look at him at work, touch him, email him constantly. I may not be as clever as you, but I'm not stupid.'

Oh but *I* am, I think. I am so, so stupid.

'So, I'm having an affair with a married man, so what?' What did it matter now, anyway?

'So, what would your mother say?' she screams.

'It was good enough for yours!' I scream back.

We stand there, both in floods of tears, and I think, how did the summer come to this? How did I fuck it up so completely?

'Look, I don't even care that much,' screams Lexi. 'I even protected you! When we went to the barbecue, I saw how pissed you got, how nervous you were but I felt sorry for you, Caroline, I hated to see you squirm. When you looked at that shelf of books, desperately trying to come up with one, I covered for you.'

'What are you talking about?' I say, my mind racing back through that hideous afternoon, but it's drowned in alcohol.

'It was *me* who said *Fever Pitch*, I tried to save you.'

'But I don't, I don't . . .'

'No, you don't remember, because you were drunk out of your brains, but it was *me*, and then it backfired, and I felt awful, more thick and stupid than I already fucking feel most of the time.'

'So, you protected me?'

'Yes!'

'So, why didn't you tell me?'

'Because I was scared you'd think I was meddling. Because you're my big sister who I looked up to, because I love you, Caroline. *Hello.* I came here to sort *my* head out, but then saw how tits up your life was and I pitied you, and I didn't want to accept it. You've always been so perfect, done your A levels and gone to university. Done everything all right, been the "clever" sister. Then I get here and see the truth and I just felt, God, *you're* the one who needs *my* help!'

I stand there, sobbing. She was right. Spot on. My life was a mess, a total fuck up. I was deluded and stupid and incapable of even knowing what was good for me. Go and hug her, I think. Hug her and say sorry. Tell her you love her and that she's right, you're going to sort it out. But something stops me – pride? – I don't know.

'I'm going to bed,' I say and I close her door.

CHAPTER TWENTY-TWO

When I get up the next morning – Monday morning – Lexi isn't in her bed. She's taken her bag and her coat and there's no note. I call Toby. It's only 7.10 a.m. and I know he won't pick up, but the urge to speak to him is overwhelming.

He does pick up.

'Hi, it's me,' I say.

'Hello, you.'

By the traffic in the background, I know he's already left for work.

'Listen, I'm having a crisis . . .'

'What sort of crisis? Don't tell me you can't make this meeting?'

Meeting. Shit. Pitch meeting with Robertsons. Biggest client after Schumacher. It's all out of the window now.

'Lexi's gone missing. I've just got up and she's not in her bed . . .'

'Well she's probably gone to the gym or for a walk. People are allowed to leave the house, you know.'

'Yeah, but you don't understand, she's with Clark – the ex. At least, I thought it was her ex, or they'd fallen out or something, but he turned up in London. I came home last night to find them in bed together and then we had a massive row and now . . .' I'm gabbling; I can feel the threat of tears. 'I don't know what to do!'

'Right, just a sec . . .' he mumbles.

The line goes quiet then I hear him say, 'Yes, with an extra shot please.' He's in fucking Starbucks ordering coffee!

'Listen, it doesn't matter!' I snap.

'Well, no, it does, obviously it does,' he backtracks. I hear the emergence of traffic as he leaves the coffee shop. 'It's just, what are you going to do? Because, unfortunately, we've still got this pain in the arse meeting and if you're not going to be coming – which is *fine* – then I need to call them, you know, now-ish . . .'

I don't say anything. How could he be so heartless? So unbothered?

'Look, I'll have to go down into the tube now,' he says. 'But you just do what you have to do. I'll take care of the meeting, okay?'

'Shall I call you later to tell you if I find her?' I ask, but I'm talking to nobody. He's already hung up.

I stand there, clutching the phone. Who can I call now? Martin? Nope. Not any more. I've screwed that one up, good and proper. There's only one other person in the world I can call. One more person who has any chance of being any help. But as I lift the receiver, I realize I've never called him in a crisis before, so I'm not sure how this is going to pan out.

'Dad?'

'Caro! How are you, honey? Are you? Oh . . . you're not okay, are you?

And for the first time in my life, I realize I am crying down the phone to him.

'What on earth's the matter?'

'It's Lexi, she's not here. She's gone missing and it's all my fault!'

'Okay, try and calm down.' There's fear in my dad's voice.

There's never fear in my dad's voice. 'First of all, when did you last see her?'

'Last night,' I sob. 'I got home to find she was with that tosser ex.'

That he was naked in her bed, I want to say, but think better of it.

'We had a huge row and I kicked him out, then when I got up today she wasn't here. Now she's probably with him – God knows where – and he's bad news, Dad. Really bad news.'

'Hang on, hang on.' Dad's doing his tapping his forehead thing. 'Who's the tosser ex? Who do you mean?'

'Clark! Clark Elder. He came to London – he came to find her. He's trying to get back with her!'

'Well, why didn't you say that?' says Dad, his voice light now. 'That puts a totally different light on things. Clark's a good guy, Caroline. A really good guy, and I should know because I employ him; he's one of our best speakers.'

'But he's not, Dad, not good. That's where you're wrong. He's a well-known drug dealer and he's been done for GBH and he's been inside and he's a conman, a total fraud.'

'Who told you this?'

'Martin. He knows him from way back. There's even rumours he was involved in more serious stuff.'

'What sort of more serious stuff?' says Dad, concerned now. He loved Martin, and he knows he speaks sense.

'Just . . . not very nice stuff.'

There's a long pause.

'Right, stay there,' says Dad. 'I'm coming down. We'll find her, okay?'

It's a good job Dad does decide to come to London, because half an hour later, things take a turn for the worse. The rain is lashing down when the phone goes. It's Lexi. She's calling from a payphone and sounds utterly distraught.

'Carolineyou'vegottocomequick.'

There's so much snot and tears and the sound of the rain that I can't make out a word she's saying.

'Lexi? Is that you?'

'Yes, I'm at Brixton Police Station. Clark's been arrested.'

'*Arrested?* What for?'

'Something terrible, Caroline, something really terrible.'

Dread fills my veins like tar.

So it turns out that whilst I was dead to the world, emotionally drained from my own little dramas, my sister was in a crack den in Brixton with a man on the run. She's sitting, huddled in a coat in the police station reception area when I get there, and her skin looks almost translucent, she's so pale under the harsh strip lights.

'I really thought he loved me but I'm scared,' she says when we've hugged and we've cried and I tell her that's the closest to a heart attack I've ever been in my life.

'It's not your fault,' I say, holding her. 'It's not your fault, okay?'

After I'd gone to bed, she'd gone out into the night. Clark had phoned and told her to meet him in a pub in Brixton. They'd gone to a house, a huge, wreck of a house, full of people who didn't seem to know one another, and loud, banging music.

'They were drinking,' she says. 'Lying about on beds and smoking this stuff. I told Clark I wanted to go home, but he started to get all agitated. He said he'd come all the way to fucking London, the least I could do was stay, but I hadn't even *asked* him to come to London, I didn't even *want* him to. Then they were weighing this stuff out. I was starting to get really scared then . . . he was doing some sort of deal, you know? There was banging on the door and the police barged in and they were like, "Are you Clark Elder?" Then

225

they put him in handcuffs and they did all that "You do not have to say anything, but it may harm your defence if you do not mention when questioned something which you later rely on in court", and then they said they were arresting him for date rape!'

I put my arms around her and hold her tight as she cries and I feel a love I've never felt before, and it seems to be crushing my chest. Afterwards, I get us both a tea from the machine and she sits, sipping it, shakily. She stares at her hands, and then she says, 'Caroline, can I tell you something? The thing is . . .' When she looks up, her eyes are full of tears. 'I think that's what happened to me.'

Lexi has to give a statement before she goes, and I am left sitting on the red plastic bench, thinking, staring into my tea.

I am her big sister, her big sensible sister, and yet here I've been all summer, thinking I have demons to fight, when all the time she's been fighting the biggest demon of all. I've failed, I realize that now. For the first time in my life, I've properly failed.

'Dad!'

Lexi comes out of the meeting room and I'm still in a sort of trance when Dad barges in through the door, tanned within an inch of his life, his hair in need of a cut as always.

He holds out his arms to us.

'Dad, you came! How come you came?' squeals Lexi.

As I hug him, I am crying and beaming all at the same time.

We're in KFC now, sharing a family bucket. It's the first time in our lives we've had a 'family' meal, just us two and Dad. The rain's stopped and a shaft of sunlight has broken across the white Formica table. Outside, on the street, you can hear the sound of tyres on tarmac.

'Listen, I want to know what happened,' says Dad to Lexi. 'Tell me what happened.'

So Lexi goes through it all again, the squat, the drinking, the drug deals and police raid. It seems ridiculous, sitting here, sharing out baked beans. It's too big a drama for such an everyday place.

Dad goes quiet and I look over at him to see there's a tiny string of saliva hanging out of his mouth, that he's sitting there crying. Lexi gets up and puts her arms around his neck.

'Oh, Dad. Come on. Don't cry, please. Not in here.'

I feel like I should be doing something too, but suddenly I'm fifteen again, Dad's crying and I've no idea what to do, I'm frozen to my chair.

'I'll be okay in a minute.' Dad sniffs, patting Lexi's arm. 'But I want to say something and I want you both to hear me out, okay? I've failed you. I've been a crap dad, and there's absolutely no excuse.'

'Dad, you have not,' says Lexi. I sip on my Coke.

'I have, hun, you don't need to humour me, just let me finish, okay?'

He gives a big sigh, then when he starts to talk, decades of stuff pour out of him, stuff I've never heard before, and I listen intently. He never wanted kids, not really, and when I was born, he felt completely out of his depth.

'We brought you home and you cried for three weeks,' he says. 'Every time I picked you up, you cried even more. Your mum said I was doing it wrong, so I just gave up. I loved you to pieces, Caro, but I always felt inadequate, like I could never quite live up to your expectations.'

I am dumbstruck. Did I really have such high standards that I made my own dad feel inadequate?

He and Mum were already having huge problems by then, he continues; she wanted a husband he felt he could never be, and now he felt he was a father that didn't make the grade, either.

'I was desperately unhappy. Then, when I met your mum,

227

Lexi, everything fell into place. When she fell pregnant with you, I was over the moon. This was my chance to be a good father. But I screwed it up again, don't you see?'

'What?' says Lex. 'No, you didn't screw it up!'

'I did. Just in a different way. I was so bloody happy, so blind with love for my new life, that I was self-absorbed. And I forgot to be a father again.'

Lexi frowns; she can't take this in. I think about how forgiving she is and I feel a rush of love.

'I wanted you to like me, Lex. I was so desperate to be your friend, but I realize that's the biggest disservice you can do to a kid.'

'But you've been a great dad. You *have* been my friend.'

'Your friend, maybe. But your father? I don't know about that,' says Dad, picking at his fries. 'I was Hippy Dad, letting you see men twice your age, believing I was being liberal when you were crying out for barriers. I didn't ask the right questions when you were upset, because I was scared of the truth, and now look what's happened. Your mum and I always said you could do anything, but what, exactly? We didn't guide you.'

'Two Family Buckets and a Regular Fries!' someone shouts in the kitchen and, for a second, the intensity of the conversation is lost.

Then, Lexi says, 'But I dropped out of sixth form, Dad. I disappointed you. I didn't make you proud, not like Caroline.'

I look sheepishly into my drink – if he knew, if only he knew . . .

'Oh, you have made me proud,' he says. 'Very proud indeed.'

Lexi goes outside to call her mum, so it's just Dad and I sitting there. I don't know what to say, and yet, I feel I have thirty-two years worth of stuff to say.

Dad makes it easy.

'You must be so bloody angry with me,' he says.

I shrug and stare at my drink. I'm worried if I start talking I might cry and never be able to stop. But this is an opportunity I might never get again, so I say:

'I just missed you, Dad.' And he reaches out and puts his hand on mine. 'I felt like I'd lost you when you left Mum and us and *then* when you had Lexi . . .'

'I know, sweetheart,' he says. A tear rolls down his face.

'You remember the first time I met her? The first weekend I came to stay with you after she was born? I *hated* her,' I say, and as the words leave my mouth, it feels like a mountain of cement that's been sitting on my chest for seventeen years has just been lifted. 'I loved her like I had never loved anything in my life and hated her all at the same time.'

'And now?'

'Oh, God, now, *now*, I'd die for her,' I say.

Dad nods his head and smiles like he knew this all along.

'Well, I love her too, but she's not you, Caroline, and she never will be. Shall I tell you a secret? There's nothing like your first-born. You can love another child, of course you can, and I love Chris, too, but you never experience the sheer wonder of meeting your first-born.' He looks at me from under his quick, grey eyes. 'And you will always be a wonder to me, even if I have been useless at showing it, do you know that? I'm so proud of you, Caro. So proud of the woman and the sister you've become.'

I watch as Lexi comes back through the front doors of KFC, bringing with her the welcome smell of fresh rain, and for the first time in my life, I feel like a proper sister. I feel pretty proud of me, too.

CHAPTER TWENTY-THREE

Dad goes the next day. There's an alternative health trade fair in Guildford and Healing Horizons have a stand.

'I won't go,' he says at breakfast. 'Your mum will be there, Alexis, and this is where I should be, being a dad, looking after you two, not bloody waffling on about changing your life to people when I've no idea what's happening in my daughters' lives.'

Lexi and I both laugh, I don't know why. Maybe it's just the childlike way he says it, like he thinks he has to completely turn over a new leaf, be 'Superdad' all of a sudden.

None of us can really change at the end of the day, I suppose. Dad will always be in cloud-cuckoo-land, a little wrapped up in himself, and maybe I'll always be a bit spiky, not quite the open, charming book that Lexi is proving to be. Deep down, a part of me has always blamed Dad for my disastrous love life. But there's only so long you can do that, isn't there? Before you just bore yourself rigid and need to get on with things.

Perhaps I'll always have a little gap that my father never quite filled. But he can't fill it for me now, anyway, it's too late. So I say:

'Dad, go.'

Healing Horizons makes him happy, it makes him feel good, it's filled his hole.

'Yeah, Dad, don't stay, please,' says Lex, laughing. 'I don't think I can deal with any more hippy bonding, or breakdowns in KFC, or any more heart-to-hearts. I think I'll be all right now.'

Dad sits there for a second, breaks the top of his egg off with his spoon. 'Well, I know when I'm no longer needed,' he says, eventually, then we all burst out laughing. 'I'll bugger off then. You're on your own, kids.'

Dad's gone and I have a little laugh to myself as I imagine him at his Healing Horizons stand, knowing yesterday he was a wreck in KFC. I go and lie down on my bed. I'm taking another day off, a personal day, and so is Lexi. I rang SCD yesterday and told them that we had some urgent family problems we had to sort, that we'd be in on Wednesday. I turn over, and that's when I notice my notebook on the side table and pick it up.

It seems like an age away now since I first started writing the To Do list. Even the handwriting looks different in places, (the mad scribblings of an unhinged control freak, perhaps?).

I lie on my bed, listening to the soft cry of children playing somewhere in the distance, and I start to read, and it's only as I do that I realize I'm smiling, the slightly knowing, slightly cringing smile of an adult reading their teenage diary entry.

Make something with quinoa.

Sort out photo albums (buy photo corners).

Get drippy tap fixed . . .

It's like I'm not just remembering the stupid tasks I set myself, but the memories surrounding them. I remember the quinoa dinner, the way the hard little pellets stuck in my throat, the all-consuming fear I felt at the prospect of going to the barbecue and the desperation that Lexi came too. I wanted her to be a human shield that day and that's exactly what she was, it's just I was so wrapped up in alcohol-fuelled humiliation that I didn't even notice. Get drippy tap fixed . . . I remember that day too, the way the sun shone in through the kitchen window, the way Martin's builder's bum poked out from underneath the sink, making me feel uneasy that he was there in my house – which was once our house – helping me.

There's a knock at my door, Lexi's soft voice.

'Hi. Can I come in?'

She opens the door. She looks drained from the previous day's events. In her heart pyjamas, she sits on my bed and smiles at me.

'What are you doing?' she says.

I close the book.

'Oh, just reading this rubbish,' I say. 'It's nothing, really.'

'Come on,' she says. 'What is it, can I see?'

'It's my To Do list,' I say. 'My brilliant To Do list!'

'Read it,' she says. 'Go on, I'm interested.'

'Okay,' I say. 'Promise you won't laugh?'

She does and I do. I read bits of it aloud and it feels more ridiculous than ever.

'Make something with quinoa.'

She smirks.

'Oi!' I say. 'You promised you wouldn't.'

'Well, that was disgusting,' she says, 'truly revolting. What else is on there? Come on, this is fun!'

'Go to art event . . .'

'What, the pictures of soil?'

'Yeah, that'll be the one. Buy photo corners,' I say.

'I can't believe you make lists about this stuff.'

Then, out of nowhere, I start to cry.

'What's wrong?' she says.

'Oh, I don't know, I just really screwed up. You know, I did those photos the other night and I just ended up in tears.'

'But why?' she says and I lean my head on hers.

'Because there were so many photos of us, Lex, you as a baby, me the mardy teenager, and I realized I'd wasted so much. When I should have been loving you, my cute little sister, I just resented you, I wished you weren't there.'

She looks at me with wide eyes. 'You resented me?' she says. 'But I never felt that, Caroline, ever, not ever.'

'Really?' I say, in disbelief. 'That never came across?'

'Really,' she says. 'If you did, you made a fantastic job of hiding it.'

We lie on my bed and we say nothing for a while, then she says, 'I've got an idea.'

'Oh God!' I groan. 'Am I going to like this?'

'Let's make a new one, a new Master list. You made one for me and now it's your turn.'

I tear a page of A4 from the pad beside me and then, sitting on my bed, we make a new To Do list – this time, Lexi's one for me. She writes – as I sit there, nodding my head – in her fat, teenage writing with the circles for Is.

1. Let Martin go and stop stringing him along. Apologize to him about not telling me the truth – that it was you – Caroline Steele – who called it off, not him.
2. End it with Toby. Just do it, it's over anyway.
3. Go and see your mother. Tell *her* the truth about Martin, she deserves to know.
4. Sell the wedding dress. It's gone, past, history. Put it on eBay and stop living in the past.

CHAPTER TWENTY-FOUR

No. 1: Stop stringing him along . . .

It occurs to me as I walk to meet Martin that evening that everywhere in Battersea holds fragments of us; the ashes of our relationship are scattered everywhere.

It's been raining again; a sudden, summer downpour and even the way the clouds look – a giant, white mountain gliding like an iceberg to reveal new blue sky – reminds me of him, of Sundays together at home when the weather would clear up and the evening held new promise.

I loved those evenings, especially last summer, our last one together when I knew in my heart that Martin and I were not going to make it and rainy weekends holed up in the house could feel interminable. On those evenings, the post-shower sunshine was like a comfort blanket that I could snuggle under just that bit longer: just one more walk around the lake in Battersea Park. One more ice cream together at the café by the lake; one more Kir Royale at the Duke of Cambridge.

One more day before I tell him.

God, I've dragged this relationship out. It's been like the last, painful days of a terminal illness sometimes: the last walk, the last summer, the last kiss. No matter how sure I was that he wasn't the One, that I couldn't marry him, I couldn't end it either. It was during those rainbows, the blasts of sunshine, that I got the fleeting rushes of hope – maybe, just maybe . . . before the light dimmed again and slid beneath a cloud.

But there's to be no more maybes. No more wishful thinking or drunken sentimentality. Lexi's right. You can't keep people. They're not to be collected, preserved like jams. Sooner or later, you have to let them go.

This is what I am on my way to do now and why I am filled with a new sense of promise – a different kind – the promise of release, of finally letting go.

Martin suggested meeting in the Duke but that didn't feel right – too many good memories. So we're meeting at the Latchmere on Battersea Park Road.

He's one of only three people in there when I arrive, standing at the bar, one foot crossed over the other, arms folded, pint of bitter in hand. Body language closed.

'Sorry I'm late,' I say, breathless. 'I set off, then it started spitting again and I'd forgotten my umbrella so I went back and–'

Martin blows air through his nose.

'It's default mode with you, isn't it?' There's a snipe in his voice I've never heard before. 'You're not even late. I was early.'

'Sorry.'

He wipes his brow with a shaky hand.

'Whatever. Let's just sit down.'

We take our drinks to a squishy brown leather sofa by the fireplace, me perching on the edge of the seat, my stomach clenched tight.

'So, what is it you wanted to say?' he asks, as if this is a business meeting and he wants to get this over with as quickly and painlessly as possible. I search his face for signs of warmth but there are none. It's in that moment that I know how much I've hurt him.

I clear my throat; this is even harder than I thought it was going to be.

'I just wanted to say, I'm sorry.'

'Right. For what?' He narrows his eyes at me.

'For lying to Lexi for starters, or at least for evading the truth. She's been so mean to you and it's all been because of me, because I wasn't brave or big enough to just come clean.'

Martin pulls his chin back and purses his lips, as if, if he didn't contort every muscle in his face and hold it tight, it might crumple. He might cry.

'Why didn't you just tell her?'

'I was a coward, Martin, that's why,' I answer. 'You know me . . .'

He says, 'I thought I did.' It makes me want to cry.

'I was the big sister living in London, the achiever, the one who never fucked up or disappointed people, but I have disappointed you.'

'Yes, you have.'

'After everything that's happened, me calling off the wedding, you moving out, the last thing you deserved was that. You deserved nothing but honesty . . .'

Martin moves nervously in his seat, his eyes shifting from side to side as if he's scared of what he might be about to hear next.

'Which is why I've decided to be honest with you. I mean *completely* honest. I have something to tell you, Martin.'

Just as the words are about to leave my mouth – *the relief*. God. Why didn't I just do this before? I've been so scared of cutting all my ties, burning all my bridges, I've been so selfish and disingenuous. If I'd have just told him this sooner – when he asked me in the Duke all those weeks ago, it would have given him the message loud and clear.

'I'm seeing someone', I say, finally.

Martin looks as if he's going to throw up.

'How long?' he says.

'Six months,' I say.

'*Six months*. Who?'

'Toby.'

'*What?*' This time it's almost a whisper. 'Toby, who you work with? Toby Delaney, who I've met?'

I nod my head slowly.

'But he's *married*.'

'Yes.' For some reason, the enormity of this fact hadn't struck me. It was secondary to me. Surely the fact I was seeing someone was the main thing? Oh, but no. Martin's looking at me as if for the first time – and not in a good way – as if the last fourteen years have meant nothing, because I am not the woman he thought I was.

'He's *married*, Caroline.'

'I know.'

'He has a *wife*. Who you have met, I believe?'

'Yes, and she's lovely.'

'So you've been having an affair with someone else's husband? With a married man? You, of all people?'

'Well yes, but . . .' I don't know what to say. It hadn't occurred to me that the fact he was married would be an issue, *the* issue. I hadn't thought that would be the thing he would focus on or even care about really. But there's a look on Martin's face, his lip is curling, his nostrils flared. Disgust. He's disgusted with me! This is the man who's always thought I could do no wrong, who has put me on a pedestal, his Caro, and now? 'You've disappointed me.'

He says it so quietly.

'Sorry?'

'I said, you've disappointed me. I'm shocked, actually. Of all the people in all the world . . .' He's shaking his head, he can't take this in.

'Martin, I didn't mean it to happen, for God's sake. I never

237

meant to fall for a married man, I didn't mean to fall in love . . .'

'You're in *love* with him?' He blinks hard at me.

'Yes. I mean, I was, I am . . .'

'Jesus Christ, Caroline.'

I am crying now.

'I should have told you earlier, I should have told you ages ago when it started but I – I just couldn't. And I was so confused and such a mess and kept thinking I could stop it, but I couldn't. I know it's wrong but I just couldn't help myself.'

Surely this isn't fair? He's overreacting? I feel like I've committed the most heinous crime in the world. Like I've murdered someone, for God's sake. He doesn't say anything, he just frowns at me – that look again – like I'm a stranger, like he never really knew me at all. It makes me feel dirty and ashamed and heartbroken. I have lost him.

'I tried to stop.' I'm sobbing now. 'I tried to do the right thing but I couldn't help my feelings, Martin.'

He gives a cruel laugh.

'You know what?' he says. 'I'm pretty sick of your feelings. The way *you* feel. Women think they can get away with anything. They think they can hurt people and sleep with who they want and fall in love with whoever they want because of their feelings, because, oh, they're *emotional*.' He gives a sarcastic little shake of his head. 'But what about what is *right*? And what about my feelings? You know, this whole thing, the calling off the wedding, this whole year stringing me along?'

'Stringing you along?'

'Yes. Stringing me along. Don't pretend you didn't know what you were doing. It's all been about your feelings, Caroline. All about you.'

I put my face in my hands.

'I know, I'm sorry.'

'Oh, I feel so guilty,' he starts. 'Oh, it's such a shame it didn't work out. Oh, wouldn't it be great if it could work out? Maybe I hadn't had long enough to get my head around the idea of getting married, even though we'd been together for *fourteen* years. Maybe, just maybe? And I believed you – you gave me hope. I still *hoped*, don't you get it? I listened to what you said and I thought maybe, too. I thought it was just a matter of time before you came round, that it was all worth fighting for.'

'I'm so sorry, Martin . . .' I reach out and put my hand on his arm but he moves it away.

'I even tried to move on,' he says, 'but you wouldn't let me. I had a chance with Polly and I blew it because of you – I pushed her away. You called me up when Lexi went missing, you seemed so jealous of Polly – I mean, why were you so jealous about Polly if you don't love me any more?'

Because I was jealous. It's not that simple, Martin. It's just not that simple.

'I took all those signs and I thought they meant something, but really it was all about your guilt and your regrets and you, you, you, when you had no intention of getting back together with me, when all the time you were shagging a married man!'

Martin never uses words like shagging and it sounds faintly ridiculous.

We sit in silence. In the whole time we have known one another, we have never been lost for words. My heart is beating, my skin crawling with self-loathing. I've been so stupid and self-absorbed, so plain inconsiderate of his feelings. All the time I thought I was just feeling those feelings – the guilt, the regret, and the jealousy I felt towards Polly – I was actually speaking them aloud. I was transferring it all to him and, all the time, he was reading into everything I said.

Martin sighs.

'Look, Caroline,' he says. His tone is softer now, more like his normal one. 'I don't blame you for dumping me, for calling off the wedding. It hurt like hell but that's just life – there's no right and wrong in falling out of love with someone. It just is. But having an affair with a married man? I simply cannot believe . . .'

'I know. I know what you're going to say.'

'The number of times we've talked about your mother,' he says, more fatherly now. 'How it destroyed her life, *your* childhood. How you lost your dad because of an affair, how you saw your mum lose all her confidence in life and in men.'

I squeeze my eyes shut. He is right. So right.

'That's what happens when people let their feelings rule everything – that's all I'm saying, really. And I'm no model of perfection. I know I can be a fastidious bore and probably patronising at times, but I really believe that sometimes, no matter how much you don't want to, you just have to do the right thing, even if that's not necessarily the right thing for you.'

We leave the pub after one drink. We've said everything there is to say and this wasn't a social occasion. The air is cool and damp after the rain; you can almost detect the faint, smokiness of autumn threatening to arrive.

We stand outside, me with my arms folded, Martin with his hands in his pockets.

''Bye then,' I say.

'Yeah, 'bye, Caro,' says Martin.

He goes to kiss me on the cheek but I interrupt him. 'Look, can I just say . . .'

'Do you have to?' he says, not unkindly. 'Because, to be honest, I'm not sure I want to hear it.'

I look at him. His face is open and kind, not even a flicker of malice. A little piece of me will always love you, I think.

'Okay,' I say to him. 'Okay, I know.'

And then I kiss him, lingering slightly too long on his cheek and then I walk away and I don't look back.

I don't feel like going home immediately, so I take a little detour down Albert Bridge Road. It's lined with trees in their height of summer fullness, the tall, redbrick mansion blocks glowing under a fingernail moon.

I close my eyes and inhale the scent from the park on my right, which is shrouded in eerie darkness now, at this time of night.

'*I can't believe you.*' I say it out loud to myself. I can't believe how you could have got it so wrong. Fucked up so monumentally.

I've spent my whole life resisting being sucked under by love, shadow boxing rather than being hit in the face because I was scared of the pain, and then I choose to do it with a married man. I surrender everything for someone I can never have and who probably never wanted me. Not really.

In some deluded way, I thought that telling Martin I was seeing someone would be all very big of me. It would give him the message it was never going to happen between us. I never considered that him being appalled that I was seeing a married man would overshadow any sort of effort to 'do the right thing' by me. If both Lexi and Martin think sleeping with someone else's husband is so wrong then maybe they're right. No, they *are* right. The question is, can I even pull myself away?

I turn left down Prince Albert Street towards home. It's surprisingly quiet this close to the river side of Battersea at this time of night, just the faint coo of a wood pigeon and the odd, half-hearted rev of a black-cab's engine as it trundles down the deserted streets.

I'll just pop into the Spar, I think, buy a pint of milk so I can have a cup of tea when I get home, but just as I am going in, I hear a familiar voice.

'Hey, Caroline.'

I notice the shoes first: grubby, red Converse, the laces undone. I look up. It's Wayne, wearing the oily, out-of-shape jumper and carrying a loaf of white bread and a Spar plastic bag.

'Hi,' I say. There are those eyes again: such an unusual pale-green colour flecked with black. I self-consciously put my hand to my face – this is the last person I want to see when I'm looking like crap, my head too full of Martin to have a polite conversation.

'So what are you . . .?' We both start to say then laugh, nervously.

'I just met a friend at the Latchmere.'

He peers at me, concerned.

'Are you all right?' he says.

'Yes, I'm fine, anyway, um . . . *Wine*?' I say, indicating the bag he's holding, which is clinking now, next to his leg. 'Quiet night in?'

'Yeah, I got some news, today. I got a job. In Sheffield. I'm trying to decide whether to take it.'

Something funny happens; my heart takes an unexpected little dive, so small and unexpected that I don't even recognize it.

'Sheffield, hey? Wow, that's a long way. So what's the job?'

'Web design, back doing what I used to do. It'd mean an end to the novel writing and the boat and all this,' he says, looking around him. 'But I don't know if I can turn it down. It's regular money, a job, and these are scary times . . .'

My mind is blank. For a minute, I don't know what to say.

'Well, I guess you have to take it then.'

His eyebrows flicker. Did I say the wrong thing?

242

He smiles. 'Yeah, I guess so,' he says. 'Can't wait for ever for a break. Hanging around a boat, no fixed income, pretending to be some sort of tortured artiste!'

I laugh. I don't want to stop the conversation here, but I've run out of words, of energy. So I say:

'Nope, I guess you might be waiting for ever.'

'Exactly,' he says. 'Well . . .'

'Yeah . . .'

'I'd better get going. There's a vast quantities of wine to be got through, life affirming decisions to be made.' He touches my arm. 'See you then.'

'Yeah, have a good one, um . . . let me know when you might be going.'

Then he kisses me on the cheek and he walks off towards Battersea Bridge, leaving me standing outside the Spar trying to remember what I was getting.

When I get home, to a still, dark house, Lexi in bed, I make myself a cup of tea and turn on my computer. In my inbox, there's an email. It's from Wayne.

Dear Caroline,

I hope I didn't scare you, jumping out from nowhere like that. I, myself, can think of far worse people than you to meet on a dark street corner but you may not feel the same way, and for that, I apologize. Anyway, it occurred to me whilst I was rambling on, no doubt nonsensically, that you'd make the perfect first reader for my book. Just so you know, I've not shown it to anyone and oscillate between having the most amazing dreams that I win the Booker prize (I know, I know!) and then waking up in a cold sweat, thinking I just wasted a year on something that's total shite. There doesn't seem much in between, but I came to the conclusion that I should at least get a second opinion. So, do your worst. Or just press delete, if you don't have time and I'll try and track down another poor, unwilling soul. BTW It's teenage fiction.

Yours

W. F. Campbell (do you think just the initials work?)

X

I smile – he was amusing – and click on the attachment.

Love is a Battlefield: Kevin Hart's Reports From the Frontline of Love

I liked the title – even if it was a bit of a mouthful. *Love is a Battlefield*, eh? Clearly, Pat Benatar references. I approved wholeheartedly.

I open it and randomly start reading halfway down the page.

There had to be a way to get Lucy Briers back. What did Ryan Kaye have that I didn't? Despite a dad who owned a carpet company (big wows – my dad laid carpets) and a face like Emilio Estevez (I couldn't see it myself. I thought he had more of a look of Keith Chegwin). Then that night, when Mum and me were having tea – Findus Crispy Pancakes – my brother Daz brought home a book about Arnold Schwarzenegger and it all became clear. Muscles. That's what Ryan Kaye didn't have that I did – well not yet, but I would. The next day, we bought weights from Argos, some protein drinks from the pound shop and there commenced our intense regime. Three hours per day, every day of the school holidays, we'd workout in the back garden following the Arnold Schwarzenegger book for inspiration. Mum would hang the washing out, occasionally tutting at us in our underpants. But I didn't care; Lucy Briers would soon be mine. She'd be eating off my rippling torso in no time.

It's only when I look at the clock, that I realize it's 1 a.m. and that I've been reading for an hour and a half and I think I'm already a little bit in love with Kevin Hart.

244

CHAPTER TWENTY-FIVE

Antoine eyes me from behind reception, his ice-blue eyes darting up from his computer screen, like I'm a child that he needs to keep a check on.

I sit on the Dali-esque, high-backed red velvet sofa, clutching my overnight bag and smile back at him, weakly. I take my mobile out of my bag – just to look like I'm doing something really – and check my mobile again, but nothing: not a text, not a missed call. Just me sitting here, switching it off and on again in case there's something wrong with it when the only thing that's wrong with anything is my head. What the hell am I doing here?

'Every-sing is okay, Madame Steele?' Antoine enquires eventually, after I have given him my hundredth fake smile.

'Yes, all okay,' I say, but the risk of tears is becoming more real by the second. Just one more sympathetic smile from a camp, French concierge and I will dissolve, start wailing like a banshee.

Today, Wednesday, is the 'book club'(whatever the hell that means any more) and I have been sitting here, in the foyer of the Malmaison Hotel, waiting for Toby for twenty minutes. Idiot.

Part of me, the part labelled 'do the right thing', not to

mention 'self-preservation', decided last night, after the evening with Martin, that I wasn't going to come today, that I just wasn't going to show up. But here I am, here I bloody well am, stuck to the seat even though every logical molecule of me is saying: 'Go. Go now! Remove your backside from the chair and walk out of the door!'

He's not going to come, I know it. But I still can't move. Love is a law unto itself – why did I never see that? It couldn't really give a monkey's about rules, logic or what is right. Christ, I'm no better than an addict robbing his own mother for his next fix.

'You are waiting for Monsieur Steele?' says Antoine, suddenly.

And he's not even fucking here. I have made myself feel like shit for absolutely nothing.

'How did you guess?' I reply with a weak smile.

I was going to end it anyway, that was never in question. I just wanted to do it in person, in the flesh. Okay, that's bollocks, I wanted to *touch* his flesh just one more time.

But he's not coming and, as the minutes tick by and Antoine's sympathetic glances become more intense, I feel even more moronic sitting here with my overnight bag.

With each of the three relocated book clubs at the Malmasion, the contents have dwindled; as each new hope has been dashed, my efforts have waned. The first time we came, I brought three lingerie collections – pretty, slutty, sporty – like this was a Miss World Contest – four pairs of shoes (did I think I was going to get a chance to change during the night?) and all the oral hygiene products I could lay my hands on, including a preview bottle of Minty Me breath freshener, which Toby thought was a bit sad, like mixing work with pleasure, but which I pointed out wasn't exactly the same as me bringing a jar of mango chutney if say Patak's were my client.

I think of us at that first 'on location' book club here at the Malmaison and think how different the whole picture was then: us giggling, him holding my hand, so dry and warm, us collapsing into giggles in the lift at Antoine's absurdly strong French accent.

Antoine must see the tears fill my eyes because he gets up and walks over to me with that absurd, camp walk of his. It's like Antoine is one of those caricature drawings that Toby got done in Brighton, but a walking, talking, real-life version.

He sits down next to me and moves in conspiratorially.

'Are you okay?'

'Couldn't be better,' I say, thinking, ground, swallow up. It's so obvious what's happening here. This is so humiliating.

'He is not coming?' he asks, looking at me from under enormous, doll-like black lashes.

'No,' I say, looking at the ground. 'It doesn't look like it, anyway.'

Antoine nods slowly, then inhales dramatically through his long, equine nose.

'*Écoute*,' he says, touching my arm. 'I 'ope you don't sink I am prying. I certainly make no judgement about ze way people conduct zer private relationships within the walls of zis 'otel – God *knows*, I've tarted myself around Lond-on.'

A nervous giggle escapes, then, again, the threat of tears.

'But I 'ave a lot of experience of men,' he continues, keeping his voice down. 'Probably more zan you . . .'

'Oh definitely more than me.'

'And one develope a sixth sense for these things, zat's all I'm saying,' he says, touching my arm. 'And I am not sure that Monsieur Steele – 'e is not Monsieur Steele, is he?'

I shake my head. 'No, he is not Monsieur Steele.'

'I am not sure 'e is . . . what is it you English say? A good . . .?'

'A *good* egg?'

'Yes,' he says. 'One of those.'

Just then, there's a beep as a text arrives and I nearly jump out of my seat. I look at Antoine who pats me on the knee and goes back to reception.

I press 'read'.

Please let it be him. Let it be Toby saying he's so sorry to have kept me waiting but he's been stuck on the tube, there was a fatality on the line and he'll be with me any minute.

It's not. Instead, there are just seven words. I know because I read every one over and over again.

Sorry can't make it. Something came up. x

It's been four days since Brighton and today was my first day back in the office. I hadn't noticed anything too different. I'd felt reassured after the 'I love you' that things were okay, *more* than okay. That things had moved on past me having to be paranoid. Even though he hadn't answered the question I'd asked him about loving Rachel, I'd hoped I was safe. Clearly, nothing could have been further from the truth.

I look over at Antoine, my eyes swimming with tears, but he's busy talking to a guest, so I just get up quietly, put the phone in my bag and walk outside.

It's still broad daylight, the air sweet and warm, the faint hum of mopeds everywhere, the city so alive and I am here, with nothing to do for the evening. I stand there for a second, thinking what to do next, then, without putting too much thought into it, I press 'call'. What the hell – I've lost my dignity now, what else is there to lose? I can't believe he thinks he can just send me a text like that and get away with it. I mean, 'something came up'? That is so lame. What 'thing' ever comes up right at the last minute that means he can't at least speak to me in person? Helpfully, as his phone rings out, I run through these possibilities in my head: Rachel's found out, he's seeing someone else, he's decided he just doesn't want to see me any more. I decide this line of thinking

248

is not altogether healthy or helpful. He doesn't pick up anyway, so I give up.

I walk towards Blackfriars Bridge, the most beautiful bridge in London if you ask me, the lights of the Southbank twinkling, my case trundling behind me on the tarmac like a child being dragged home from a party that their mother got the wrong date for.

CHAPTER TWENTY-SIX

It's Monday – five days after I was stood up at the Malmaison by Toby – and the night of the Annual Product Sales Awards. I'm up for Salesperson of the Year in the health and beauty market section – get me! Janine put me in for it, which is high praise indeed from the Iron Lady in Joseph Trousers. Up until a few weeks ago, I would have been pathetically excited about it, too, but recent events have put a dampener on things. For the first time in my life, I am failing to get a high from work. A potential award for selling breath freshener doesn't quite seem to be cutting it any more.

Thoughts of Toby are taking up all my energy. It's ridiculous, an affliction, a kind of OCD. He's the first thing I think about when I wake up and the last thing I think about when I go to sleep. When I'm drying my hair, I'm thinking about him, when I'm talking to someone on the phone about dental floss, I'm thinking about him. When I'm designing a pie-chart on PowerPoint, I'm attributing sections to him: sixty per cent chance he's still in love with Rachel, twenty per cent chance he does actually love me, two per cent chance he'll ever leave his wife. When I'm not thinking about him, I'm thinking about them together and it's driving me *insane*.

The day after he stood me up, I questioned him about it in the office.

'So what was this "something" that came up?' I asked him as he tried to walk past me in the corridor. He looked tired and stressed – maybe he was ill. Damn it, I even cared about him when he was being a prize cock.

'Are you all right?' I asked.

'Yeah, fine,' he said, touching my arm. I felt a murmur of desire. 'Listen, I'm really sorry about last night.'

'You should be. Forty minutes I waited there, Toby. Whatever it was – an unmissable episode of *Glee*, sudden attack of food poisoning, attack of cowardice, perhaps?' He didn't even flinch. 'You could have at least called me.'

'Rachel wasn't well and to leave her would have just looked dodgy. I was annoyed, to tell you the truth. I was desperate to see you.' He got hold of my hand. 'It's been over a week since I snogged you, Steeley, do you know that?'

God, I wish he wouldn't say things like that.

'What was wrong with her?'

'Migraine.'

'Right.' Likely story.

'She gets really bad ones: flashing lights, sickness, the works. She was off work all day.'

I frown. This didn't really add up.

'Right. So if she was off work all day, why didn't you tell me earlier that you probably wouldn't make it?'

Toby gave a short, hurt laugh.

'Oh my God, you don't believe me, do you?'

'Yes,' I lied. 'Yes, I believe you. I think. Actually, I don't know what to believe any more. I just don't know why you had me make the journey all the way there, sit in the foyer waiting for you like a total lemon, then text me forty minutes after you were supposed to arrive?'

He sighed and rubbed his forehead.

'Oh God, I know, I know . . .' He sighed. 'She was being very irritating, to be honest. One minute she was saying go, I'll be fine. The next she was flailing about on the bed, whingeing for me to stay with her. It just got later and later.'

I still wasn't convinced.

That was on Thursday. Now it's Monday and Toby staggers out of the Men's Room of Grosvenor House on Park Lane just as I'm walking to the bar. There's a red wine stain down the front of his shirt and his flies are undone.

'All *right*, Steeley. Nice frock.'

He leans in to give me a kiss on the cheek but misses so I get a Lucky Strike flavoured slobber in the ear instead.

'Where've you been?' I say. I have to shout over the noise of a thousand overexcited sales people already half-cut on cheap plonk. 'I've been looking for you all over. I wanted to practice my speech on you.'

'Me and a few of the lads went to the pub first; couldn't face five hours of this shit.'

'Oh,' I say, feeling ever so slightly hurt and idiotic standing here in my full-length gown like the Annual Product Sales Awards are actually the Oscars.

Toby loses his footing slightly and staggers backwards. God, he's pissed.

'Anyway,' he slurs. 'Giz a little sample of this speech, then.'

'I've kept it quite short,' I say, perking up. 'Just outlining how Schumacher and I negotiated, my strategy, that sort of thing.'

Toby grins, his eyelids heavy, then breaks into a cruel little laugh. 'Wow, get you, Little Miss Confident. You really reckon you've nailed this, don't you?'

I feel myself go red. Ever since I was nominated for this award, Toby has behaved like a total arse. At first, I brushed off his one-word 'lickarse' emails and his 'you're so spawny' comments as harmless banter. Back then, I was grateful of any sort of banter. But now it's just rude, frankly. I'm beginning to think Janine's right.

'I think you might be just jealous,' I say. 'And really drunk. Oh.' I reach over and patronizingly arrange his quiff, which has gone fluffy and looks rather ridiculous now. 'And I think you'll find your flies are undone.'

I stride off, eyes squeezed shut. That was good, Steele! I think. Don't ruin it by turning back. Deep down though, as I climb the stairs to the top tier of the Grosvenor House Ballroom, where a queue of other girls poured into shiny, satin dresses wait at the bar, I feel a horrid spread of disappointment in the pit of my stomach, a pang of humiliation that I can't shake. Since last week's book club that never happened, since Brighton really, I see it now, I can't deny that Toby's been distinctly off with me. Not much in the way of flirtatious emails, no brushing hands in the corridors or clinches in the kitchen, not even any pen throwing in the last few days. In fact, by the way he set up almost all his meetings out of the office last week, you'd think he was avoiding me.

You might also think I'd be pleased, that it would make things easier, given that I'm going to dump him soon. Soon. Very, very soon.

But it's far easier said than done and a tiny part of me (scrap that, every last cell of me) has been holding out for a miracle, clinging to the hope that at some point, perhaps tonight when he saw me in my off-the-shoulder Coast dress that I now feel overdressed in, or up on stage, collecting my award, he'd really fall a little bit in love with me. He'd choose me over her. But now he's so drunk and clearly so unimpressed by it all that it would be a miracle if he even made it until my category without collapsing in a pool of his own vomit. Was it too much to expect him to be a bit proud of me?

Still, now's not the time to think about all this, I tell myself, standing here in the queue. This is work, your big night. The night you've been focusing on all year. So where are your powers of compartmentalization now, Caroline Steele? What happened to the girl who was able to separate her life like laundry, just a few months ago? Now it feels like everything's in a gigantic chaotic heap that, rather than sort out, I just keep adding to.

I take another glass of champagne from the tray of free ones laid out on the bar. This has got to be the last one, I tell myself, if I'm not going to be tripping up on stage, or doing a Judy Finnigan, my bra hanging out for all to see. The ceremony starts in fifteen minutes.

'I hope that's going to be your last, missy.'

I turn around to find Health and Safety Heather, resplendent in an enormous crushed-velvet dress and bolero ensemble, evidently reading my mind.

'We're counting on you. You're our only hope.'

'Oh thanks, but honestly, please,' I say, modestly, but inside I'm quietly confident. My pitch to the judges went well and Janine made noises that I was definitely in for the running – maybe I deserve some good luck?

'I'm serious!' Heather shouts, grabbing my arm. 'That award has got your name on.'

I've come to rather like Heather of late; we've bonded over our monthly fire-marshal meetings and First Aid courses – oddly, they've been light relief from the tension of the Toby and I situation – and if you can get past the fact that Heather is the most interfering woman you're ever likely to meet, the sort who thinks nothing of asking you about your bowel movements in front of your colleagues, you see that she has a heart of gold.

'Come on, you.' Heather takes me by the arm, away from the bar, and we weave our way through the forty or so numbered tables all laid with crisp white tablecloths and floral centrepieces, candles casting everyone in a flattering light.

This is my first Annual Product Sales Ceremony – in past years, for one reason or another I've not been able to attend, and it hadn't much bothered me because I'd never been up for an award before. Already I can see that the tribes are out in force. The lads from Leyton-Blanche – basically a load of pissheads who sell lager to the supermarkets. The Reimans crew, distinctive if only because they're all female – they sell disposable nappies and other baby products to the supermarkets. And then the banking lot – the 'wanker bankers', as Shona calls them, the WBs being the epitome of everything she hates – getting stuck into the champers before anyone's even won anything.

We wave at all the SCD clan as we approach our table – a number seventy-seven sticking out of the middle. 'All the sevens, seventy-seven, this is our lucky night,' says Heather with what I'm beginning to think is a worrying level of confidence. Still, my name place is next to Janine.

'They always put you next to the boss if they think you're going to win,' Shona said with typical dryness when we arrived. 'It's so that when they call your name out, they can gush that you've always been their prodigy and make you feel guilty that you should spend your prize money on booze for the table rather than keep it for yourself.'

I rolled my eyes. Shona was such a cynic. If you ever wanted honesty, Shona was your woman.

Everyone's sitting at the SCD table now, and the seating plan is like this: me, Janine to my right and after her Shona. Lexi is on the left of me, sporting her new, tight purple dress from Jane Norman and the highest, most brilliant shoes you've ever seen. She looks gorgeous.

I watch her as she chats to Charles, opposite. I see how poised she is, how a little frown line develops in her forehead as she listens intently. Lexi has grown-up so much, I think.

My little sister. My very own confidante. She's been more excited than me about this event. I feel like I owe her. Oh God, please let me live up to her expectations, at least tonight.

So, there's Lexi, followed by Heather and Marta and after that, in order of drunkenness, the boys: Toupee Dom, hairpiece combed for the event, Charles from marketing, and then Toby, who is wide-eyed and seems to be finding Marta enthralling for the first time in his life, which tells me he may have had something more than a wee when he went to the toilets just before.

The lights dim. 'You all right?' whispers Janine in my ear. 'Remember, if you go up – well, *when* you go up – take a second to look straight ahead so that they can take your photo for the internal magazine, okay?'

I feel a bubble of anticipation rise in my throat.

Mine is the third category. Before me is 'fast-selling consumer product of the year' then the 'financial products' section won by a bloke from the wanker bankers table with hair like Simon Le Bon.

Jimmy Carr is compering, but most of his jokes fall embarrassingly flat on the ears of a straight sales audience, particularly the nappy girls on the table next to us. Something tells me that deadpan, wrong humour, isn't really their thing. I look over at Toby. His face seems to be getting redder and sweatier by the second, his voice louder and more obnoxious. He looks like he's going to combust. He heckles Carr until Carr makes a joke at his expense – something about him being a fucking Eton Mess. Everyone laughs, except me.

Please don't get chucked out, Toby, I plead silently, or heckle me or spoil my moment because, if you do, I don't think I'll be able to forgive you.

And then suddenly it's my category.

'Now for Health and Beauty . . .' announces Carr. 'And the shortlist is . . .'

There's the familiar drum roll music as he gestures to the huge screen behind him.

MACKENZIE BOOTH FROM GLAXOSMITHKLINE!

Mackenzie's grin bounces onto the screen and his table goes wild.

GSK are renowned for sweeping awards.

'We'll nail him, no fucking problem,' Janine whispers in my ear. My lips break into an involuntary smile.

CAROLINE STEELE FROM SKIDMORE-COLT-DAVIS!

The table vibrates as everyone whoops and cheers and bangs the table with their fists and I grin like an idiot. Maybe that award would hit the mark after all.

'Go Caro! Go Caro!' shouts Lexi, shaking her hands from side to side like she's shaking a cocktail. I smile, but I'm not taking it in, I'm too busy looking over at Toby – what the hell is he doing? Taking a Lucky Strike out of his cigarette packet and putting it behind his ear? Oh God. If he leaves the room to smoke now I will kill him.

'And last but certainly not least . . .' Carr holds the room in suspense for a second before calling out the name of the final contender.

RACHEL DELANEY FROM HUNTERHEWITT!

What? My heart thuds horribly. I stare open-mouthed at the screen, at the honey-haired girl with the beautiful, wide smile that I know I recognize, but I can't quite compute.

Rachel? Rachel was up for the same award as me and Toby didn't *tell* me? He'd known – he *must* have known! Their marriage wasn't so bad that she wouldn't have told him – I mean, he looked after her when she had the migraine, for God's sake!

I feel my face burn. I look over at Toby but his seat is empty and I can just see him flitting between the tables as he makes his way to the exit.

257

Janine nudges me in the side.

'Remember to smile,' she says, but I can't reply. If I speak I might cry.

'And the winner is . . .'

I can literally feel my heart threatening to burst out of the Coast dress now.

'Make sure your dress isn't stuck in your knickers,' Lexi whispers loudly and everyone laughs but I can't say anything, my lips won't move.

The room falls unbearably silent save for the rustle as Carr opens the golden envelope.

'. . . RACHEL DELANEY FROM HUNTERHEWITT FOR HER CAMPAIGN WITH . . .'

I don't hear the rest of it – it's drowned out by applause and shrieks from Rachel's table, anyway, where she is being mobbed by a throng of colleagues. She eventually breaks free and walks to the front. She's wearing one of those trendy, body-con dresses, black with shimmering oyster-pink panels, which looks like you're wearing your underwear on the outside. It clings to her perfect hourglass figure as she sashays onto the stage, her stacked heels showing off her toned, lean, calf muscles, her blonde hair pulled back tight to show off her cheekbones.

'Is that Toby's wife?' I hear Charles say to Toupee Dom. 'Well, she's a *very* pretty girl, isn't she? Hasn't he done well?'

Nobody except Charles is clapping at our table; people are mumbling about the injustice of it all, 'so unfair', 'better luck next time'. But the words are like the last bit of air escaping from a withering balloon, a tape running out of battery. And if I look at anyone I'll cry, and I can't cry here, I must *not* cry here. So I stare straight ahead, clapping a freeze-framed smile on my face.

Toby is nowhere to be seen.

* * *

Shona and Lexi are being so sweet, it's unbearable. Despite my efforts to control myself, I am a mass of snot and tears, standing at the bar throwing vodka down my neck.

'It's not the fact I didn't win,' I'm snivelling between gulps of air.

'We know it's not,' soothes Shona. 'We know it's not that.'

'It's just the fact he didn't tell me – and he must have known – why didn't he tell me?'

Shona grabs hold of my arms and makes me look at her. 'Coz he's a knob-end, darling,' she says. 'A total A grade cunt.'

Like I've said, you could always count on Shona not to mince her words and at that moment, like many more before them, I really loved her.

Lexi's standing behind her, her eyes full of compassion and something else too – possibly fear. Poor kid. It must be like watching your mum lose it.

'He probably knew it would be hideous, you being in the same room as, you know . . .' Shona grimaces. 'His *wife*.' Bless Shona. She's trying so hard not to spell it out, not to bring up the small matter that she warned me this would happen; that I should have ended it yonks ago. 'So he decided not to deal with it at all and just got wasted instead.'

'Yeah, I reckon he's been shitting himself about this for weeks,' adds Lexi. 'He was off his face before we even got here.'

I look up at them. Maybe they were right. Maybe this is why he didn't turn up to the Malmaison last week, why he's been so funny about this awards thing all along. It would kind of make sense.

Shona hands me a napkin and I blow my nose then throw it dramatically onto the floor.

'Fucking hell, look at me! I'm like a cliché of the bad loser at a work awards do. Pissed and crying in a crap OTT dress.'

Shona rolls her eyes.

'Now everyone's going to think I'm crying because I didn't bloody win. How embarrassing is that?'

Lexi folds her arms and sighs at me, all matter-of-factly.

'I wouldn't worry about that,' she says. 'Janine's done one. Probably gone home to defrost or something. Heather and Charles have disappeared for some heavy petting in a darkened corner and the rest of 'em are making far bigger tits of themselves than you could ever hope to, dancing to Phil Collins. So I reckon you're all right.'

At that moment, I loved her, too.

Shona and Lexi go back downstairs and I wander off to the Ladies' to try to bring some semblance of normality to my face.

I try Toby's mobile again but really – what's the point? He's gone. Off his head somewhere. He doesn't love me, and he probably never has, I just have to stomach it. So I'm standing in front of the mirror, phone clamped to my ear with one hand; the other wiping away mascara with a bit of tissue when a familiar face appears in the mirror next to me.

'Hello, Caroline.' She peers at me, just to check it is me. 'Oh, *honey*!' The genuine compassion on Rachel's face kills me. 'Oh God, you're not upset about . . .?'

'What? God no!' I force a laugh; this was *hideous*. 'No, no, just um . . . something else . . . PMT. Over-emotional. Drunk too much.' She looks at me – so kindly, so genuine, I want to thump myself in my stupid swollen face and make it swell for a very long time.

'So been there, honey,' she says. 'All a bit too much?'

I smile, weakly. *Just run now, Caroline. Make your excuses, leave now.*

She goes into the toilet, reels off some toilet roll and hands it to me.

'It's all a fix anyway,' she says. 'All a load of bollocks,

these awards, that's why Toby's buggered off, he always hates these ceremonies.'

I dab at my face and look at her from blurry, tear-filled eyes.

'Congratulations, anyway. You really deserved it,' I say. 'And I love your dress.'

She shrugs. 'It's just an old Top Shop number. Bit tight to be honest. Haven't been able to eat all night.'

Why the hell did she have to be so nice?

'Do you fancy a drink?' she says. 'Everyone from Hewitt's is pissed out of their heads and I can't really be bothered going back to our table.'

No, I think, no I do not. I want to turn around, run home, shut my door, drink my own weight in vodka, and not wake up for a week.

Two minutes later, we are sitting down with drinks.

She puts her hand on my arm. 'Seriously, hun,' she says. 'I hope you're not upset about the awards because I really couldn't give a toss. This . . .' she holds the award up. Some crap glass, pyramid-shaped thing. 'It means bugger all, in the grand scheme of things.'

I take a large gulp of wine; if I was going to get through this I needed to be as drunk as her, if not more.

'You're very sweet,' I say, 'you're really sweet. But it's not that, really. I know it must look like that. You must think I'm a total sad case!'

'Not at all,' she says. 'Actually, I really like you, Caroline. It's official!' she says, holding her glass up to chink with mine. 'Toby was always going on about you and now I can see why.'

This was *hell*.

'I feel like you're a woman's woman, you know? Like I can tell you anything.'

I nod weakly.

'And I'll tell you why I don't give a shit about this pap award and why you shouldn't either,' she says, taking another huge gulp of her wine. She was drunk; I could see that now, her pretty hazel eyes trying to focus on me. She smiles at me, sadly. 'I lost a baby last week. Last Wednesday, I had a miscarriage. Kind of puts things in perspective . . .'

At first the facts don't compute, my instincts are just to hug her – which I do, manically and tightly. But then slowly, like the horrid first moments of reality when you finally come to after a drunken, misspent night, all the bits fall into place. A baby. Their baby. My lover's baby. I was fucking Toby when his wife was *pregnant*? *He was fucking me when he knew she was pregnant?* Like a wife driven mad with suspicion, riffling possessed through her husband's wallet, I riffle through my memory. Last Wednesday. That was book club night. 'Something came up,' he said. Something came *up*? He was in hospital with his wife as she lost their baby – that's what he calls 'something came up'?

She doesn't register my horror – course she doesn't – she just keeps talking.

'Basically, we'd been trying for ages . . .' I'm watching her mouth move but I can't hear the words. 'I'm thirty-nine next month – I'm five years older than Toby – he's my toy boy! Don't know if he's ever told you that?'

My head moves but my face is rigid.

'I knew time was ticking when we got together and I've always wanted kids, it's everything to me. So we were trying, we'd been trying for something like eighteen months and nothing, I'd begun to think that was it, forget it. We had tests, nothing came up, we were doing all the ovulation tests, I gave up drinking. Our sex life was basically reduced to me peeing on sticks and sticking my legs in the air after sex. Then it happened.'

'When?' It just shoots out. I'm still riffling through the memories, putting everything together.

262

She narrows her eyes.

'Oh, well, sixteen weeks ago to be exact . . . Then, when I was away in Scotland on a business weekend and Toby was in Brighton – I called him because I'd started to bleed and I was terrified . . .'

I feel a trickle of sickening realization drip down my spine. Brighton. The hotel. The phone call he took from her whilst I was looking at my reflection in the bathroom mirror – it was all coming back to me. How jittery he was when he came off the phone, how he was desperate for sex, how he told me he *loved* me. When all the time it was guilt and fear driving him, and I was nothing more than a packet of cigarettes, a double shot of gin, something to relieve the anxiety.

She doesn't stop talking.

'As you can imagine, we were thrilled – well, I was thrilled – Toby, I don't know, he's gone off track a bit lately, and I worry I've pushed him into it.'

She could say that again. Poor Rachel. Poor, poor girl . . .

'The bleeding stopped for a bit but then, last Wednesday morning, I started to get cramps and then to bleed really heavily and then . . .'

She stops, catches herself.

'Sorry, you must think I'm insane, I'm sorry, like what is this pissed mad woman, oversharing with me for?'

'No, no!'

'It's just I wanted you to know, even though I know you're not upset about the award thing, that it truly means nothing to me. Truly, I couldn't give a shit. I don't care about work, I just want a baby, to be a family, to be happy. That's what I'm getting at really. You know?'

'Yeah, I do,' I said, my eyes filling with tears.

And I did. Rachel and I had that in common.

CHAPTER TWENTY-SEVEN

Now I know what I know, I don't want to drag this on a moment longer. It's like a tumour is lying dormant in me and I just want it out. Toby was not at work the day after the awards or the day after that. Something about 'a heavy cold', Shona said. As if. Heavy hangover more like. News travels fast and everyone in the office knows that big Clive, the managing director of SCD, who made a cameo appearance at the awards on Tuesday, was out in Soho with Toby that night on a massive bender involving copious amounts of drugs and a session in a lap-dancing bar. So, whilst his wife was home alone, mourning the loss of his baby, Toby was no doubt snorting coke whilst some pneumatic blonde writhed between his legs.

Not that I know any of this for sure, since my only means of contacting him during the last forty-eight hours has been by text and, learning from past mistakes – the 'I love you too' text after Brighton and various others including one where I meant to write *I miss kissing you* but I was so drunk I actually wrote 'kicking you', which is apt, really in the circumstances – I have restrained myself to one very dignified one, just asking him to meet me here, today, next to the golden Buddha in Battersea Park.

Anyway, I'm sick of texts. I'm sick of not being fully present because I'm too busy listening out for the beep-beep of my phone and a text from him. I'm sick of thinking about him and not being able to live my life because I'm stuck in this go-between of what I wish something was and what it is. I'm sick of the obsessing about Rachel and occasionally hating her when, ordinarily, she would be someone I'd love as a friend.

That's not me.

It's August now. The first of the trees are yellowing and the river, which has been motionless for so long, the banks bone-dry, is gliding along with a late summer breeze. I look below me, at the sloping, manicured lawn leading to the promenade where couples take an evening stroll, hand in hand along the Thames, and wonder where I went wrong.

Everything in my life that I've worked for, I've got. The GCSEs – ten As no less. What a clever girl. The A levels, the first class degree and the top job in a blue chip company. But love? Love is the only real prize, and no amount of tutoring or sticking your head in books makes you good at that. You have to learn on the job, I get that now.

I've wasted so much time. I'm thirty-two now, more than a third of the way through my life, and I've clung onto the things that are wrong for me, and not grabbed the things that could – if I were brave – *really* make me happy.

I sit down on one of the stone benches at the foot of the statue, tuck my legs beneath me and check my phone to see if Toby's running late, but nothing. I wonder if he already knows what's up. I wonder if Rachel told him she told me.

He's ten minutes late now, but I'm past caring. I love to look at London like this, across the wide, sparkly river, rather than from inside the claustrophobic streets of terraces, from inside my house where I seem to have lived too much of the last decade. I lean back and close my eyes. There's the end of summer in the air – the damp, smokiness again and it feels delicious. I've always loved autumn, that back-to-school feeling, the promise of a new beginning – and this is mine. This is mine.

I look at my phone, fifteen minutes late now. Maybe he's not coming, I think. And then:

'What have you got up your sleeve, Steeley? Bringing me here?' That familiar lisp. He appears from nowhere, kisses me on the cheek. He's wearing long shorts and a pale pink, creased shirt. He's sweating, too. Pure Carlsberg by the smell of him. He sits down beside me, leans back, then takes a Lucky Strike out of his pocket and lights one.

'So,' he says patting my thigh. 'You cool, yeah? You all right? Where's my picnic, anyway, Steeley? Or are we just going for straight *al fresco*?'

He giggles, that public schoolboy giggle that's beginning to make me want to punch him, until he sees my face and the smile fades.

'Everything all right?'

'How's your heavy cold?' I say with the emphasis on 'heavy'.

Toby sniffs, on cue, very un-cold like.

'Seems to be clearing, actually,' he says, taking a long, hard drag on his cigarette. 'This morning was a shocker: bunged-up, sore throat, hacking cough. Tragic.'

I hug my knees, watch a barge as it drags its great weight along the water.

'Gosh, you two really are in the wars, aren't you? You with your heavy cold, Rachel with her migraine.' I'm sniping, I know I am. I don't want to bring Rachel into this but I can't help it. I tilt my head to look at him and he stops, cigarette halfway to his mouth.

'What's that supposed to mean?'

'Oh come on, Toby. We need to talk.'

'Talk?' He strokes my cheek but I shrug him off. 'You've got me all the way here, just to talk?'

I look at him now, that inane grin on his face, and I feel like slapping it, I really do.

'Jesus, Toby. Just stop lying, will you? You're unbelievable.'

He snorts.

'Lying? Lying about what?'

'You weren't ill today, there's nothing wrong with you. Except a very shaky morality and no conscience whatsoever.'

'What's this about?' he says, blowing smoke out sideways.

'You *know* what this is about.'

'Oh for fuck's sake. So I pulled a fucking sicky. So I lied about a cold. Big fucking deal!'

I glare at him. 'You still don't get it, do you?'

'Oh, hang on.' Toby starts jabbing his finger at me. 'I get it, I know what this is about. You've been talking to Clive, haven't you?'

Like I said, unbelievable.

'I don't give a shit about Clive.'

'No, but you give a shit about what we got up to, don't you? You're totally pissed about that?' He smokes the last of his fag and stubs it out. 'So we went to a lap-dancing bar.' It doesn't mean anything. It's just a laugh. I didn't snog anyone, or pay for sex, or put my head in between anyone's tits.'

My feet slap the hard concrete in frustration.

'God, you're a dickhead.'

Toby laughs.

'It's a lap-dancing bar, not a brothel, Steeley, and who are you now, anyway? My wife?'

I stop. I try to speak but my mouth just opens wider, nothing comes out.

'No, I'm not,' I manage eventually, standing up. 'Thank God. But I sincerely pity the woman who is.'

267

The minute I start walking away, I regret it. I haven't finished the argument, haven't said even half of what I wanted to say but I am so incensed I couldn't sit there any longer. Thankfully, Toby comes after me, I can hear his stupid deck shoes slapping the promenade where I'm striding off now, towards Chelsea Bridge.

'Look, I'm sorry, okay?' he shouts from behind me. 'I'm sorry I said that. I'm a twat, you're right. But Monday night was totally innocent, seriously and I think you're a beautiful woman, Caroline. And I – I have very strong feelings for you, in fact I love you, I do, it's just . . .'

I turn around and wrap my cardigan around me, tightly, in exasperation.

'It's nothing to do with the bloody lap-dancing bar! Just stop lying, Toby. Christ. What's wrong with you? Do you think I was born yesterday?'

He stops, lets his hands, which were placed theatrically on top of his head as he squeezed his eyes shut – a gesture I can't help thinking he's seen in films – down by his side.

'You don't love me, Toby, you never have,' I say, half laughing, it's so obvious to me now. 'You love your wife, not that you behave like you do most of the time. And don't say you can love two people at the same time because I'll hit you.'

'But I – I do love you,' he says, walking towards me.

'Do you? It's funny how you only ever say that when I'm walking away or not having sex with you, isn't it? Well, anyway, it's tough if you do because I don't love you any more, and maybe I never did, maybe I was just infatuated.' Then I hit him with it. 'I know about the miscarriage, Toby.'

His smile slides right off his smug little face.

'How?'

'Because Rachel told me.'

'Rachel?'

'Yes, Rachel. You know? Your wife? The one who was at

the awards ceremony and won an award that you didn't even tell me she was up for – not that either of us give a crap about that now. The one you left on Monday night to go on a two-night bender, five days after she lost your baby?'

Toby is speechless, for the first time of knowing him, he doesn't know what to say.

'Do you know what?' I say. It's like, I've started now and I may as well go hell for leather. There's really nothing left: no pride, no love, not even much hurt any more, so I might as well let it all out. 'I'd almost convinced myself that what we were doing was okay. That it was okay to sleep with someone's husband. Rachel was just an annoying woman you talked about, and that didn't matter because you were going to leave her anyway – ha! How deluded was I? But then I met her, and I saw what a lovely person she is and how ungrateful you are, actually, to take a woman like that for granted. And then I felt extra terrible, and I beat myself up so much. But I was madly in love with you by then, God only knows why! And for some mental reason, I still clung onto the hope that you'd leave her; that somehow, all the things you said about her, all that stuff about her being self-obsessed, work-obsessed, never giving you enough attention, all that bollocks, were true and you'd decide you wanted me. But all the time, all the time we were meeting for the book club, having baths together at the Malmaison, fucking, frolicking about in the sea in Brighton, you were trying to realize your dreams of becoming a family. But do you know what I think?'

'No,' he says. 'But I'm guessing you're going to tell me anyway.'

'I don't think they were *your* dreams, I think they were only Rachel's. I think you were shit scared. Rachel's thirty-eight, smart, knows exactly what she wants. She wanted a baby before it was too late but at five years younger, and

269

about three decades in mental age, you just couldn't hack the commitment.'

'I – I don't know about that, I think that's a bit unfair!'

'But listen, Toby, that would have been okay on its own. There's no shame in being scared of a major thing like having a baby if you'd have gone and talked to your wife about it, but you didn't. You had an affair.'

Toby jabs a finger at me.

'Hey now, so did you! It takes two to tango, you know.'

'Oh, I know that,' I say. People walking along the promenade are giving us a wide berth, staring at us, but I don't care. 'And don't I fucking well regret it? Don't I wish more than anything in the world that I hadn't? I am certainly not blameless, but you? Toby, come *on*! What sort of man has an affair with someone when he's going for fertility tests with his wife? When his wife is *pregnant*?'

Toby flops his head back, he can't bear this, I know he can't. Like a child being told off, he just wants to put his fingers in his ears and get to the next fun part, for it all to go away.

'Tell me the truth about something, Toby. Just for once in your life, try to tell the truth.' I say. Rachel's already confirmed it but I want to hear it from him. 'That day in Brighton, when we were in the hotel room and Rachel called. She told you she was bleeding, didn't she?'

'Um, yes.'

'And then you wanted sex because you felt guilty and wanted a distraction and then, when I wouldn't have sex with you, you told me you loved me but you didn't mean it, did you? That's why you freaked out and ignored me when I texted that I loved you too. Do you know how used and shit that made me feel?'

'Oh, Steeley, but I did love you . . .' Toby walks closer towards me.

270

'And stop calling me Steeley.'

'Okay, Caroline, then,' he says, pathetically. 'Caroline, I do love you, I'm just . . .' he screws his eyes up and slaps his forehead with the palm of his hand dramatically – again something that reminds me of a gesture in a film. 'I'm so confused.'

I shake my head and start walking again. He really was fucking unbelievable.

'Course you're confused!' I shout behind me. 'You're confused because you want your cake and to eat it too. But I can't be shared, Toby. I am good enough to be taken whole, thanks very much.'

We're climbing up the steps to Chelsea Bridge now, Toby trotting behind me, trying to keep up.

'Look, I'm sorry. I can see how I might have come over like a prick in all this, and I don't want you to think I'm a prick because I'm not, really I'm not.'

I stop and turn to him. He's sweating and out of breath now. He looks a right state, and for a second I have the gratifying feeling of not finding him attractive any more.

'I'm sure you're not. Not all of you, anyway. Maybe your little toe has some integrity. But you've behaved so much like one in the past couple of months, Toby. I mean, all that stuff you said about Rachel having a migraine, calling her irritating and saying she was "whingeing" when she was in hospital having a *miscarriage*? Having sex with me when your wife was worried she might be losing the baby – *your* baby? How low can you stoop? How can you possibly expect me to have any feelings, any respect left for you at all?'

I start walking up the steps again. When we get to the top, I keep walking but Toby stands on the bridge, shouting over the traffic at me.

'But I was scared! I didn't know what to tell you. I didn't want to lose you.'

271

I turn around. He looks suddenly small now, dwarfed by the enormous bridge that stretches behind him and the huge, sweeping sky the colour of blood-orange.

'But you *have* to lose me, don't you get it? We can't *do* this any more. I don't *want* this any more. It's wrong, Toby.'

'But, wait, Caroline, just wait. Maybe we can . . .' he's doing the hands on the head thing again.

'Go back to your wife, Toby. Go home to her because she's wonderful, and you don't deserve her. I was never right for you, anyway. Do you know why?'

He shakes his head.

'Because I need too much. More than you could ever give me. Do you remember when we were in my kitchen and you said all that stuff about how you loved me because I was like a bloke? Able to compartmentalize things? That I didn't have "constant irrational emotions", and I agreed? Well, it was all rubbish! All total bollocks! I've had nothing but irrational emotions all year and I'm not like a bloke in any way, shape or form. I'm not in control, or aloof, or the woman you thought I was. I was just scared, and a mess, but I'm not scared any more, Toby, and I just want to love and be loved, now. I deserve to be loved, and you can't give it to me, not just because of the small matter that you're married, but because you need so much yourself.'

He stares at me. He knows he's lost.

'So go. Before you lose her, too. You've got away with so much already, it can't be long before your luck runs out.'

And then I turn, leaving Toby standing on the bridge, and I finally feel like I've said everything I wanted to say. As I walk home, I feel so light, it's like the gentlest breeze could take me now, pick me up off this bridge and carry me somewhere else.

CHAPTER TWENTY-EIGHT

'Well, well, well,' says Lexi when I finally emerge from the changing room of Warehouse, wearing a tulip-shaped blue floral dress with an enormous belt. 'The lady has a waist. And pins! Blimey. Look at you with your pins up to your armpits.'

I look at myself in the mirror.

'Shut up,' I say. I've always been useless at taking compliments. 'Who are you? Gok Wan? Are you going to make me stand naked in the window of Selfridges next?'

It's three weeks since I finally ended it with Toby on Chelsea Bridge and I'm on Oxford Street shopping with Lexi.

We've done the nail bar in Top Shop and ransacked H&M, completely shamed ourselves on the Designers Lingerie floor of Selfridges:

'Fifty quid for a gusset?' Lexi had shouted at the top of her voice whilst holding up a Moschino G-string. 'I think I'll go commando!'

This is the best fun I've had in months. This is what having a sister is all about, what I imagined. Two of the four points on Lexi's Master list for sorting my life out done and I already feel lighter, I owe her.

Lexi is sitting down on the floor where she has been for

the past half-hour, while I've tried outfit after outfit. She pulls at her cheeks and groans, comically.

'Come on now, Caroline, stop it with the false modesty. Let's get the dress. Please! I haven't got all day, you know.'

'I don't know,' I sigh, eventually. 'I never go anywhere to wear it.'

Lexi says nothing. I watch her through the mirror. She's got her tongue in her cheek and is looking distinctly *guilty*.

'Lexi Steele, what's going on?'

She starts to smirk. Her little rosebud mouth breaking into the naughtiest smile.

'Nothing.'

'Bollocks. I know that face. What have you got up your sleeve, you little schemer?'

'Weeeell . . . I wasn't gonna tell you till we got home. Until I'd got some booze inside you, to be fair.'

I laugh out loud.

'So you had to get me pissed to tell me? It must be bad!'

'Promise you won't kill me?'

'I'm promising nothing of the sort.'

'Okay, well promise you'll keep to your word? You know, the conversation we had the other night about you trying new things, taking some risks, not being such a . . .' she grimaces in an effort at tactfulness. 'Control freak,' she says, eventually, and I feel a little pang of hurt. Was I really that bad? 'Basically, I've set you up on a date.'

'*What?* When?'

'Tonight. In about four hours time, to be exact.'

I rub my forehead as I try to compute.

'Right, so who is this date?'

'He's off Match.com.'

'Lexi!' I fall against the wall.

'You promised! You said, you were going to take all opportunities, try everything once.'

'B-but . . .' I'm stammering now. This was ridiculous. 'How on earth did you manage to intercept my account? Set me up with someone?'

'Easy. I told the truth. I found someone I thought you'd like and I emailed him, saying that I was your sister, that you were hilarious and charming and a *right* little sexpot . . .' I don't believe this. What was she *like*? 'But that you were also shy and would be a spinster for eternity if someone didn't take action.'

My mouth falls open.

'Okay, I didn't say the spinster bit but I did say the rest.'

'And?' I was intrigued as well as flabbergasted now.

'He confirmed, yes, you were a right little sexpot and that he'd be happy to go on a date with you.'

'So, you've basically logged onto my account and acted like my wing-woman?'

'Mm-mm. It would appear that's true, yes.'

I don't really see the point in arguing. This was the new me, after all, the new gung-ho me, who went on blind dates, willy-nilly, exuded an air of casual relaxation, was completely at home in her own skin. Someone who didn't clean the inside of taps with a toothbrush, or line jars up in the kitchen. Or sleep with married men. Or make endless lists. Well, maybe just the odd one. As I'm lying in the bath before I set off that evening, a cucumber face mask cracking on my face, I can't resist making one very short one. Just to calm the nerves. Lexi had been through it with me, her being far more experienced in the dating arena than me at seventeen, which was pretty tragic when I looked at it like that.

I sat up in the bath, careful not to get my notepad wet, and wrote them down.

First Dates: The Rules.
1. Be yourself
2. Smile a lot
3. Use open body language
4. Ask open questions, too, such as (I practise this bit aloud): 'How do you feel about Zanzibar as a holiday destination? Rather than 'Zanzibar? Yes or no?' If in doubt, make a joke of it
5. Do NOT get too drunk
6. DO NOT talk about ex-partners
7. Definitely no shagging (or, in fact, any sort of sexual contact except snogging)

It's only minutes before leaving that I have a change of heart on the outfit front.

I stand at the top of the stairs, wearing the midnight blue shift dress that Wayne gave me, Lexi standing at the bottom.

'I've decided that, although I like the dress we bought today, I'm going to wear this instead. What do you think?'

Lexi's face lights up. A slow, delighted smile spreads across her face.

'But I thought you didn't buy it in the end?' she says.

'Wayne gave it to me – a sort of olive branch for the hand-on-heart fiasco – I forgot to tell you. Do you think it's all right?'

She rests her chin on the banister and looks up at me with her big, dark, eyes. 'All right? I think it's perfect. Very, very, very cool. You look awesome.'

Awesome? Well that wasn't bad. Especially coming from a seventeen-year-old.

'Really?'

'Really.'

'Not too mutton-dressed-as-lamb?'

'Nope.'

'Not too smelly-charity-shop?'

'Definitely not!'

'Not too thirty-something-trying-to-be-seventeen?'

Lexi groans. 'Just go! He's gonna be waiting for you.'

'But what if he's awful? What if he's like, four feet tall and got a colostomy bag he hasn't told me about, or a fake leg or he's racist or he smells or he's deathly boring, or he thinks *I* smell and I'm deathly boring or . . . Oh God, I can't bear it!'

'Jesus Christ!' Lexi shakes her head in despair. 'Just *insane*. Text me and I'll call you, okay? Sudden, acute appendicitis. You have to leave immediately and rush me to hospital. *Easy*. Now go.' She shoos me down the stairs. 'Go on, get out, woman. *I* can't bear it, never mind you!'

I leave, tottering in new, excruciatingly painful wedges from Dorothy Perkins, towards Battersea Park Station, my Marianne Faithfull dress brushing the tops of my bare thighs, and I am filled with a reassuring fizz of excitement about the evening. I am going on a date, a blind date and apparently I look awesome. This was all good.

I give myself a pep talk as I walk through Aldwych towards Drury Lane: 'It's just a date, Caroline, not an appearance on *Question Time*. Relaaaaax. I take out the First Dates checklist from my jacket pocket and have a quick run through: be yourself, smile, do not get too drunk. How hard could it be? Very, I decide by the time I get to the restaurant. My heart is pounding, my mouth feels like it's been freeze-dried. Quick as a flash, before anyone can see, I turn to my reflection in a parked car window, lift up my arms and my fears are confirmed: two round sweat patches. Just brilliant. Oh well, as long as I didn't go giving him any high-fives.

The restaurant looks inviting. It's still light but on the verge of dusk and the pretty foliage that creeps on trellises around the arched doorway looks extra green against the milky sky. Lanterns burn outside, a placard featuring golden cherubs hangs above the door and, inside, the cavernous space flickers with cosy candlelight. A dream location for a first date; Lex has done well.

Then I walk inside. It's not that there's anything wrong with the inside, just that it was sort of . . . well, *novel*. There was definitely a theme going on, but what that was exactly was anyone's guess: fake-gilt chairs, crushed red velvet table-clothes and, on the ceiling and panels along the sides, murals depicting scenes of Roman gods.

There is a long table down the middle, full already of a rowdy, foreign crowd. Puppets hang down from the ceiling – a little macabre, like something out of the film *Chucky*. But it was what was around the sides of the restaurant that gave the theme away, because elevated on the second 'tier', which could only be reached by staircases around the side, were pretend opera boxes where people sat dining.

I pull the hem of my shift dress down. Maybe I should have worn a bosom-enhancing floor-length number instead? Something that made me look more like Lesley Garrett.

'Can I help you, madame?' A waiter in black bow tie approaches.

'Yes, thank you. I'm looking for . . .' Shit, I didn't know who I was looking for. Then I remembered what Lexi said. 'He's upstairs, I think.'

The waiter gives me a knowing smile. Clearly, I had INTERNET DATER emblazoned across my face.

'That way,' he says, gesturing to steps leading to one of the opera boxes. I climb them, feeling a new creep of perspiration under my arms. There's only one person sitting there and I recognize him immediately, his hair newly cut against the nape of his neck.

'Wayne?'

He looks round.

'Caroline? Oh my God! What are you doing here?'

'What am I doing here? What are *you* doing here . . . Oh . . .' It suddenly dawns.

'I can't believe . . .' He's pointing at me now, laughing. 'That Lexi Steele, that sister of yours, she is a *right* one.'

'You're telling me.'

He looks at me, that long-enough-to-make-me-look-the-other-way look.

I say, 'Well, I must say, your profile was very misleading. [*If in doubt, just make a joke.*] You said you were tall, good-looking and had all your own hair.'

Wayne tugs at his straw-coloured mop. 'How dare you? This is my very best hairpiece. Can't do much about the height thing, I'm afraid. I stop here . . .' he gestures to where the table comes up to his waist. 'I'm ALL torso. As for the good-looks bit, well you girls are so fussy.'

I laugh. So, he's funny. And good-looking. More good-looking even than I'd remembered. He's caught the sun over the summer and has cute new freckles over his nose. He's wearing an expensive looking powder blue jumper under a biker jacket – a definite improvement on the oily cable-knit. It makes him look sexy, effortless. Not too try-hard.

He smiles – that same warm, infectious smile – and I feel a sudden thrill: I was on my first date for years and it was with someone I fancied. What were the chances of that? According to Shona, who'd spent years Internet Dating before she met Paul, you were lucky if they were within a decade of the age they said they were. Underneath the excitement, however, I am also gripped with panic. What if he had been hoping for a six foot Swedish beauty called Anneka to walk through the door and he got me: a five foot five nervous wreck with – currently – an excessive sweating problem? What if he's going to have to have words with Lexi?

I know what she will have been thinking: my tragic sister needs some dating practise. Wayne's going to Sheffield soon – perfect for a no-strings practise run before I start the intensive bloke-finding programme with her and she gets a bloke for good. But what would Wayne make of giving up his evening for me? I would hazard a guess he'd been hoping for something more exotic for his last London fling . . .

Or maybe not, I don't know. Because when I sit down, he leans back in his chair then looks comically under the table so that I instinctively wrap one wedge-clad foot, self-consciously, around the other.

'Can I just say, you look . . .' He blows air through his lips. 'A knockout.'

I grin at him like a lunatic. Was he taking the piss?

'Beautiful dress, by the way.'

I loved the way he said beautiful – dropping the 'Ts'.

'Thank you, it was a gift from someone with impeccable taste.'

I look around at the funny little faux-opera box we are sitting in – like something out of *Alice in Wonderland*. We are sat on benches, with a table between us covered in what Martin would definitely identify as 'ethnitat' – a multi-coloured hessian number with tassels and frayed edges. Encasing us, as if we are on the set of a school play, are swathes of sun-and-moon printed fabric and, opposite, obviously to look like theatre props, is a collection of clocks and dusty old books, arranged in haphazard little piles. I looked at the menu: Greek, or was that Turkish? Or Moroccan? It was hard to tell.

The starters come – dollops of hummus and huge slabs of halloumi and soggy courgette – and we politely begin, sharing from each other's plates.

Wayne takes his jacket off and rolls up his sleeves. There was the tattoo again. Who was Justine? One of these days I would ask him about her.

I say, 'I've started reading your book.'

Wayne puts his fork down and looks at me expectantly.

'And?'

'I love it!'

'Seriously?' he says, delighted. 'You're not just saying that?'

'No, believe me, I'm the world's worst liar. I think it's sweet and touching and really funny.' I start to giggle as I remember bits. 'I love, love *love* the scene where Kevin goes to Argos to buy dumbbells, which he can barely carry home, then starts copying the Arnold Schwarzenegger video in his back garden in a bid to bag that total bitch, Lucy Briers.'

Wayne laughs too.

'She is a prick tease, that Lucy Briers, isn't she?'

'Brilliant creation. Totally brilliant. And it's just so sweet.' I carry on, enthused now, in my element. 'The Arnold Schwarzenegger thing, it totally made me fall in love with Kevin. You can completely imagine this scrawny 13-year-old, desperately pumping iron in his underpants in the back garden, whilst his mum hangs out the washing, rolling her eyes.'

Wayne smiles and pokes the food around his plate. We both know it's pretty grim but we're too polite to say.

'I'm really flattered you liked it,' he says. 'Such an experienced reader as yourself. Whilst you're here, can I ask you what you thought of . . .?'

But then he's interrupted by the arrival of a group of drunk, raucous girls, all wearing hard hats, boiler suits and fake moustaches. MEL'S ERECTION PROJECT is emblazoned on the their backs.

We look at each other

'Hen do,' we say in unison and Wayne flops his head dramatically on his table

'It's not your fault,' I laugh. 'Blame Alexis Steele. She's the one who booked it!'

281

We try to have a conversation, but it becomes more and more impossible what with Mel's Erection Project chanting beside us, embarrassing the Hen with a quiz about her sex life. Now and again, random words come at us: Masturbation! S&M! Crotchless knickers! And at first we try to ignore it, then realize that's utterly futile and ridiculous and start pissing ourselves instead, putting in our penny's worth: 'Nipple tassels!' I shout out of the side of my mouth. 'Gimp mask!' says Wayne.

But things take an even more farcical turn for the worst, because then we hear it. Opera. Someone singing *opera*? And then, as if this night couldn't get more surreal, there's a woman with an enormous heaving bosom, singing tonsil-quivering opera at the top of her voice, right next to our table. The hens start to squeal. I don't know how to react.

'Oh Jesus,' says Wayne. 'Do you think we should go?'

We pile outside laughing.

'Jesus Christ, I thought her left breast was going to make an escape for it at one point!' says Wayne. 'Teenager's taste, eh? And it looked so promising at first. I thought Lex had got it bang on the money.'

'I think Mel's Erection Project did it for me,' I say. 'That really topped it off.'

We catch our breath. The light has fallen and the sky is bruise-coloured. All around us, theatreland is waking up.

'So what do you fancy doing now?' says Wayne.

'What, me?'

He laughs.

'No, that pensioner over there.'

I am so used to nights out with Martin, where everything is pre-planned, pre-booked, offers from the *Standard* ringed in highlighter, that this completely throws me.

'God, I was hoping you might have some idea?' He smiles at me, hopefully, and I feel bad to let him down.

282

'Sorry, I'm a bit rubbish, never really venture outside SW11.'

'Really?' he says, surprised.

'Really.' I wince

'Well, I reckon now we've got you north of the river, we have to make the most of it. So, Caroline.' He eyes me up. 'Miss Faithfull, in that lovely dress of yours, what do you want to do now?'

'What, like, anything?'

'Yeah, what would be your ideal night? Fuck it, we're on a date, aren't we?'

I laugh. I love his directness about the situation; it makes me feel wanted.

'Oh I don't know,' I say, feeling terribly self-conscious, rubbish at this spontaneity thing. 'Picnic in a moonlit park, walk along the river, some cool, dingy rock bar I've never been to, tequilas, dancing, outrageous, drunken harlot behaviour?'

His eyes widen.

'I'm joking, of course. I'm already too pissed for date one.' I catch myself. 'Not that there's necessarily going to be another one . . .'

He smiles. 'So let's do it,' he says.

'Do what?'

'What you said – your perfect night out. I've got a magic carpet, you see, I can take you anywhere.'

I tut. 'Now, you're just showing off.'

'Ah, but I'm not.' He starts to walk. 'Come over here.'

He takes me by the hand and I note how nice it is just to hold a man's hand who isn't someone's husband – and leads me to a motorbike bay on the opposite side of the road – so that's why he wasn't drinking much. Panic rises in my chest.

'Oh no, ah-ah.' I shake my head. 'I don't do motorbikes. I'm sorry. I went on one once in 1992. The guy was mental.

He had a total death wish. We went about a million miles per hour and I swear I saw my life flash before me – I thought that was it, over, finito. I started to say goodbye to everyone I love in my head, think about who might come to my funeral. I got off that motorbike, I was sheet white, sheet white, Wayne, and I . . .' I stop. He's laughing at me, actually bent over laughing at me.

'What?' I say.

'Nothing, it's just . . .' He composes himself. 'That was seventeen years ago. I think, maybe, it might be time to give it another go?'

'So just hold onto me, or hold onto the side and lean with the bike, okay?'

'Okay.'

We're on the bike. I can't believe he got me on the bike. Putting the helmet on was embarrassing enough, me getting it stuck somewhere around my ears. And then he starts the engine and he revs it so much that I squeal helplessly from within my visor, a muffled, desperate squeal like I'm being attacked. Could this be the most embarrassing first date ever?

Then, then . . . It's amazing. I don't know what happens for the next half-hour, but I'm on a motorbike and I feel like I'm flying.

We race through Aldwych, pass coach trips of middle-aged ladies going to see *Grumpy Old Women* at the theatre and here's us, I think, young, carefree, on a growling, daring machine and I feel light and heady, like I'm in a French film.

We wind along the Strand, darting in and out of buses. At one point I actually feel the heat of a red bus brush my bare thighs and clench every muscle in my body, screaming with a mixture of delight and terror.

Wayne keeps turning his head and shouting something to me, but I can't hear him above the crawling, honking, heaving traffic. The air smells of burnt sugar. I grip on even tighter. It's only as we turn into Waterloo Bridge that I realize what it is he's trying to say.

'You've got your hands around my neck!'

'Sorry. I can't help it!' I shout back as the wind hits my face so hard it makes my cheeks shake.

'Hold onto the . . .'

'What?'

'Hold onto the sides!'

'But I can't!'

'You have to. You're gonna fucking strangle me!'

So I loosen my grip, slowly, gingerly – here goes, here I come – And with all the fearlessness I can muster, every last scrap of courage I possess, I take my shaking hands from around his neck and place them around his waist. It feels terrifying and thrilling. It feels like I just leapt out of the plane – except there's no parachute. How the hell was I staying on this thing? But wow! *I get it now*. We are flying over Waterloo Bridge and I am doing it. I am leaning with the bike! It reminds me of the time I went for a trial day's diving. If I could just relax, let go of the ever-present threat of death for a second, it was the most beautiful thing I had ever seen.

And this is beautiful. This city I live in that yawns at either side of us now is so beautiful. Boats glide beneath us, so tiny looking as they make it out into the wide mass of water, glittering with a golden, sinking sun. The river curves to the left, fairy lights string the Victoria Embankment, a neon sign glides across the smooth façade of the National Theatre: AFTER THE DANCE SHOWING NOW . . .

Down below, everything seeming to unfurl so slowly and gracefully, whilst up here, if I dare to open my eyes for a second, the city flashes before me at the speed of lightning.

I can feel the warmth of Wayne's body beneath my

fingertips, the vibrations of the engine on my thighs. Every now and then I catch his face in the wing mirror. He's grinning at me.

We turn along York Road, the London Eye appearing like a tricycle wheel that a giant left by mistake in the middle of London. There's a 24-hour shop and Wayne parks up. 'Supplies?' he says. 'For the picnic in the park?'

So we park up and go inside, but I can't get my helmet off, so I'm walking around in this brightly lit grocery store, looking and feeling like an astronaut just landed on planet earth.

'Er, Wayne? I can't get my helmet off.'

But my voice is muffled beneath the visor and he can't hear me so I just give up. It's only as I'm standing behind him in the queue, paying, that he realizes and almost wets himself laughing.

'You've been in this shop all that time and not been able to get your helmet off?'

'I did try to tell you.'

We put supplies in the back box and carry on: over Westminster Bridge, the Houses of Parliament backlit now by a red sun, hovering like a hot-air balloon. We almost hug the statue of Winston Churchill, we're leaning so much around Westminster Place. There are the protestors against the Iraq War, camped outside Parliament. A teenage girl shouts at us from the window of a pink limousine. Foreign students take pictures of themselves outside some important building or other. Everywhere there is the sound of the city: the perpetual honking of horns, the gaseous, wheezing sigh of the buses as they stop and start – one great, pulsating heart that we are right in the middle of.

We eventually get to St James's Park where we picnic under a weeping willow, Buckingham Palace just visible over the tops of the trees. Everything has stopped now, but the sound of the journey still rings in my ears.

After eating, we both lie on the grass. Wayne folds his arms across his stomach. They're toned, and I stare at them. I want to touch them. I watch his chest rise and fall, his eyelids flicker, the light of the moon drifting across them. His mouth is wide, slightly open, like he's inviting me to kiss it. You're gorgeous, I think. It's like this thought has always been in the peripheries of my mind and yet it's only now that it's fully crystalized. A snog would be nice, I think, just to put my lips on his right now and taste him. But what with him driving and me deciding that to get leathered all on my own might be a bit wrong, we're stone-cold sober. Control yourself, Steele. Steal yourself . . .

No. 4: Ask open questions . . .

'So,' I sigh.

Wayne smiles without opening his eyes.

'Who is Justine? Tell me about Justine.'

'Ah, this,' he says, stroking his tattoo. 'My battle scar. Justine was my fiancée.'

'You were *engaged*?' I sit up on my elbows and he opens one eye.

'Don't look so surprised.'

'So what happened?'

'She dumped me. Three months before our wedding.'

'Oh.' I shift on the grass, I feel my heart beat. 'Why?'

'She just fell out of love with me – unbelievable, I know, but we wanted different things. She wasn't right for me, and it's okay, I'm over it now.'

'You must have been gutted! Were you very in love with her? How long were you together?'

'Blimey, that's three questions, the answers to which are yes, yes, and eight years.

Eight years?

287

'But like I said, we were wrong for each other. It was the best thing that ever happened to me although I couldn't see that at the time.'

I want to ask questions and more questions. I think about Martin and I. Would Martin ever come to feel that way in time? I hoped so.

Wayne pauses, looks up at me through shrewd green eyes.

'I used to make these lists,' he says. 'Reams and reams of lists about my future. I used to make them as a kid, too, about stupid things like *Cars I will own in my lifetime in ascending order of price.*'

'Like Kevin Hart,' I say.

'Yeah. Like Kevin Hart.'

'So anyway, when I got older and particularly when I was with Justine, I became obsessed about "Stuff I want to do" lists. But after a while I realized they were just keeping my head above water; that I made them to stay sane.'

I give a little laugh. This all rang so true. Maybe all that time Wayne was saying that people who made lists were masking some deeper unhappiness, he was right, when I just dismissed him as a self-help bore.

'Justine would never, ever want to do the same things as me; we were going in different directions.'

'So what sort of things did you have on these lists?'

'Oh, live in London for a while, travel around America, write a book. But then one day I realized they were just dream lists, that by committing this stuff to paper was a bit like a wannabe writer talking about writing – it wasn't the same as actually *doing* it. In a way, Justine finishing with me was a blessing in disguise because it was only once I was on my own and heartbroken that I felt driven to start to make things happen.'

'So, that's when you moved to London and started writing the book?'

'Yes – and travelling. I rode around Africa on that old heap of metal last year.'

I watch him, both his eyes closed again, and think how much I admire him. I would never do anything as bold as to drive around Africa on a motorbike. I could hardly drive around London without having a hernia.

'So, do you think you'd ever get the tattoo removed?' I ask.

He grins.

'No way, it's my battle scar, this,' he says. Then, hand on heart in comedy mock-drama, 'The pain, Caroline, it's part of me.'

I giggle. He opens both his eyes this time, and a slow smiles creeps across his face.

'Plus, she's not alone, I'm afraid.' He lifts up his top. There's a tacky little heart tattoo with an arrow through and the name Tracey on it, on his right hip bone.

'Oh my God!'

'And this . . .' he bends forward and there's one along the base of his back that reads, Christabel, She's a Rolling Stone.

He pulls down his T-shirt and grimaces at me. 'I mostly regret that one.'

I shake my head, laughing in disbelief.

'What were you thinking of! And Christabel?! Sounds like you made her up!'

'What you saying?' he laughs. 'I lost my virginity to Christabel. She went like a train, did Christabel.'

I jab him in the arm. 'Wayne Campbell!'

'Seriously, we were the real-life Romeo and Juliet, doomed teenage sweethearts. Me the local motherless urchin from the council estate, her the daughter of a barrister.'

'Motherless?'

He closes his eyes again. 'Yeah, Mum died when I was fifteen. Breast cancer. It's okay, it was a long time ago now.'

289

I look at him in awe, study his face, his eyes flickering beneath the lids. Wayne I decide, is not like anyone else I know. He is so open with his feelings, so straightforward. I feel embarrassed, me with my middle-class parents who may not have been sane but were alive at least. What had I endured? Divorce. Big deal. And yet Wayne seemed so much more of a happier person than me, a functioning, positive person.

'Wow. You've really been through it, haven't you?'

He shrugs. 'Worse things happen. At least I had a mum for most of my childhood, a great one too.'

There's a pause, and I am aware of not getting too heavy. If he wants to tell me more about his childhood, he will.

'So what of this little floozy Christabel, then?' I say, handing him a piece of bread.

'We ran away'

'You're kidding!'

'Nope. Dropped out of school and ran away to a kibbutz. I wanted to get away from my life, she wanted to be with me, but her parents disapproved because I was this little ruffian, not good enough for their little girl, you know, all that nonsense. So we ran away to Israel.'

'Bloody hell, is there anything you haven't done?!'

But it's all falling into place, the tattoo, the dropping out of school, the affinity he must have with Lexi, the lists he made. The life lived. I feel like Wayne Campbell is emerging, right here, in St James's Park, like he's handing me pieces of a jigsaw puzzle to complete the whole.

'Anyway, enough about me, what about you?' he says, squinting up at me. 'Ever had your heart broken?'

I pause, did I want to tell him this? Could I tell him about Toby? Had Lexi done so already?

'Yes,' I say, eventually 'yes, I have . . .'

Like he can read my mind, his eyes widen, then he says, very slowly:

'Ah, Toby.'

'Yes,' I say. 'Toby. But he was my lucky escape.'

And then, almost as if we both know we've had all we can take of heart to hearts and picnics in parks and life stories and anecdotes, we hit the town and get the sort of drunk that is definitely not allowed on first dates. (Rule Number Five broken.) We start off in a bar called ScooterCaffe near Waterloo doing beers and tequila chasers amongst the vintage Vespas and the old motorcycle parts and the pretty bunting strung up on the ceiling and, then, when we decide we're nowhere near drunk enough and the night is yet young, we hit an all-night drinking den in Hanway Street where ridiculously trendy clientele with their ironic satchels and their angular fringes and brogues drink beer out of vintage teacups. It's the sort of bar I'd never be seen dead in normally, but I don't care, I'm having the time of my life. We've broken every rule there is to break now: Don't get too drunk (5), don't mention ex-partners (7) but there's one main rule left to break.

So I am back at his place now, on the boat and all I know is that I want him, more than I have wanted anyone, ever. My dress is off within minutes of getting below deck, all my own doing, and I am sprawled, arms back, on his hammock. He kisses me.

'God, you're beautiful,' he says. Then he kisses my belly and I quiver, every last inch of me.

I grab him under the arms.

'Make love to me,' I say. 'I want to be made love to.'

Tender. Not 'seedy mistress sex'.

He kisses me, and he's the best kisser, changing his stroke between so soft it's like gossamer and firm and purposeful.

We're moving together now, our pelvises pushing against each other, our breathing quickening.

'We don't have to do this,' he says, looking me in the eyes.

I put a finger to his lips.

'Will you just shut up? I am very busy.'

Wayne giggles at me.

'And drunk,' he says. 'We're very, very drunk. Oh, but you're so pretty.'

'Am I?'

'Ridiculously so,' he says. 'And with the sexiest legs I've ever seen. It's been all I can think of since I first clapped eyes on you in that dress, in my stall.'

'Well, if it makes you feel better . . .'

'Oh, I couldn't feel any better than I already do.'

'I fancied you from the first moment I saw you, too, even if I didn't know who you were, even if you took the piss out of my list making.'

'Well, we all know why I took the piss out of that, don't we?' he says. And then I'm in some other zone. On some other plain.

Afterwards, we lie rocking gently in the hammock. I am breathless with arousal, my body still shaking.

'Well, that's got to be the best sex I've ever had in my life,' Wayne says, incredulously, laughing.

'Me too,' I say. 'God, we were good!'

I squeeze him, inhale his scent: that slightly woody smell of the boat's woodburning stove and the scent of St James's Park in summer, all rolled into one.

We lie still, and I watch his contented face, slack now with approaching sleep.

What now? What will become of Wayne Campbell and me? In the porthole above us, I can see the pink dawn creeping in. I'll have to go home, soon, I think, back to my sister, who will ask me about the Rules. We broke every last one of them and I couldn't care less. The minutes tick by. I don't want to leave, I think. I just don't want to leave.

Wayne turns to me, the gorgeous creases around his eyes, deepened by tiredness now.

'You're not worrying, are you?' he says.

'Worrying? About what?'

'About tomorrow, this. You won't sober up and regret it, will you?'

I smile, curl my leg around his.

No, I won't regret it. If this was what one-night stands were about, 'reckless sex', then I wonder why I've not done more.

'Well, anyway,' he says, tidying a strand of hair behind my ear when I don't say anything, 'it's not like we have to worry about it. I'm off to Sheffield soon so you won't have to see me or bump into me all the time.'

Sheffield. I hadn't thought of Sheffield for the entire night until now. He was right, of course, the fact he was going was all for the best in the long run. I'd done it. I'd had a one-night stand with someone (not married) and now it wouldn't get all complicated. There'd be no tears and, 'Where are we taking this?' This couldn't be taken anywhere, it was just here, right now. This was all we had.

'So, when do you go?' My voice sounds sleepy, extra muffled down here below deck, like we're in a little cocoon.

There's a pause, a very long pause.

'Three weeks,' he says.

Three weeks. Twenty-one days.

CHAPTER TWENTY-NINE

So by the time Sarah Rawlinson dumped me, my heart was already a hardened mass of scar tissue. Plus, I had a new actual scar on my face after a scrap I'd had with Ryan Kaye after the under-16s night at Crystal Ts and too many Southern Comforts . . . Life couldn't have got much worse.

I close the page and finally turn my light off, my eyes stinging from reading. I'm slowly falling in love with Kevin Hart – or was it just because when I read it, I heard the voice of his creator?

I lie in the darkness of my bedroom, thinking: I can't fall in love with Wayne Campbell. I just can't. There are various reasons for this and I list them in my head.

1. He's called Wayne. Period. How could I ever fall in love with a man called Wayne? I think of all the other famous Waynes I know: Wayne Rooney, Wayne Sleep, Wayne Hemingway. I imagine introducing him: 'Hi, this is my boyfriend, Wayne.' No, I couldn't go out with a man called Wayne, could I?

2. Then there was the tattoo. Sorry, the *tattoos*. Did I ever, in my life, see myself with a man with so much body art, let alone that dedicated to ex-girlfriends? His

body was a shrine to his exes, for God's sake! Still, there was something endearingly shameless about a man who felt the need to mark his body with evidence of past broken hearts. Clearly, this was not a man afraid of his feelings.

3. The dubious occupation(s): the novel-writing (not published); the part-time job in a shop. This went against everything I ever stood for as a woman who needed stability and pensions to sleep at night. A woman so risk averse, I had stayed in the same job for a decade.

But I can't stop thinking about Wayne. This wasn't supposed to happen. Mind you, sleeping with a married man wasn't supposed to happen, either. Or getting engaged to Martin. I'm beginning to wonder what *is* supposed to happen. The thing that's confusing me is, wasn't this a one-night stand? Because if it was − which I'm pretty sure it was, it *had* to be, he's going to Sheffield in three weeks − then I don't think I'm supposed to feel like this. I'm sure (although obviously I'm no expert, never having had a one-night stand), I'm supposed to feel like, 'Way-hay! Go, girl', and all that girl power malarkey. I am a thoroughly modern chick who just had drunken, meaningless sex with someone just because I can. So there.

I'm sure it's supposed to be all about the sex, but that's it. This *is* all about the sex. The sex was bloody brilliant! And I'm sure that's not supposed to happen on a one-night stand, either, is it? Isn't it supposed to be all strange houses, strange smells and noises, excruciatingly embarrassing break-fasts even though five hours earlier you had your nipples in his face? But there was nothing strange about sex with Wayne. Nothing. Everything about sex with Wayne was familiar and yet exciting and amazing, like arriving at your favourite holiday destination with all your best friends, knowing you are guaranteed to have the time of your life.

We breakfasted like we did this every day, me in just my pants and his T-shirt, up on deck. Then I walked home, barefoot, in my dress; my stupidly high wedges that had torn my feet to shreds swinging by my side and my thighs still aching from the motorbike . . . amongst other things. The sun was high in the sky, the pavement already warm beneath my feet. I could still taste him in my mouth, smell him in my hair, and I found myself having one of those rare, fleeting moments of joy that actually made me cry. A diamond-in-a-rock-face moment. Gosh, haven't had one of those for a while.

'Er, missus?' Lexi called from her bedroom, as I tried to creep past it to mine. 'Miss Dirty Stop Out. We need a debrief.'

It was all she could do not to laugh out loud when she saw me.

'What? Nothing happened!' I said. 'We were just listening to music back at his, it got late so I stayed over.'

'Mm-mm.' She nodded, a dirty great grin across her face. 'So, what happened to your chin?'

'What's wrong with my chin?' I grabbed the mirror from her dressing table. 'Oh *shit*!' Lexi was now doubled over with mirth. My chin, or what was left of it, looked like I'd been at it with a pan scourer. 'His bloody stubble did that to me!'

'So you *so* snogged?!'

I bit my lip.

'Oh my God, you shagged? You broke *all* the rules!'

I sat down on her bed and pointed at her, warningly.

'He's going to Sheffield, nothing can come of this, lady, and let me tell you, I am not proud of my behaviour . . .'

'Don't lie,' she said. 'You are.'

'We had a good time. For what it was.'

'Which was?' She was fluttering her eyelashes at me now and I didn't quite know what she was getting at.

'A one-off. One night of fun . . .'

She put her head in her hands and groaned, dramatically.

'He's going to Sheffield, Lex, what can I do? Things happen for a reason. Wrong timing. I thought you knew that, anyway?'

'But you *liked* him?'

'Yes.'

'So my match-making skills were good?'

I hugged her. 'Alexis Steele, they weren't just good, they were brilliant. Thank you . . .' I kissed her cheek repeatedly, like an overbearing aunty. 'Thank you, thank you, gorgeous sister of mine. What am I going to do without you?'

She raised on eyebrow.

'What are you going to do without Wayne Campbell?' she said.

So I feel like a teenager again, except I don't, because something is stopping me and that something is thoughts of Rachel. They were there when I went shopping with Lexi, they were there even when I was with Wayne, and they are there at work, whenever I look at Toby, which is not often now since he has taken it upon himself to move desks. He will barely even look at me. There are long, loud conversations on the phone to his wife, shows of his newfound commitment − and I'm glad, genuinely glad. I meant what I said. She's the only one for him. But for me, the aftermath is a bit like being on holiday knowing you have a dissertation to write. There's a gnawing, uneasy feeling like something bad's going to happen. I stole another woman's husband for a year and there's no fallout? It all seemed too easy. And I was right, because on the Tuesday after my date with Wayne, this happens:

I come back from lunch to find the office deathly quiet and Shona at her desk in tears. Toby is leaning on the back of his chair, his head bowed, his knuckles white. Christ, had someone died?

'What's happened?'

Silence. Just the sound of typing. I look over at Lexi for some clue, something, but she just gives me a sympathetic smile.

Shona says, 'Caroline, I need to speak to you. Now, in private.'

My blood starts to rush with nerves. What the hell was going on?

That's when I notice it. The odd flicker of an eye up from a screen, a snatched glance. People are looking at me.

I look at Shona, then Toby. 'Just tell me,' I say. I'm panicking now. Maybe someone really had died. 'God, is it one of my parents?'

Toby lifts his head up and it's only then that I see that he's been crying too.

'No, it's *Rachel*, for fuck's sake'

'Rachel?' I say. Rachel had *died*?

Then the realisation catches me like a chill wind. My body goes cold. She *knew*. Of course she knew.

For a nanosecond I actually toy with the idea that this could be a dream, a horrid dream, then become aware of Heather standing at the photocopier in her fire marshal tabard, pretending not to listen. You don't get anything as subtle as that in a dream, I think. In a dream, Rachel would be standing there at the copier with a knife in her hand. Or my mother. I didn't know which was worse.

My hand goes to my mouth.

'Oh God,' is all I can manage.

'Yes. Oh God,' says Toby, glaring at Shona. She's still crying, and still wearing her coat from lunch.

'Look, let's just go outside for a minute, shall we?' she says to me. Then she gets up and I follow her, feeling everyone's eyes burn into my back.

We're outside now, on the elevated smoking section, looking out towards Edgware Road.

'Shone, tell me. Whatever it is, I promise, I don't blame you.'

And I meant it. Rachel knew now, what did it matter how or when?

'We met for lunch,' starts Shona. Her voice is shaking. She puts her hand up to her mouth and her fingers are shaking too. 'I thought it was a bit strange, her wanting to meet me for lunch when she doesn't know me that well, but I thought it might be something to do with Toby. That maybe she wanted to throw a surprise birthday party for him, or something, *anything*. I wouldn't have agreed to go if I'd have known, because like I've always said, I knew this would happen. I knew I was an appalling liar. I knew if I was ever put on the spot, I'd fuck up. That's why I tried to warn you.'

Down below, the traffic crawls along the Edgware Road, I can just make out the sprawl of Hyde Park in the distance. This all feels so unreal; I can't believe it's come to this.

I get hold of her hand.

'It's okay, you don't have to justify it. I don't blame you. Just tell me, what happened?'

'Well, she just came out with it, didn't she? I got to the café and she was already crying . . .'

I close my eyes. How could I have possibly ever thought I could get away with this.

'She said, "Shona, you have to tell me. Is there something going on between Caroline and Toby?"'

I picture her sitting there, the strength it must have taken her to ask for the truth. Her searching Shona's face for clues, how Shona must have felt. God, I could die.

299

'And I had to tell her, Caroline. I had to. I couldn't lie to her . . .'

'Shona, it's *okay*. Course you couldn't.'

She starts sobbing again and I put my arms around her. This was such a mess, such a horrid, complicated mess.

'It's not your fault. It's *my* fault. I didn't listen, did I? I didn't listen when you told me to get out of this?'

'Rachel's told him to move out.'

Oh God. That was big, that was different.

'She says he has to have his stuff gone by the time she gets home from work. Janine knows,' she says, head bowed, face like stone. I nod my head.

'And everyone else in the office?' 'Yep,' she says. 'And everyone else.'

I keep my head down until lunch and I'm not invited to the weekly round-up meeting. 'I just think it's probably best today,' Janine says, discreetly, hand on my desk. 'Just until everything calms down.'

I am a scandal in my own lunch hour. Talk about a fall from grace. To think that this time a few weeks ago, Janine couldn't get enough of me, that I was teacher's pet. That I was her hope for the Sales Award.

Now, I have been outed as a mediocre sales manager – can't even push bloody mouthwash worthy of an award – and a wanton harlot of a mistress. Not bad for a few weeks work.

Things go from bad to farcical, when Schumacher drops the Minty Me account. Turns out that during my ridiculous, nervous showing off at the Barbecue of Horror about winning the Minty Me account with Schumacher (don't know what I was thinking, as if Rachel cared, as if she gave a shit!), I let drop how cheap we'd got it on the shelves, how much profit Darryl had – in his generosity – inadvertently made for the company.

Rule Number One of sales: never let a buyer know how good a deal they gave you.

Turns out Lexi hadn't quite grasped this.

'But I thought I was giving him a compliment,' she says, confused, when I finally get out of her exactly what she said, which was, *'You make us the biggest profit out of all our clients!'*

(Headthunkdesk.)

But I don't care, not like I once did. I really couldn't care less. So I'd lost Toby, I'd lost Schumacher, I'd lost my dignity, and I was probably going to lose my job.

Lexi and I go to Pret à Manger on Baker Street for lunch. I feel dirty and ashamed, like I was just found snorting coke off the toilet seat. And to think my little sister came here for me to set an example to her? It's just too grim to contemplate.

She's being unbelievably gracious and grown-up about it. Every day, she impresses me. It's me who asks her advice these days.

I pour soy sauce on my sushi.

'Do you think I should call Rachel?' I say.

She looks at me like I'm mental. This is what I love about Lexi. There's no stroking your ego, or well this, or well that, it's just 'that's the shittest idea I've ever heard' or 'that is genius'. If you want a true opinion, ask a teenager, that's what I've learned.

'Are you mad?' she says.

'I don't know, am I?'

I couldn't really tell any more.

'Yes! Think about it. Think about your mum. Would she have loved it if my mum called her and said: "Hey, Gwen! I've been having sex with your husband, but I'm sorry, truly I am, can we be friends?"'

When put like that, she had a point.

'Anyway, why do you want to call Rachel?' she said.

I thought about this. Why did I want to call Rachel?

'Coz I bet it's not to make her feel better, is it? I bet it's to make *you* feel better.'

She was right of course. She always is these days.

I stir my coffee and look out of the window at everyone walking past. Normal people getting on with normal lives. The thought of going back into that office, today, day in, day out, dealing with the gossip and the scandal and the seeing Toby every day, I didn't know if I could handle it.

'Maybe I should hand in my notice,' I say.

Lexi gasps. 'Don't you dare! You're going to have to just walk in there, hold your head up high and get on with it. It'll all blow over soon, these things usually do.' Turns out she was right about that too. When did she get so goddamn mature?

This whole mess has made me think about Martin, too. When the Rachel thing blew up, I wanted to tell him. Not because I wanted to off-load on him, but because I wanted him to know – I wanted him to know I didn't get away with it. I wanted to thank him, in a way, for making me see the light!

It turns out he had some thanking to do too. Something I hadn't expected.

We meet in a café in Battersea Square and I tell him about Toby, about Rachel and everything that's happened. I tell him how sorry I am about calling off the wedding – and it's only as the words come out of my mouth, that I realize I've never actually said them before. I've never told Martin I'm sorry – not about calling off the wedding, anyway. We've never really talked about that.

He sits and he listens. He looks relaxed and calm today, sitting in the sunny window, stirring his coffee. Then he says:

'I loved you for so long, do you realize that?'

I am aware of the past tense. I *loved* you.

'Do you remember the day we met? That soggy field in bloody Hebden Bridge? You despairing of Pippa coz she'd got drunk the night before and whined all the way round the orienteering course?' I laugh at the memory. God, I was square. 'I thought you were exquisite,' he says. 'There with your cagoule pulled tight and your little serious chin and the way you went all red in the face when people weren't being as sensible as you liked.'

'Bloody hell. I hope I've moved on.'

Martin smiles.

'You were different, Caro. You didn't follow the crowd or feel you had to rebel. I fell in love with you that day, and I stayed in love. I thought you were the girl for me and you broke my heart.'

'Martin, I know I did.'

It's taken me until now to be able to hear those words and not start to cry.

'I never stopped hoping after you called off the wedding, you know. For the past year, I've kept thinking, maybe, just maybe . . . I longed for you. I clung onto every last hope that at some point, you'd change your mind. I thought perhaps if I did this, if I did that, if I helped you out with DIY and helped you with the Clark thing, you'd fall in love with me again, but now I know nothing I did would change your mind, you just didn't love me any more and that's no more your fault than mine.'

I smile, sadly.

'I put you on a pedestal, Caro, you could do no wrong, but, you know what? I see now, that you're just a human being – a lovely one – but just a human being and that you're not perfect at all. In a way, you telling me about Toby, you having an affair with someone else's husband – I was so shocked – but also, well, it made me fall out of love with you and I guess for that I'm grateful.'

'Great,' I say. 'So you basically realized I am a deeply flawed human being with a very dubious morality.'

Martin laughs.

'That about sums it up, yes.'

And then I laugh too, lean forward and kiss him on the cheek.

'I'm sorry for breaking your heart. I'm sorry if I ruined your life . . .'

He rolls his eyes.

'God, you really are an egomaniac, aren't you?' he says. 'You haven't ruined my life. My life's only just starting.'

CHAPTER THIRTY

I'm coming back to myself. Bit by bit, I'm coming back. I'm still getting used to it. At first, it felt like something was missing until I realized that the something that was missing was Toby and Martin. It's not like I've forgotten them – maybe you never forget the people you hurt and who hurt you, maybe they scar you for ever. Your battle scars. But I've let go, and things I haven't thought about for so long, since before this summer and the affair, have started to creep back into my consciousness, like colour into a photograph: old friends – I've got back in touch with Pippa. My health, the news, who's winning *The X Factor*. Normality has returned. My mind is mine again. But I've one last thing to tick off Lexi's list. My mum – I need to see her.

So I'm driving north up the M1 – just me, my little Nissan and my shoddy car stereo that cuts out every other song and the rest of the time rattles and buzzes like a blue bottle. Normally, this would annoy the pants off me, have me shouting obscenities at the dashboard. Normally, I would have had to sort it out before I could contemplate a run to Sainsbury's never mind a six hour drive to Harrogate.

But something strange has happened to me of late, a sense of calm has descended, a sudden ability to drive with a rattling car stereo and sleep knowing there's an inch of dust under the bed. I say 'of late' like it was gradual, but it was very definitely sudden. I woke up one morning, and there − it was like someone had turned off the noise, the earth had stopped quaking. For the first time in a long time I feel at peace in my own skin.

I take a swig of the Diet Coke resting precariously by the gear stick, turn the radio up and wind my window down, so that the breeze, warm as a hairdryer, whips my hair about my face. It feels good. It's 5 September today − next week, it's Lexi's eighteenth birthday and then she goes back to Doncaster. The earth has had a whole summer to heat up and the landscape has that parched, hazy look of a painting by an old master − perhaps something by Vermeer − a sleepy scene depicting rural simplicity. Pale fields dotted with cows and the odd, verdant bush stretch out at either side of me. The poplars, like quills, lean in the breeze.

Then I pass Ferrybridge Power Station, smoke billowing from its four great cooling towers − a reminder, along with the telegraph wires criss-crossing overhead, that it's 2009 and we have had the Industrial Revolution. Still, I know I'm on the home stretch once I get to Ferrybridge. Normally, it's here that I start to get anxious at the prospect of a whole weekend at Mum's, us two rattling around in that depressingly empty bungalow, lifting my feet so she can vacuum endlessly whilst making snippy comments about Dad.

This time, however, I don't know, I've got a good feeling about it, like this visit might be different. There was something about her tone on the phone last night.

'Get here early so we can have the whole day together, yes?'

This wasn't like her at all. Normally, she doesn't stipulate any conditions. It's as if she's just desperate for me to come at all and doesn't want to risk it not happening by being demanding, which I must admit has niggled me in the past. Why can't she just say, 'I'd *love* to see you' rather than me having to read her mind? Detect her neediness. I might have been more ready to come if she'd been less scared of asking, but then, all my life, Mum's been scared of most things.

And I've been a terrible daughter – not seeing your own mother for the best part of a year? I have a sudden urge to get there – to see my mum – and I cross into the fast lane and put my foot down.

I roll into Coppice Avenue – the quiet road of uniform dormer bungalows on the outskirts of Harrogate where I grew up, just after eleven thirty. Mum is standing barefoot in the driveway, waving.

I get out of the car and the quiet hits me. As does my mother's outfit.

'Well, that was pretty speedy, darling,' she says, putting an arm around me and pulling me tight.

Darling?

She never uses terms of endearment; that was always Dad's job. A job he took very seriously indeed with his honeybuns and his sweetpeas and his flowerpots and chicken pies. Secondly, she looks *great*. I swear to God, my mother looks hot. She's had a warm brown colour put on her salt-and-pepper hair, which has been styled out of her usual 'middle-aged mum short do' into something that wouldn't look out of place on Fiona Bruce. The elasticated blue trousers that always reminded me of operating theatre scrubs have gone and in their place is a stylish linen tunic in taupe – the sort you might buy in East or Monsoon – clinched in with a bronze belt, over a pair of leggings. My 57-year-old mother in a pair of leggings!

I look her up and down, amazed.

'Mother, you look *fab*!'

She beams, coyly.

'Do you think so?'

'*Er, yes.*' I shield my eyes from the sun so I can get a good look at her. 'The whole thing, the hair and this top and these *leggings*. Hello. Legs. Mother!'

'Well, I thought it was about time I made an effort.' She sticks her leg out in front. 'Roger in the newsagent's said I had very shapely calves.'

'And Roger's not wrong,' I say, marvelling at her, following her inside the house. 'I wish I looked that great in a pair of leggings.'

The entrance hallway of my youth hasn't changed since 1986 when we moved in: the thick beige carpet with the loud, red leaf patterns, the telephone table with the shell-shaped directory that you press and it pops open, something I'd do over and over again whilst on one of my marathon phone calls to Pippa ('Get off that bloody phone! You only saw her last night!' I can still hear Mum shouting from the kitchen now). The mahogany sideboard with Mum's collection of ceramic frogs and the pictures of me and my brother, Chris, on our graduation days hanging above it. Chris looks quite presentable – if ponytails on blokes are your thing. I on the other hand look tragic. I'm wearing my glasses and my right eye looks like I've been punched repeatedly (the prospect of my parents coming to stay had meant I'd got uncharacteristically obliterated the night before and slept with my contact lens still in). I am bloated in the face, sheepish, hung over. If it weren't for the mortar board, it could be a police mug shot.

I look at it, despairingly.

'Yes, it always was a shame about that contact lens,' says Mum before taking me by the hands. 'Oh but it's *so* nice to see you.'

There was definitely something going on!

We go through to the square kitchen with it's old-fashioned tiles with the cockerels on and the big Formica table with the spindly chairs, where I remember learning news of my sister's arrival almost eighteen years to the day.

Everything is as it has always been, and yet the house feels different, like someone has opened all the windows and let the summer in. Light blasts through the hallway, the radio blares. There are breakfast things left out – marmalade and a margarine-covered fork. In thirty-two years of knowing my mother, she hasn't once left the breakfast things out past 9 a.m. Nor does she eat marmalade.

She hovers around, watching me as I fill the kettle, tugging at her new hair, as if she hasn't quite got used to it yet, as if layers feel like the equivalent of plastic surgery.

'Tea?' I say, holding up a tea bag.

Mum looks at me with a quivering smile, her hands go self-consciously to her neck.

'Um, actually I thought we could go to Betty's.'

To my knowledge, in all her twenty years of living in Harrogate, Mum hasn't been to the town's famous tearooms once – certainly not with me. Mum is suspicious of anything that is an 'experience', and 'experience' to her equals over-priced, and that included McDonalds (I would have literally *slain* for a McDonalds party when I was a kid but to no avail), Alton Towers (never been) and Betty's tearooms.

'Why would I want to spend the best part of £10 on a cup of tea and a scone, when I can have one at home for a fraction of the price?' she said more than once. But then she also once watched a documentary about the Nile and the Pyramids and said, 'Why would I want to go and see the Pyramids now I've seen them on the telly?', which, in retrospect, I think kick-started Dad's affair with Cassandra and her enormous watercolour smocks.

They went on a cruise down the Nile the following summer.

'Fine by me, I love Betty's,' I say, filling up the kettle. 'There's no rush, though, is there?'

A pause, just the sound of the tap running.

'Well, actually, I thought it would be nice to avoid the lunchtime rush.'

'Well, this is nice, isn't it?' sighs Mum. After ten minutes queuing, (and not a squeak of complaint from Mum), we get a seat in the Montpellier Café area of Betty's tearoom on a cappuccino-coloured leather banquette, looking out onto the busy street.

I've been to Betty's many times with my friends (in the same vein as us having dinner parties where we dined on tuna pasta bake, it was part of us pretending to be grown-ups) and it always reminds me of a very elegant Italian ice-cream parlour: spacious, high-ceilinged, colour palate of vanilla and gold, and marble floors where staff in waistcoats and smart red cravats scurry about industriously.

I order the open crab sandwich, followed by a raspberry macaroon (basically an orgasm in sugar form). Mum just orders tea.

'I'm not doing wheat,' she says, when I give her a funny look. 'Makes me puff up these days and I need to get rid of this, Caroline Marie.' She pats her stomach. 'It cuts right into the belts, for one thing.'

Belts. When did Mum start wearing belts? Or fashion accessories of any kind?

She sits up and rearranges the belt, rearranges her fringe again. She seems agitated, excitable. Mum is rarely excitable,

There's a group of ladies next to us; one, a woman with a leathery face and black hair who looks like she might be a palm reader, leans over.

'I'm guessing you are mother and daughter?' She smiles

310

and we smile back. 'We're all old school friends,' she says, gesturing to the other ladies sitting with her. 'This is my last supper before my chemotherapy starts. Breast cancer,' she whispers. 'Not looking good. They've found cancerous nodules in my lungs, one rib looks black. I've been under every damn machine there is and I haven't even started treatment yet.'

I watch Mum. Usually, this would be her worse nightmare – a mad stranger oversharing? But she puts down her teacup.

'My friend had cancer . . .' she's saying. 'Cancer of the bladder. She thought she had three weeks to live and she's still here, six years later. So, it just shows you. You've just got to stay positive, that's all you can do.'

Was this actually my *mother*?

The food comes; Mum rearranges the plates on the table and looks around the room as if she's being surveyed.

'So come on, you haven't told me,' she says. 'Where's Lexi this weekend?'

'She's working on a market stall,' I say, cutting into my sandwich.

'What sort of stall?' says Mum.

'Vintage stuff, furniture, clothes. The guy who runs it is lovely,' I add, rather unnecessarily.

'Well, how lovely. How nice, to have found a little summer job, isn't it?' I wait for some sort of snipe about Lexi, about Dad, but there's none. 'And how is it going? With Lexi, I mean? How's it been all summer? I've hardly spoken to you.'

I still wonder where this is going. We're on Lexi ground now, which means Cassandra ground, which means Dad ground, which means dangerous ground. And I want to tell her about Martin, I owe it to her to tell her the truth. I need to keep this sweet.

'You know what, Mum? Actually, it's been great. Well, most of the time. Always interesting, anyway.'

'I bet you've been able to teach her a thing or two, haven't you?' she says, pouring tea. 'Kept her on the straight and narrow? She always was a loose little cannon, that one, just like her mother but in miniature form.'

'Actually, she's taught me a thing or two.' I shrug, trying to sound casual.

'Really?' says Mum. 'And what do you mean by that?'

What did I mean by that? I tried to order my thoughts in my head, how I was going to put this. Suddenly it seemed a far bigger deal.

'Well, you know . . .' Talking to Mum about feelings was hard, I remembered now. 'Having her to stay, it's sorted my head out. Life's been a bit, well, all over the place of late.'

'I know how you feel,' she says, looking around.

Silence. Say it, Caroline, I think. Just tell her the truth – it's not like she's going to start shouting here.

'Mum, I've got something to tell you. Something I've been meaning to tell you for a while . . . You know Martin?'

She claps her hands together.

'Oh my God, you're not back together?'

'No. Sadly. Sadly, I'm not. But, there's something I didn't really tell you . . . about Martin.'

'What? He's not gay, is he? I knew there must have been some reason for him to just go off the boil like that.'

'No, he's not gay, Mum. And *he* didn't go off the boil. I did.'

Mum stops mid-drink and blinks.

'What do you mean, darling?'

'I was the one who called the wedding off. Even though I didn't tell you that. I told you it was the other way round . . .'

It's ridiculous, I feel like a criminal who's just come out to their mum. (Hey Mum. You know that serial robber that's been all over the papers recently? Well, it's me!) Like in those few words, I just smashed every notion she had of me as the perfect daughter. The sensible, reasonable, academic daughter. But I'm not perfect – Martin's already cleared that one up.

Stunned silence for a second.

'So, why?' asks Mum.

Did she mean, why couldn't I marry him? Or, why did I lie?

'Why did you call the wedding off?'

Just tell her the truth.

'I wasn't in love with him. I just couldn't do it. As the wedding got nearer, I tried to imagine us being together for ever and I couldn't – I knew I wanted different things, that he couldn't give me what I needed.'

'Which is?'

I wasn't expecting this and for a minute I'm thrown until suddenly, like a light out of nowhere, it becomes dazzlingly clear.

'Someone who lets me be me, rather than tries to be my father.'

And it was true. I lost my dad to Cassandra and Lexi and jumped straight into the arms of Martin who was basically another father figure. I loved him, but I outgrew him.

Mum looks at me; she's trying to compute. Just fill the silence, keep filling the silence . . .

'I – I felt so guilty,' I begin. 'All that money wasted, all that excitement about the wedding, I felt I'd let you down. I know how much you loved Martin . . .'

Mum takes my hands in both her hands, strokes them with her thumb.

'Yes, but I love *you* more,' she says. 'You're my *daughter*, you silly banana [only Mum would say something like silly banana at a time like this]. Your father and I only ever wanted you to be happy. To think you didn't feel you could talk to us, that you thought we'd be more worried about the money

313

than your happiness?' Her eyes start to water. 'Well, that hurts.'

I sit there, holding her hands, *feeling* like a silly banana. And I'd spent a year drowning in guilt? Thinking she'd disown me, or shout at me, or be bitterly disappointed if I told her the truth? When all the time, she was my mum. Of *course* she was. All she'd ever wanted was my happiness. I'd underestimated her.

She's still holding my hands, still stroking me with her thumb and it feels lovely, reassuring.

'You know, marriage is a serious thing,' she says. 'I mean, I wish your father and I hadn't just launched into it like we did; we were totally incompatible from the start. At least you had the good sense and the courage to get out of it before it started. You were brave. Really brave.'

That's the second time someone has said that to me.

'So, you're not annoyed?'

'Oh, livid. No, course I'm not annoyed!' She looks at her watch. 'Actually, I've got something to tell you too.' She sweeps her new fringe across her face and looks around the room. 'I've got a friend.'

'Friend?'

'Oh, a boyfriend then.'

'Oh, *Mum*!'

I feel a sudden swell of happiness in my chest. It takes me quite by surprise. It all made sense now. The new clothes, the new hair, the house that felt full and bright for the first time ever. It was because she was happy.

'Well, I'm definitely happ*ier*,' she says, with typical understatement when I put this to her.

'So, so what's he like? Is he nice?'

I want to ask her endless questions. I'm impressed! Intrigued. At thirty-two, I struggled to get a boyfriend and she managed to bag one at fifty-seven?

He was a good 'un, too. A right silver fox. I found that

314

out when he walked through the door of Betty's approximately twenty seconds later.

Things I Learned about My Mum's New Boyfriend (my mum's first-ever boyfriend) that Afternoon.

He was called Charlie.

He was fifty-three (toy boy, too. Bloody good work!).

He wore stylish but sensible clothes: a corduroy jacket, M&S jumper, jeans and brogues and a genuine smile.

He was a paramedic (calm, practical, great in a crisis).

And looked like he could model for a life insurance advert. ('A dead ringer for Richard Chamberlain, no?' said Mum, proudly. 'In his *Thornbirds* days?')

He loved DIY and carpentry.

He was the absolute polar opposite to my dad in every single way.

And he made my mum ridiculously happy.

I'll never forget the look on her face when she introduced us:

'Caroline this is Charlie. Charlie, this is my daughter, Caroline . . .'

It was so full of hope − like a teenager introducing their boyfriend to their parents for the first time. She was all flustered; her hands kept going to her new hair. When Charlie went to the toilet, he kissed her. He'd even miss her in the loo?

Turns out old Charlie's become a bit of a regular fixture at Coppice Avenue. Hence the marmalade.

After half an hour or so, Charlie gives Mum another kiss − me trying really hard not to stare − and goes to see his daughter. Mum and I sit on the slope of grass in front of the war memorial just outside Betty's, and continue our chat. Mum's open, she's relaxed. I've never been able to talk to her like this in my life. I think about telling her about Toby.

I'd done to Rachel what Cassandra had done to Mum, after all, maybe Mum would have some advice from the other side? I decide no, though. Some things even your mother doesn't need to know. The affair was over now – what was the point in confessing all? I needed to move on.

After all, she had.

The sun's come out now. Mum lies back on the grass.

'So, what do you think of Charlie?' she asks.

'I think he's great, Mum. Really, great.'

'The polar opposite of your father?'

'Er yeah, just a bit.'

'I don't think your father ever erected a piece of flat-pack furniture in twenty-two years of marriage to me. Charlie erected an entire dining room in one afternoon.'

We both start laughing.

Neither of us says anything for a while. I watch the clouds drift above us, just enjoying being here and feeling, for the first time in my life, like an equal to Mum. Like we're two women trying to make the best of things.

Then she says:

'It must have been tough for you growing up. Us two as your parents. Me depressed, your father feckless.'

I think about Wayne. 'At least you were there,' I say. 'At least I had a mum and dad – very good ones in lots of ways.'

She turns her head.

'Do you think so?' she says.

'Course I do. You loved us, didn't you? You did your best.'

'I beat myself up for so many years,' she says. 'Worried what the divorce did to you and Chris. Did it screw you up? Make it difficult to settle down? Did you miss your father being around?'

'Oh probably,' I say. 'But let's face it, there are worse things that can happen to a child than a divorce. At least I got a sister out of it.'

She smiles. I wonder if she realizes now, that this is how I see it. That Lexi's a positive thing to come out of all of this, not some bloodied by-product of a messy war.

There's a pause, then she says:

'Do you know what, Caroline? I'm not angry at him any more.'

'Who?' I say.

'Your dad,' she says. 'Your stupid bloody father! I was probably as unbearable to live with as he was. I nagged him, and we just didn't appreciate where each other was coming from in the end. No point being bitter for the rest of your life, though, eh? Or feeling guilty?'

'No,' I say. 'Don't feel guilty on my part, Mum.'

I think that's probably the most sensible thing she's ever said in her life.

Mum's going for a drink with Charlie that night, so I leave at 6 p.m. For the first time ever, though, I'm not gagging to get back in the car and would have stayed for longer if I could. But that's the point, I couldn't. I couldn't because Mum had stuff to do and her own life now. She didn't need me so much and, in a funny old way, that made me feel closer to her.

It's still warm and humid and Lexi's sitting on the front doorstep under the glare of a street-lamp when I get back, wearing beaten-up boots and a stripy dress. The sun's low in the sky, casting an orange glow over the front of the house.

'And how was Gwen?' she says, as I get out of the car.

'Oh, distinctly less embittered. Looking great. *In love*.'

Lexi frowns, incredulous. 'No fucking way!'

'Yes, fucking way.' I open the boot. '*And* he was cute.'

'What, you met him?'

'Yup, he's called Charlie.'

'Young Charlie, eh?' says Lexi.

'Well he's not that young, he's fifty-three.'

'But she's got a boyfriend, though. Gwen's got a man!'

'I know, miracles do happen, hey? You never know, it might be me one of these days.'

I try to get past her to get into the house but she puts her arm out.

She's got to tell me something, she says. Something that can't wait.

'Wayne goes to Sheffield on my birthday,' she says.

My heart stops.

'Oh?'

'They told him they want him to start earlier than planned, so . . .'

My hands shake as I try to get my keys in the door. I don't know what she expected me to say. So, he was leaving earlier than expected.

Lexi stands up and blocks my way to the door. What on earth was she playing at?

'It's awful, Caroline. You have to stop him!'

I roll my eyes and try to push her gently out of the way.

'Lexi, he's a free man, a big boy. He knows what's right for him. I can't *make* him do anything.'

'But you're so right for each other!' says Lexi, exasperated, standing square in front of the door now. 'He told me about the date. We talk, you know. He told me, and he said, and I quote, that it was "magic". He thinks you don't care, he wants you to stop him going to Sheffield. He wants to make a go of things with you but he just hasn't got the guts to come straight out with it.'

My heart is racing now. I stand with the key in my hand. My hands are still shaking.

'And, has he actually said as much?'

'Well, no, but . . .'

'Well, there we are,' I say, pushing her out of the way again.

'But don't you see, *you* have to take action. *You* have to say what you feel.'

'How do you know how I feel?'

'Right.' She's got her head in her hand now. She's taking this role very seriously. 'But you care about him, right?'

Care about him? I thought. Did thinking about him every minute of every day, count as caring? Reading each chapter of his book, over and over again in the hope of absorbing some sense of him, not of Kevin but Wayne? Closing my eyes and imagining kissing him again, like some teenage female version of Kevin Hart, for goodness' sake. Reliving every second of the picnic in the park . . .

'Yes, I care about him,' I say.

'Oh, thank *fuck* for that. So call him. Now. Before it's too late.'

I shake my head at her.

'Lex, I know you mean well, but this is not some film. This is real life and in real life, you don't run to airports, or to people's houses, or houseboats for that matter, in the pouring rain, declaring your undying love, telling them not to go and expect them to not think you're batty, okay?'

Lexi sighs and removes her arm from the side of the door.

'Now, can I get into my own house, please?'

CHAPTER THIRTY-ONE

Lexi's eighteenth birthday is one of those glorious September days. The sun is low and glittering. The trees, so full and green as I remember them from the day she arrived, are sparser now and tinged with gold. I am in my bedroom, wrapping Wayne's leaving present: a notebook. A5. Fabric. With a picture of a vintage Vespa on the front – nothing special, really, but it reminded me of him and I want him to continue writing. *Love is a Battlefield: Kevin Hart's Reports from the Frontline of Love* is stuck in my head now and I want it to live on.

I take a silver pen: *For Kevin*, I write inside the front cover. *May he live on and win his battles! I shall miss you, Caroline* xxxx

It's been two weeks since our date and that lives on in my memory, too. It feels like a dream now, the feeling of the engine drumming into my thighs, that delicious thrill mixed with terror as I finally managed to extricate my arms from around Wayne's throat. The way London zipped by like a lifetime before me. Sometimes, when I think of us lying in that hammock, the pink dawn through the porthole above us, Wayne's warm body next to mine, I can't help but catch my breath. Was that really me? Caroline Steele? Did that really happen?

But this is right. This is the way things are. Experiences we have are all the more potent because they can't last for ever, after all. I want to box up that night and inhale it, but all good things come to an end. Bittersweet and all that.

There's a knock at the door.

'Can I enter, madame?' says Lexi.

She comes in and I push the present underneath the duvet.

'Hey!' She smiles, head curled around the doorframe. She looks like the archetypal Londoner these days: gone are the gold leggings and the flashy T-shirt. In their place, a jaunty blue beret that highlights her eyes and a little vintage dress. 'Is that another present for me?'

She jumps onto the bed and paws the tissue paper.

'Get off!' I say. 'Give that to me!'

'Aha, so it *is* for me?'

'No, it is not! You've had your presents.'

She looks at me, mock sternly. 'Come on,' she says. 'So who's it for?'

'It's for Wayne,' I say, taking the package and unwrapping it. 'A leaving present. Do you like it?'

She takes it in her hand. I tense. *Don't open the front cover.*

'It's perfect,' she says. 'He's gonna love it.'

Then she takes both my hands and I know what she's going to say.

'You know, it's not too late. You could call him. Call him now. Tell him not to go. I know he'd listen to you, Caroline, I know . . .'

I put my arms around her.

'Alexis Steele, for a seventeen-year-old girl — sorry, an *eighteen*-year-old girl — you're such an old romantic. But sorry, I'm not going to call him.' I shrug. 'It's okay. I'm okay about this, you know, and it's not like Sheffield is Africa, is it? We can go and see him, me and you. I could come up and see you

321

in Doncaster and we could go together to Sheffield, take him out on the town. It'll be fun.'

She smiles, sadly. 'Okay. I guess you're a thirty-two-year-old woman and you know your own mind.' Something inside me flinched. 'But you liked him, didn't you? Perhaps *more* than like?'

'Yes,' I say. 'I really like him. But, you know, you can't keep everyone, Lexi, and I'm just glad I met him, you know? I have you to thank for that. Wayne Campbell turned out to be pretty good for both of us, didn't he?'

She gives a sad smile.

It's 2 p.m. and in half an hour we're meeting people in Battersea Park for a birthday picnic for Lexi. They've got a fairground up in the park today, so it's going to be extra special, extra fun. A great big sendoff, because this time tomorrow she'll be back in Doncaster. The summer, over.

A sound like a lion roaring. Lexi's mobile. She sits up on her knees and answers it, then starts to giggle.

'Ha, ha, very funny,' she's saying. 'I bet I can guess what it is. What? No way! Did you? Okay, okay. Oh, and bring your camera,' she says. 'I want a picture of us both to take home.'

Jerome.

Since she finally got Clark out of her life, she has become very friendly with the boy she met on the train and I can't help but think that things have come full circle. If the Clark thing had never happened – if this whole summer hadn't happened – maybe she'd have stepped off the train and into a summer fling with him? Not that they're having any kind of 'fling', of course. She's adamant about that. But they've taken to hanging around London together, taking arty photos of the city and of one another, going to markets and exhibitions, far more cool and cultural than any installation art about 'Otherness' by Jergen bloody Rindblatten could ever be!

She comes off the phone.

'Jerome, eh?' I tease and she rolls her eyes.

'One hundred per cent platonic. Thanks very much.'

And that's great, I think, that's perfect, really. Friends with someone her own age who likes her for her. This is how it's meant to be.

We lie back on the bed.

'I can't believe you're leaving me,' I say. 'What am I going to do without you?'

'Oh, get back to normal life, have a clean house, *no* fun! Get a bloody *boyfriend*,' she says, nudging me in the side.

'Oh, and I will, don't you go worrying your little head about that. I'm a changed woman. You watch, I'll be married in a year, massive do at St Paul's Cathedral to some member of the aristocracy, you my head bridesmaid, resplendent in vintage, me wearing a gigantic meringue.'

She gasps. 'Oh my God, we forgot! The wedding dress. The last thing on the list!'

She's right, we were going to sell the wedding dress, flog it on eBay, give it to a dress shop, burn the damn thing. It smells of fags, anyway.

But lately, I've been thinking of Wayne and his tattoos. His battle scars. The stories that make up his life. Poor bugger will never be able to get rid of Tracey or Justine or Christabel, but he doesn't seem to want to, either. They are part of him, like the dress and the wedding that never happened are part of me, really. They're my story, too.

'Actually, I've kind of had a change of heart about that one,' I say. 'I think I'll keep it after all.'

'Really?' says Lexi, wrinkling her nose.

'Yeah, you never know, when you marry Jerome you can wear it!'

'Shut up,' she says, rolling her eyes.

* * *

We're downstairs now. The sun-filled lounge is full of cards and balloons; it's twenty minutes till party time, twenty-four hours before Lexi goes and it feels likes the official end of summer. I feel suddenly exhausted, like I've lived a lifetime in this house.

The bell goes. 'That'll be that there Jerome Montaigne!' says Lexi in her 'exaggerated Yorkshire' voice, hopping towards the door excitedly, but I know there's a chance it might be someone else.

The five whole minutes of yelps and squeals and hysterical laughter confirms I was right. A full-figured, cherubically pretty blonde stands in my hallway holding a Best Friend 18 Today balloon and an enormous bunch of flowers.

'Carly Greenford. Oh. My. God! What are you *doing* here!' Lexi looks like she might wet herself with excitement.

They dance around the hallway, hugging one another until they collapse in a frenzied heap on my rug.

'Happy?' I laugh. I'm applying lipstick in the hallway mirror. 'She's a trouper, that one. I only called her yesterday and she dropped everything.'

Lexi hugs me so tight she nearly winds me.

'Happy?' she says, looking at me through the mirror, and, for the first time in my life, I see similarities between us. Something about the serious chin, the little rosebud mouth. 'This is the ultimate birthday present. The best, ever. You're a genius! Thank you.'

We put Carly's flowers in a vase, then Jerome arrives and takes some photos of the birthday girl. Finally, we're ready to go.

Lexi opens the front door to a blinding sun.

'Let's do this,' she says. 'Let's have it, people!'

But I hold on behind.

'You go onto the park, I'll find you in a minute.'

There's just one thing I have to do.

* * *

The letter sits on the windowsill. It arrived yesterday, a small, cream envelope, thick with paper.

The postcode is Clapham. I only know one person who lives in Clapham. But from the elegant, feminine writing, I know it's not from him.

I sit down at the kitchen table and open the letter. The house is suddenly quiet now and I have a sudden pang of dread, like, this is how it's going to be from now on.

My hand goes to my mouth as I start to read.

Dear Caroline,

You must wonder why the hell I am writing this letter. *I* wonder why the hell I am writing this letter. I guess I meant what I said when I met you at the awards bash: despite everything, I think you are a woman's woman, deep down. And I want to talk woman to woman to you now.

It's funny how you can get people so wrong, isn't it? The first time I met you, I thought you were adorable: genuine, funny, down-to-earth. Turns out you were shagging my husband behind my back. I should hate your guts, but I don't. I've asked myself why this is and can only come to the conclusion that it's because, for the last few weeks, at least, I've been too busy hating myself.

You see, I got Toby wrong too — except I didn't — I knew from the start, but I ignored my instincts. I don't know if Toby's ever told you this (I would assume not) but he was with someone when I started seeing him. He'd been with her three years, in fact. So you see, this is another reason why I can't, I *don't* hate you. Because I was you once. I slept with another woman's man too! I kept believing he would leave his girlfriend, too — just like you. Only in this case, he did. Consider you've had a lucky escape.

I feel like I've had a lucky escape, too, and I suppose this

325

is why I wanted to write – to say thank you. Seem mad that, no? You must think I'm unhinged. Shouldn't I be hurling insults? Reams and reams of why you're such a bitch? But you see, whilst I've certainly spent many an hour lately thinking you're a bitch, ultimately, you saved me. I'm thirty-eight now and all I want is a baby. Time is running out. If you hadn't had had an affair with Toby, and if I hadn't found out, we would be trying for another baby now, and maybe this time we wouldn't have lost it.

But maybe there was a reason we did, because I can't have a baby with Toby: he will never, ever change. And I would rather be childless now, and know there's a chance I will one day have a baby with a good man, than pregnant and condemned to having one with a man who will only ever break my heart.

He would have broken your heart, too, Caroline; I think he probably did. But I have broken the chain. *You* broke the chain. The best thing we can do now is get on with our lives and not allow history to repeat itself. Only we can change the course of our love lives, only we can change our story, because Toby will never change the course of his. I just wanted to tell you that.

Rachel

I sit there, my hands shaking, tears rolling down my face. She was so brave. So brave and so honest. Had I ever been that brave and honest in my entire life?

I fold the letter back up and put it in its envelope. Then I wash my face, reapply all the make-up that's slid down my cheeks, take Wayne's present from where Lexi left it on the bed, and walk to her party.

The park is throbbing with life and noise. The fairground is set up around the bandstand – waltzers, Dodgems, a terrifying zig-zagging thing that flings you around and then upside down. There are stalls along one side selling burgers and hot dogs. The air smells deliciously of candyfloss and fast-food grease.

I look at my watch. Half past two. In fifteen minutes, Wayne will be down here to collect his leaving present, say his goodbyes and that will be it.

'I've got something for you,' I'd said to him. 'It's nothing big – don't get too excited – but it's something I thought you could remember this summer by, each time you use it.'

Dave was going to get a new boat partner when he heard Wayne was leaving, but since Wayne's been manning his shop at Camden Market (and, I like to think, since Lexi's been working her magic), he reckons he's made enough money to set himself up for a bit and he's going to move out and get a flat somewhere instead. Turns out the novelty of sleeping in a hammock wears off after a while.

I can hear Lexi's squeals from a mile off. She's being thrown around on the waltzers, Jerome one side, Carly on the other, head pinned to the back of her seat by G-force, eyes squeezed shut in an expression of pure, delighted abandon. After Clark's arrest, she told Carly the truth about her and Clark. Turns out, in true teenage form, that Carly thought that Lexi and Clark were having the sex life of the century – that they were swinging from the chandeliers! The lies we tell for the sake of our pride . . .

Out of my peripheral vision, I see someone in top-to-toe cream get up from the sea of picnic blankets around me and stride towards me. My dad. He's wearing leather sandals, a linen suit and a red T-shirt that says ANIMAL on it, and I think how sweet and vaguely ridiculous he looks. He flings both arms around me, the champagne from his glass sploshing on the grass.

'Caro. Hello, honeybun. How are you?'

'I'm good, Dad,' I say, kissing him back, then wiping off

the champagne dribbling down my dress. 'Great you made it down here. Perfect day or what?'

Cassandra's waving at me from the picnic basket; two large, bangle-laden arms and a vision in lilac tie-dye. I wave back and she raises her glass.

'Well, Cassandra's pissed,' I say, and Dad laughs out loud.

'Birthday Girl's not far behind,' he says, gesturing towards Lexi.

I look over at my sister. She's off the waltzers now, staggering, still dizzy, arm-in-arm with her posse, a bottle of champagne swinging louchely from her hand.

She's definitely decided not to go back to sixth form. She starts on a business course next week instead, but something tells me she's going to be all right. More than all right. It turns out, after all, that my sister is a sales and negotiations genius. Some sort of whiz kid at people skills.

After we lost the Schumacher account, Lexi single-handedly won it back. I came back to work from lunch one day to find my little sister in the meeting room with Darryl Bum Smacker having a power meeting all on her own!

'What the hell?' I yelped to Shona.

'I know. They've been in there an hour,' she said.

Without telling me, the little so-and-so had arranged a meeting with Darryl, explained about the profit slip up, navigated her way through a minefield of negotiations with the sort of charm most people can only dream of, and won the Minty Me account back.

We did a deal: SCD would pay more for Minty Me and he stopped with the sexual innuendos and making people feel uncomfortable. Lexi had come straight out with it: 'Basically, Darryl, when you do that, people think you're a letch.' A feminist icon, in her own lunchtime!

So a Diploma in Business Management and Enterprise starts

next week. 'Tomorrow, Doncaster market. Next year – the world!' Lexi joked when she got the letter. And I'm so proud of her. It's all her doing, at the end of the day.

'She's happy, that kid, you know?' says Dad. 'She's a changed girl since she came to London. All thanks to you, of course.' He nudges me on the arm.

'I think she just learned how to make herself happy, Dad,' I say, as Lexi throws her head back and necks straight from the bottle. 'And to drink professionally, it seems.'

Since our chat in KFC, Dad seems so much more relaxed, less manic. Like he's realized he doesn't have to overcompensate any more, that it's okay to be him. That I forgive him.

He passes me a plastic glass, fills me up with champagne, and we stand there laughing at Lexi as she drags her friends from ride to ride.

Then suddenly, a familiar voice . . .

'Fancy a go on the Dodgems, Trevor?'

I freeze. *My mother. My mother talking to my father?*

It was always a risk to invite both parties. They haven't been in the same room for twenty-two years. To be honest, when Mum said she would come, I started to get panicky. 'Charlie's going to drive,' she said, proudly. (Now she had a driver, I'd never get rid of her.) But to come to Lexi's birthday? When she knew Dad was definitely going to be there, too? Now, this was progress.

And then the most miraculous thing happens; Dad answers Mum's little joke and they start to talk. I mean talk, actually *talk* (and even laugh a little), and for the first time since I was fifteen years old, I realize I am watching my parents have a conversation.

I leave them to it. Ten minutes now. Just enough time to get a drink before Wayne gets here, but the words from Rachel's letter are reverberating in my head and I've already got an idea what I might do.

Only we can change the course of our love lives . . .

I bump into Lexi and Jerome hand in hand on the way to the stall. She's all breathy and overexcited and high on her birthday.

'Is he here yet?' she says. 'Have you seen Wayne yet? Don't let him go before he says goodbye to me, too, will you?' Then she's dragged off to go on the Dodgems.

I stand at the queue.

Only we can change our story . . .

There's a pat on my back. 'Hello, Caro.' I turn to find Martin standing there. He and Lexi have had a few phone chats about Clark, since it all came out. She feels terrible about how mean she was to him – even if it was all my fault – so she invited him to come down today. Well, actually, she invited Martin *and* Polly.

'Hey, Martin, how are you? Is . . .?'

'Yes, she's over there,' he says, proudly, gesturing to Polly queuing at the drinks van.

Martin and Polly are officially going out now. I've seen them sitting outside the Duke two Saturdays in a row. He always was a man of habit.

'How's it going?' I say.

'Well,' says Martin, 'really well. We're going on holiday next week, two weeks on a French cooking course in the Dordogne.'

He's beaming from ear to ear and I think how long it's been since I've seen him smile like that.

'That's great, Martin. That's really great.'

'Yes.' He nods. 'Yes, it is.' Then he says, 'You know, I think she might be it – The One, Caroline.'

His eyes are shining. And I'm glad, *so* glad.

I give him a peck on the cheek. 'Oh, Martin,' I say, 'I'm so pleased for you.'

Turns out he was right, I hadn't ruined his life at all, that it was only just beginning, that all he needed was to be set free. It turns out I wasn't The One after all, was I? I was the one before The One.

There's a slightly too long silence. I know what I want to say, but dare I? I don't know if I should ... Sod it, I think, I may never get another chance.

So I say:

'Martin, you know something?'

'No, what?' he says.

'Polly's a very lucky lady. *I* was lucky, too. That's all I really wanted to say.'

'Lucky?' he says, bewildered.

'To have you love me,' I say.

And he smiles and looks towards Polly. He knows he has to go now, that this might even be the last time we have a proper conversation because that's how it goes. That's how relationships go. And so he hesitates, he looks at me and says,

'And a part of me probably always will.'

I've got my drink now and I'm walking back through the fairground towards our party. I can hear the faint squeals of people being thrown upside down on some ride or other, and Amy Winehouse blasting from the speakers.

Then, he's walking towards me. He's smiling, waving, and I wave back. I feel the tissue paper of his present in my hand and I put it behind my back.

He's right in front of me now. He gives me a hug.

'All packed?' I say.

'Yeah, just Dave left in the hammock and a load of boxes.'

I laugh. I see his eyes dart to the hand behind my back and the present, but he doesn't say a thing.

I think about the letter lying back at home. *Only we can change the course of our love lives, only we can change our story, because Toby will never change the course of his.* The words fill my head.

We start walking.

'So, how's Birthday Girl?' he says.

'Oh, pissed.'

'I should think so, too.' He laughs. 'It *is* her eighteenth birthday.'

'You say that, but I was sober as a judge on my eighteenth birthday. I had a ceramic-painting party for Christ's sake!'

Wayne cracks up laughing.

'A ceramic-painting party? Jeez, you really were square, weren't you? A late developer, I'd say. Making up for lost time now.'

'Do you remember your eighteenth birthday?' I ask as we walk.

'Oh yeah.' He grimaces. 'Oh, that one was bad. I got dumped on my eighteenth birthday. Lucy bloody—'

'Briers?' I interrupt, jokingly but he nods, resignedly.

'As a matter of fact, yes.'

I stop.

'What, and you didn't even change her name?'

'Not hers, no,' he says. 'I particularly wanted revenge on that little minx.'

I start to giggle and I peer at him, coyly. 'So can I ask – the weights and the working out in the back garden?'

He grimaces. 'Yep, that too, I'm afraid. Never did get a six pack.'

'So, Sarah Rawlinson?'

He laughs.

'Oh no, no. Lucy Briers is where the autobiography ends. Everyone else who broke Kevin Hart's heart, I totally made up.'

A pause. We both know he has to go soon. There are new people moving into the boat and the removal van's arriving. Give him the present now, I think, whilst we're talking about

332

the book. Just do it! But I can't seem to move my hands from behind my back. So I say:

'Do you want to go on the waltzers?'

And he looks at me and pulls a face.

'You? On the waltzers? Wow, you really have come over all daring since you went on my bike.'

So we do, the tissue-paper wrapped present lodged between us. As well as something else as loaded as a gun.

I scream as our carriage spins so much I think it might come right off and sail into the air.

Wayne is laughing with a mixture of fear and delight. He takes my hand in his, our heads are pushed right back, and for a second I dare to open my eyes. Above us, clouds whip and spin, the sunlight bounces off the park's golden Buddha sending golden discs into the sky like meteors.

Change your story. TAKE A RISK. Otherwise, you may never know.

We step down giddily, still hand-in-hand, and Lexi comes over, says her goodbyes.

'You're nothing without me, Campbell!'

She slaps him on the back and he picks her up.

'You bet, Steele. You'll be taking over the world before we know it. One day, I'll be able to say, Alexis Steele? A great friend of mine!'

Lexi goes, so then it's just Wayne and I alone, next to the bandstand.

'I guess this is it, then?' he says.

'I guess it is,' I reply. 'I guess it's goodbye.'

I bite my lip. I can still feel the present in my hand. Please don't, I think. Please don't. Not now.

But he doesn't. He just leans over and, very gently, he kisses me on the lips. I kiss him back, and I linger for every last millisecond, breathing him in. And then he's gone, he's walking away from me into the crowd.

333

'Phone me, yeah?' he calls back to me.

'Oh, absolutely. Absolutely will.'

'Goodbye, Caroline.'

'Goodbye, Wayne.'

Wayne. Still a bloody awful name. But I'd decided it suited him now that he'd made it his own.

I watch as he makes his way through the fairground, I turn the present over in my hand, and go back to the party.

Ten minutes go past. Fifteen. I've almost lost hope at twenty-eight minutes. Then my mobile goes.

He says:

'Hi.'

'Hi.'

'It's me.'

'I know.' I laugh.

'So, um, I didn't take my leaving present.'

'You didn't?'

'No.'

Silence. It goes on for ever. My heart punches against my ribs.

Then eventually:

'So, shall I come back and get it?'

You can change your story. But you have to be brave.

'No,' I say. 'I've decided I'm not going to give you a leaving present after all.'

'Why?' he asks and I drive off the edge.

'Because I don't want you to leave.'

Epilogue

Where are they now?

Lexi Steele is the proud owner of *Movie Star Bride,* a vintage wedding dress shop in Doncaster, and was last year named Local Businesswoman of the Year by the *South Yorkshire Times*. When she's not working or giving motivational talks to young entrepreneurs, she likes to rock out to Gossip in her pyjamas with flatmate Carly Greenford. Lexi and Carly are both currently single and very, very happy about it.

Gwen Steele lives self-sufficiently with Charlie Gaunt in a cottage in Otley. Charlie recently started work on converting their loft where Gwen will run her new ironing business. Gwen currently has a good line in maxi dresses. Leggings being so last year . . .

Trevor and **Cassandra Steele,** with the blessing of their kids, moved to the Greek Island of Zante where they now live in a yurt and run Healing Horizons courses. Lexi and Carly visit often, to giggle throughout Cassandra's reiki classes and get drunk on ouzo.

Toby Delaney is currently Account Manager at Pearl's Biscuits, where he is shagging the intern. He hasn't read a book in two years.

Rachel Gregory (formerly **Delaney**) now lives in Shropshire where she runs an Interior Decoration Business with boyfriend Al. She is expecting their first child this autumn.

Shona Parry is now single and still works at Skidmore-Colt-Davis.

Darryl Schumacher never asked her out for dinner again.

Martin Squire and **Polly Green** recently moved into a new-build in Surbiton. They hope to open their French restaurant, Ooh la la!, by Christmas (and to have perfected their choux pastry).

Wayne Campbell's debut teenage novel, *Love is a Battlefield: Kevin Hart's Stories from the Frontline of Love*, was published in January. He marries the love of his life, Caroline Marie Steele today, at 3 p.m., at St Peter's Church in Harrogate. The bride will wear an original Sixties shift dress from *Movie Star Brides*. Honeymoon: a motorbike tour of Belize. Future home: Two-bed flat, East Dulwich, London.

Caroline Marie Steele recently had CS 4 WC 4 EVA tattooed on her backside.

Ask
Katy...

Do you have someone in your life who was the *One Before the One*?

Um… not really since I haven't found The One or even 'A One' yet! I have certainly been lucky enough to meet a lot of lovely men in my life who have shaped me and who probably all appear in this novel in some guise or other.

You talk of Caro's mid-twenties crisis in the book. Referred to in the press as the quarter-life crisis, a relatively new phenomenon. How did you survive this challenging period of your life? And do you have any pearls of wisdom to pass on?

My twenties were mainly wonderful: job of my dreams, a LOT of boozing, loads of fun flat-mates and friends, just what your twenties should be about... However, it seems I still managed to be emotionally tortured for most of them! It's only now, in my mid-thirties, that I wonder what the hell I was worrying about. My main pearl of wisdom therefore would be – relax and enjoy because it only gets worse!

In *The One Before the One* you bring in that classic Katy Regan humour. What comedic writers, or other mediums, have inspired your writing?

For me, humour is what makes writing really enjoyable but I don't necessarily prefer comedic novels. I do, however, prefer an authentically funny voice that comes from character rather than the narrator trying to impress us with flowery, complicated writing. Ruby Lennox in Kate Atkinson's *Behind the Scenes at the Museum* is one of my favourite, naturally funny characters as are many of the characters in Nick Hornby's books. I think I get most of my comedy inspiration from my mates, though – they're hilarious – and I'm always getting myself into some sort of scrape which offers brilliant, comedic material for writing.

Do you, like Caro, have a tattoo on your backside?

Absolutely not. I'm thoroughly boring and have no body-art whatsoever. I do know two good friends with tattoos of names on their body though and think they're both terribly cool…

If you were not a writer, is there another career that you'd like to give a go?

Many, but I am one of these people whose talents are very 'niche'. I am generally incompetent at everything else and that's not me being charmingly self-deprecating, it's just a fact!

Have you devoured Katy's first book yet?

Tess Jarvis' rules for life have always been somewhat relaxed…

1. Never go to bed before your last guest has left
Tess and Gina's flat has a jacuzzi so it's the obvious location for a party … every night.

2. Make great friends and keep them close
Though not actually in your bed. Tess and Jim's claims that they are 'just good friends' has everyone's eyes rolling.

3. Look on the bright side of life
After all it could be so much worse. Tess's job interviewing the nation's catastrophes proves this every day.

4. Don't wait for the weekend to wear your fancy knickers (although be warned, this can lead to all manner of messes…)
Tess has always been one to wing it but she's fast realizing that her bank of blag is running out of funds. At 28, is it time to grow up? Maybe having a baby with your best friend isn't the best way to start…

marie claire

Glossier, Smarter, Sexier

WIN!

A day behind the scenes at *Marie Claire* the UK's biggest selling monthly fashion magazine

Join the *Marie Claire* team at their fabulous London offices and find out what really goes into putting the magazine together each month. Katy Regan will also be on hand to whisk you out for lunch after treating you to a masterclass in blogging.

Simply log onto
www.marieclaire.co.uk/competitions
to enter

SUBSCRIPTION OFFER:

3 issues of

marie claire
for just £1